PRAISE FOR SUE MARGOLIS'S NOVELS

ORIGINAL CYN

"Hilarious . . . Margolis' silly puns alone are worth the price of the book. Another laugh-out-loud funny, occasionally clever, and perfectly polished charmer."—*Contra Costa Times*

"Delightful . . . fans will appreciate this look at a lack of ethics in the workplace."—*Midwest Book Review*

"Has something for everyone—humor, good dialogue, hot love scenes, and lots of dilemmas."—*Rendezvous*

"A perfect lunchtime book or, better yet, a book for those days at the beach."—*Romance Reviews Today*

BREAKFAST AT STEPHANIE'S

"With Stephanie, Margolis has produced yet another jazzy cousin to Bridget Jones."—*Publishers Weekly*

"A heartwarming, character-driven tale . . . a hilariously funny story."—*Romance Reviews Today*

"A comic, breezy winner from popular and sexy Margolis."—*Booklist*

"Rife with female frivolity, punchy one-liners, and sex."
—*Kirkus Reviews*

"An engaging tale."—*Pittsburgh Post-Gazette*

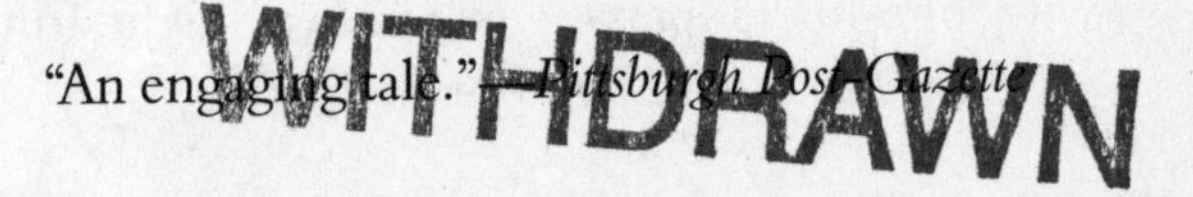

APOCALIPSTICK

"Sexy British romp . . . Margolis's characters have a candor and self-deprecation that lead to furiously funny moments. . . . A riotous, ribald escapade sure to leave readers chuckling to the very end of this saucy adventure."—*USA Today*

"Quick in pace and often very funny."—*Kirkus Reviews*

"Margolis combines lighthearted suspense with sharp English wit . . . entertaining read."—*Booklist*

"A joyously funny British comedy . . . a well-written read that has its share of poignant moments . . . There are always great characters in Ms. Margolis's novels. With plenty of romance and passion, *Apocalipstick* is just the ticket for those of us who like the rambunctious, witty humor this comedy provides."—*Romance Reviews Today*

"Rather funny . . . compelling . . . brilliant send-ups of high fashion."—*East Bay Express*

"[An] irreverent, sharp-witted look at love and dating."
—*Houston Chronicle*

SPIN CYCLE

"This delightful novel is filled with more than a few big laughs."—*Booklist*

"A funny, sexy British romp . . . Margolis is able to keep the witty one-liners spraying like bullets. Light, fun."
—*Library Journal*

"Warmhearted relationship farce . . . a nourishing delight."
—*Publishers Weekly*

"Margolis does a good job of keeping several balls in the air at once."—*Southern Pines (NC) Pilot*

"Satisfying . . . a wonderful diversion on an airplane, pool side, or beach."—*Baton Rouge Magazine*

NEUROTICA

"Screamingly funny sex comedy . . . the perfect novel to take on holiday."—*USA Today*

"Cheeky comic novel—a kind of *Bridget Jones's Diary* for the matrimonial set . . . Wickedly funny."
—*People* (Beach Book of the Week)

"Scenes that literally will make your chin drop with shock before you erupt with laughter . . . A fast and furiously funny read."—*Cleveland Plain Dealer*

"Taking up where *Bridget Jones's Diary* took off, this saucy British adventure redefines the lusty woman's search for erotic satisfaction. . . . Witty and sure . . . A taut and rambunctious tale exploring the perils and raptures of the pursuit of passion."—*Publishers Weekly*

"Splashy romp . . . giggles guaranteed."—*New York Daily News*

"A good book to take to the beach, *Neurotica* is fast paced and at times hilarious."
—*Boston's Weekly Digest Magazine*

"This raunchy and racy British novel is great fun, and will delight fans of the television show *Absolutely Fabulous*."
—*Booklist*

Also by Sue Margolis

Neurotica

Spin Cycle

Apocalipstick

Breakfast at Stephanie's

Original Cyn

SUE MARGOLIS

Gucci Gucci Coo

DELTA TRADE PAPERBACKS

GUCCI GUCCI COO
A Delta Trade Paperback / June 2006

Published by Bantam Dell
A Division of Random House, Inc.
New York, New York

Cover design by Melody Cassen

Book design by Ellen Cipriano

Library of Congress Cataloging in Publication Data
Margolis, Sue.
Gucci Gucci coo / Sue Margolis
p. cm.
ISBN-10: 0-385-33899-6
ISBN-13: 978-0-385-33899-8
1. Pregnancy—Fiction. 2. Jewish women—Fiction.
3. London (England)—Fiction. I. Title.

PR6063.A635 G83 2006 2006040161
823/.914 22

Printed in the United States of America
Published simultaneously in Canada

www.bantamdell.com

BVG 10 9 8 7 6 5 4 3 2 1

For my husband, Jonathan,
who's always there when things go wrong for me.
The man's a bloody jinx.

Gucci Gucci Coo

Chapter 1

Ruby Silverman shuffled down the gynecologist's table and maneuvered her feet into the stirrups. As she gazed steadfastly at the ceiling and listened for the tart snap of the doctor's rubber gloves, she tried to take her mind off what was happening by returning to the game she had been playing in her head—seeing how many words she could find in *speculum*.

So far she had six—cup, mule, plum, clue, lumps and slump. Her seventh, eulum, wasn't a real word, of course, but she'd decided to allow it, since it sounded to her like some obscure body part prone to enlargement or inflammation.

"Any tenderness here?" the doctor asked crisply, pressing down on one side of her abdomen. He had yet to reach the internal part of the examination, but it could be no more than seconds away.

"No. Nothing."

Pus! That made seven.

The doctor, whose name she'd forgotten, although she knew it was hyphenated, was the archetypal English hospital consultant: late fifties, unkempt eyebrows in urgent need of a trim, expensive but conservative gray suit, ditto the tie, precious little by way of bedside manner.

Usually Ruby placed great value in a doctor's bedside manner, but on this occasion, the lack of it didn't bother her. In fact she saw it as a bonus. The idea of a nonboyfriend man—even one who was a gynecologist—having access to all areas of her body was bad enough; one who was overly charming—or, God forbid, young and good-looking—would have had her making a bolt for the door.

Because of her reservations about male gynecologists, the doctor she usually saw for her annual nether region checkup was a woman. Dr. Jane Anderson was a forty-something, easy-to-talk-to, mothering soul with untameable hair and a comforting lack of fashion sense. Ruby wouldn't go so far as to say she enjoyed their encounters, but she always felt reasonably comfortable with Dr. Jane. Today, though, she was off sick and Dr. Double Barrel was filling in for her.

"Periods regular?" It was more of a command than a question.

"Yes."

"Urination?"

"Fine."

"Bowels moving?"

She thought about trying to lighten the atmosphere by replying: "Yes, to East Grinstead actually." She decided against it, as Double Barrel didn't appear to be overendowed in the humor department. Instead she just nodded.

"Any STDs in the last year?"

"What? No. Absolutely not."

As Double Barrel carried on prodding and pushing, Ruby abandoned her speculum word game for a minute to consider how odd it was that despite St. Luke's being the trendiest, most progressive private maternity hospital and well-woman clinic in London, its male doctors—or at least this one—were as distant and aloof as in any ordinary hospital. She couldn't imagine chatting away to DB the way she did to Dr. Jane. On the other hand, maybe male gynecologists kept their distance on purpose because they were aware that affability might be misinterpreted.

Whether Double Barrel was the exception or the rule, his manner wasn't stopping women flocking to St. Luke's in Holland Park for all their ob-gyn needs. Since it opened five years ago, it was forever being extolled in the broadsheets and upmarket glossies as the "Bentley of birth centers." The upshot was that the number of patients on the hospital's books was growing almost daily.

The maternity unit in particular was hugely popular. Women who wanted natural childbirth instead of being pumped with drugs, along with those who preferred to wander—obstetrically speaking—even farther off the beaten track by opting for the £10,000 birthing pool, doula and champagne breakfast package, were falling over themselves to get into St. Luke's. Because the competition for rooms was so fierce, most women picked up the phone to the admissions department the moment the pregnancy testing stick registered positive.

The way Ruby saw it, St. Luke's patients fell into three categories. First there was the megarich Kabbalah and crystals brigade—the ditzy, enlightenment-seeking British celebs and Hollywood stars living in London who hired shamans (along with the doulas) to be present at the birth and ate their placentas—although Ruby secretly believed they hired the shamans to eat the placentas.

Then there were the middle-class, organic-vegetable-consuming, *Guardian*-reading women who liked the idea of St. Luke's being a center of medical excellence as well as progressive. At the same time, though, they felt that paying for medical treatment severely compromised their left-wing principles. They got over this by going to St. Luke's and then writing long, guilt-ridden, but ultimately self-justifying articles in *The Guardian*.

Finally, there were the ordinary women who didn't have much money to spare, but saved what they could and went without holidays so that they could have their babies at St. Luke's. These were the women who had decided they'd had it up to here with public hospitals and clinics where they were forced to sit for hours on end in grubby green waiting rooms, TV blaring in the corner, carrying a wire supermarket basket containing their underwear, only to be seen by some disinterested junior doctor who barely looked up from his notes and addressed them as if their IQ were lower than their dress size.

Because her parents had struggled financially when she was growing up, Ruby liked to think of herself as "one of the people" and therefore part of the last group, but these days—even though she wasn't remotely obsessive about reading the *Guardian* or buying organic food—she knew that she had more in common with the second.

RUBY HAD ONLY agreed to see Dr. Double Barrel after the receptionist explained that Dr. Jane was off with a serious virus and she wasn't sure when she would be back. Since Ruby's checkup was already overdue because of her summer holiday, she decided to try and overcome her hangup about male gynecologists and take the appointment with DB. Maybe she was wrong about them and they got no more pleasure looking up a vagina than a car mechanic did looking down into an engine through the cylinder head.

Since Double Barrel was seeing Dr. Jane's patients as well as his own, he was running late and Ruby had been forced to wait over an hour.

In that time she'd drunk three cups of strong black coffee, which had made her feel even more jittery. It had also made her want to pee every twenty minutes. When she went to the loo the last time, there was no paper left and she'd had to go rooting around in her bag for tissue.

She also read *Hello!* magazine. Twice. Like many intelligent women she tried to convince herself that her interest in celebrity gossip was strictly ironic. The truth was she devoured it. Seeing who was pregnant, who had lost or gained weight, cellulite or wrinkles, or who had turned up to a film premiere done up not even like the dog's dinner, but worse—as the dog's doggy bag—nourished her the way chocolate did before her period. A candid snap of Kate's orange peel thighs, a shot of Gwyneth's eye bags—even if it was a trick of the light—could set her up for a whole week.

Ruby's fascination with celebrities, however, extended beyond mere curiosity. She had a professional interest. One of the reasons she was especially curious about who had just got pregnant or had a baby was because like St. Luke's, much of Ruby's clientele was made up of celebrity mothers.

Ruby ran and part-owned Les Sprogs, the exclusive mother and baby shop in Notting Hill. British and American stars, along with all the trust-fund mummies, came for the designer maternity and baby wear (Ruby had just taken delivery of her first consignment of Baby Gucci, which was flying off the shelves), the old-fashioned Silver Cross Balmoral prams at nearly £1,000 a pop, the all-terrain buggies and the cute sterling-silver egg containers for "my first curl."

As she flicked through *Hello!,* she came across a small piece about the Hollywood actress Claudia Planchette. The headline read: "Claudia Expecting Special Christmas Delivery." The article was accompanied by one of those snatched paparazzi-style shots—clearly reproduced from one of the tabloids—of her striding away briskly from St. Luke's prenatal department, her head down, her nauseatingly neat bump encased in tight Lycra. So, Ruby thought, unlike the first time she gave birth, Claudia wasn't going back to L.A. That meant Les Sprogs could be about to acquire yet another wealthy, high-profile customer.

Ruby had always possessed a head for business. Nobody in her family knew where it came from. It certainly wasn't her parents. Her mother, Ronnie—short for Rhona—was a well-regarded artist. Once a year she would have an exhibition at a trendy gallery in the East End. She might sell three or four paintings and make a few thousand pounds. Sometimes she sold none.

Ruby's dad, Phil, was a freelance commercial artist. He and Ronnie had met at art school, during Ronnie's first term. Phil was four years older and in his final year. It was an odd coupling, Ruby always thought—the hippie-dippy fine art student and the commercial artist. Ronnie always explained it by saying it had been lust at first sight. It was only as the relationship developed that they realized how they complemented and completed each other. She was the young, contemplative idealist, while he was more grounded and practical.

A few months after they met, Ronnie discovered she was pregnant. There was no question for either of them of not keeping the baby. Instead they got married in a civil ceremony, to which only Ronnie's sister, Sylvia, and a handful of their friends from art school were invited.

After Ruby arrived, Ronnie dropped out of art school to become a full-time mother. The three of them lived in a tiny rented flat in Balham, where the only bedroom served as sleeping quarters, nursery and study. It was here that Phil designed artwork for soap powder boxes and cereal packs.

Thirty years on, he was still doing it. He had always been reasonably successful and in demand, but it wasn't until the last ten years or so that he'd hit the Kellogg's, Nestlé, Procter & Gamble league. Until then, the companies that employed him were very much at the lower end of the market. His creations were strictly Happy Shopper. He must have done their custard creams and dishcloth packets for twenty years.

Throughout her childhood, her parents lived from one Spar or Happy Shopper check to the next. What made it worse was that because of the feast-or-famine nature of their lives, they could never afford to set money aside for taxes. The upshot was that her parents were constantly in debt as one cash flow crisis segued into the next.

Although Ruby was always aware that her dad worried incessantly about money, her mother never seemed that bothered. At heart Ronnie was a bit of an art school hippie who insisted it was vital to keep one's eye on the "big picture"—the demolition of the rain forests, the destruction of the ozone layer, globalization—rather than worry about a few late payments to the Inland Revenue.

As an armchair Buddhist—that is to say she read books on the subject, but never went so far as to join a group—she also believed that "the universe" would provide. Every time the bank threatened to withdraw their overdraft, she used to "chant for a check." Occasionally the universe provided. More often than not, it didn't. When it didn't, Ronnie would phone her gallery owner buddies and beg some wall space.

Ruby remembered one occasion when she was about fifteen when her parents' sole source of credit was their Ikea store card. For a month the only sustenance to be found in the deep freeze was Swedish meatballs, Johanssen's Delight and vodka.

Ruby only became aware of her parents' impoverished, boho existence when she was about ten or eleven. Until then she thought everybody came from homes where the wooden floors were splattered in oil paint, the sofas were beaten up and broken beds were propped up on piles of telephone directories. Slowly it began to dawn on her that most of her friends came from homes with carpets and that when you went into the kitchen, it didn't smell of turpentine because there were paintbrushes soaking in the sink alongside piles of dishes. Nor were there charcoal marks on all the paintwork and half-finished canvasses propped up on nearly every wall.

None of her friends had mothers with wild red hair who only ever wore workmen's dungarees covered in paint. They certainly didn't have mothers who picked them up from school in a fluorescent orange VW camper covered in Campaign for Nuclear Disarmament stickers and then sang along—very loudly and very badly—to Joni Mitchell's "Big Yellow Taxi" all the way home.

Most teenagers are embarrassed by their parents and some might say that Ruby had more reason to be embarrassed by hers than most. But her friends really liked Ronnie and Phil and enjoyed coming to the house. The whole disheveled hippie thing appealed to the kind of kids who were scolded for getting a speck on the cream linen sofa. Since her friends seemed to think her mum and dad were the coolest in the neighborhood, Ruby saw no need to rebel—at least not in the conventional way.

She didn't shout much or have tantrums. What she did was develop a passion at high school for business studies. Her dad's state of constant distress over money left its mark, and after the Ikea card incident, she was determined that she would never experience the financial insecurities she'd known growing up.

Even during her university vacations she was busy building her first business. Although she lacked her parents' artistic talent, she had inherited some of their creativity. She had an eye for jewelry and bric-a-brac, which she started buying and selling at antiques fairs. Her profits built slowly but steadily. After university—having discovered that it was the ethnicky pieces that attracted people most—she rented a large Transit van, which she and her then boyfriend, Dan, drove to Marrakesh and loaded up with Moroccan lamps, bowls, rugs, candleholders, jewelry and embroidered kaftans. When she got back she took a stall at Camden Market and shifted the lot in a few weeks. The business took off and pretty soon she was going on solo buying trips to Morocco while Dan minded the stall.

Then she and Dan broke up. He'd wanted to get married and although she loved him she felt that at twenty-two they were too young. Soon after the split, all the trendy interiors shops started getting into the Moroccan thing and prices at the local markets rocketed. She battled on for a few months, but eventually she was priced out.

Then by pure chance, the week before she was due to give up the stall, she found herself sitting in the dentist's waiting room, flicking through an old *National Geographic*. A picture of Guatemalan peasant children caught her eye, although it wasn't so much the children—beautiful as they were—that struck her. It was the clothes they were wearing: the glorious multicolored jackets, skirts and dresses. The brilliant pinks, oranges and greens clashed and yet worked spectacularly at the same time.

Two days later she was on a plane. A week after that she found a small village clothes-manufacturing cooperative and figured she could offer the workers double what the profit-hungry U.S. importers paid them and still have a decent income.

As the business took off, Ruby realized that once again she had found a gap in the market—albeit in children's fashion rather than in interiors. On top of that she was doing her bit for fair trade.

Trendy, slightly whole-grain young couples in strange vegetarian shoes and rainbow sweaters couldn't get enough of the Guatemalan outfits—particularly the baby romper suits, which Ruby had specially commissioned because she thought the fabrics looked just as stunning on newborns as they did on older children. As well as clothes, Ruby sold glass dream catchers and embroidered bags, which she had adapted so that they came with compartments for baby bottles, nappies and packets of wipes.

She wasn't sure why, but selling baby wear gave her enormous pleasure. Ever since she used to babysit for neighbors' children when she was at school she knew she loved kids, but there was more to it than that. She suspected it had something to do with all the excitement, the sense of hope and new beginnings, that surrounded pregnancy and childbirth.

Ruby had always longed for a baby brother or sister, but despite desperately wanting more children, Ronnie had only managed to produce Ruby. After a year or so of trying for a second child, the doctors discovered she had seriously blocked fallopian tubes, which couldn't be cleared by surgery. It was long before the days when IVF was commonplace, so Ronnie was sent home and told to be grateful to have conceived one "little miracle." Ronnie's sister, Sylvia, who was four years older, suffered from the same condition, but for her there would never be a miracle and she remained childless.

As a child, Ruby was a precociously reflective little soul. Not only did she feel sad for herself that she had no brothers or sisters, but she also felt sad for her mother. These days she couldn't help wondering if there was something about working at Les Sprogs, where she was constantly surrounded by pregnant women and babies, that filled an emotional gap and reminded her of life's possibilities.

Thanks to Dr. Jane those possibilities were even more

real. A couple of years ago—urged by Ronnie—Ruby had undergone a series of scans and tests, only to be told by a gleeful Dr. Jane that she had most definitely not inherited her mother and Aunty Sylvia's dodgy fallopian tubes.

When the baby and children's wear started to take off, even more good fortune came her way. Stella, one of her mother's cousins—married to a filthy rich art dealer—heard about Ruby's market stall on the family grapevine. She happened to be looking for a new venture to add to her business portfolio and offered to put up 90 percent of the money to open a mother and baby shop. She made it clear that her interest was purely financial and that she wanted no part in the day-to-day running of the business. That would be Ruby's responsibility.

Of course Ruby leaped at the offer and she and Stella had several meetings to discuss setting up the business. Stella was an elegant, rather haughty woman with a spectacularly taut face and a child substitute in the form of a yappy pooch named Blanche. Their first meeting took place over coffee at The Sanderson. The moment Stella spotted Ruby, she rose to her oyster suede heels, her wide mouth a barely upturned crimson gash. As Ruby shook her hand she was aware of Stella's chilly gray eyes giving her the Sloane Street once-over.

Ruby explained how she wanted to make the shop egalitarian with an ethnic twist—sort of Mothercare meets Body Shop. Ronnie had warned her daughter that Stella's experience of ethnic didn't extend beyond the best table at La Gavroche and that she balked at words like *egalitarian* in the same way that she balked when Harvey Nicks had the audacity to run out of demitasse sugar sticks. Ruby chose to ignore her mother and remained convinced until the moment she met Stella that she would be as thrilled by her vision as she was.

Of course it wasn't to be. Ruby's vision left Stella

distinctly underwhelmed. She dismissed it with a languid wave of her exquisitely manicured hand and explained that she had something far more grand in mind. She then outlined her own idea, which was to fill the shop with Flanders lace christening robes and monstrously expensive dry-clean-only baby clothes. She was convinced that trying to compete with a national mass-market corporation like Mothercare was ridiculous and that the only way they could make a go of the business was to go small and exclusive.

By the end of that first meeting, Ruby had decided there would be no point pursuing a business relationship with Stella. They had a completely different image in mind for the business. On top of that, Stella was a snob and the kind of person who would want her own way all the time. The whole thing would end up a disaster.

But as the days went by, Ruby couldn't quite bring herself to phone Stella and tell her she didn't want to go into partnership with her. The truth was that although she had a bit of capital, she didn't have enough to take a lease on a shop, decorate it and fill it with stock. When she contacted her bank they agreed to lend her only a fraction of what she required because she didn't have five years' worth of accounts. (Ruby had only got around to taking on an accountant and keeping proper sets of accounts in the last two or three years.)

It also occurred to her that Stella's plan for the business did make financial sense. As for the woman's none too appealing personality, Ruby decided that the way to handle her was to avoid conflict, go along with her and to slowly introduce her own ideas. It was a case of compromise or carry on with the market stall. In the end Ruby decided to compromise.

The new business struggled for a few months. Mainly through snobbery and habit, women tended to stay loyal to the old established Chelsea and Kensington mother and baby shops. But gradually things picked up and since by now Stella and her husband had moved to New York where Stella was busy with other business projects, Ruby felt confident enough to introduce a few dream catchers here and there and the odd Peruvian hat with the long flaps at the sides, as well as the Guatemalan dresses and romper suits. They walked off the shelves.

The day before Stella's twice-yearly visits from across the pond, all ethnic items were secreted away in the stockroom. From time to time, Ruby considered telling her about her experiment and how successful it had been, but she knew this would mean having to face a huge amount of flak. Even if Stella could see that the ethnic merchandise was making the company money, it wouldn't stop her getting livid with Ruby for going behind her back and demanding they be removed. She would insist that Ruby was alienating the rich and stylish Les Sprogs clientele and encouraging instead the namby-pamby-friends-of-the-ozone-layer brigade. She would go on to argue no doubt, that since the latter didn't possess anything like the wealth of the typical Les Sprogs customers, the business would be in the hands of the receiver within six months. Ruby, loath to jeopardize her relationship with Stella, saw no need to rock the boat.

"BEFORE I TAKE a smear, I'm just going to examine you internally," Dr. Double Barrel said. His voice was pretty matter-of-fact, but as she turned to look at him, she couldn't help noticing he had managed to raise the corners of his mouth. She was on the verge of making a nervous joke about her cervix with a smile, but thought better of it. "OK," she replied. She was staring at the ceiling again, playing her word game. There it was. Finally. The snap of the rubber glove. She felt his fingers inside her. Even though he'd warned her of what he was about to do, the suddenness made her flinch. "Ceps," she blurted.

"Sorry?" Double Barrel said vaguely. His mind was clearly on what he was feeling rather than what he was hearing. "What did you say?"

God, how did she go about explaining her speculum word search and that *ceps* was her latest discovery?

"Ceps," she repeated. "So, er, do you like ceps, doctor?"

Double Barrel's head shot up from between her legs. His face had turned pink. "Do I like sex? Look, maybe I should call in a nurse to chaperone."

"No, no," Ruby cried out, the color on her face now matching his. "I said 'cèpes.' They're mushrooms. They're my favorite. I was just wondering if you liked them, that's all."

His frown caused the doctor's bushy eyebrows to knit. Judging by his expression he was clearly wondering if she was quite all there.

"Not really. No," he said.

As she watched his head disappear again, she gave a faint, nervous laugh and mumbled something about them not being to everybody's taste.

"So, er..." she began, desperate to engage him in conversation since she couldn't think of any more speculum words, "...what do you do when you're not being a doctor?"

"I like to play a bit of squash," he said.

She had no idea what to say next, since she knew nothing about squash.

"So, are you any good?" she ventured.

"I get by. I was much better when I was younger."

She winced again as she felt the pressure of his fingers pushing and turning inside her.

"So you like to keep your hand in," she said. No sooner had the words left her lips than her hand flew to her mouth. Fabulous. On top of the cèpes faux pas, she was now suggesting to the male gynecologist, who was at this very moment examining her cervix, that he liked to keep his "hand in."

"No, er, that came out wrong. What I meant to say was..."

But DB didn't appear to have noticed her blunder. He simply continued his excavation. "Umm, that's most odd," he muttered after a few seconds.

"What's odd?" She was starting to feel edgy. "Is there something wrong?"

"Hmm, this is certainly a first," Double Barrel continued. His tone was curious rather than panicky, which Ruby found a relief. Then again, doctors never panicked. At least not British ones. American doctors were all: "OK, we have to get you into the OR stat or you're gonna die." British ones took a much more gung-ho line, believing that bravado gave hope and lessened the blow. Consequently, they would regard you over their pince-nez, and employ a string of cricketing analogies to indicate that things were looking less than hunky-dory.

As she waited to hear DB announce that from an interuterine perspective she was up against a rather sticky wicket, she turned to look at him. It took a few seconds for her eyes to focus on the tweezers he was holding and what was contained between them. The horror of what she could see being displayed in front of her, combined with all the caffeine she'd consumed in the waiting room, was causing her pulse to skyrocket. Her heart seemed to be beating out a tachycardic Morse code that said, "Get me out of here. Please, just get me out of here."

She let out a feeble "Oh dear" as her mind spun back to her last visit to the waiting room loo. She remembered the empty loo roll and how she'd had to use tissue from her bag.

Clearly there had been something stuck to the tissue. That something had come off on her and must have somehow worked its way up inside her.

Double Barrel regarded the tweezers and raised a bushy eyebrow. "Extraordinary place to find a postage stamp," he said.

Chapter 2

Ruby's heart carried on beating out its tachycardic Morse code: A stamp. In my vagina. My gynecologist just found a stamp in my vagina. Omigod, I cannot believe this is happening.

The worst part was that she had to lie there for a few more minutes, saturated in embarrassment, while Double Barrel did the Pap test. She thought she ought to explain to him how the stamp got inside her, but when she tried, all that came out was a garbled, strangulated mess of half-sentences. After three faux pas in ten minutes, her humiliation was complete and she could barely put one word in front of another.

To her surprise, DB handled the situation rather well. He patted her hand in a paternal way, told her not to worry and that these things happen. But she could tell from his concerned, patronizing smile that frankly these things didn't happen, and any remaining doubts he may have had that she was a basket case had vanished.

All Ruby wanted to do was get the hell out of DB's consulting room. The moment he left her alone behind the curtain, she grabbed her underwear and skirt. She had them on in seconds. Her tights were going to be too much of a fiddle so she rammed them into her bag. In less than a minute she was striding out toward the door.

"Er, Miss Silverman, before you go," DB called to her from behind his desk, forcing her to turn round and offer him a smile. "I just want to let you know that everything seems fine. You should get the results of your Pap test in the next few days, but your cervix looks perfectly healthy and I don't anticipate any problems." He stood up and extended his hand toward her. "So, we'll see you again in a year."

Barely able to look him in the eye, Ruby took his hand. "Absolutely," she said, forcing her face onto full beam. "Wouldn't miss it."

As she closed the door, she found herself glancing at the name plate. Of course, she remembered now. That was who he was: Dr. Steven Babbington-Gore.

DECIDING SHE WAS in desperate need of some water and a sit-down, Ruby made a beeline for the drink machine in the hospital foyer. As she started rooting in her purse for the right change, her mobile rang. Grappling with her bag, purse and phone, she dropped a handful of coins onto the floor. Somehow, she managed to press "connect."

"Hi, it's me." It was her best friend, Fiona. "I just wanted to say thank you again for the pirate outfit. Ben absolutely adores it. Last night after you'd gone he refused to take it off. He even insisted on going to bed in it."

Ben was Fi's oldest son. Her second, Connor, was a month old. Yesterday had been Ben's third birthday. Ruby knew that his grandparents were buying him the Playmobil pirate ship and she thought he might like a pirate outfit to go with it.

"I feel so guilty," Fi went on, "because it's already filthy."

"He's a little boy," Ruby said from the floor, where she was on her knees gathering up coins. "It's bound to get filthy."

"Rubes, you sound a bit tense. You all right?"

Ruby shuffled across the floor in order to gather up a couple of pound coins. "As all right as I can be, having just experienced the most humiliating twenty minutes of my entire life."

"Blimey, what happened?"

"OK—you know I had an appointment this morning for my annual gyne checkup..."

Fi gasped. "Omigod, your gynecologist made a pass at you."

"No."

"Oh, yeah, I remember—your gynecologist is a woman." She paused. "Bloody hell. *She* made a pass at you!"

"No, it's nothing like that—but as it happens, Dr. Anderson was away and I did end up seeing a man. Anyway..."

"Oops, hang on a tick, Ben says he needs to do a wee... That's it, darling, off you go and fetch your potty... OK, so go on. I'm all ears."

"Right, so there I am with my legs in stirrups when..."

"No, sausage, when you sit on the potty, you have to tuck your willy in, or the pee will go everywhere. Here, let me show you. Soppy Grandma bought you a girl's potty without a guard at the front, didn't she? Hang on a sec, Rubes, I have to go and rearrange my son's penis."

By now Ruby was on her feet and brushing floor dust from her skirt.

"Sorry about that." Fi came back, slightly breathless. "Since Connor arrived, Ben's completely regressed. He's back in nappies at night and I've had to start potty training him all over again. Found a turd under the kitchen table this morning."

"Wow! Lucky old you." Ruby laughed.

"The visiting nurse says it's because he's feeling jealous. Apparently it's quite normal for children to go on a dirty protest after a new sibling arrives. It's wearing me out, though, because I'm having to watch him all the time to check he doesn't pop a poo into the cutlery drawer or my handbag...OK, so you were saying."

This time Ruby got to the end of her story. "And you'll never guess what Double Barrel was holding."

"Good God—what?...Oops, hang on a minute, Ben's just brought me his potty...Clever boy! That's a lovely wee for Mummy. And only a tiny bit went on the sofa. Well done...So what was he holding?"

"A stamp. Can you believe it? The doctor pulled a postage stamp out of my vagina."

"You are kidding."

"Nope."

"My God. You must have been mortified." She paused. "But I suppose it's reassuring to know you've got a first-class vagina." Fi had started to giggle.

"Ha, ha. Very funny," Ruby came back.

"Sorry, I couldn't resist it. Look, don't worry about the stamp. Doctors get to see all sorts of weird stuff. I read this article recently about how mothers have to be careful because little girls are always sticking pebbles and bits of Lego up them." At this point Fi said there was something else she needed to talk to Ruby about, but needed to hang up because the cat was sniffing round the potty full of pee and the baby had woken up. "I'll call you later."

"OK," Ruby said.

"And don't forget what I said about little girls."

"Yes, but I'm not two," Ruby said. "I'm thirty-two. I'm a thirty-two-year-old woman who had a postage stamp in her vagina." But Fi was gone.

As Ruby pressed "end" she looked up to see a man dressed in blue surgical scrubs standing next to her. She found herself taking in the trendy ultrashort dark hair and long sideburns, the nut-brown eyes set into the gentle smiling face, the fact that he was about her own age . . . the fact that if he had been standing there for more than two seconds, he must have overheard her conversation with Fi and known about the stamp in her vagina.

"Pardon me," came an American accent, "but I was wondering if you were planning on getting anything from the drink machine. The thing is, you've been here awhile and I was kinda hoping to get a cup of coffee."

"Oh, God, yes of course," she blurted, her face prickling with beet-red blush. "You go ahead. I've changed my mind."

"Sure?"

She nodded and waved him in front of her.

"Thanks," he said. He smiled again, only this time she noticed. She couldn't tell if he was just being polite or stifling laughter about her vaginal stamp. She decided he was probably laughing and that a few minutes from now her recent predicament would be the subject of canteen hilarity. Unless of course Double Barrel had already blabbed, but since he hadn't struck her as having much of a sense of humor, he was unlikely to be the bantering, joke-telling type. On top of that he had come across as the kind of doctor who took patient confidentiality very seriously.

She wasn't convinced that the young American doctor standing in front of her was quite so lacking in the humor department. She decided she had to convince him that he hadn't heard what he thought he'd heard.

The doctor took a steaming polystyrene cup from the dispenser, smiled at her again and started to move away.

Shuffling from foot to foot, Ruby nodded toward her phone, which she was still holding: "I, er . . . I was chatting to my best friend just then. She's . . . she's a stand-up comic. And . . ." And what? God, where was she planning to take this? "And . . . er . . . some executives at the post office have asked her to do a gig at the end of their annual conference next month. I've been helping develop some new material."

"Really?" he said. "Sounds great. Very original."

It was possible he believed her, Ruby thought, but it seemed more likely that he was simply going along with the story to save her blushes. Not that it had worked, since her face was still burning with embarrassment. Suddenly his pager went. His hand shot to the waistband of his hospital scrubs.

"Sorry, gotta go," he said. He took a hurried sip of his coffee. Then he placed the cup on top of the drink machine, alongside all the other barely touched cups of coffee, clearly abandoned by colleagues whose pagers had also cut short their coffee breaks.

She watched him turn and begin striding out toward X-ray. For a moment her embarrassment subsided as she noticed the way the blue cotton of his scrubs outlined his perfect rear.

Chapter 3

When Ruby got back to Les Sprogs, there wasn't a single customer in the shop. Even though the business was doing so well, she couldn't stop herself worrying when there were no customers. Today, though, she was less concerned. First of all it was a Monday morning and Mondays were always slow. Second it was raining, and third, all the other shops in the street were empty.

Chanel was leaning against the counter, her head buried in one of the downmarket glossies she always liked to read. "Pisces," she announced, noticing Ruby walking into the shop. She stabbed the horoscope page with a finger. "That's me... hang on, this looks interesting: 'Jupiter, planet of good fortune, is about to align with Venus, planet of romance. This could signal a windfall, not to mention a long awaited boost to your love life.' Wow. You know what I reckon?"

"What?" Ruby said, taking a sip from the bottle of water she'd just picked up at Starbucks—to rid herself of all the caffeine she'd soaked up at the hospital. She placed a large cappuccino on the counter for Chanel.

Chanel acknowledged it with an "Ooh, cheers, I've been gagging for a coffee." Then she straightened. "OK, I reckon this means somebody's going to die and leave me enough money to pay for those collagen injections I've been wanting in my G-spot."

Chanel had been with Les Sprogs since it opened. Officially, she was Ruby's number two, but apart from the accounts, which were Ruby's province, they pretty much worked as a team. They shared everything from serving customers and dealing with phone and e-mail orders to stocktaking and going out to fetch the coffee. At Christmas and during sale time they took on temporary staff to help out, but mostly they managed on their own.

Stella always used to get sniffy when she found Chanel reading magazines because she said it created a bad impression. Since Chanel was meticulous about only doing it when the shop was empty and since she worked her socks off the rest of the time, Ruby never minded. The truth was that Stella wasn't overly keen on Chanel and had never wanted to take her on.

"Are you mad?" Stella had snapped at Ruby after Chanel's interview—to which she had insisted on coming even though she had agreed to leave the hiring and firing to Ruby. "We can't possibly have somebody like that working here." The words *like that* had been put in italics.

It seemed that she had taken one look at Chanel's bosomy size fourteen frame, encased in tight stone-washed denim, her brassy blonde highlights and her very, very visible panty line, and practically had an attack of the vapors.

"She looks like an Essex barmaid," Stella went on. "And then there's her accent. Her vowels are flatter than roadkill and her grasp of grammar is nonexistent. I simply refuse to employ somebody who can't even decline the past participle of the verb 'to be.' Doesn't she know that the second person singular is were, not woz?"

But Ruby had seen beyond the clothes and Chanel's deficiency in the declension department. In Chanel Stubbs, she saw a chatty, warmhearted soul, who clearly adored children. She was thirty, had been a nanny for ten years before applying to Les Sprogs and came with outstanding references. When Ruby asked her why she had given it up, Chanel explained that she had just got married and that the long, unsociable hours meant she didn't get much time with her husband.

As she listened to Chanel talking about her work as a nanny, a plan formed in Ruby's mind. It occurred to her that Les Sprogs needed a unique selling point, something that made it different from all the other mother and baby shops in London. One way of achieving this, she thought, might be to make it somewhere that attracted not only women but their children, too. From the heartfelt way Chanel talked about the children she had looked after—she was in regular touch with all of them—Ruby thought it was fair to assume that little ones loved her as much as she loved them. Chanel, she decided, would be a huge hit with customers' children.

Then fate stepped in to prove the point. Halfway through the interview—which was being conducted at the back of the shop—a friend of Stella's turned up with her three-year-old. Stella insisted on breaking off for a few minutes to chat to her. What happened next was typical of Stella. She introduced her friend to Ruby, but not to Chanel. She also completely ignored the little girl. It was only when Blanche, Stella's yapping pooch, jumped up at the child, scaring her and making her cry, that Stella was forced to acknowledge her.

"Oh, that's just her way of showing she likes you," Stella cooed, making no attempt to remove the dog, which was still pawing the child. It was the little girl's agitated mother who scooped up the dog, handed her to Stella and suggested the animal might be in need of a walk. While Stella got affronted, but carried on smiling in an attempt not to show it, Chanel knelt down to the child's height, shook her hand and said: "Hiya, I'm Chanel. What's your name?"

The child turned and buried her head in her mother's skirts, but Chanel persevered. "Wow, that's a beautiful dolly you've got there. Isn't she the one I've seen on the telly? Doesn't her hair grow by magic?"

The little girl looked back at Chanel and rewarded her with a hesitant nod.

"Can you do the magic and make her hair grow?" Chanel asked her.

Another nod, but this time there was a smile as well.

"Do you think you could show me? I'd love to see it."

A couple of minutes later the child, who finally revealed her name to be Freya, was sitting on Chanel's lap chatting away with her as if she'd known her all her life. Ruby felt really guilty breaking them up to continue the interview.

Ruby was left in no doubt that Chanel would be perfect for Les Sprogs. Her references had said she was a hard worker and on top of that she had proven how well she got on with children.

Stella took some persuading, but after Ruby had worked on her gently but consistently for a week, she threw up her hands, said "OK, on your head be it," and agreed to give Chanel a month's trial. For her part, Ruby acknowledged that Chanel's stonewashed jeans probably wouldn't play well in Notting Hill and she agreed to introduce a staff uniform. Ruby had pale blue T-shirts made with the scarlet Les Sprogs logo across the front, which she and Chanel wore over smart black trousers.

Although she kept promising to be more hands-off as far as the business was concerned, Stella found it impossible. Much as Ruby had expected, she turned out to be an almost pathological control freak and insisted on being consulted at every turn. Irritating as Ruby found this, she was forced to admit that if she had invested as much money as

Stella had invested in Les Sprogs, she might well have become a pathological control freak, too.

Long before the Chanel issue, though, they'd had another major difference of opinion. They hadn't been able to agree about how the shop should be decorated. Ruby envisaged a modern minimalist feel with lots of primary colors and the walls covered in giant black-and-white photographs of pregnant women, babies and children playing. Stella wanted the Martha Stewart, weather-boarded house in Maine look: natural wood floors, painted dressers, squidgy check linen sofas, teddies and Beatrix Potter mice wearing aprons and wire-rimmed glasses dotted about the place.

As usual Ruby had fought for her vision, but without getting into a full-blown confrontation with Stella. On this issue, though, Ruby was finding it particularly hard, since she was convinced her approach was the right one.

It was her father, Phil, who finally convinced his daughter to pull back. He said shop design was essentially packaging and that he knew from his own experience how important it was to give the customer what she wanted, rather than force your own vision on her. Even though he agreed with Ruby that the image Stella had in mind was twee and dated, he could also see that it was cozy and reassuring. "It harks back to an era—albeit a nonexistent one—of happy, wholesome families gathered round the pine kitchen table eating Mom's apple pie. It's the Notting Hill Billies meets the Ingallses. You just watch how it pulls in the punters." Of course he was right.

Ruby's climb down over the shop design issue was immediately rewarded by Stella's announcing her departure to New York. These days—because of all her business commitments over there—she visited Les Sprogs no more than once or twice a year. Finally she was leaving Ruby to run things alone.

Occasionally she would phone, but it was only to touch

base. If Chanel happened to take a call from Stella, she was always her chatty self, but their conversation never lasted more than a few seconds. Ruby knew that it was Stella, as she would cut the conversation short since she merely tolerated Chanel. Even though Stella was now in no doubt about how popular Chanel was with the customers and their children, it wasn't in her nature to back down and admit she may have been wrong about not wanting to take her on. Whenever she visited the shop, Stella greeted Chanel with the kind of distaste that Jerry Seinfeld reserved for Newman. Ruby assumed it was the same when they spoke on the phone.

In true Chanel style, she refused to let Stella get her down—particularly as she hardly ever saw her. Nor was she ever rude to her. She understood that if she were rude or started a row, it would have affected Ruby's relationship with Stella. Then Ruby would have no choice but to let Chanel go.

So, with a good-natured smile and muttering something barely audible about it being "the icicle" on the phone, she would hand the receiver to Ruby. Then she would go and find some shelves to tidy.

"C'MON," RUBY SAID, re Chanel's proposal to have collagen injected into her G-spot. "You wouldn't really have injections up there, would you?"

Chanel thought for a second. "Dunno. They said on this plastic surgery program that you have the most amazing orgasms afterward. Only problem is that if I went for it, Craig would go ballistic. He'd be worried sick about it all going wrong."

Chanel's husband, Craig, was a London plumber who made a fortune. He was a huge ex-navy, rugby-playing bear of a man with a heart every bit as big as Chanel's. He would have lassoed the moon for her if he could. Collagen injections aside, whatever Chanel wanted, Chanel got. Not that she asked for much. She wasn't the demanding type. Nevertheless, she only had to mention in passing that she'd seen a kitchen in Ikea that she liked and it was hers. Ditto bathrooms, lounge furniture and jewelry.

Chanel returned Craig's love by refusing to take off the gold Chanel earrings he had given her on their wedding day. For her, the interlocking Cs stood for Chanel and Craig and were a symbol of their eternal love.

She also cooked him a "proper meat and two veg man meal" every night when she got home, ironed his boxers (not that he'd ever asked her to) and generally fussed and doted over him as if he were a helpless baby.

Chanel was no fool. She knew that in many ways Craig had become her surrogate child and she his, but neither of them could help treating the other the way they did. Until a baby came along, which, with the failure of one IVF attempt after another, seemed less and less likely, each remained the center of the other's life.

"Ironic, isn't it?" Chanel often said. "I come from a family of six. Mum only had to look at me dad and she'd be knocked up. My sisters are the same. All breed like blinkin' rabbits. Then there's me: one miscarriage and that's me lot."

Ruby once asked her how she could bear to work in a mother and baby shop where she was constantly surrounded by children and pregnant women. Chanel had shrugged. "Dunno, suppose by rights I should want to run a mile," she said. "But I love babies and kids and I'm buggered if I'm gonna run away and let my problems get the better of me. I just know me and Craig 'ave to plow on with the IVF and that one day it will be me standing the other side of this counter trying to decide which Moses basket to choose." Chanel paused. "Bloody hell, I must sound like some obsessed nutter." Ruby told her she didn't sound at all like a nutter, just utterly determined.

Despite Chanel's courage and bravado, there had been two or three occasions when Ruby had noticed her in the stockroom pressing a Babygro or tiny woolen cardigan to her cheek. Each time her eyes had been full of tears.

"SO," CHANEL SAID now, "your checkup at the hospital go OK?"

Ruby let out a tiny sigh. "You may as well know. You'll only hear it from Fi the next time she comes in." She explained about Dr. Double Barrel and the stamp.

"You know," Chanel said, apparently not in the least bit shocked by what she'd just heard, "I used to go out with this bloke who was really into sex toys. Only, because neither of us 'ad much money, we used to improvise. Instead of Chinese love balls I used to make do with an 'ard-boiled egg."

Ruby looked at her, incredulous.

"Of course, you 'ad to keep the shell on," Chanel went on. "If you'd peeled it, it would've disintegrated. Anyway, one day the egg got stuck and I ended up in the emergency room, so I know how you must've felt. It was the most embarrassing two hours of my life."

"I can see that," Ruby said, "but I bet you didn't have the added humiliation of some gorgeous American doctor overhearing you on the phone telling your friend that you had a stamp lodged in your vagina."

"Omigod. How gorgeous?"

"Very."

"What on earth did you say?"

Ruby told her. Chanel burst out laughing, but was nevertheless hugely impressed by Ruby's quick thinking.

Chanel was still commiserating between giggles, when a

couple of customers came in. They were typical trustafarian mummies: ski-slope cheekbones, expensive highlights, each with a little Gucci bag slung over one shoulder. Even though it was cold and raining they were both wearing sunglasses—albeit as hair bands. One of them had really taken the early September chill to heart and was wearing a three-quarter-length fake fur coat.

"Blimey," Chanel muttered to Ruby. "I wonder 'ow many Muppets 'ad to die for that." Ruby shushed her, but it was as much as she could do to stop herself bursting out laughing. The other thing Ruby loved about Chanel was her irreverence.

From their slightly awkward body language and the unfamiliar way they were chatting, Ruby got the impression the women didn't know each other that well and that they had probably bumped into each other outside the shop.

The woman in the coat was about six months pregnant and had a toddler in tow. The other was carrying her newborn in a leather and sheepskin Bill Amberg papoose. The papoose hinted to Ruby that the woman was a natural-childbirth-St.-Luke's mother. The too-posh-to-push brigade never used papooses because they spoiled the look of their clothes. Instead they favored the Porsche buggy.

The toddler, a little boy, was whining and demanding to be given the packet of potato chips his mother was holding.

"Not until you say the magic word, Finn. What is it? Pl... Pl..."

Finn turned down the corners of his mouth and folded his arms in defiance.

"Come on. Say it. Say the magic word. Pl..."

"Plain!" the child exclaimed, holding out a tiny chubby hand. Since he couldn't have been more than three, it was clear to Ruby and Chanel that this had been said without a hint of sarcasm or cheek. His mother didn't see it that way. Just as she was about to explode with fury, Chanel stepped in and suggested she take the child off to the play area. Introducing a play area with a miniature slide, climbing frame and pedal cars had been Chanel's idea. It had also turned out to be a stroke of absolute genius. It was another reason mothers returned to Les Sprogs again and again.

Coat woman was beginning to calm down. "Ooh, isn't that exciting," she cooed to her son. "Now then, off you go with the nice lady while I browse." Finn took Chanel's hand and the two of them trotted off. "Oh, by the way," coat woman called out after Chanel, "Finn's educational psychologist says he is gifted, so he might find the Play-Doh a bit beneath him."

Neither Ruby nor Chanel reacted. They were used to shallow, haughty women like the coat and their long-suffering trophy brats. It was at times like this that Ruby wished she had been able to fulfil her dream of opening a more mass-market baby shop with an ethnic, Body Shop–style spin. She had even come up with a name for it: Baby Organic. She would often lie awake and let her imagination run away with her as she imagined herself pioneering the first global baby-wear chain, which sold affordable clothes—and maybe later on, even baby food—made entirely from organic products.

The two women made a beeline for the Gucci baby wear. They oohed and aahed over the fabulously expensive outfits. Finally the coat selected a pair of blue suede baby slippers with a £100 price tag. As the pair carried on picking things up and putting them down, Ruby caught snippets of their conversation. At one point the coat patted her bump and informed papoose woman that she had booked herself in for a planned cesarean at the Portland.

"Oh really?" papoose woman simpered, her tone giving more than a hint that she was about to claim the moral high ground in this conversation. "So you're not going to do it naturally, then? Such a shame. I always think natural childbirth is better for the baby." She looked down beatifically and stroked her baby's head. "But of course your mind has to be centered and you have to be in a place where you see the labor as work rather than pain. Not everybody is capable of doing that. When I had Serendipity I went for seventeen hours without any drugs. But it was worth it for the whole water-birth experience. And then afterward we buried the placenta under a tree in the garden."

"That's absolutely fine," the coat came back, her languid smile no disguise for the venom she was clearly feeling, "if you don't mind the aftereffects. Personally, I always worry about the structural damage caused by natural childbirth. Your husband may not mind finding your hallway a great deal roomier than it once was, but I know mine would be less than happy." At this point the women exchanged taut, tension-charged smiles and went their separate ways. For the next ten or fifteen minutes each looked round the shop alone. In the end neither woman bought very much. Papoose woman bought a dream catcher and a pair of newborn Navaho moccasins. The coat bought Finn a £40 T-shirt with "I'm a genius" written across it.

There was only one more customer before lunch, but Chanel managed to sell her a Silver Cross Balmoral pram and a whole load of nursery furniture and baby clothes—including half a dozen Guatemalan romper suits.

"Kerrr-ching," Chanel declared after the woman had gone. Chanel was on commission and worked out the sale had earned her over £50. She insisted that lunch was on her.

They sat eating bacon and fried egg sandwiches in the tiny kitchen area at the back of the shop. The filling had been Ruby's idea—not that Chanel had objected. Like Ruby, she was always up for a bacon sandwich smothered in ketchup, but of the two of them, Ruby was far and away the worst junk food junkie. Ruby was the only person she knew who had watched *Supersize Me* and salivated throughout.

Afterward she demolished two Big Macs, large fries and a Coke.

She was aware that for somebody committed to opening a baby-wear shop devoted to all things organic, her love of junk food was—to put it mildly—something of a contradiction. These days, though, she'd stopped trying to explain it. She reasoned that vices were part of being human and lusting after fatty, processed comfort food was hers.

To her credit, she did try to limit her intake of rubbish. She had no wish to end up with a quadruple bypass before she reached menopause, or turn into one of those wobbly-arsed lard people you saw on documentaries about Texas. Tonight she would atone for the bacon sandwich with a chickpea salad in a low-fat dressing, but it wouldn't give her anything like the same olfactory satisfaction or serotonin hit as a hamburger.

While they ate they glanced up at the CCTV screen from time to time, looking out for customers.

"Ooh, look," Chanel said, picking up her magazine again. "Claudia Planchette's expecting again."

"I know," Ruby said. "There was a piece about it in *Hello!*"

Ruby looked down at the picture. It was very different from the *Hello!* photograph. In that one she had been caught unawares with her hair all over the place and no makeup. In this—clearly posed—picture she was a vision of fresh-faced, high-cheekboned loveliness—or as Chanel put it: "Bloody 'ell, look at her. She's got the hair, the figure, the tits, everything."

Ruby pointed out that the star was six months pregnant and even though she looked pretty stunning she wasn't exactly her usual svelte self. Chanel grunted, turned sideways and pointed at her not inconsiderable stomach. "She's six months gone and she looks smaller than me. God, why do some women get all the blinkin' genes?"

Ruby laughed and told her it wasn't about genes, it was about being rich enough to have dieticians, personal trainers and makeup artists on tap.

Chanel kept staring at the photograph. "So, where's her spiritual guru, then? That Raj Bhojan or whatever he's called. You never see her in a photograph without him in tow." Claudia wasn't simply a staggeringly rich Hollywood actress and mother of Avocado, aged two, she was also a self-proclaimed seeker after truth and spiritual enlightenment.

"Probably off somewhere, putting drops in his third eye," Ruby remarked. Chanel laughed so much she almost choked on her sandwich. She carried on devouring the article and reading bits out to Ruby. "Blimey, get this: 'St. Luke's has agreed to Planchette bringing in her own Ghanaian midwife to deliver the baby. After the birth, in an ancient Ghanaian ritual, the midwife will bury the placenta in the garden of Planchette's £7.5 million home to ensure the child doesn't wander from its roots.'

"So, what do you think she'll call this one?" Chanel went on. "My money's on Lychee or Quince. Or Pomegranate. Pomegranate Planchette. It's got a certain ring about it, don't you reckon?"

They spent the next couple of minutes convulsed with laughter as they came up with even more bizarre names like Paw Paw and Papaya.

"Oh, by the way," Chanel said when they couldn't think of any more, "I forgot to mention . . . Strange coincidence—while you were at St. Luke's this morning, one of their hospital managers rang to speak to you."

She explained that the manager, whose name was Jill McNulty, was in charge of the prenatal department. She wanted to know if Ruby would be prepared to give a regular talk to first-time mothers about what they needed to buy for a new baby. "I think you should do it," Chanel went on. "It'd be great PR for the shop."

"And not only that," Ruby said with faux brightness, "it would give me the perfect opportunity to bump into Dr. Double Barrel. Not to mention the American doctor."

"Oh, come on, you won't see either of them. When you arrive, this Jill woman will probably whisk you straight into a lecture room and afterward there'll be a quick cup of something herbal and disgusting and you'll be on your way."

Ruby let out a long slow breath. "I suppose you're right," she said. "I'm just being silly. I'll give Jill McNulty a call. It'd be daft to pass up a chance like this."

Chapter 4

That evening Ruby should have been having dinner at Laura and Jack's. She hadn't seen them since they got married a few months ago. They were old friends from her Camden Market days. Jack still ran their stall selling art deco glass and porcelain, while Laura now worked for a small arts theater in Islington where she was in charge of wardrobe. She had rung Ruby to say that Jack was cooking Thai and that she was inviting actors. Seriously cute actors, she'd said.

Then, last Saturday, Ronnie had phoned Ruby at the shop and also invited her to dinner on Monday. Ruby said she would love to have come if she hadn't already accepted Laura and Jack's invitation.

"I don't suppose there's any possibility," Ronnie began tentatively, "that you could beg off."

"I guess I could," Ruby said, "but what's so special about me coming on Monday? I can make any other night next week."

"It's just that your dad and I decided on the spur to take a short trip to Rome next week and Monday's the only night we've got free before we go."

Ruby asked what was so vital it couldn't wait until they got back the following weekend.

"There's just something I have to tell you, that's all."

"But why can't you tell me now?" Panic suddenly engulfed her. "Mum, there's nothing the matter, is there? You're not ill, are you?"

"I'm fine. Honest—and Dad's fine, too. It's nothing like that. Please just say you'll come. I wouldn't ask if it weren't important."

"OK, but can't you just give me a clue about what's going on?"

"I'd rather not over the phone and anyway I've really got to run." Ronnie couldn't get off the line fast enough. "I'm meeting a couple of girlfriends for lunch and I'm late. Bye, darling. See you Monday." That had been it. End of conversation. Her mother had hung up.

For nearly three days Ruby had barely stopped thinking about what could be so important. Now, driving toward her parents' house in Hendon, she was still trying to work it out. The most likely answer was that her parents were going to announce that they had come into some money. But if they'd had a windfall, surely they would have been bursting with the news. They wouldn't have kept it a secret.

She knew there was an inheritance in the offing, but Ronnie and Phil had been perfectly open about it. Grandma Esther, her father's very elderly and ailing mother, had died a few months ago. Maybe she had left a fortune that nobody knew about.

Ruby had always assumed—along with her parents—that Grandma Esther didn't have much more than a few savings and the flat in Hackney where she and Ruby's late Grandpa Leo had lived for the last forty years. Her grandparents' glove manufacturing business had made them a reasonable living, but Ruby never got the impression it had done that well. Phil had always been nagging them to expand and buy more up-to-date sewing machines and cutting equipment, but Grandpa Leo refused to believe new equipment would increase his output. The truth was that neither Leo nor Esther was particularly bright. In the twenties, just after they got married, they decided to emigrate from Germany and make a fresh start in New York. They bought boat tickets from some shyster travel agent and ended up in London, thinking it was New York. Family legend had it that they spent the next three months looking for the Statue of Liberty.

Nope, Grandma Esther had left no great fortune. Ruby was sure of it.

If her parents hadn't had a windfall and neither of them was ill, she had no idea what the big secret could be.

She felt mean having the thought, but ever since Ronnie's call, Ruby hadn't been able to stop herself muttering that her mother's news had better be worth her having canceled on Laura and Jack. Now that Ruby was finally back in the saddle dating-wise, she didn't take kindly to missing a chance to meet severely cute actors.

Until recently, romantically speaking, she had been going through a bit of a dry spell. Not that this had been forced upon her. It was very much self-imposed.

It had taken her a good three months to get over her last boyfriend, Matt. During that time she'd continued to see her girlfriends, but she hadn't been remotely interested in meeting new men.

The sad part was that Ruby and Matt had only been going out for eight weeks when the publishing company he worked for offered him the job in Australia. If they'd known each other longer—a year maybe—they would have had a bit of history to fall back on.

Nevertheless, during the short time they had been going out, both had declared their love for each other and were determined to give the relationship across two continents thing a try. She promised she would fly out every couple of months and he said he would do the same. But because of the distance and the jet lag, it was impossible for Ruby to "pop" to Sydney for the weekend, and going for any longer meant leaving Chanel on her own to run the shop.

What made it worse was that since Matt had gone to Sydney to set up an entire new arm of the publishing company, it was impossible for him to take much time off at all, let alone disappear back to London for a week at a time.

Even though they phoned and e-mailed constantly, after a couple of months, the strain of not seeing him got too much.

After several tearful, late-into-the-night discussions with Fi, she ended it with Matt. Not in a letter or e-mail. That would have been unspeakably cruel. Instead, she flew to Sydney. Over a candlelit dinner at one of those trendy Paddington eateries, packed with blissfully happy, doe-eyed young couples, she took his hand and told him as gently as she could that she didn't think things were working out.

When he said he was struggling with their relationship, too, she felt relieved. It made the whole thing easier to talk about.

Then, after dinner, they went back to his flat and ended up making love. This threw them both into a tailspin of confusion and they stayed up the entire night going round and round in circles trying to find a formula, some way of salvaging it and making it work, but it always came back to the same thing: neither was prepared to put the relationship before their careers.

Just before dawn they decided to take a stroll by the harbor. At one point they sat down on a bench, both staring out into the early morning mist. When their eyes finally met a few minutes later, they knew it was over. They clung to each other and cried.

Despite the clinging and the crying, it was clear to Ruby that there must have been something missing between them from the beginning. Otherwise, surely they would have found a way to make it work. If she'd really loved Matt she would have given up Les Sprogs in a heartbeat and flown out to be with him. If he'd loved her, wouldn't he have offered to give up his job and find a new one in London? When she gave it some thought, it slowly dawned on her that their relationship had always been a bit odd. Why had she never questioned the amount of time they spent talking about work? The truth was that when they weren't making love, they were talking shop. It wasn't humor, affection and a shared view of the world that had bound them together. It was ambition.

Understanding this didn't stop her feeling sad for ages after the split.

For a while they phoned and e-mailed, but pretty soon communication petered out.

It was only in the last few weeks that she'd felt like dating again, so she'd accepted every party invitation going and had even gone on a couple of disastrous blind dates organized by Fi.

Because Fi was almost obsessive about not losing touch with friends from university and even school, she knew tons of people. It wasn't so bad when Fi suggested a blind date with one of her old friends. The problem came when the guy in question was a friend of a friend and Fi didn't have any information to go on—other than "apparently he's really nice."

Ruby had gone on two blind dates with men Fi didn't know firsthand. One turned out to be forty-five, which wouldn't have been a problem if it hadn't been for the hairpiece. All through dinner, he kept urging Ruby to tug it to feel how real it was. The second spent the entire evening telling her about his depression and how his shrink said it stemmed from his fear of changing. Ruby decided that this explained his working for the Department of Social Security since graduating, as well as the stains down his shirt.

Fi was the sister Ruby never had. They'd met at Manchester University, where they both studied English. They'd clicked immediately and pretty soon they were staying in each other's rooms until the small hours, drinking cheap wine and talking about boys and sex.

One particularly boozy night in the first year, they got into a daft competition trying to remember the lines from all their childhood Dr. Seuss books. Ruby was positive she could recite the whole of *Fox in Socks*. She got as far as "Gooey goo for chewy chewing! That's what that Goo-Goose is doing" and couldn't get any further. Fi won because she was able to finish *Fox in Socks* as well as remembering large chunks of *Green Eggs and Ham*.

Somehow, from here the *Green Eggs and Ham* society was formed. Each week a group of English and philosophy students would meet to discuss why *he* would not eat them on a train or on a plane and whether *he* had an eating disorder brought on by an emotionally abusive relationship with *that Sam I am*. Between ten and twenty students showed up every week and afterward they would all go out for a curry and get slaughtered.

After they graduated Ruby set up her market stall at Camden Lock and Fi became an English teacher. She was talented and dedicated and pretty soon she was made head of the department.

Then, four years ago, Laura and Jack moved and invited Ruby to their housewarming party. Ruby took Fi along and Fi met Saul, one of Laura's "seriously cute" actor friends.

Ruby took an instant liking to Saul and couldn't have been more delighted when Fi announced a few months later that they were in love.

Fi's widowed mother, Bridget, now in her late sixties, had always been determined that each of her five daughters should marry "a professional and a good Catholic." One by one they had all let her down. Two had got hitched to beer-gutted builders, for whom religion held about as much interest as aromatherapy. One had married a Muslim social worker and another was living in sin in Woking with a podiatrist. As it happened, the podiatrist was Catholic, but in Bridget's eyes, so far down the food chain, career-wise, that it made no difference.

Fi had often told Ruby how pressured she felt to do right by her mother. When she finally plucked up the courage to break the news and tell her that she was not only marrying an actor, but a Jewish actor, Bridget turned white and had to grab the back of a chair to stop herself from collapsing. Then, gazing up at the ceiling, she crossed herself three times and pleaded with the Holy Father to take her now.

In the months leading up to the wedding, Bridget was forever on the phone, begging Fi to call it off. Ruby would never forget visiting Fi one particular evening and sitting listening to her on the phone to Bridget. For over an hour Fi tried to placate her. Finally she got furious and put the phone down on her mother. No sooner had she done this than the phone rang again. Fi could see from the caller display that it was Bridget.

Fi begged Ruby to take it. "You know how much she loves you. She'll listen to you. Just tell her what a great bloke Saul is and how much we love each other."

Ruby took the phone, but she barely got a word in.

"Sweet Jesus, will you tell me how could she do this to me?" came Bridget's hysterical voice with its heavy southern Irish accent. "God knows marrying some layabout actor is bad enough, but to hitch her wagon to a heathen. You know it was the Jews that betrayed our Lord. How could she commit such a sin? Has she no thought for her mortal soul?"

"You know, Mrs. Gilhooley," Ruby said, "I'm Jewish."

"Ah, yes, I know darlin', but you weren't one of them heathen Jews that crucified our Lord."

"But Mrs. Gilhooley, I don't think Saul was exactly standing there cheering with a two-shekel bucket of popcorn and a can of diet ass's milk."

Neither Ruby's reason nor Fi's tearful begging and fury got through to Bridget.

Saul's parents, on the other hand, had no problems with their son marrying a Catholic. They weren't particularly religious and were happy for the wedding to take place in a Catholic church and for the ceremony to be conducted by a priest and a Reform rabbi working in tandem.

When the big day came, it all went off rather well. Much to everyone's surprise, Bridget turned up—albeit red eyed, wearing black and clutching her rosary—and if anybody overheard one of Saul's elderly uncles muttering about the rabbi being so Reform he was a Nazi, nothing was said.

Admittedly, things did get a bit sticky at the point in the service where the priest asked if anybody had any objections to the marriage. Ruby couldn't help noticing one of Fi's brothers practically getting Bridget in a half nelson and threatening to strangle her with her rosary beads if she so much as opened her mouth.

BACK IN THE car, Ruby was pulling up outside her parents' house.

Phil answered the door. She kissed him hello and hung her coat on the end of the banister. Whenever she came home she never failed to notice how much the house had changed in the last few years. Since Phil had started to earn decent money, it was barely recognizable. OK, the place was still full of clutter, the familiar smell of turpentine hung in the air and it was clear that cleaning still wasn't a top priority chez Silverman, but now there was a posh kitchen, newly laid wooden floors, fresh blinds and trendy furniture. The house had never really felt comfortable when she was growing up. Now it did.

Her dad had changed, too. There was a lightness about him, which she had rarely seen when she was younger. Now that money wasn't tight, he was able to relax. He'd started exercising and watching his weight. For years, worry had caused him to comfort-eat confectionary and fatty foods. Ruby often wondered if watching her father eating unhealthily had kick-started her love of junk food. These days, though, he was a good thirty pounds lighter than a decade ago. His hair, now almost entirely gray, was cut into a fashionable crop. The absence of middle-aged spread, along with the edgy specs and well-cut jeans, didn't make him look younger than his fifty-five years, just a well-preserved fifty-five.

"What's that?" Ruby said, noticing a small clear plastic ball lying on the hall table.

Phil's eyes lit up. "It's the most fantastic toy. One of your mother's girlfriends came over with her grandson and he left it here. Now I can't stop playing with it." Phil loved toys and gadgets. When Ruby was a toddler, he had bought her a clockwork train set for her birthday. Years later when she challenged him about it, he said he had done it because he was a male feminist who believed buying little girls dolls severely restricted their view of the world. Ruby was certain he had bought the train set for himself.

He picked the ball up off the table. "There's a computer inside and it plays twenty questions with you. Go on, think of an object. Hard as you like. I guarantee it'll get it."

"Hang on, before I do that, I need to talk to you about Mum. It's driving me mad. What's this big secret she's been keeping?"

His huge grin left Ruby in no doubt that he was bursting to tell her.

"Grandma Esther didn't end up leaving you a fortune in her will, did she?"

"I wish," he chuckled.

"So, what is it?"

"I think we should wait for your mum. She's upstairs in her studio. I'm sure she won't be long."

"But you know what it is, right?"

"Oh, yes," he chuckled, rolling his eyes. "I know."

"And it's good news. Nothing bad has happened."

"Let's just say it's taken a bit of getting used to. OK, no more digging. Now then, you have to think of an object."

She thought. "Really hard, you say?"

"Yep. Hard as you like."

"OK. Capybara."

"Capy-what?"

"Capybara. It's a semiaquatic South American rodent. There was this mad girl at my school who was obsessed with them. Her bedroom was covered in pictures of capybaras."

"Oh, come on, be fair. How's it going to get capybara?"

"You said it could get anything."

"Yes, but not some weird rodent nobody's ever heard of." He seemed to decide the time had come to change the subject. "Tell you what, why don't you go upstairs and let your mum know you're here?"

Ruby started to climb the stairs, leaving her father to see if by any chance the twenty questions gadget could guess capybara.

A few years ago her parents had converted the loft into a workspace for Ronnie. The two giant windows meant it was flooded with light all day.

Ronnie was wearing her trademark workman's overalls, covered in paint. Her long red hair was pulled back and held in place by a large tortoiseshell claw clip. A few loose strands hung around her face, making her look girly and coquettish. Ruby could hardly believe her mother was fifty. Of course she dyed her hair now and she had a few fine lines at the corners of her eyes, but nothing deep enough to be called crow's feet. And although she had put on a bit of weight around her middle in the last few months—which most women seemed to as they approached menopause—she was still leggy and slim. But it wasn't just her physical appearance that made Ronnie seem so young. It was her vibrancy, her facial expressions, that indefinable something behind her eyes.

All of Ruby's friends' mothers were in their sixties. Some were even older. They tended to be thick-waisted and heavy of hip, with bosoms that in recent years had become singular rather than plural. People were always shocked the first time they met Ronnie. For her part, Ronnie rather enjoyed the flattery and being told she didn't look remotely old enough to have a daughter who was in her thirties.

The reason Ruby's friends' mothers were older than Ronnie was that they hadn't got pregnant at eighteen and eloped with their art student boyfriends.

RUBY LEANED AGAINST the doorframe and looked around the studio. As her eyes wandered, she breathed in the familiar smell of oil paint and turpentine. There were canvasses everywhere, mostly propped up against the walls. Surfaces were strewn with old sketches, ends of charcoal and long discarded paper palettes dotted with tiny cracked peaks of oil paint.

In the middle of the room her mother was standing in front of a canvas dibbing and dabbing at her latest painting.

Ruby was so proud of what her mother had achieved. Unlike Phil, who had been in his final year at art school when Ronnie got pregnant, she had been forced to abandon her degree after the first year. She then chose to stay at home—in their grotty rented flat—to look after her baby. She did her bit to make ends meet by stenciling kitchen units and nursery walls in posh Hampstead homes. Despite that, Ronnie never lost sight of her ambition. As soon as Ruby started school, she applied for and got a grant, which enabled her to go back and finish her degree. Her paintings may not have earned her a great deal of money, but in so many ways, Ronnie had been and still was Ruby's role model and inspiration.

As usual, this painting was an abstract consisting of great swathes and gashes of color. Ruby liked it. She liked nearly all of her mother's paintings. They were so full of energy and spirit. It was hard to tell, but to Ruby's eye the painting looked pretty much finished. The canvas was big—six feet by eight, maybe. Since it was too big for an easel, it was up against the wall like all the others. All Ronnie's paintings were large. Some were even larger than this. She said small canvasses made her feel hemmed in and restricted.

Ruby remembered being about eight when she first asked her mother what her paintings were about and what the bizarre patterns and shapes meant.

Ronnie had put her on her knee and the two of them had sat for what seemed like ages, talking about the painting she was working on. "Tell me how you feel when you look at it," Ronnie had said. Ruby replied that she liked the bright colors and that they made her feel happy. "That's it. Then you've got it. If art makes you feel something—anything at all, then it's succeeded. We live in a world obsessed with meaning and explanation. As you go through life, Rubes, you'll realize that not everything has a meaning and sometimes that can be hard to understand."

"You mean like people getting killed in earthquakes?" Ruby said. "And Hilary Newsham in my class getting appendicitis and nearly dying?"

Ronnie smiled and kissed her—presumably for being so perceptive at only eight. "Yes, things like that."

RUBY STOOD RECALLING that conversation and watching Ronnie as she stepped back to consider her latest work. The dominating color was hot pink with explosions of blue, yellow and emerald green.

"So, does it have a title?" Ruby said, walking into the studio.

Ronnie spun round, hand clamped to her chest. "God, you made me jump," she cried. "No, haven't got one yet. I'm still thinking." As she spoke she shoved the pointy end of her paintbrush through her hair, Geisha style, and wiped her hands on a piece of old rag. Then she kissed Ruby hello. "I'm so glad you could make it, but I feel really guilty about asking you to cancel on Laura and Jack. Are you very angry with me? You have to tell me if you are. It's so unhealthy to bottle stuff up."

How long had it taken Ronnie to lapse into therapy mode? A minute? Along with dabbling in Buddhism, she'd been seeing a shrink on and off for fifteen years. It was Phil who had begged her to go—although he now admitted that he was living to regret it. Back then he had found it impossible to keep up with Ronnie's constant optimism and gung-ho—"the universe will provide"—attitude to life. He said it was like living with "the sodding Dalai Lama." He told Ruby he felt desperately guilty getting frustrated with somebody who was permanently happy, but he couldn't help it. Nor could he help the fact that his problem with Ronnie was partly related to his own despondency about money.

Early on—with the help of Clive, her therapist, who she was still seeing—Ronnie had discovered that her constant optimism was connected to her father—whom she adored—walking out and going to live with another woman. She rarely saw him after that because the new woman in his life resented his relationship with Ronnie. The trauma and hurt of losing him explained why she ran off and got married at eighteen. It also explained why she steadfastly refused to allow any more pain in her life and had remained irrationally positive and upbeat when she and Phil were hard up.

These days, she found it much easier to admit when things weren't going well. The irony was that neither she nor Phil had very much to worry about. Their finances had improved beyond recognition, they had a strong marriage and a daughter who thought the world of them, and they were both healthy. Although her father had died a few years ago, just as she and Sylvia were trying to build a new relationship with him, Ronnie's mother had found new love late in life and was now married to a retired dentist and living in Marbella.

The downside to Ronnie's therapy was that she had become addicted not only to self-analysis but to analyzing everybody else as well.

"So, are you OK with coming here for dinner?" Ronnie said again, trying at the same time to rub a stubborn patch of red paint off her middle finger. "You sure you're not bottling up a whole load of angry feelings?"

"Mum, I'm not angry. Promise. Oh, and before you ask, yes, the shop is still doing fine and no, I don't feel guilty about what I've achieved and yes, I do believe that everybody is entitled to succeed."

"Now you're making fun of me," Ronnie said, making a sad clown mouth.

"I know, but I need you to understand that it comes from a truly good place," Ruby said, smiling and still teasing.

"And what about the Matt thing. Is it getting any easier? Does it feel like you're ready to move on?"

Ruby had become aware lately that the moving on bit was code for "isn't it about time you found a serious boyfriend slash husband and settled down." Ronnie would have been hurt and angry if anybody had dared to suggest she was a typical Jewish mother. After all, she had never been the type to sit at home breast-feeding her daughter matzo balls. She wasn't needy or demanding. When Ruby was at school she always encouraged her efforts rather than put pressure on her to be the best. To this day Ronnie had never made a single negative comment about her daughter's appearance or weight. The upshot was that Ruby had grown up with her self-esteem in pretty good shape.

Until now Ronnie had also never interfered in Ruby's romantic life—although she always made it clear she was happy to talk about it if Ruby wanted to. Then, when Ruby split up with Matt, a change seemed to come over Ronnie. Ruby had detected a panic descending on her mother. It was clearly something she was aware of and battled against—hence the tangential sideways comments, rather than head-on references to Ruby's lack of a man. Her remarks tended to be along the lines of, "Darling, are you OK? I mean *really* OK? You know I really worry about you being on your own." Or, "So and so's daughter has just moved in with her boyfriend/got married/had a baby and she must be two or three years younger than you."

Ruby had told her mother a few times that she felt she was putting her under pressure to find a man. Since Ronnie had been in therapy for so long and was used to "getting feedback," she knew she wouldn't see it as an attack.

"You know, you're right," Ronnie had said. "I have been

putting pressure on you. This is definitely something I need to look at in my sessions with Clive. I think I'm starting to panic that you may never find a man and settle down. But my need to see you in a relationship is my problem, not yours. I'm transferring my anxiety onto you. Why would I do that? What's stopping me from giving you permission to live your life however you choose? I'm wondering if there's something in my past that makes it impossible for me to own my anxiety."

And so it went on. Ronnie and Clive were still working on Ronnie's anxiety transference issues, but it didn't seem to be doing much good. Hardly a phone call with her mother went by without her mother making some oblique but nevertheless pointed reference to Ruby's single status. Sometimes Ronnie would catch herself doing it and apologize. When she didn't, Ruby simply took a deep, calming breath and let the comments go.

RONNIE SWITCHED OFF the bright studio light and the two women headed toward the stairs.

"So, come on, Mum," Ruby said. "What's going on? What's the big secret? Dad's refusing to say anything and I'm dying to know."

Just then the doorbell rang. Ronnie's eyebrows knitted. "Who can that be?" she said as they listened to Phil opening the front door. Ronnie leaned over the banister to see. "It's your Aunty Sylvia," she said to Ruby. "I wasn't expecting her. This is going to make things a bit awkward. Your dad and I really wanted you to ourselves tonight."

When they got downstairs, Aunty Sylvia was handing her coat to Phil.

"Thought I'd just pop in and say a quick arrivederci before you went off to Rome." She kissed Ronnie and then stood wiping the lipstick smudge off her sister's cheek.

She turned to Ruby. "And how's my favorite niece?" she said with a gentle pinch of Ruby's cheek. "Still working with our dear cousin. Of course you know what's wrong with Stella, don't you? Heart problem. She doesn't have one. "

Ruby laughed and said she didn't hear from her much since she'd moved to New York.

Aunty Sylvia turned to Ronnie. "You know, when I got here I had to drive round for ten minutes looking for somewhere to park."

"Oh, I usually chant for a space," Ronnie said. "Always works."

"Really? Maybe I should start chanting for a husband."

Sylvia Lieberman—she had kept her ex-husband's surname—was Ronnie's older sister by four years. She was PA to a West End theatrical agent and looking for love. For the last decade—ever since her divorce—it had evaded her, so she comfort-ate instead. The upshot was that she weighed 200 pounds. Even though she was heavy, she shared Ronnie's artistic flair and was by no means without style. Her hair—cut every five weeks by Roscoe, he of Roscoe and Belle—was dyed an even more vibrant red than Ronnie's. Everybody agreed it was the perfect accessory to her loud, ballsy personality.

She wore expensive, well-cut loose layers, which showed off her hourglass shape but didn't cling in the wrong places. Tonight she looked particularly elegant in an olive-green wrap-over A-line dress and matching pointy suede boots.

EVERYBODY TROOPED INTO the living room. Ronnie took one sofa, Ruby and Aunty Sylvia claimed the other. Phil didn't sit down. Instead he took the twenty questions ball out of his pocket.

"It crashed just as you went upstairs," he said to Ruby. "Seems to be working again now... So, these capybaras—are they meat eaters?"

"No. They're vegetarian. If my memory serves me correctly they live on grasses, melons and squashes."

"OK. And are they nocturnal?"

"Don't think so."

Aunty Sylvia turned to Ronnie. "A capy who?" she whispered. "What's going on?"

Ronnie rolled her eyes and explained about the computerized ball that could play twenty questions. "I have no idea what this animal is they're talking about.... Phil, please. Can't you leave it alone for just a minute and come and sit down?"

"Hey, Phil," Sylvia said, laughing, "see if it can get Elvis, or better still, a lox bagel... or... or a thong."

Phil raised a hand in front of him as if to say "hang on." A couple of seconds passed before he spoke. "This is amazing! I don't believe it. Look. It got it. Capy-blinkin'-bara. It worked it out." He passed the ball to Ruby and pointed to the display.

"See if it can get chiropractor," Aunty Sylvia said. "I've just found a new one. He's brilliant. In fact he's so good the last time I saw him he practically offered me a cigarette afterward." She winked at Ronnie before adding, "You should try him."

By now Ruby was fidgeting in her seat. She was desperate to get the conversation off chiropractors and thongs and back to whatever it was her mum and dad wanted to tell her. "So, come on, you two. When are you going to let us in on the big secret?"

"Big secret?" Aunty Sylvia said. "What big secret? I didn't know about any big secret."

"We'd planned to tell Ruby first," Ronnie said, "but I'm sure she won't mind you being here."

Phil went over to the dining table on which there stood an unopened bottle of champagne and some glasses.

"Ooh, so it's good news, then," Aunty Sylvia said, clocking the bubbly.

"None for me," Ronnie called after Phil. "Water's fine."

"How come you're not drinking?" asked Sylvia. "It's me who has to watch the calories, not you. You have a husband. Me, I'm starting to think I'm never going to find a man and fulfill my dream of buying a double burial plot.... Come on, have a drink."

"No, I really don't fancy alcohol at the moment."

"Gawd," Aunty Sylvia snorted, adjusting the cushions behind her back, "anyone would think you were pregnant."

The champagne cork popped. Ronnie's face broke into a huge grin. "Actually, I am... that is, we are," she said.

"Yeah, right," Aunty Sylvia came back. "So, come on, what's the real reason you're not drinking?"

"I told you. I'm expecting a baby."

There was a few seconds' silence while Ruby and Aunty Sylvia waited for Ronnie to say: "Aha, gotcha. Had you going for a minute there, didn't I?" But she didn't. In fact she didn't say anything. While Phil poured the champagne, she just sat smiling.

"God, you're not joking, are you?" Ruby said, her voice little more than a whisper. She swallowed hard. "You really are pregnant." She and Aunty Sylvia exchanged bewildered glances. "Are you sure? I mean, can you even have a baby at fifty? OK, Cherie Blair did it at forty-five, but even that was pushing it."

At this point Sylvia got up and went to sit next to Ronnie. "Rhona, darling," she said gently, putting an arm around her sister. Sylvia always called Ronnie by her proper name when she had something serious to say. "This is just the menopause. It's your body playing tricks on you. And don't forget you have blocked tubes. It's highly unlikely that you really are pregnant."

"Well, I am," Ronnie said. "Over four months. I've had two scans. I'll show you the pictures in a moment. I hated waiting this long to tell you. It's been awful, but we wanted to hang on until we got the results of the amnio. They've just come through and everything's fine."

"But what about your tubes?"

Ronnie shrugged. "My doctor says one of them may have spontaneously unblocked itself. It's more likely that the original diagnosis was wrong."

Ruby felt herself sink back into the sofa. How many times in her life had she uttered the phrase "I don't believe it" and not really meant it? Well, this time she meant it. She couldn't take it in. She literally couldn't believe it.

By now Phil was handing round champagne glasses. "So, aren't either of you going to congratulate us?" he said.

Ruby put down her glass and leaped from the sofa. "Oh, God. Sorry. It was the last thing I'd imagined, that's all, and I'm still in shock." Despite this she managed to put an arm around each of her parents and kiss them in turn. "Wow, I'm going to have a baby brother or sister!"

"Thirty-two years—it's the perfect age gap," Aunty Sylvia piped up.

"OK," Ruby said, giggling at the age gap remark, "here's the deal."

"What?" Ronnie came back.

"First, we don't share a room. Second, we get the same amount of pocket money and third, as the eldest I get to go to bed when I like."

Ronnie burst out laughing. "Oh, I think we can manage that."

Instead of joining in with the levity, Aunty Sylvia was suddenly looking uneasy. "I don't for a second want to rain on your parade, but are you two absolutely sure about this? I mean you'll have a teenager in the house when you're in your midsixties. It's not going to be easy."

"We've thought it all through," Phil said. "I think we have a fair idea of what we're letting ourselves in for."

"And you know how much we've always wanted another child," Ronnie went on. "I agree it might have been better if it had happened a decade or so ago, but we're both healthy and fit. I'm sure we'll manage."

"My God, you'll be having labor pains and hot flashes at the same time," Sylvia said, shaking her head. This made everybody laugh again.

"Well, if you're happy I'm happy," she went on, her face finally breaking into a broad smile. She got up and hugged Ronnie and then Phil. "You are OK with this, aren't you?" Ronnie said to her sister. "I mean, this is my second child and I know how much you always wanted children. I've been really nervous about telling you in case you felt uncomfortable with it."

"OK, I admit it. Even ten years ago I would have been as jealous as hell. But I'm fifty-four. I've started to grunt as I get out of an armchair. I can't eat anything fried after six o'clock and the only pill I take these days is to control my cholesterol level. The last thing I need is a screaming baby, nappies and sleep deprivation. Believe me, you are welcome to it."

Ronnie turned to Ruby. "And what about you, darling? You might not realize it now, but when this baby arrives you may find yourself struggling with some pretty uncomfortable feelings. I don't want you to feel that we are pushing you out of the family or that we won't love you as much. You are our first baby and always will be."

"Mum, please, I'm thirty-two years old. I appreciate the thought, but I do have a life. I'm hardly going to get jealous of a little baby. And you know how I always wanted a brother or sister. Admittedly we would have had more in common when I was a bit younger..." She started to giggle.

"So, do you want a boy or girl?" Aunty Sylvia asked Ronnie. Before Ronnie had a chance to say anything, Aunty Sylvia added, "Ooh, and have you thought about names? I picked up *Tatler* the other day and there was a picture of this little boy called Heathcliff. It's such a romantic name. On the other hand, I'm not sure Heathcliff Silverman really works. I suppose you could always call him Cliffy for short. Now, then, if it's a girl, what about Aida? Or Taittinger, that's unusual."

Ruby was aware that her mother was looking as if she were under siege. She decided to get the subject off names. "So, where are you having the baby?"

"The local hospital has been pretty good so far, although I think your dad would prefer me to be at St. Luke's. Problem is it's just so expensive." The baby talk carried on for an hour or so. Finally Ronnie announced that dinner was ready. "Sylvia, why don't you stay?" she said. "It's your favorite—ricotta and spinach cannelloni, and Phil's about to open another bottle of wine." She didn't need asking twice.

"I have news, too," Aunty Sylvia said later on, as Phil got up from the dinner table to top up her wineglass. "I'm seeing a new man."

"Hang on," Ronnie said, "what happened to your last new man?"

"Brian? He was still hung up on his ex. I tried to be patient. I listened. I held him when he cried, but in the end it did no good, so I ended it."

"What about the one before him—Max? He sounded nice."

"He was—except he had to touch everything ten times

and smell it. I got him into cognitive behavioral therapy. He did it for a bit, then he gave up. Oh, and he sat down to pee."

Phil looked up from his cannelloni. "What's so wrong with sitting down to pee?" he said mildly. "It's the only way men of a certain age can empty their tank. These days, I sometimes have to . . ."

"Dad, please," Ruby broke in, grimacing, "too much information."

"I disagree," Ronnie said. "Important health issues like this need to be discussed, not swept under the carpet. Society needs educating. People should understand that some men sit down to pee because they have reached middle age and are having problems with their waterworks. Others simply prefer to sit down. What right have women to deny them that choice? For so many men, choosing to pee sitting down is the truth that dare not speak its name and I think it's about time we got rid of the stigma."

"You should write a letter to *The Times,*" Aunty Sylvia said. "You could spark off a national debate."

"I hate it when you mock me," Ronnie came back. "All I'm saying is that—"

Sensing the onset of sisterly friction, Ruby decided it was time to change the subject. "So, Aunty Sylvia," Ruby said. "Who was that chap you went out with before Max? I seem to remember he was a biker."

"Harley David. God, he was gorgeous. I really fancied him until he took me out on the bike and I saw what was written on the back of his leather jacket. It said, and I quote: 'If you can read this, the bitch fell off.' Sexist didn't begin to describe the man. I spent weeks debating the issue with him. I even bought him *The Female Eunuch*. He just laughed."

"Why is it every man you go out with turns out to be a project?" Ronnie said. "You know, I think it has something to do with our father. You couldn't make him a better person. Then he died and you were forced to give up trying. But you continue the struggle with other men."

"Maybe." Sylvia shrugged.

"So, tell us about this new chap," Ronnie said.

Sylvia put down her wineglass. "Well, his name is Nigel and he's an independent financial adviser. Believe me, what this man doesn't know about the best-rated mutual funds and tax efficient portfolio management isn't worth knowing."

Ronnie remarked that he sounded unusually normal and grounded for Sylvia.

"You're right. Funny, I hadn't thought about it."

"I think that subconsciously you have decided you're tired of taking on projects."

"So, is he good looking?" Ruby interrupted.

"I'll say," Aunty Sylvia grinned. "He's tall and slim with these gorgeous gray-blue eyes."

"And it's serious?" Ronnie said.

"Getting that way."

Ronnie asked how old he was. Sylvia responded by taking a glug of wine, then another. "Oh, he's about my age—a few years younger maybe."

Ruby could practically see her mother's antennae flapping. "So, what are we talking?" Ronnie said. "A couple of years?"

"A bit more than that, maybe."

"How many more?"

"Ten. Fifteen, maybe. I'm not sure."

"Come on—is it ten or is it fifteen?" Ronnie asked, shooting an anxious glance at Phil.

"Actually, it's seventeen."

"He's seventeen years younger than you?" Ronnie repeated, her voice rising with disapproval.

"Coo coo ca choo, Mrs. Lieberman!" Ruby cried.

"Wow, good for you. God, my Aunty Sylvia's got herself a boy toy."

"Does he know how old you are?" Ronnie said.

"Yes. No. Well, sort of. I've told him I'm forty-two."

"But you're fifty-four. When are you planning to tell him the truth?"

Phil tapped his wife's arm and reminded her this really was Sylvia's business, but she ignored him.

"Ronnie, this is so unlike you," Sylvia said. "You usually see the positive side of everything. I thought you'd be happy for me. For the first time in ages I'm having fun."

"I'm sorry. I just don't want to see you get hurt, that's all."

Sylvia reached out across the table and patted her sister's hand. "I know I have to tell him my real age," she said. "And I will when I feel the time is right. Now, please, can we just leave it?" Clearly eager to change the subject, she turned to Ruby. "So, maybe it won't be long before you have a baby. Of course it would help if you found a man. If you leave it much longer I'll be coming to your wedding in an urn."

Aunty Sylvia positively relished her role as surrogate Jewish mother, and unlike Ronnie, she made no apologies for it.

"Sylvia, please," Ronnie came back. "Right now, Ruby's busy building her career. A man will come along when the time is right. The universe never gets these things wrong."

Ruby couldn't quite make out what this statement meant. She decided there were two possibilities: either her mother and Clive had finally made a breakthrough in her therapy, and from now on Ronnie was going to stop making barbed comments about Ruby's single status, or it was an indication that Ronnie found it easier to get impatient with her sister's Jewish mothering than she did with her own.

It turned out to be the latter. A couple of hours later, as

Ruby and Aunty Sylvia were leaving, Ronnie tugged her daughter's sleeve.

"Don't worry, darling," she whispered. "Every night, without fail, I chant for a man for you."

She then slipped a slim square package into Ruby's bag. "Open it when you get home," she said.

Chapter 5

Ruby lay in bed, gazing up at the shadows on her bedroom ceiling. So, at the age of thirty-two, she was going to have a baby brother or sister. How weird was that? The news still hadn't quite sunk in. Would he or she look like her? What sort of a relationship would they have? She decided that since the age difference ruled out the traditional sibling relationship, she would take on the role of fun aunty figure—a bit like Aunty Sylvia, only more cool.

If it was a girl, Ruby would take her out for "princess days." When she became a teenager, the two of them would meet for lunch and gossip about their parents, who by then would be getting old and eccentric. Ruby would listen to all her boyfriend problems. From time to time she might even babysit for Ruby's own children. If of course Ruby had any. That involved finding a man. Suppose she didn't? Suppose it never happened? No, she absolutely mustn't think like that.

"I am ready to accept positive change in my life right now," she whispered. "I am beautiful and vibrant in my uniqueness. I am a child of the universe who deserves to love and be loved. I am capable of finding love."

Ronnie's package had contained a CD called *Discovering*

Love Through Inner Empowerment. It consisted of daily affirmations delivered by a softly spoken, impossibly sincere Texan woman whose directives were accompanied by warbling, atonal New Age music. According to the blurb on the cover, she had been "a sex worker for twenty years, until she pulled herself back from the brink and turned her life around."

Ruby had been about to throw the thing in a drawer and forget about it, but curiosity—fueled by there being nothing on TV—got the better of her. She found herself sliding the CD into the player.

She listened for a couple of minutes before turning it off, snorting with cynicism and unable to believe that Ronnie, even with her mystical tendencies, could have fallen for this kind of claptrap.

Now, here she was, half an hour later, lying in bed reciting the affirmations she'd just been sniggering at. She justified it in the same way she justified keeping a four-leaf clover in her purse or listening to Chanel's astrological predictions. It was all harmless fun so long as you didn't take it too seriously. And maybe, just maybe, affirmations weren't so stupid. Perhaps, by repeatedly telling herself how great she was, she might improve her chances of meeting the man of her dreams.

THE NEXT MORNING, she called in at Fi's, bearing croissants and *pains au chocolat*. She had an appointment at eleven with Jill McNulty, the hospital administrator in charge of St. Luke's prenatal department, and Fi's was on the way.

She couldn't wait to tell Fi that Ronnie was pregnant. More than that, she needed to talk about it. Last night, as she was falling asleep, she'd been convinced she was OK with the news. This morning, having dreamt that she'd gone to visit her parents, who didn't recognize her, she wasn't so sure.

Fi lived in the tiny terraced cottage in Hammersmith that she and Saul had managed to buy with the bit she had saved and his "yogurt money." Like most struggling actors he leapt at any commercial that came his way. For a start there was always the possibility—however slim—that playing an animated yogurt pot or pizza could lead to the offer of a proper acting role. More important, commercials were financial lifesavers. They tended to pay megabucks for a couple of weeks' work. The downside was that since he never knew when the next job would appear, he had to make the money last—often for a year or more.

For the last couple of months he'd been working at the National. He had a bit part in *Hamlet*—a role he described as "third codpiece." During that time he'd also recorded a couple of advertising jingles. Saul had a great singing voice. He'd had a few minor singing roles in West End musicals, but family and friends who had seen him perform were surprised he'd never landed a leading part. He made no secret that this was a major ambition.

With Fi now a full-time mother, they needed every penny he earned to pay the bills. When Ben was born three years ago, Ruby had insisted on making them a present of a crib and a buggy, for which Fi in particular was immensely grateful. Ruby got the feeling that Saul on the other hand, although he made all the right noises, was a bit uneasy with the gift. It occurred to her that his pride had been dented and that he might feel she was treating them like a charity case.

As far as Ruby was concerned, the gift had been generous but not particularly lavish, since with her business contacts she'd ended up paying even less than the wholesale price. Nevertheless, she was perturbed by Saul's reaction and mentioned her fears to Fi. Fi was adamant that Ruby should take no notice. "The hunter-gatherer hasn't had any work for a few months and it's starting to get to him."

But Ruby had taken notice. She had a huge soft spot for Saul and she knew how serious he was about proving to Fi's mother that even a heathen actor could provide for his family. Ruby didn't want to upset him. When Connor was born she gave Fi a couple of gorgeous baby outfits and left it at that. The pirate costume she'd bought Ben for his birthday had cost fifteen quid from the Early Learning Centre.

THIS MORNING, FI opened the door pale and puffy-eyed from lack of sleep. Her long blonde hair, which looked like it hadn't been brushed or washed for a couple of days, was pulled back into a scrunchy. She was wearing an ancient Juicy Couture tracksuit offset by a sick-encrusted cloth slung over one shoulder. Cradled in her arms was a beatific, slumbering Connor. Ruby gazed at him with his mop of black hair—just like Saul's—sucking two fingers in his sleep.

"OK, I know he looks positively edible right now," Fi jumped in without even giving Ruby a chance to say hi, "but don't be fooled. The little so-and-so has been screaming his head off nearly all night."

Ruby kissed her friend hello. "God, you look knackered." Fi led the way down the hall to the kitchen. Ruby asked her if Saul could give her a break this morning so that she could catch up on her sleep. Fi shook her head. "He's got an audition for a commercial. Don't worry. I'm fine. I slept back in July."

"God only knows how my mum's going to cope," Ruby said, sitting down at the kitchen table. She couldn't help noticing that the kitchen was a mess. The surfaces were littered with piles of unwashed plates and pans, plus an assortment of bibs, pacifiers and half-empty feeding bottles. A heap of dirty laundry sat on the floor in front of the washing machine.

"How d'you mean you don't know how she's going to cope?" Fi said, flicking the switch on the electric kettle. "Has somebody asked her to look after their baby?"

"Not exactly," Ruby replied with faux nonchalance, a smile hovering at her lips. "Actually, she's pregnant."

"Yeah, right." Fi gave a half-laugh.

"No, honestly. My mother is having a baby."

Fi came over to the table and sat down. "C'mon. This is some kind of wind-up." Connor, who was lying over her shoulder, started to whimper. She began rubbing his back.

"Nope. She's due in January."

"But how did she get pregnant?"

"Usual way, I suppose."

"Duh. I meant how did she manage it at her age, and didn't you once tell me she had blocked fallopian tubes?"

Ruby explained that one of Ronnie's tubes might have spontaneously unblocked itself.

"I just can't get my head round this," Fi said. "You're going to have a baby brother or sister. At thirty-two. It's unbelievable."

At this point Ben came bursting in. He was wearing Bob the Builder pajamas and the hat and eye patch from the birthday pirate outfit Ruby had given him. He smelled slightly of pee-soaked diaper. Fi clearly hadn't got round to changing him from the previous night. "My godda baby bruvver," he piped up. "Him's called Connor and he does ukky rabbit poos and he makes pukes on me."

"I know, sweetheart," Fi said. "But he doesn't mean it. And you like Connor really, don't you?"

Ben picked his green plastic pirate sword off the table and began waving it violently in the air, perilously close to Connor's head. "No," he announced. "He can stay for eleventeen more days. Ven we have to send him back to his own garden."

Fi gently removed the sword from her son's hand and put it down on the table. She gave Ruby a shrug to indicate that she had no idea why Ben assumed that Connor had originated from, or belonged in, a garden. "Probably all tied up with the j-e-a-l-o-u-s-y thing." Ben was now demanding to have his sword back. "Tell you what, sweetie," Fi soothed, "why don't you get up to the table and do some Play-Doh?"

Ben gave a vigorous nod and climbed onto a chair. As he knelt at the table, he began pulling the plastic lids off the tubs of Play-Doh.

"I can really understand how Ben feels about Connor," Ruby said with a half-laugh.

Fi asked her what she meant. Ruby explained how, when her mother had announced that she was pregnant, she had laughed at any suggestion that she might feel jealous. "Then, last night I dreamed that I went round to my parents' and they didn't recognize me. Old as I am, I can't help feeling I'm about to lose my mum and dad to this new baby and that they're about to push me out of the nest."

Fi made the point that Ruby had, in fact, left the nest at eighteen when she went to university.

"I know," Ruby said. "But when I woke up this morning, the feeling just seemed to overwhelm me. I keep trying to stop it, but I can't. The other thing I keep thinking is that I'm thirty-two and it's me who should be getting married, having babies and getting all the attention. Not my fifty-year-old mother. I think I'm a tiny bit jealous of her, too. No. Correction. If I'm honest, I'm a lot jealous. I know she didn't get pregnant on purpose, but it's like she's stepped onto my turf. God, do I sound utterly pathetic and self-centered?"

"Maybe, a bit," Fi said. "But I'm sure most women in

your position would feel the same. The natural order of things is for couples to have children and then at a certain age they become grandparents. They don't try to compete with their children by having more babies. In your family the natural order has got skewed and you feel you have no place. Not only has it come as a shock, but it's also pissed you off. Look, you only found out a few hours ago that Ronnie's pregnant. You have to give yourself time to get used to it." She patted the back of her friend's hand. "It will get easier. Honest."

Ruby nodded. "I know. But the other thing I'm worried about is her health. I don't know much about it, but I imagine that carrying a baby at fifty can be really risky."

"Yes, but at her age she'll have the most senior and experienced doctors looking after her. They'll be on the lookout for problems and they'll be monitoring her. They won't let anything happen to her."

"But what about the baby? I know Mum's had the amnio and all the other tests, but suppose there still turns out to be something wrong with it? These tests aren't infallible, are they?"

"No, they're not, but with the right care, the overwhelming likelihood is that they'll both be fine."

Ruby let out a slow breath. "I just hope you're right."

Fi decided to put Connor in his crib. While she went upstairs, Ruby finished making the coffee and chatted to Ben, who had been busy molding Play-Doh.

"So, what are you making, Ben?" Ruby said, opening one of the kitchen cupboards and looking for a plate to put the croissants on. She was out of luck. There wasn't a clean plate to be had.

"My is doing green eggs and ham." He held up two green lumps of Play-Doh and another flatter, pink piece. "You like some?"

"I'd love some," Ruby said, turning on the hot tap and

starting to rinse a plate covered in dried-up masala sauce. "You know I used to read *Green Eggs and Ham* when I was little."

"Dat Sam I Am," Ben announced gravely, "he's a bad boy." He maneuvered himself down from the table, toddled over to Ruby and offered her some green egg to try. Crouching down to his height, she put it up to her mouth and made yum-yum noises. "Those are great eggs, Ben. Brilliant."

"You give this one to your mummy." He handed her another egg.

"Oh, thanks, Ben. I know she'll love it." Ruby slipped the egg into her trouser pocket.

"Do you have a mummy wiv a zsgusting fat tummy and bloody stretchmarks?" It was clear from Ben's bright, unperturbed expression that he was simply parroting Fi's words and had no real idea what he was saying.

Fi appeared just in time to hear what he had said. Her face immediately became filled with panic. "Oh, Gawd, now Ben's picking up on all my anxieties," she whispered to Ruby. "I can't get anything right. Seeing me all pathetic and feeble is going to make him feel even more insecure than he already is."

"Come on, Fi, he's fine. He's just repeating stuff. Stop beating yourself up. You'll get your figure back. It's just going to take a bit of time, that's all."

At this point Ben announced he wanted his blanket. He jumped down from the table and ran off toward the living room to find it, losing his pirate hat as he went.

Fi reached for the *Daily Mail,* which was lying on the table and covered in Play-Doh bits. She swept them away and prodded a picture. "But how do all these Hollywood celebs get their figures back so fast? I mean look at Mia Ferrari. She only gave birth a month ago and here she is at some premiere in a dress I couldn't have got into even before I was pregnant." Fi squinted at the picture. More prodding. "Look, she's not even wearing a bra. See how high her nipples are. My boobs are practically down to my knees. And look at my stomach." Fi lifted her tracksuit top and yanked a flap of fatty stomach over her trouser waistband. "It'll take me at least six months to get rid of this lot and even then it never really goes back to how it was."

Ruby took the plate of pastries over to the table. "Look, you know as well as I do that these women have dieticians and fitness trainers. You're tall, you've got blue eyes I would give an arm and a leg and a fair amount of offal for and you've always had a wonderful figure. There's no reason why you shouldn't get it back."

"Yeah, but when?" Fi said, giving a throaty laugh and biting off a chunk of croissant. "It's the breast-feeding. I just can't stop eating. Maybe I should just carry on stuffing my face until Connor's weaned and then get all the fat liposuctioned."

"God, I wish you'd change the record," came a male voice. The two women looked up. Saul had walked in. "Rubes, please knock some sense into my wife and tell her how beautiful she is. I keep doing my best to convince her, but it's like talking to a brick wall."

"I'm doing my best," Ruby said, "but she won't listen to me either."

Saul stood behind Fi, placed his palms on her shoulders and bent down to kiss the back of her neck. "You know, you're still my shiksa goddess," he said, getting all smoochy and forcing Ruby to look the other way and pretend she hadn't noticed.

"You mean that?" Fi said.

"Like you have to ask. Look, I've got the audition for the fish-sticks commercial at twelve. I should be back by three.

Then you can go for a nap and I'll tackle the washing up. You OK with the kids until then?"

"Stop kvetching." Fi loved practicing her Yiddish. "I'll be fine. Go, break a leg, already."

Saul turned to Ruby. "Tell me honestly, do I look like Captain Bird's Eye to you?"

The truth was that Saul looked nothing like Captain Bird's Eye, who was always cast as an avuncular, ruddy-faced old sea dog. Saul was a young, olive-skinned Semite more suited to the role of biblical hero. Those being in short supply, he usually ended up singing advertising jingles or being cast as a Mafia henchman or dodgy kebab seller.

"Maybe they're trying to change his image," Ruby said, trying to sound positive. "Perhaps they want somebody a bit more dashing and swashbuckling." With his dark beard and matching long hair—grown especially for the part in *Hamlet*—Saul certainly looked pretty dashing.

He laughed, picked Ben's tiny pirate hat up off the floor and perched it on his head. With a flamboyant gesture he grabbed the plastic sword from the table and did a couple of fancy moves. "Yeah, I reckon I could buckle a bit of swash," he said.

"Wow, you look sexy in that hat," Fi giggled.

"Never say I don't know how to turn you on," Saul said, bending down to kiss her again. Just then Ben came back carrying a tatty and rather grubby bit of old crib blanket.

"My hat! My sword! Daddy, gib vem back. Vey is for likkle boys, not for big mans."

"Sorry, Ben," Saul said, placing the hat back on his son's head and handing him the sword. "I only borrowed them for a second." He scooped Ben up and gave him a hug and a kiss. "Now then, you be a good boy for Mummy until I get back."

Ben nodded and then lunged at his father with the

sword. Saul responded with a wonderfully comic performance of being mortally wounded—complete with mad eye-crossing and desperate gasping for breath—all of which had them in hysterics.

AFTER SAUL HAD gone, the two women sat drinking coffee. For a while Ben went back to making green eggs and ham. Then he got bored, climbed onto Fi's lap with his blanky and began sucking his thumb.

"So," Ruby said, "what was the other thing you wanted to tell me on the phone yesterday?"

"OK, you know Connor had jaundice when he was born and the doctors said we had to delay his circumcision at least a month..." She broke a *pain au chocolat* in half and offered a piece to Ben, but he didn't want it. He was beginning to nod off. "He's exhausted. Connor kept him awake last night, too, poor little mite...Anyway, we're finally doing it next week. Of course you're invited."

"Fabulous," Ruby said, laughing. "There's nothing I love more than watching a baby get part of his penis lopped off."

"Ruby, you're Jewish, you're not supposed to give me a hard time over this. We're going to have enough trouble with my mother. Don't you remember the fuss she kicked up when we had Ben done? She thinks circumcision is utterly barbaric."

"And she may have a point."

"I know. I know. And I'm not completely, totally comfortable with it—you remember the state I got into before we circumcised Ben, but Saul's been done and there was no way we wanted the boys looking different from their father. It just didn't feel right. Anyway, that's not the issue. The point is that in order to keep the peace, I planned not to invite

Mum to Connor's circumcision. It was only after I'd booked the rabbi that I remembered we'd invited her to stay. She's going to be here all next week."

"Can't you make an excuse and put her off?"

"Not really. She's been visiting my sister in Vancouver and she hasn't seen Connor yet. She's really looking forward to coming and she's even been getting on a bit better with Saul since we told her we were going to name the baby after my dad. Now everything's going to go back to how it was. Thing is, I really don't want to delay the circumcision any longer. Apparently, the older the baby, the more painful it is.

"She is going to raise the blinkin' roof just like she did last time. Saul and I are planning to have a firm and frank talk with her, but I suspect it won't be enough and that on the day she'll reprise the sackcloth-and-ashes role she performed at our wedding and Ben's circumcision. So, I was wondering if you could help keep an eye on her and try to make sure she stays calm and doesn't cause a commotion. I'm scared to death she's going to insult the rabbi or disrupt everything with some terrible outburst. My brothers and sisters will be around, but they're family and she won't think twice about playing up in front of them. With you she's far more likely to behave herself."

Ruby said she hadn't had much luck in the past trying to calm Bridget down, but she would do her best. "I'll tell her all the male royals are circumcised. That'll impress her."

"It might actually. Apart from you, the queen's the only heathen my mother's got any time for. And thanks, Rubes. You don't know how much I appreciate this." She took a sip of coffee. "So, what's going on with you—apart from your mother being preggers?"

"Oh, you know... same old same old... Shop's fine, got this appointment at St. Luke's—you know the one I was telling you about on the phone . . . What else? Oh yes, after the Double Barrel thing, this really cute American doctor overheard me on the phone telling you about my vaginal stamp. I got out of it by saying you were a stand-up comedian and that I was helping you put together material for a gig you were doing for the post office."

Fi simply stared at her wide-eyed. "That would be brilliant if it weren't so totally unbelievable."

"OK, what would you have said? I had to come up with something. I couldn't let him think that Double Barrel really had found a stamp in my vagina."

Fi said she got the point. They sat for a few moments, drinking their coffee. "By the way," Fi said eventually, "haven't you got another blind date tonight?"

Ruby's face brightened. Despite her past experiences with the men Fi had fixed her up with, she was allowing herself to feel enthusiastic about this one. His name was Duncan. As usual Fi had never met him. All she knew—via her friend Soph, who had known him for years—was that he was gorgeous. He was also a novelist, which Ruby thought sounded intriguing—not to mention rather sexy.

"You know, Rubes," Fi went on, "I've got a really good feeling about this one. I'm really sorry about the others. I admit a couple of them were a bit unfortunate."

Ruby thought back to the one before last and said a man with a great head of hair, nearly all of it in his nose and ears, was more than a "bit" unfortunate.

"So, where are you meeting Duncan?"

Ruby said he'd left a message on her answer machine suggesting a neighborhood Italian restaurant in Battersea.

"What did he sound like on the phone?"

"Couldn't tell, really. He left a very short message and when I rang back to confirm everything, his voice mail was on. So, we haven't actually spoken."

"I just know this one is going to work out. Promise you'll phone me the minute you get home, to let me know how it went."

"Don't I always?" Ruby smiled.

"Call as late as you like. I'm bound to be up with Connor. This is the best excitement I've had in ages. It so beats breast-feeding and watching daytime talk shows about men who sleep with goats and the women who stick by them."

JILL MCNULTY WAS a jolly, welcoming soul with an accent that could have cut crystal and impeccable, old-fashioned manners. Ruby decided she was probably no more than forty, but she gave the impression of being much older. It was partly the accent and the manners, but it was also her conservative clothes and excessive neatness. Her bobbed hair, which had not so much as a strand out of place, was covered in so much lacquer that it looked like a blonde cotton-candy helmet. Her manicured nails were covered in a thin coat of neutral pink varnish, allowing her perfectly shaped half-moons to show through. Her navy woolen blazer was the kind that could be put in a car crusher overnight and still spring back into shape the next morning.

Once she had thanked Ruby profusely for coming, she insisted on making her coffee. She disappeared to the staff kitchen. When she came back she was carrying a tray of freshly brewed coffee in a pretty pink-and-gold bone china pot. The cups, saucers and milk jug matched the pot and there was a paper doily on the plate containing carefully arranged shortbread fingers.

From behind her desk, with its legal pad, fountain pen and silver-framed family photographs placed at anally precise angles, Jill explained how she thought Ruby could help St. Luke's expectant mothers. She said that first-time mothers were always telling the midwives that when it came to buying baby clothes and equipment they felt overwhelmed by the choice. "Of course a lot of our mums are awfully well off," she said as she began pouring coffee, "and simply buy everything and the best of everything at that. But a fair few are on a budget and really need some advice. That's where you come in. I thought you could help them with their decision making. Should they opt for a pram or a buggy, or both? Is a baby bath really worth it when you can put the baby in the proper bath with you? What are the pros and cons of cloth diapers?" She handed Ruby a cup of coffee and invited her to help herself to milk and biscuits.

She went on to say that she envisaged small informal groups of about a dozen or so mothers and thought they had enough newly pregnant women coming onto their books to justify Ruby giving talks a couple of times a month.

"On top of a fee, the hospital is more than happy for you to promote Les Sprogs and sell maternity clothes and baby wear after the talks."

Ruby was delighted by this and said that in order to encourage sales she would offer everything at a discount.

Jill showed Ruby the sunny room full of comfy chairs where the talks would be held. Afterward they went back to her office to firm up dates.

Just as she was about to leave, Ruby noticed that Jill had a copy of *OK!* magazine lying on her desk. The picture of the film star on the front page caught her eye.

"Isn't that China Katz leaving St. Luke's with her new baby? Wow, look at her in her hipster jeans. She looks amazing. I noticed Claudia Planchette's booked in to have her baby here, and didn't Mia Ferrari give birth here, too? There was a picture of her in the *Mail* this morning. She was at some premiere looking thin as a twig. My friend Fi's just had a baby, and she was seething with jealousy. What is it about this hospital that all your patients look so slim so soon after giving birth? Are they doing sit-ups in labor or is there some instant weight-loss drug you're giving them?"

It was meant as a joke. Ruby had assumed Jill would smile, roll her eyes and then make the usual point about how unfair it was that all these women had personal chefs and fitness trainers. Ruby hadn't been prepared for the reaction she got. Jill's face clouded over and her sunny manner was replaced by a sudden and severe cold front. She didn't look cross so much as anxious. "We never discuss our patients," she said, minutely repositioning her pen and legal pad. Then she covered the magazine with the coffee tray. "Or their treatment."

"Goodness, no, of course not," Ruby said, embarrassed that she'd brought up the subject of celebs. She knew how fiercely hospitals like St. Luke's guarded the privacy of their high-profile patients.

"We always worry that gossip might end up in the newspapers." Although Jill was smiling, her voice and body language betrayed her unease. "Once that happens we are in danger of losing our reputation and our patients." Ruby noticed that Jill's face was starting to look flushed.

"I completely understand," Ruby said. But although she appreciated the sentiment, she didn't understand Jill's extreme reaction to what had been a fairly insignificant faux pas.

They continued to chat about practical arrangements such as Ruby needing an identity pass in order to get through hospital security, but the atmosphere was tinged with awkwardness.

It was only as the meeting came to an end that Jill began to relax. "Well, good-bye, Ruby, and see you next week." Ruby took her outstretched hand. "Absolutely. I'm looking forward to it."

She headed down the corridor toward the lobby, still

trying to work out why Jill had been so jumpy on the subject of celebs. She could only assume that the hospital management had put the fear of God into the staff about gossiping and that Jill was constantly on her guard, petrified of being caught and getting the sack. What a desperate strain that must be, Ruby thought.

As she passed through the prenatal department she noticed a wire rack stacked with pregnancy and childbirth pamphlets. One caught her eye: *Pregnancy and the Older Woman*. Putting Jill McNulty and her problems to the back of her mind, she picked it up and started reading as she walked.

Apparently, a pregnant woman of fifty who had previously given birth was classed as a geriatric multigravida. If that didn't sound unpleasant enough, there was worse to follow. Words like *diabetes, hypertension* and *preeclampsia* leapt out at her. She was so engrossed that she wasn't watching where she was going.

The next thing she knew she was colliding with another body.

"Oops, God, I'm so sorry," she blurted, aware that she had made contact with a man's back, pushing him forward and causing him to lose his balance. In the second or two it took him to right himself and straighten, she registered the blue scrubs and became aware that she had bumped into a doctor. He spun round, clearly wanting to see who had crashed into him. Her eyes began to focus on his face, which was registering surprise rather than anger. It was him—the cute American doctor who knew all about her vaginal stamp. As she felt her cheeks begin to flush with embarrassment, she prayed he wouldn't recognize her. Some hopes.

"It is you, isn't it?" His surprised expression had become a smile of recognition. "The woman from the coffee machine?"

"Oh, yes, of course... The coffee machine... Yesterday," she said, doing her best to give the impression that the previous day's encounter had made only the vaguest dent in her memory. "Look, I'm so sorry about bashing into you. I was miles away. Wasn't watching where I was going. I hope I haven't done any damage."

"I'm fine. Please don't worry."

She couldn't help noticing the way the corners of his eyes creased when he smiled and how sexy it made him look.

"Well," she said, suddenly aware that she had been staring at him, "I won't hold you up. You must have loads of patients waiting for you."

"Actually, I'm on a break. I've been in surgery all morning—two hysterectomies and a cesarean." It was then that he noticed the leaflet she was holding. *"Pregnancy and the Older Woman,"* he read. "Well, if you're an older woman, you sure had me fooled. When's your baby due?"

Ruby laughed. "I'm not pregnant. What my mother thought was menopause turned out to be a baby. I was doing a bit of research on her behalf."

"Wow, that must have come as a bit of a shock to everybody. How do you feel about having a baby brother or sister?"

"A bit weird, really. I think it's going to take me a while to get used to the idea."

"I'll bet."

"I'm also a bit worried that because of her age, something might go wrong,"

"That's understandable. But obstetrics has moved on so much in the last few years. There's no reason why she shouldn't have a completely problem-free pregnancy and labor."

"I hope so." She couldn't help thinking how kind it was of him to take the time to reassure her.

"So, you here with your mom?"

"No, actually I'm here on business." She explained as briefly as she could about Les Sprogs and St. Luke's having taken her on to give talks to expectant mothers.

"You're going to be a regular visitor, then?" She was sure she noticed his face light up.

"Looks like it," she said.

"I'm Sam Epstien, by the way." He extended his hand.

Epstien. So, he wasn't just a doctor, he was a Jewish doctor. She was being chatted up by a handsome Jewish doctor—albeit one who specialized in vaginas. She daren't tell her mother—at least not about the Jewish part (she'd be fine with the vaginas). Much as her mother loathed the traditional Jewish mother stereotype, she wouldn't be able to resist becoming giddy with excitement. There was no doubt in Ruby's mind that she would be straight on the phone to Aunty Sylvia. Before you could say "wedding planner," Aunty Sylvia would have broadcast the news all over North West London.

"Ruby Silverman," she said, shaking his hand and registering its warm firmness and how it completely enveloped hers.

"So, you're American, then?" Dah. Could she have asked a more redundant question? It was nerves. She always got anxious when she found herself in conversation with men she fancied.

"You guessed," he grinned. He explained that he was working at the hospital as part of an exchange program, which meant he swapped places with a British doctor. He had been here six months and had another six months to go.

She asked him how he was enjoying being in Britain. He said he was loving it. This was followed by one of those uneasy silences. Ruby hated silences and always felt the need to fill them. "My friend's got her post office gig tonight," she blurted. As the words left her mouth she wanted to stuff them back inside. What on earth had possessed her to say that? He was bound to ask her more questions, which meant she would end up compounding everything by telling more lies and getting herself into even deeper water.

"I would be so nervous having to get up in front of an audience and tell jokes," he said, leaving Ruby wondering if he knew that the whole post office scenario was a lie and was humoring her to spare her blushes.

"Right, well anyway it's been lovely, er, bumping into you again," she said, "but I really should be getting—"

"I was just about to grab a bite in the canteen," he said. "The food's nothing fancy, but since I've been here I've become addicted to the Lancashire hot pot. I don't suppose you'd care to join me?"

Of course she wanted to join him. She wanted very much to join him. After all, he was desperately handsome and then some. He was tall and broad-shouldered. She could see he worked out. And he had the warmest brown eyes. She even found herself forgetting that he was a gynecologist. But what if he brought up the post office thing again?

He seemed to sense her hesitation. "Or there's a great little Italian place across the street, if you'd prefer," he said. "They make a mean lasagne."

She was on the point of saying yes, having decided that she would have to tell him the truth about her vaginal stamp. It was cowardly and wimpy not to tell him. Plus lying wasn't really in her nature. She was busy thinking that in the restaurant, with a couple of glasses of Chardy inside her, she just might be able to find the courage to come clean, when her mobile rang. It was Chanel to say Henry the bookkeeper had just arrived at the shop to start work on the tax returns and had a string of urgent queries, which she couldn't answer. Ruby had been sure that Henry wasn't due until later that afternoon, but she'd clearly got it wrong.

"Look, tell him I got my times confused and that I'm really sorry. Make him a cuppa and I'll be there in twenty minutes."

Not being able to have lunch with Sam made her feel sad and relieved in equal measure. "I'm sorry, Sam, but there's a problem at the shop. I really do have to get back."

"That's a shame," he said, with what felt to Ruby like genuine disappointment. "Look, maybe I could give you a call sometime and we could meet up for a drink?"

"Sure," she heard herself saying, "I'd like that." She reached into her bag, took out a business card and handed it to him.

Ruby walked away, her entire body pricking with excitement and anticipation.

Chapter 6

"So, if 'e phones to ask you out, you gonna go?" Chanel carried on bagging up the day's takings—not that their cash payments amounted to much, since most customers paid by credit card.

"I don't know," Ruby said. Being holed up with Henry the bookkeeper all afternoon, she had been bored witless and her mind had started to wander. By now she was having second thoughts about going out with Sam Epstien. "I know he is totally gorgeous, but let's not forget that this is a man who spends his day looking up women's vaginas. What kind of a man does that?"

"Are you saying he's a pervert?" Chanel asked.

"What would you call a woman who spent all day examining men's penises?"

"Lucky!" Chanel cackled. Then she thought for a moment. "On the other 'and, I s'pose yer penis isn't much to look at, per se. I would need some extra incentive—like Brad Pitt or George Clooney on the other end of it."

Once they'd stopped laughing, Chanel went back to filling the money bag. During the silence that followed, Ruby started to think about how she really ought to tell Chanel about Ronnie being pregnant. The truth was, she didn't want to say anything. It seemed so unfair that Ronnie was expecting a baby at fifty while Chanel and Craig were trying so hard for one and nothing was happening. There was no getting out of it, though. Ronnie often turned up at the shop looking for a present to give a friend's new grandchild. It was only fair that when she came next, Chanel wouldn't be shocked and upset by the sight of Ronnie plus her bump.

Chanel was utterly gobsmacked by the news, but at the same time, genuinely pleased for Ronnie.

"Ah, I'll send her a card. God, somebody must really want to be born, that's all I can say." Chanel was all smiles, but it was clear to Ruby that she couldn't get away fast enough. She was making noises about having to get home because she was doing Craig a special roast beef dinner with all the trimmings.

"Chanel, please don't run off. You know, it's OK to be upset."

"I'm not upset. I'm fine. Honest." She turned and headed toward the kitchen to fetch her coat.

Ruby followed her. "I'm sorry. I shouldn't have said anything."

Chanel turned round. "Don't be daft. Of course you should. It's not your job to protect me." She seemed to be fighting to hold on to her emotions. "Look, you might as well know, I got my period this morning. That's the sixth lot of IVF that's failed."

"Oh, Chanel, I'm so sorry. I don't know what to say."

Chanel shrugged. "Nothing *to* say. We just 'ave to keep going, that's all. I've been pregnant once. I know we'll get there in the end." She was saying the words and putting on a brave face, but Ruby could tell this latest setback had come as a body blow.

"What does your doctor say?"

"I phoned 'im this morning. He wants us to knock the

IVF on the 'ead. Pretty much said me and Craig woz flogging a dead horse. Still, what does 'e know, eh? Doctors are always getting stuff wrong, aren't they?"

"Of course they are," Ruby said tenderly. "Having said that, what about trying one of the fertility specialists at St. Luke's?"

"I've tried. They're all booked up for months. Plus Craig's done all the research, and as far as IVF goes, St. Luke's 'as about the same success rate as our bloke in Harley Street."

Ruby nodded. "It was just a thought. . . . You know you didn't have to come in today. I would have understood if you'd wanted to take time off."

"Nah, I'm better at work. Keeps me occupied. And we'll get pregnant eventually. I just know we will."

Ruby put her arms round Chanel and gave her a hug. It was something she had never done before. She was worried that Chanel might see being comforted as a sign of weakness and push her away, but she didn't. As they stood, locked in their embrace, Ruby tried to think of something positive to say. She realized, of course, that there were no words of comfort. There was nothing she could offer to make the pain go away.

When the phone rang, Ruby's inclination—since they were closed—was to let it ring. Chanel insisted one of them answer it. "OK, I'll get it," Ruby said, taking a tissue from her pocket and handing it to Chanel.

It was Stella phoning from New York to say she'd just heard that Claudia Planchette was pregnant.

"I know," Ruby said. "I read about it yesterday in *Hello!*"

"Fine. Whatever." God, Ruby thought, would it hurt the woman to at least feign interest in what other people had to say? "The point is," Stella continued, "I've just had the most wonderful idea. Why don't you drop her a line—I have her address in London—and offer to close down the shop for her one afternoon so that she can pick out a layette and all her baby equipment."

Ruby wanted to make the point that this was brown-nosing in the extreme and that if she was going to suck up to this extent, she might as well throw away the Hoover, but she wasn't so blunt. She simply suggested that offering to close the shop might be seen as a bit over the top and put Claudia Planchette off coming to the shop at all. She also made the point that when it got round that they had closed the shop for a celeb, it would antagonize their other customers. "It would also upset the other VIPs who come in here. They'd want to know why we don't offer to close down the shop for them, too."

"The reason we don't close down for anybody else is that none of them gets $20 million a picture. The woman is obscenely rich, for crying out loud. We can't afford not to do this."

As usual Stella got her way and Ruby agreed she would write a letter.

By the time Ruby had finished speaking to Stella, Chanel had her coat on and she seemed to have perked up. "My 'oroscope said Taurus would be affected by Mercury opposing their natal moon. Apparently everything gets better toward the end of the month when Venus, planet of 'armony, returns to the midheaven angle of my chart." Ruby could see that behind the bravado she was still deeply troubled, but her emotional drawbridge had been pulled up. Chanel wasn't going to talk about IVF or babies anymore. It was clear to Ruby that it was the only way she could cope.

SHE GOT HOME to find Ivan the Terrible on his knees in the loo. He was busy packing up his tools. The floor was covered with bits of copper piping, as it had been for days, and the basin was still hanging off the wall.

"Hi, Ivan. How's it all going?"

"No good," he said with a grave shake of his head. "We hef problee-yem."

"Oh, dear, not another one."

One hand on the loo seat, Ivan heaved himself to his feet. He was in his fifties, well over six feet, with a barrel chest and cropped fair hair that was starting to go gray. He reminded Ruby of an aging Russian cosmonaut. Of course, Ivan was not and never had been a cosmonaut. He was a plumber-cum-general-handyman who had recently emigrated from the Ukraine with his wife and teenage children.

Ruby had been in her flat in Shepherd's Bush just over a year. When she decided it was time to start remodeling the bathroom and kitchen, she'd asked Chanel's Craig if he could do the work. Much as he'd wanted to help out, he couldn't. He was so busy that he simply couldn't find the time.

One of Ronnie's neighbors had recommended Ivan. She was full of praise for his work and said he was friendly, honest and reliable. He was also cheap. It was only when Ivan started work that Ruby realized why he was cheap. He was slow. And not just a bit slow. Ivan was breathtakingly, mind-numbingly, gobsmackingly slow. He was so slow he could have plodded for the Ukraine. It seemed that Ronnie's neighbor hadn't been bothered by this because she was an elderly widow and grateful for the company.

Remodeling the bathroom should have taken ten days, tops. It had already taken nearly three weeks and there was still the tiling to do when the plumbing was done. Heaven only knew how long the kitchen was going to take. Ruby had thought about looking for somebody else to do the work, but she'd decided against it. Ivan might be slow, but he was good at what he did. Before taking him on, she'd been to look at Ronnie's neighbor's new kitchen and been hugely impressed.

There was another upside, though. Once the kitchen and bathroom were finished, there was no more work to be done. Everything else was finished. The rewiring had been done. Ditto the painting and decorating. Last week, new wooden floors had gone down and a few days ago her brown leather sofas had been delivered along with new blinds. All she needed to think about now were cushions, rugs and lamps. The fun part.

She loved her flat—especially now that the renovations were coming to an end—because it was cozy and womblike. It was her refuge, her safe haven when the going got rough. Of course, she knew that it was too small. She badly needed a study so that she could move her computer and all her papers off the dining room table. She also hankered after a garden—somewhere to sit with a glass of wine on a warm summer's evening. She wanted to smell lily of the valley, honeysuckle and sweet peas. Since it was a top-floor flat, she had thought about converting the loft and maybe seeing if she could get permission from the council to build a roof terrace. But she'd been so busy doing the place up and running the shop that her plans hadn't extended beyond her head.

Ivan was standing in front of Ruby now, red faced and breathless from the effort of getting to his feet.

"You sure you're feeling all right?" Ruby said gently. She suspected that Ivan had a heart problem. She'd broached the subject of his breathlessness once or twice, but Ivan always insisted it was caused by nothing more than the mild asthma he'd had since childhood.

He inhaled deeply and straightened. "No worry. I em good now."

"Sure?'

He nodded.

"So, how's the loo coming along?" It was a redundant question, since she'd just passed the toilet sitting in the hall, still in its wrapping. If she hadn't had a guest loo she wasn't sure what she would have done.

"Bollocks," Ivan announced.

"Blimey, things that bad, eh?"

"I do not understand," he said, arms outsretched, palms turned heavenward, "the English bollocks."

"I'm not sure they're much different from Ukranian ones," Ruby replied, wondering precisely where the conversation was going.

"But I just buy new ceestern yesterday and already the bollock it ees kaput. The overflow keep on overflowing and I cannot feex eet. I think bollock is too small."

A light went on. "Oh, you mean ball cock. My ball cock is kaput."

"Da, that is what I say... bollock." Ivan had only been here a few months and his plumbing vocab wasn't yet up to speed.

"No, Ivan, it's pronounced ball cock, not bollock. Bollock is something quite different."

"Yes, bollock. Eet is what I say."

"No, Ivan, it's not..."

"I go back to plumber's merchant tomorrow and return bollock and ask for new one. Then maybe I feex it."

She wasn't sure how to approach this. "You know, Ivan, I don't think you'll get much joy asking the bloke behind the counter for a new bollock. Might be better to ask for a replacement cistern."

"Ah, yes, thees is good. But still I tell him, his English bollocks are too small. In my country we have much bigger bollocks."

Ruby cleared her throat. "Good, well... excellent. I think I'll just leave sorting this one out to you."

Once Ivan had left and she'd swept up some of the mess

he'd left in the bathroom, there was no time to write the letter to Claudia Planchette. She made time, though, to put in a quick call to Chanel. She didn't want to pester her, but she was worried about her and simply wanted to check that she'd got home OK and was hanging in there. Craig answered and said he was taking her out to dinner and that they were determined to find a new doctor. Ruby said nothing. Despite having suggested to Chanel that she make an appointment with one of the doctors at St. Luke's, she couldn't help thinking now that they were clutching at straws.

After she got off the phone, she went into the bedroom to choose something to wear for her date. The room was just about big enough for her bed and a small wardrobe. Since it was so fashionable again, Ruby had wanted to hang patterned wallpaper. Fi had convinced her that a pattern would make the room seem even smaller, so Ruby compromised. She bought a couple of large wooden panels and covered those in fancy seventies aubergine and olive wallpaper instead. She hung one over her bed in place of a headboard. The second she put on the far wall facing the door, so that people noticed it the moment they walked in. Everybody, including Ronnie, said how well the wallpaper panels worked. What Ruby didn't say was that she'd nicked the idea from *Changing Rooms*.

Ruby's wardrobe was overflowing—not because she was always buying clothes, but because the wardrobe was so small and because she hadn't had a clear-out in ages. She knew the rules. If you haven't worn an outfit for more than a season, dump it, but she never could. There was always that vague feeling that maybe high-waisted tapered jeans and bat-sleeve sweaters might have their day again. The fact that bat-sleeve sweaters had only ever had a very brief and less than triumphant day in the first place always seemed to escape her.

She opened the mirror door and began sliding clothes along the rack. A gorgeous novelist definitely deserved her best shot. She paused briefly at a low-cut scarlet dress before wrinkling her nose and moving on. Too tarty. It practically screamed: "take me now!" She continued along the rack. Finally she pulled out a halter-neck top in pale raspberry silk. It was sexy without being too full-on. She teamed this with a pretty beaded A-line skirt in a slightly darker shade. She even managed to find a dusky pink halter-neck bra and pants. Not that she was planning for things to go any further than dinner, but coordinating underwear always made her feel good.

She left everything on the aubergine and olive duvet and went to run a bath. As she soaked in the tub, she burned lavender and jasmine candles, which was the nearest she had got so far to a garden.

When she arrived at Bella Roma—right on time—Duncan wasn't there. She wasn't too put out, since he'd phoned the restaurant and left a message apologizing and saying he was stuck in traffic.

The maître d' offered to show her to her table, but she decided to go to the loo first.

There were two cubicles in the ladies' room, one of which was occupied. She took the second and sat down to pee. Suddenly she heard a voice coming from the next cubicle. "So how are you?" Ruby stopped in midpee and frowned. Assuming there was some weird woman in the next cubicle, she didn't say anything.

"No, come on," the voice said again. "You all right? Please, speak to me."

Ruby did some nervous throat clearing. "Yes, I'm fine."

"I've been so worried about you."

"Really? That's kind, but there's no need."

"Everything OK at work?"

"Erm, yeah . . . couldn't be better. Shop's pretty busy."

"So, what are you doing now?"

"Umm, just having a quick pee, actually. You?"

There was a brief pause. Then Ruby heard the voice again. "Listen, Justin, I'll have to call you back, babe. There's some daft tart in the next cubicle answering all my questions."

Desperate that the woman in the next cubicle wouldn't see her and think she was completely barking mad, Ruby finished peeing, rinsed her hands and fled the ladies' room as fast as she could.

When she got back into the restaurant, one of the waiters told her that Duncan had arrived and pointed out a table at the far end.

As she walked through the restaurant, she had no idea that the woman from the loo was following her. Suddenly she felt a sharp tap on her shoulder. She turned round. Standing in front of her was a brassy-looking woman in her midforties, wearing tight black leather pants and a crimson trout pout. "Excuse me," she blasted Ruby, so that the entire restaurant could hear, "is this how you get your kicks, hiding in toilet cubicles joining in other people's private phone conversations? I mean, how sad is that? Don't you have a life?"

"Sorry. It was a genuine mistake," Ruby ventured. "I honestly thought you were talking to me."

"Yeah, right. Like I'd start talking to some strange woman in the next cubicle. What do you take me for, some kind of weirdo?"

Ruby wanted to say that actually she *had* taken her for a weirdo, but seeing how angry the woman was, she felt it was wiser to say nothing.

The woman delivered something that was clearly meant to be a haughty sniff but came out more as a piggy snort.

With that she turned on what Ruby couldn't help noticing were rather cheap, excessively high heels and teetered back to her table where a group of equally brassy, St. Tropez-ed women friends were waiting.

Ruby was aware that everybody in the restaurant had stopped eating to watch the exchange between her and the woman. Now, as they turned back to their food, she found herself glued to the spot, her face burning with embarrassment. She seriously considered making a run for it. What was the point of staying? Her gorgeous, sexy novelist was bound to think she was some kind of nutcase with a public toilet fetish.

Against her better judgment, she continued toward the table. It was curiosity that spurred her on. She simply couldn't resist seeing precisely how gorgeous Gorgeous Duncan was—not that he would be remotely interested in her now, after what had just happened. She took a deep breath. "I forgive myself my past mistakes," she muttered, remembering her affirmations. "I am beautiful and vibrant in my uniqueness."

As she approached the table, all she could see was a man sitting with his back facing her, his body bent over toward the floor. He appeared to be struggling to pull something from a large black leather holdall. So engrossed was he that Ruby decided there was a distinct possibility he hadn't overheard her contretemps with the brassy woman.

She watched as he continued to do battle with the overly full bag. Finally, Mary Poppins–like, he produced one of those beaded seat covers favored by taxi drivers. With great precision, not to say solemnity, he stood up and began arranging it over his chair.

Ruby waited for him to finish. Then, doing her best to conceal her amusement and disbelief, she introduced herself.

"Oh, hi, I'm Duncan," he said, taking her outstretched hand. "Nice to meet you. Soph's told me all about you." It was his voice that struck her first. It was a low monotone. He hadn't said much, but she could already tell that listening to him was going to be like listening to a car engine stuck in second gear.

They sat down and Duncan immediately began rolling his back and shoulders over the beads of the seat cover. "Oh, that feels good," he said, starting to rotate his head as well. "It's so important to get the right lumbar support."

Ruby immediately felt rotten about sneering. Poor chap clearly had a bad back.

"It must be awful being in constant back pain," she said.

"I'm not in any pain. There's absolutely nothing the matter with my back... yet." He wagged a finger in front of her. "But as I always say, prevention is better than cure."

It turned out that Duncan had just hit forty and as a result had become obsessed with the health effects of getting older. Over drinks—wine for her, mineral water for him—he treated her to an artery-by-artery account of how the cardiovascular system deteriorates during a person's fifth decade. As he spoke, she noticed his heavy forehead and elongated chin. With his fringe that had been separated into "curtains," she couldn't help thinking he looked—not to mention sounded—like a funeral director stuck in a nineties-style rut. It was clear that Soph's idea of gorgeous was nothing like her own.

"So, I hear you're a novelist," Ruby said, anxious to get the conversation away from Duncan's physical decline.

"Yes, I write murder mysteries."

Now this sounded promising.

"I've completed six so far," he went on. Wow, he was successful. Better and better. "And all of them in my own, made-up language."

Ah. Oh... kay. "In your own language? I see. So, um, who's your publisher?"

Duncan said he didn't have a publisher as such, but was living in hope of getting one lined up shortly. He then went to great pains to describe the fundamental building blocks of his made-up language, which was called Brogan.

By the time the profiteroles arrived she was proficient in conjugating the verb "to be." "Well done!" he enthused. "Now, then, let's move on to the verb 'to do' or 'to make.' This is an irregular OL verb: *anrol*. So, I make is *eb anrol*. You make—familiar form—is *ip anrola*. He, she and it makes is *sa anrols*. See if you can remember any of that."

Over espresso they covered the perfect and the imperfect tense, as well as the subjunctive. By eleven she could bear it no more and told Duncan that she'd had a wonderful evening, but really needed to get home as she had an early start. He offered to give her a lift, but, petrified he would try to seduce her by teaching her the genitive or ablative, she insisted on calling a taxi.

As they waited outside for a cab, Ruby sensed that Duncan was psyching himself up to saying something. Her heart sank. Any second he was going to suggest they go out again and ask her for her phone number. Naturally she would give it to him on the grounds that it would be too mean not to. She would then go home and spend all night trying to invent plausible excuses for not going out with him.

Several minutes and at least a dozen cabs went by—all with their for-hire lights off—but instead of asking for her number, he stood rolling on the balls of his feet, nattering on about how chilly the nights were getting now they were into September. She was about to put him out of his misery and simply hand him her card, when he said: "Look, Ruby, you are very nice and please don't take this the wrong way, but as I always say honesty is the best policy and the truth is I don't think there's much chemistry between us."

Relief shot through her. "Oh, right," she said, thinking that for the sake of politeness she ought to at least sound disappointed.

"You see, I demand very high standards in the women I go out with. I look for a sharp, probing mind. I need somebody who will challenge me, somebody who can appreciate that in creating this new language of mine, I am in fact attempting to create a new reality."

"I see."

"The thing is that when I was trying to engage with you over semantic roles and clustering syntactic positions, you didn't seem that interested. I'm sure that in many ways, you're not a boring person, but—"

"Hang on, you think *I'm* boring?"

"Just a little, maybe, but please don't take it to heart. I would hate you to see this as a rejection." Before she had a chance to say anything, Duncan was hailing a taxi. The next thing she knew, he was holding the door open for her. "There is a man out there for you, I just know it. As I always say, every pot has its lid." With that he slammed the door shut.

"Where to, love?" said the driver.

WHEN SHE GOT home, Ruby tried ringing Fi to inform her that as long as she lived she would never go on another blind date—at least not one Fi had organized—but the phone was off the hook. That could only mean that Connor was asleep and she didn't want to be disturbed.

She brushed her teeth and took off her makeup. Then she fell into bed and began reciting a new affirmation—one she had just made up. "I am not boring. I have never been boring. I never will be boring. I am scintillating, articulate and intelligent. In company I dazzle people with my wit and insight." She must have recited this a dozen times or more. Then she fell asleep and dreamed that she was teaching Sam Epstien how to conjugate the Brogan verb "to neck."

Chapter 7

"Chanel, can I ask you something?" It was the following morning and Ruby and Chanel were getting ready to open the shop.

"Course."

"Do you think I'm boring?"

"You? Boring?" Chanel said. "You're the least boring person I know."

"Really?" Ruby could feel herself blushing at the compliment.

"Of course, I don't mind when you go on for hours about how yer mum analyzes you, but I can see it might get some people down. And then there was that time when that bloke cut you off on the motorway. You didn't talk about anything else for days."

"But he nearly killed me. I was in shock. You'd have been the same if it had been you he'd cut off."

"And whenever you've got the slightest sniffle, you don't stop moaning..."

"OK, but apart from the mum thing, the near-death experience on the motorway and my tendency to be a bit needy when I have a temperature of 103, I'm not boring?"

"Definitely not. What's all this about anyway?... Oh, 'ang on, it's got something to do with your date last night, 'asn't it?"

Ruby admitted it had.

"Bit crap, was it?" Chanel said.

Until now Ruby had been dusting the countertop. She stopped, can of Pledge in one hand, duster in the other, and pretended to become lost in thought. "Hmm, I'm not sure that 'a bit crap' quite gets to the nub of it, really. I think 'catastrophe' would be a more accurate description."

"Oh, right. So, better than some of the other dates Fi's fixed you up with, then?"

Ruby managed to laugh. Then she told Chanel about Duncan. Chanel wasn't amused. "A novel? In 'is own made-up language? And 'e 'ad the nerve to call you boring?" She shuddered. "Total weirdo if you ask me. I wouldn't have 'ung around, I tell you that much."

"I have to admit, he was a bit strange..."

"Yeah, like Jack McFarland's a *bit* gay."

Ruby began sorting through the mail while Chanel unlocked the front door. "Look, I know it's short notice," Chanel said, "but would it be all right if I took a couple of hours off later on? It's just that I phoned this new Harley Street specialist just before I left this morning and by some miracle 'e's got a cancellation at twelve. If me and Craig don't take it, we'll 'ave to wait until November for another appointment."

Ruby said of course she could have the time off. "Like you have to ask," she smiled.

"Great. Ta. I'll make up the time. Promise."

"Don't be silly," Ruby said, throwing some junk mail into the bin. "You work hard enough as it is."

The door had been open less than a minute when Fi walked in. She looked frazzled and exhausted. "Hi, Chanel," Fi said, giving her a kiss on the cheek.

As they pulled away from their embrace, Chanel stood back to take a look at Fi. "Gawd, when did you last get a decent night's sleep, 1485?"

"Something like that," Fi said.

By now Ruby had joined them. "Hi, sweetie," she said to Fi. "What brings you here? And who's in charge back at the ranch?"

"Saul, but I can't stop. I'm on my way to Waitrose and have to get back for Connor's next feed. I just stopped in to say I'm really sorry about—"

"You know, Cancers need to watch their immune system," Chanel broke in, shaking a warning finger at Fi. "If you don't get enough sleep, you're going to get seriously run down."

"Tell that to Connor when he wakes five times in the night. By the way, he adores the crib mobile you got him. Thanks again, it was such a lovely thought."

"My pleasure," Chanel said, waving a hand in front of her. "Now come over here and sit down." She led Fi to one of the chairs they kept next to the counter for heavily pregnant women.

Fi and Chanel had real soft spots for each other. Before Connor was born, Fi would sometimes help out at the shop during sale time and she and Chanel had hit it off straight away. Chanel loved mothering people, and Fi, having received precious little by way of affection from Bridget, rather enjoyed it. Plus, Chanel made her laugh.

"Right, don't know about you two," Chanel said, "but I'm feeling a bit precaffeinated. I'm off to do a coffee run." She took her purse out of her bag and turned to Fi: "You look like you could do with a cup."

Fi protested that she needed to get to Waitrose and didn't have time for coffee, but Chanel managed to tempt her with the promise of a chocolate éclair.

After Chanel had gone, Fi turned to Ruby: "Look, I just had to come in and say sorry about Duncan," she said. "Soph rang. Last night must have been miserable."

"I admit I was a bit cross at the time—particularly when he said I was boring, but I'm starting to see the funny side."

"He said you were boring? Cheek. I don't think you're at all boring. OK, you do have a tendency to go on about your mum. Then there was the time that bloke nearly ran you off the motorway. You bored on about that for weeks. And when you're ill you're pretty boring..."

"Yeah, yeah, but *basically* you don't think I'm boring, right?"

"Absolutely. Look, last night was all my fault and if I were you, I'd be furious with me. All I can say in my defense is that I had no idea what Duncan was like until Soph rang me last night. She was in such a state. She'd suddenly realized how wrong it was to set you up with him without telling you what he was like. She told me all about him—the made-up language, the obsession with health, everything. Apparently he's a lovely bloke when you get to know him, but he's just a bit eccentric and not very at ease socially."

"You don't say," Ruby said, examining the giant vase of white lilies on the counter and breaking off a damaged leaf.

"She told me that both his parents are physics professors. He was one of those hothouse child prodigies and the experience left him a bit peculiar. I'll find you somebody else. Promise. My friend Kate's got a mate who knows this conductor."

"Orchestra or bus?" Ruby asked, only half joking.

Fi blinked. "Now you come to mention it, she didn't say."

"Look," Ruby said, "when I told you I didn't want to go on any more blind dates, I really did mean it. I love it that you care about me and want me to find somebody, but let's just give the blind dates a rest for a bit, eh?"

Fi looked disappointed. "OK, perhaps you're right," she said.

Ruby decided to change the subject. "So, is Saul the new Captain Bird's Eye?"

"Not exactly. They said he was too Semitic looking and didn't his agent know they were looking for somebody to advertise fish suppers and not the Last Supper."

"Ouch—seems a bit hard."

"I know, but he's got another couple of auditions lined up, so he's not too down.... How did things go at St. Luke's?"

Ruby explained about bumping into Sam Epstien again.

"Epstien," Fi repeated, brow knitted. "That's funny, Saul has Epstiens in his family. And I'm sure there's an American branch. This Sam didn't happen to say if he was a Teaneck, New Jersey, Epstien, did he?"

"No, we didn't actually get round to that," Ruby said with gentle sarcasm.

"Shame. I mean, they could be related.... On a second thought, scrub that. I'm almost certain Saul's lot are Ep-*steins* to rhyme with 'wines'—rather than Ep-*steens*. Two of them came to the wedding. Elderly couple. Lovely people. Now, what are their first names? Hang on, it's coming. I'll get there in a tick. Saul did tell me.... Bert? No, not Bert.... Buddy, that's it. Buddy and Irene. Big in kosher pickles, apparently."

"Really?" Ruby said with a soft laugh. "Well, I'm glad we've cleared that up."

"Oh, God, I've been wittering again. Sorry. It's lack of sleep.... So, you've got a Jewish doctor after you. Talk about fulfilling every Jewish mother's fantasy. Saul's sister married a Jewish doctor. Saul's mum always says it was the only thing that cured her postnatal depression. So, have you told Ronnie about Dr. Epstien?"

"There's nothing to tell. We chatted and he said he would give me a call. That was it."

"God, you'll have to get something special to wear for your first date. Why don't I come shopping with you?"

"Fi, I don't even know if there's going to be a date." She

told Fi what she'd told Chanel—that confessing she'd lied about her vaginal stamp and then having to tell him the true story would be just too embarrassing.

"Oh, come on, Ruby. . . ." It was Chanel back with the coffee. "You know you want to go out with him. Allowing your vagina to come between the two of you is stupid." Chanel wrinkled her brow. "I think that may 'ave come out wrong," she said, "but you know what I mean." She handed out cups of coffee and gave Fi a bag containing the promised éclair.

"All right, maybe I do," Ruby said, easing off the plastic lid on her coffee cup, "but even if I can get over the embarrassment issue, he's still a gynecologist."

"Tell me about it," Fi giggled. "I can't remember the last time I was this jealous. You know . . ." she lowered her voice to a whisper, "sleeping with a gynecologist is my ultimate sexual fantasy." She bit into the éclair, causing whipped cream to ooze from its sides.

"Blimey, you kept that quiet," Ruby said.

"What do you want me to do, go round broadcasting to the world that I like to have sex with my legs in stirrups?"

"You serious?" Chanel said, grinning.

Fi nodded. "Absolutely." She took another bite of éclair. "Saul found the stirrups on eBay. Some doctor was upgrading his equipment and didn't need them anymore."

Ruby was shaking her head, eyes wide with surprise. Not in a million years would she have guessed Fi was this sexually liberated. She wasn't the type. She wore Sebagos. She recycled. She worked for her local branch of the National Childbirth Trust as a breast pump agent. This was the woman who had been utterly scandalized to discover Ruby and Matt had done it in one of the changing rooms in French Connection. And two years ago, when Ruby had presented her with a Rampant Rabbit vibrator for her birthday, she'd thought it was a paper towel holder.

"This feels so weird," Ruby said. "All these years you think you know somebody and then you discover you don't. How come you never told me? I told you about me and Matt doing it in French Connection."

"I know, but this is far more kinky. Plus I knew how you felt about the whole gynecologist thing."

"Of course," Chanel chipped in, "the gynecologist fantasy is all about wanting to be dominated. It's not something me and Craig 'ave ever got into. He's a Cancer, and Cancers tend to be a bit conservative in the bedroom department, but I can see 'ow it would be pretty mind-blowing to act out."

"Too right," Fi said with a rich earthy laugh, which was so unlike her. "So, can you imagine what it would be to have real sex with a gynecologist?"

Ruby stood drinking her coffee, her eyes starting to glaze over. Try as she might to fend them off, she was having thoughts about being ravaged by Sam Epstien. Worse still, in her fantasy Sam was wearing his blue scrubs and she was lying on a gynecologist's table.

Chanel seemed to pick up on her faraway look. " 'Aving second thoughts about Dr. Epstien, then?"

The question jolted Ruby from her reverie. "No, not at all," she said, aware of how defensive she sounded.

"Yeah, right," Chanel came back, a trace of a smirk on her face.

"OK, what if I am?" Ruby said, feeling her cheeks burning. "Since when was changing your mind indictable?"

Chanel and Fi exchanged amused looks.

"Of course," Fi said, "the domination issue aside, the other reason for wanting to sleep with a gynecologist is that they really know their way around women's bits. How can they not be totally amazing in the sack?"

Ruby said she couldn't imagine old Double Barrel being good in the sack.

"You'd be surprised," Chanel said. "I bet 'e knows exactly 'ow to show Mrs. Double Barrel a good time."

Ruby grimaced at the thought.

AFTER FI HAD gone, customers began to trickle in. While Chanel looked after them, Ruby sat at the computer in the stockroom, dealing with a pile of e-mail orders. The door was open and she could hear Chanel talking to people in the shop. She was being perfectly pleasant, Ruby thought, but she seemed less chatty than usual. She was clearly getting worked up about the appointment with this new doctor.

When it was time for Chanel to go, Ruby wished her good luck and gave her a hug. "I'll keep everything crossed."

"Thanks," Chanel said, smiling, "but I've got this really strong feeling everything's going to be OK and that this new bloke is going to give us some fresh 'ope. I know it sounds weird, bearing in mind what the last doctor told us, but I can't 'elp thinking it."

"Let's hope you're right," Ruby smiled, giving her another squeeze.

Things started to quiet down in the shop and Ruby decided to pop into the kitchen and make a cup of tea. While the kettle boiled she grabbed a packet of potato chips. She'd go out for a sandwich later when Chanel got back. She was tearing open the packet when she became aware that her trouser waistband felt tight. She looked down and ran her hand over her stomach. It was bloated and straining against her trousers. Wheat always did this to her. Last night in the restaurant, the first course had taken ages to arrive. How many bread sticks had she eaten as she sat there listening to Duncan droning on? Six? Eight? Maybe more. Still, so long as she kept to protein and green veg for lunch and dinner, she'd be back to normal by tomorrow. She put the chips back in the cupboard and opened the minifridge. Inside was a raspberry yogurt, which was only three days out of date.

As she drank her tea, she pottered around the shop, tidying shelves, checking the displays and praying that this new doctor really would be able to offer Chanel and Craig some hope. As she thought about how lucky they were to get this cancellation with the fertility specialist, she remembered her Grandma Esther's attitude toward making medical appointments. If Esther phoned for an appointment and the doctor had a vacancy, she would immediately hang up. The way she saw it, all the best doctors were booked up for weeks and one with a vacancy was highly suspect. Ruby smiled to herself as she remembered her grandmother and her pals bragging about the length of time they'd had to wait for their checkups and operations.

It was nearly one before the next customer appeared. Even though she was wearing no makeup and her long blonde hair was hanging flat and unstyled, the woman—who was about six months pregnant—was instantly recognizable. Ruby could barely believe her luck. She wouldn't have to write that letter after all. Claudia Planchette, her lips forming an unnaturally plump crescent, was standing in front of her waiting to be served.

It had taken a while, but Ruby was finally used to Hollywood superstars coming into the shop. When they first began to appear she got flustered and tongue-tied. This was because she found it impossible to believe that it was actually Gwyneth Paltrow or Kate Winslet standing in front of her wanting advice on the best make of breast pump or maternity bra.

These days, she managed to be relaxed and friendly with celebrity customers, but not fawning. Unlike Stella. If she happened to be in the shop when a famous person came in, she would greet them as if she had just applied a fresh coat of unction.

"Hello," came Claudia's actressy American voice. "I wonder if you can help me. I'm looking for a maternity bathing suit?" Her statement ended with a question mark. She had the most beautiful eyes, Ruby thought. They were like a pair of almond-shaped emeralds.

"No problem," Ruby said. "Why don't you come over to the rack and I'll show you what we have."

Ruby led the way. She had just taken delivery of their winter beachwear collection, which included a range of stunning Italian-made maternity swimsuits.

"Hey, these are so cute," Claudia gushed, picking one up and holding it against her. Ruby watched her posing in front of the mirror, one foot slightly in front of the other. She couldn't resist flicking her hair and running her tongue over her lips. Force of habit, Ruby assumed. She was clearly in no doubt how high she ranked on the stunometer.

"So, sweetie, when's your baby due?" Claudia said, still admiring herself in the mirror.

The patronizing "sweetie" remark felt like nothing compared to the question that followed. It stopped Ruby in her tracks. Her eyes shot down toward her stomach. Is that what nine bread sticks had done to her—bloated her so much that she actually looked pregnant?

"Actually, I'm not pregnant," Ruby said, feeling the flush forming on her cheeks.

"You're not? Sweetie, I'm so embarrassed. I just assumed... Listen, sweetie, why don't I give you the number of my personal trainer? I'm sure he could help you strengthen those abs."

Ruby didn't know what to make of this last remark. Either the woman was so embarrassed at having suggested Ruby was pregnant that in her distress her apology had come out all wrong, or she was being starry and spiteful. Since Ruby wasn't one to see the worst in people, she decided that Claudia was doing her best to make amends for the pregnancy remark and that she would give her the benefit of the doubt.

"Here's his card," Claudia went on. "His name's Hilary, but don't be put off—the man's a brute."

"Actually, that won't be necessary," Ruby blurted. "You see, I love and accept my body and I am beautiful and vibrant in my uniqueness."

Claudia was still frowning in puzzlement when her mobile rang. "Pardon me," Claudia said to Ruby as she reached into her bag. She stabbed "connect." "Yeah? What?" she snapped. "Look, Marta, I've made it clear I do not wish to be disturbed with domestic issues during the day. If Avocado has a fever, deal with it." She covered up the phone and turned to Ruby. "I need this like a hole in the head. It's the sitter. Totally neurotic... Marta! No! Don't let her be sick on the fauteuil. It's Louis the friggin' fifteenth for crying out loud. Do you know how much it cost me to get that thing restored?... Look, can't you see she's only doing all this to get attention?... No, I won't come home. I refuse to be blackmailed by a two-year-old. I have to go. I'm in an important meeting. I'll call you."

Claudia's cold-hearted outburst left Ruby blinking in disbelief. Her mind sprang back to the *Hello!* article she'd read in the waiting room at St. Luke's. Every other sentence referred to Claudia as a calm, deeply spiritual person who struggled not to overprotect the child she adored. Ruby was beginning to understand why Claudia had been nominated for two Oscars in the last few years.

Having put her phone back in her bag, Claudia turned back to Ruby. "I have two nannies for that child. On top of their salaries they get free health care, dental, a car and plasma TV in their rooms. You'd think with all that they might be willing to show some initiative, but no. The moment I turn my back, they fall apart." She began rotating her head in wide circles. "I think all the stress is getting to me," she said. "I don't suppose you'd have some Kabbalah Spring—with a little ice and lemon, maybe?"

Although the fridge in the kitchen was stocked with bottled water and organic fruit juice, purely for the relief of flapping celebs, Ruby didn't have Kabbalah Spring water.

"I can offer you Perrier," she said.

"Is that all?" Claudia came back, still rotating her neck. "Well, I suppose I can make do."

"So, I hear you're having this baby at St. Luke's," Ruby said as Claudia alternately sipped Perrier and massaged the back of her neck.

"That's right, just like last time. The place is a marvel. With Avocado, my husband—actually he's now ex-husband—brought in scented candles. We played soothing music. In the final stages of labor, the doula actually got him to massage my vulva. I cannot begin to tell you how awesome it was. I had no idea it was possible to have an orgasm during childbirth. We are talking totally Zen experience, here. Avocado came into the world smiling and utterly at peace. I felt I owed that to her."

Ruby was tempted to say it was a shame her feelings about what she owed her child seemed to have changed so much, but she bit her tongue.

As Claudia put her glass down on the shop counter, her mobile went off again. "Marta," she screeched, "just deal with it, OK? All kids run fevers and puke. I am not coming home because my child has a bit of stomach flu."

By now Ruby was fighting back the tears. It was possible that Claudia was having an off day, but she suspected that as far as poor little Avocado was concerned, every one of

Claudia's days was an off day. "Look, maybe you should go," she said after Claudia had finished barking at Marta. "I can bike some swimsuits round to you and you can try them on at home. I'm sure you're right and there's probably nothing serious the matter with Avocado, but you never know and I'm sure you'd feel better..."

Claudia let out a sigh. "I guess you're right. I'd better go check on her, but I refuse to go until I've tried on some of these fabulous swimsuits." With that she pulled three off the rack and headed toward the changing room.

"Shout if you need a different size," Ruby called after her. She knew not to go into the changing room unless she was summoned. Women celebs in particular were very wary about being seen without their clothes. It was obvious why. They knew that in real life their bodies didn't begin to compare with the computer-enhanced, Photoshopped images that appeared in the glossies. It would destroy the myth to let people see that they had orange-peel buttocks just like the rest of the world.

"Oh, the orange is fab-u-lous! So is the violet," Claudia trilled from the changing room. "I'll take two of each." Ruby went into the stockroom to fetch another couple of swimsuits. As she came back, she had to pass the row of three curtained-off changing cubicles. Judging by the shouting coming from the one Claudia occupied, she was on the phone to poor Marta again and giving her hell. At one point Claudia must have gesticulated so hard that her hand caught the curtain, causing it to slide along the runner. She closed the curtain, apparently unaware that Ruby had seen into the cubicle. The entire curtain-moving incident was over in a flash, but it had lasted long enough for Ruby's eyes to alight on Claudia's abdomen and for her brain to register that, pregnancy-wise, things weren't quite as they should be.

The woman was wearing a flesh-colored body suit with large breasts and a six-month-pregnant stomach. It reminded her of the getup Robin Williams wore in *Mrs. Doubtfire*. Ruby was so sure that she would have put money on it. But why on earth would Claudia pretend to be pregnant?

Disturbed and confused, Ruby made her way back to the counter and started wrapping the swimsuits she'd brought from the stockroom. When Claudia emerged from the cubicle she was all smiles. Nothing about her expression suggested that she realized she had been found out. She was holding the swimsuits she'd been trying on. Ruby took them from her and carried on wrapping in silence. Her lack of words belied the frantic activity going on in her mind. She'd definitely seen it. A prosthetic stomach, right? Yes. No doubt. Claudia handed her a platinum Amex card and then began looking through a basket of hand-knitted booties on the counter. As Ruby swiped the card, her thoughts carried on churning. But she'd only seen into the cubicle for a second. How could she be so certain about something she'd seen for such a short time? In her mind a fantasy was developing, in which she was giving evidence in court about what she had seen. A wigged barrister was saying: "So, Ms. Silverman, how long did you say you'd glanced at said prosthetic stomach?"

"Er, a second. Maybe less."

"A second or less? I see. So, you are prepared to swear on oath that this woman was wearing a prosthetic stomach based on having glanced at her abdomen for a mere second, maybe less. I put it to you, members of the jury..."

And it didn't make sense. Ruby had to be mistaken. She watched as Claudia signed the credit card slip. Then she handed her the swimsuits in a Les Sprogs carrier bag. "Bye," Ruby said. "I hope we'll see you again."

"You have my word on it. I need so many things for this baby. I guarantee you haven't seen the last of me."

Stella would be ecstatic. "I hope Avocado is feeling better when you get home."

But Claudia didn't hear. Through the shop window, she had spied a taxi pulling up and was making a remarkably athletic dash for it.

Chapter 8

Ruby spent the next hour fretting and puzzling over what she had seen in the changing cubicle. She was so engrossed that a couple of times when customers approached her with a query, they had to repeat themselves before she acknowledged them.

Then, while she was flicking through a catalogue that had arrived that morning from a Parisian maternity lingerie manufacturer, she had a realization. "Of course! That's it," Ruby muttered to herself, stabbing a picture of a pregnant model in her underwear. How had she taken so long to work it out? It wasn't a prosthetic stomach that Claudia had been wearing. It was a maternity girdle. It was identical to the one she was staring at now. Back in the sixties and seventies, nearly all pregnant women wore them. They contained a stretchy webbed pouch, which gave extra support to the underside of a pregnancy bump. Forty years later they were just starting to make a comeback in Europe—particularly in France and Italy. Claudia's last movie had been filmed in Paris. She must have bought hers there. The garments had yet to catch on again in Britain, but bearing in mind the business she was in, Ruby couldn't believe she'd failed to recognize a maternity girdle when she saw one.

She couldn't wait to share her tale with Chanel. She'd have hysterics when she found out Ruby had actually been daft enough to think Claudia might be faking her pregnancy.

In the meantime she phoned Stella in New York to give her the news that Claudia had been in to buy swimsuits. "What? She only bought swimsuits? What use is that? I take it you then offered to close the shop so that she could choose the rest of her layette in complete privacy?"

"Actually, no. I didn't. She said she'd be back and I didn't want to put more pressure on her. In my experience celebrities don't react well to pushy salespeople."

"Offering to close the shop isn't remotely pushy," Stella snapped. "You would simply be flattering Claudia's ego. How can you not see that? It seems that I have to explain the simplest things to you. Sometimes, Ruby, I really do doubt your ability to run an exclusive establishment like Les Sprogs. You really must buck your ideas up. Now then, I have to go. I have a breakfast meeting." With that she hung up.

Ruby stared at the receiver. "Thanks, Stella. Always good to know I have your support."

Chanel turned up at the shop just after two. Ruby, who was in the middle of serving a heavily pregnant customer, took one look at Chanel and in an instant all thoughts of having a giggle with her over the maternity girdle she had mistaken for a prosthetic stomach vanished from her mind. It was obvious from Chanel's red face and puffy swollen eyes that the news from their new doctor hadn't been good, and this time, Chanel had let the tears come.

Craig was with her, his arm firmly round her shoulder. His height and rugby player's build always managed to dwarf even Chanel's chunky frame, but today it was even more apparent. As he smiled down at her from under his short ginger thatch, which always looked as if his barber had set about it with a machete, he looked like a friendly giant protecting a frail, unhappy child.

"Be with you in a tick," Ruby said, looking at them anxiously. As fast as she could, she maneuvered a boxed sterilizer unit into a large Les Sprogs carrier bag and slid it across the counter to the customer. "There you go, and I'll pop our new catalogue in the post the moment it comes in."

The woman said her thank-yous and headed toward the door. Ruby turned to Chanel and Craig. "What happened?" she said, her voice practically a whisper. She realized it was a stupid question, since she pretty much knew the answer, but she couldn't think of anything else to say.

"Oh, you know," Chanel said, swallowing hard, but at the same time doing her best to sound bright. "The doctor, 'e... er... 'e broke it to us as gently as 'e could...." Her voice gave out on the last word and she began biting her top lip. Craig gave her a squeeze and a reassuring smile. They were two of a kind. Like Chanel, he was determined to stay positive, but Ruby could tell he was as distraught as she was.

"New bloke pretty much agreed with the last one," Craig said, taking up the story. " 'E'd managed to get our notes faxed over to 'im. Once 'e'd read them 'e said there didn't seem to be much point carrying on with the IVF. Suggested we should think about adoption, didn't 'e, babe?"

"But surely there are other fertility specialists," Ruby said, feeling the overwhelming need to offer them the hope the doctor had snatched from them. "I mean, have you thought about trying St. Luke's again, or maybe you should consider going to America?"

"These doctors we've seen 'ave been two of the top men in the world," Craig said. "If they're saying it's time to call it a day, then we 'ave to go with that."

Just then the phone started ringing. It occurred to Ruby that this was the second time recently that Chanel had been in the middle of delivering bad news and the phone had rung. Like last time, Ruby was more than prepared to let it ring, but again Chanel insisted she take it.

Annoyed at having to abandon her conversation with Chanel and Craig, Ruby went back behind the counter and picked up the phone next to the till.

"Hello, Les Sprogs," she announced, aware that her manner sounded a bit flat and lacked its usual upbeat charm.

"Hi, is that Ruby?"

"Speaking."

"Hey, Ruby, it's me, Sam Epstien. Sorry to disturb you at work. I tried you on your cell, but it seemed to be switched off."

"Oh, hi, Sam. How are you?" Despite all her doubts about him, she was pleased he'd called, but at the same time, she was desperately aware of how offhand she sounded. "Actually, my cell's not off. The battery keeps running down. I really need to get a new phone."

"Listen, I was just wondering if you were free one night this week. I thought we could go see a movie, maybe. Or just have a drink if you'd prefer."

She glanced across at Chanel and Craig. The pair of them looked so utterly miserable. Her heart ached for them. "Sam, I don't mean to be rude, but you've caught me at a really bad time. Some friends of mine are here. They've just received some really bad news . . ."

"I totally understand. No problem. I'll call back some other time."

"That'd be great. Speak soon, yeah?"

"For sure."

Ruby put down the phone and went back to Chanel and Craig. "Sorry," she said, deciding not to mention it had been Sam on the phone. It wasn't remotely the right time. "So, you were saying how the doctor had suggested adoption."

Chanel nodded. "Yeah," she said, with a breeziness that was clearly meant to comfort all three of them, but didn't. "And we're definitely going to think about it. I mean, an adopted child is a stranger at first, but after a while you bond and in the end it's just the same as 'aving your own child. And there are so many unwanted children desperate for a mum and dad to love them. Craig agrees, don't you, Craig?"

"We'll see," he said gently. He turned to Ruby. "Look, it's all been a bit much today. Would you mind if I took the missus 'ome? I think she could do with putting 'er feet up."

Ruby did her level best to convince Chanel to take the rest of the week off, but as usual she said coming to work made her feel sane and normal and she wouldn't hear of it. "A rest—just until tomorrow—is all I need. Honest."

"OK, if you're sure."

"I'm positive."

Ruby shot Craig a look of mild despair, as if to say: "What do you do with her?" He replied with a shrug. It was clear that, like Ruby, he believed there would be no more arguing with her.

OVER THE NEXT few days, Chanel appeared to struggle to keep her emotions in check. Whenever she had a particularly sad or faraway look on her face, Ruby would ask her gently if she wanted to talk, but Chanel always brushed her off with a chirpy: "Look, stop worrying. I'm fine." Ruby knew she was anything but fine. She also knew that if she put pressure on her to talk when she didn't want to, she would get cross.

Had it not been for Ronnie coming to the rescue, Chanel might have descended into a full-scale depression. She popped into the shop one afternoon on her way back from lunch with one of her girlfriends. Ruby wasn't there because she'd gone to St. Luke's to drop off a couple of passport photographs so that the hospital could process her ID card. She'd forgotten to tell her mother about Chanel and Craig giving up IVF. Had she remembered, she would have suggested to Ronnie—whose bump was just beginning to show—that in order to protect Chanel's feelings, it might be best to stay away from the shop for a couple of weeks.

When Ruby got back from St. Luke's it was after closing time. Ronnie and Chanel were standing in the shop's tiny kitchen area. The second she saw the two women together, she started to panic. As she greeted them, she looked for signs of additional strain and upset on Chanel's face, but there were none. In fact, her face looked genuinely sunny for a change. What's more, as Ronnie was leaving, Chanel gave her a kiss and an enormous hug. "Thank you so much," she said to Ronnie. "Talking 'as made such a difference. I'm already starting to feel better."

After Ronnie left—with an organic paint chart full of nursery colors—Chanel told Ruby what they had been talking about. Apparently Ronnie had persuaded her to get some counseling to help her come to terms with her infertility. "Your mum's amazing. I wish I could talk to mine the way I can talk to 'er. You are so lucky to 'ave 'er. She totally got 'ow I'm feeling because she remembers being told 'er tubes were blocked and she couldn't 'ave any more babies. She reckons I'm in mourning for my lost fertility and she's recommended this woman therapist she knows."

Ruby asked if she was going to ring her.

"I did it while your mum was here. I've got an appointment next week."

That evening Ruby phoned Ronnie to thank her for helping Chanel.

"No problem. I was just glad to help. She was telling me about these talks you're going to be giving at St. Luke's. Sounds like they could be really good for the business."

Ruby explained. "I'm really nervous, though. I've never done anything like it before."

"You'll be brilliant, just you see. You know, the more I think about it, the more I think I should be having this baby at St. Luke's. It sounds like such a great place and your dad's all for it. I just wish it wasn't so damned expensive."

A FEW DAYS later, Ruby gave her first talk. She was so worried about being late that she set off far too early and reached the hospital at ten—half an hour before the talk was due to start. When she arrived at the room she'd been allocated, Jill McNulty was already there, arranging chairs into a perfect circle and fussing over the refreshment table. "There's coffee, tea, orange juice and water. You should have enough."

Ruby thanked her for going to so much trouble and said she was sure she would be fine.

"You know what I've forgotten? Sparkling water."

"Please don't worry. I'm sure people can make do with still."

"It's no trouble to pop to the cafeteria and get some."

"Tell you what, if there's somebody who can't manage with still water, I'll go and fetch some sparkling."

"You sure?"

"Positive."

"And you will shout if you need me? I'm only down the corridor."

"I promise," Ruby said with a smile. She liked Jill, but she couldn't help wondering if her colleagues found her constant fretting a bit wearing.

Jill disappeared back to her office, but not before she had rearranged some teaspoons that were facing the wrong way.

• • •

WITH THE EXCEPTION of a couple of women wearing business suits and a househusband-to-be with bicycle clips round his trouser bottoms, who had come on behalf of his newspaper-executive wife, the fifteen or so women who turned up for Ruby's talk were exactly as she'd expected. They were the lean, Pilates and yogacized members of the rich boho set—their neat bumps perfectly accessorized by their Fulham highlights, Fendi handbags and Ugg boots.

They were a chatty, friendly enough bunch, though, and to give them their due, Ruby thought, no less anxious than other first-time mothers. They couldn't get enough of Ruby's advice on maternity bras, video baby monitors and car seats for infants.

The only time things went a bit flat was when she tried to get a discussion going on the issue of cloth diapers versus disposables. To a woman they had already opted for cloth, on the grounds that landfill sites were already brimming over with nonbiodegradable disposables. Ruby couldn't help thinking that they might have been less anxious to claim the moral high ground had they not been about to hire nannies to scrape the baby dung off the oh-so-nonpolluting, environmentally friendly cloth diapers.

When her talk was over, Ruby invited the mothers-to-be to look along the racks of maternity and baby wear. The clothes—along with the racks—had been delivered by courier the day before. She explained that larger items such as cribs and prams could be ordered from the Les Sprogs catalogue.

As everybody oohed and aahed—particularly over the Guatemalan baby outfits, cashmere christening shawls and massively expensive organic cotton crib linen—Ruby found herself thinking how cosseted these women were and how removed their lives were from those of ordinary women.

As she listened to a woman called Plum take a call from her fitness trainer, Ruby was more certain that she wanted to move her business away from Kensington and Chelsea and into the high street.

There were already mass-market fashion companies that recognized that the markup on cashmere and organic cotton was hugely excessive and were prepared to take a cut in profits by selling them cheaper. She could do the same. Ruby remained adamant that what Body Shop had done for cosmetics, she could do for mother and baby wear.

SHE WAS PLEASED with how the talk had gone. Despite her nerves, she had been clear, articulate and had even managed to make the group laugh by likening breast pumps to farm milking machines.

"At least breast-feeding helps you lose weight," Plum-with-the-fitness-trainer said at one point. The woman was so thin that if she'd turned sideways only her bump would have remained visible.

This was the cue for everybody to join in and start moaning about how much weight they'd put on during their pregnancies.

"If I don't leave the hospital in my Chloe hipsters," somebody said, "I shall die." Ruby waited for the derisive laughter, but it didn't come. Instead there were nods of agreement from the rest of the group.

"I'm living on fruit and cottage cheese at the moment," Plum said. "I'm allowing myself a ten-pound weight gain and no more."

"But all the books say you can put on 30 pounds during pregnancy," Ruby said, appalled at what she was hearing. Her comment was met with cries of horror.

"Look," a woman with a red Kabbalah bracelet said to Ruby, "you've seen the pictures of stars like China Katz leaving St. Luke's after giving birth. Have you any idea of the pressure on women to stay thin during pregnancy?"

"But these women are film stars," Ruby protested. "Their faces and bodies are their careers. Surely the rest of us can afford to ease up on ourselves during pregnancy?"

"You'd think. Look at this." The Kabbalah woman took a copy of *For Her* magazine and handed it to Ruby. She read the cover:

> Inside: How Claudia Planchette stays so sickeningly svelte during pregnancy... plus our special diet plan helps you to be just like her and stop piling on those ugly baby pounds.

Ruby turned to the Claudia Planchette interview. When asked how she stayed so slim during pregnancy and left the hospital after giving birth without the remotest sign of a postpregnancy bump, she declared:

> It's all down to genes. I eat like a pig during pregnancy and don't put on weight. After the birth, my skin and muscles instantly spring back into shape. I'm just very lucky, I guess.

"You see, that's what we're up against," Plum said. "And after the birth I fully intend to breast-feed and diet at the same time. Everybody says it's the only way to ensure the pounds fall away."

Yet again there was a chorus of approval.

Ruby shook her head in despair. These women worried obsessively about the environment and how chemicals could poison their children and yet they were prepared to deny themselves and their unborn babies the nourishment they so desperately needed.

Plum looked at her watch. "Oops, I'm late for my spinning class. I really must get going." She said how much she had enjoyed Ruby's talk and turned to go. The rest of the women stayed on for tea and decaf, then they, too, began melting away.

Despite having sold several thousand pounds' worth of clothes and nursery furniture in just over an hour, Ruby was left feeling sad and disturbed. She knew that this group of women couldn't be unique. There had to be thousands of pregnant women out there starving themselves in order to get back into their jeans immediately after giving birth. What sickened her even more was that women's magazines were clearly encouraging them.

RUBY WAS WALKING through reception, heading toward the main doors, when she saw Ronnie coming toward her. What on earth was her mother doing here? She saw Ruby's look of surprise.

"I know, don't say it," Ronnie laughed, drawing her daughter's attention to the cheesecloth smock she was wearing over jeans. "The seventies rang and want their smock back. I found it in a vintage dress shop. Isn't it fab? It manages to hide my bump and make me feel sixteen at the same time."

"It's lovely, but that's not what I was going to say. Actually, I was wondering what brings you here."

"It was a spur-of-the-moment thing. I phoned and booked a tour of the delivery room. A lovely girl just showed me round and I have to say I'm very impressed. Your dad hasn't stopped badgering me about changing hospitals. He doesn't trust the local one. He thinks that because of my age, something might go wrong."

"I wish I'd known you were going to be here. You could have come to my talk."

"Of course, it was today. How did it go?"

"Really good, if I do say so myself."

"See, I said you'd be brilliant. I'm sorry I missed it, but I couldn't have come. The girl showing me round had organized a meeting for me with a lovely lady obstetrician. She's about my age and specializes in caring for older women."

Ruby thought it might be Dr. Jane, but it was somebody else, a Dr. Beech.

"That's great news. They'll really look after you here."

"I think you're right. Dr. Beech seems very caring and confidence inspiring, so I've decided to go with her." She added that she had just phoned to give Phil the news. "He's really pleased I'm changing hospitals, but I feel so guilty. It means he's got to cash in one of his pension plans to pay for the treatment."

Ruby laughed and said there couldn't be too many men in their fifties cashing in their pension plans to pay for private childbirth.

Ronnie laughed. "I know. The irony's not lost on him. Anyway, after I left the doctor I went to sit in on a prenatal class.... God, the women are thin. Things have changed so much since I was pregnant with you. Nobody eats these days. It's appalling. I came in eating a doughnut I'd just bought and people looked at me as if I had leprosy. Heaven only knows what harm they're doing to their babies."

Ruby agreed and told Ronnie about the article in *For Her*. Ronnie grimaced. "What kind of world decrees that the only way for women to be acceptable is for them to practically disappear? Even when they're pregnant?"

"God knows," Ruby said, shaking her head. "So how was the class?"

"Fantastic. I had a chat with the teacher afterward and she says that despite my age she can see no reason why having this baby shouldn't be a really special experience."

Ruby didn't mean to come across as pathetic and needy, but before she could stop them, the corners of her mouth had dipped southward.

"Oh, sweetie, not that having you wasn't special. It was.

I won't ever forget it. I just knew my having this baby was going to bring up rejection issues for you. Maybe you should see somebody to talk it through."

"Mum, stop worrying. I'm fine," Ruby soothed. "I don't need to see anybody. Honest. I admit the idea of having a baby brother or sister still feels strange, but I'm sure I'll get used to it."

"I know, darling, but it may not be easy and I want you to remember that you were my first baby. The first one is always special, but back then they shaved you, gave you an enema, pumped you with drugs. Now I'm being told I can give birth in water with the lights dimmed and soft music playing."

Her eyes were wide with excitement. "Rubes, I can't tell you how wonderful this prenatal teacher is. First she had everybody practicing their womb breathing. That was followed by sun salutations to energize the body. And next week she's going to get us started on our birthing mantras, which are based on Tibetan overtoning chanting. But that's not all..." She looked round to check that they couldn't be overheard. "You will never guess who's in this class."

"Who?"

"Claudia Planchette. You know, the film star. She is so beautiful. I mean *exquisite* isn't the word."

"I know. She came into the shop the other day. I knew she was booked in at St. Luke's. What did you make of her?"

Ronnie wrinkled her nose. "Not a lot. To be honest I found her a bit aloof and condescending. I kept wondering what she was doing there. She really seemed to set herself apart from the rest of the women. On the other hand, maybe I'm the one with the problem and subconsciously I feel threatened by beautiful, highly successful women. Oh, and there was something else."

"What?"

"Well, at one point she left the class to take a call on her mobile. Judging from the conversation it must have been from whoever it is that looks after her little girl. Claudia was really brusque with the poor soul. I'd hate to work for her. I didn't catch all the conversation because she disappeared into the corridor, but I got the impression Claudia isn't particularly interested in her daughter."

Ruby told her mother about the conversations Claudia had with her nanny the day she came into Les Sprogs. "I was left with the feeling that she isn't the best mother in the world."

"But you'd never think it," Ronnie said, "not from the interviews she gives in the newspapers."

By now the two women had left the hospital building and were heading toward the parking lot. They were approaching Ronnie's car when they noticed a gleaming chauffeur-driven Jaguar pull up in front of the hospital steps. The next moment Claudia Planchette emerged from the hospital and started walking down the steps toward the car. Before she got there, one of the rear car doors opened and a little girl about three—Avocado presumably—jumped down from the car, ran toward Claudia and launched herself at her. Claudia grimaced, promptly grabbed the child by the wrists and turned to the nanny, who had followed her out of the car.

"Marta, these maternity pants are a one-off from Donna. What have I told you about letting Avocado near me when she's got chocolaty hands?" Suddenly, not one but three paparazzi appeared out of nowhere. Without missing a beat, Claudia's face broke into a dazzling Oscar-night smile. She scooped up the child, who proceeded to smear more chocolate over her mother's top. This time Claudia either didn't notice or pretended not to. "Smile, baby," she cooed to Avocado, "smile." When the little mite became shy and, instead of smiling, buried her face in her mother's shoulder, Claudia's face turned to stone. She immediately handed the child over to her nanny. While Avocado was being bundled back into the car, Claudia's smile returned and she stood flicking her hair and posing for the photographers.

Ruby and her mother exchanged anxious, troubled glances. They were both close to tears.

"What a sad, loveless life that child must lead," Ronnie said. "But why would she want another child, if the one she's already got is such a nuisance to her?"

"Two reasons. First, babies are hip in Hollywood. A baby in a sling is the ultimate fashion accessory. Haven't you seen those vile articles in *Vogue* about babies being the new black? And second, being seen as the perfect mother is brilliant PR. As well as being a film star, she's a role model for her female fans."

"If only they knew," Ronnie said, shaking her head. "You just wish you could help the poor little mite."

"Don't you just."

"The woman clearly needs help. If you ask me, she wasn't loved by her own parents and now that she's a parent, she can't show love because she never learned how to do it." She took a deep breath. "Still, there's nothing we can do.... You still on for dinner next week? Your Aunty Sylvia's bringing her new man."

Ruby said she was. "Oh, by the way, I forgot to say thank you for the affirmation CD. It's... it's very interesting." She thought *interesting* was the most diplomatic word to use. She wasn't about to upset her mother by saying that even though she'd found herself reciting them, she thought the affirmations were nonsense.

"Really? That's great. I was worried because you usually snigger at New Age stuff."

Ronnie suggested they go for a cup of coffee, but Ruby said she really needed to get back to the shop. "Chanel's been on her own all morning and on top of that I have to leave early to go to Connor's circumcision... By the way, what's the etiquette? Do you take a gift? The last time I went to a circumcision I was about eighteen and I went with you and Dad. What did we take?"

Ruby had this image of leaning over Connor's crib and saying: "Congratulations on losing your foreskin. Here's a fountain pen."

Ronnie said she couldn't remember what she had taken, but it had probably been a cake rather than something for the baby.

SHE WENT BACK to the shop and worked until half past three. Then she headed home to get changed for the circumcision, which was due to start at five.

As she drove home, Ruby found herself getting more and more upset about poor little Avocado. Eventually she forced herself to think about something else. Her mind turned to Sam Epstien—as it had several times over the last few days. Despite his promise to phone her back, he hadn't. She was in no doubt that he'd interpreted her offhand phone manner as rudeness and a sign that she didn't want to go out with him. She so wanted to apologize and set the record straight by explaining about Chanel and Craig. On each of her visits to St. Luke's to take care of her ID card, she'd hoped their paths might cross again, but they hadn't.

On the other hand, part of her was relieved not to have heard from him. It meant she didn't have to suffer the humiliation of explaining to him that she had lied about her vaginal stamp.

Of course, the last time they'd met, the time he asked her to lunch, she'd mustered up some courage and decided to tell him the truth. If he did phone to ask her out—not that it seemed very likely now—she would have to force herself back into that mind-set. He was a doctor, after all.

He'd probably think the whole thing was hysterical. Surely she wasn't so emotionally fragile that she couldn't bear a laugh at her own expense.

Back home, she stood in front of her wardrobe wondering what the appropriate ensemble was for a circumcision. It was a religious event, so that ruled out anything revealing. Red was definitely out. Black was far too melancholy. It suggested one was either in mourning for the lost bit of penis or, even worse, anticipating the rabbi having some catastrophic accident with the knife. Besides, Fi's mother was bound to be in black to show how much she disapproved of Connor being circumcised.

In the end, Ruby decided to play it safe with a pale pink tweedy suit with narrow fringes around the epaulets and cuffs. Her hair, which had a tendency to be wavy, could have done with a going-over with the straighteners, but there wasn't time. Instead she tied it back.

Before she left she went into the bathroom to look for some headache pills. She'd spent the afternoon stock-taking. The stockroom was tiny and stuffy, and being there too long always gave her a headache. Usually it would have eased off on the drive home, but today it hadn't.

She rummaged through the bathroom cabinet and realized she was out of Advil and Tylenol. All she could find were some prescription painkillers left over from when she'd pulled a shoulder muscle moving a display unit at the shop. She poured a glass of water and swallowed a couple. She reasoned that since the use-by date on the box had expired six months ago, the pills couldn't possibly be as strong as when her doctor prescribed them.

The rush-hour traffic was solid all the way to Fulham. On top of that there was a ten-minute queue at Patisserie Valerie. Thanks to the painkillers, though, her headache had gone, which was a relief.

Despite the hold-ups, she made it to Fi's just after five. Even though she was only a few minutes late, she was worried that the ceremony might already have started. By now, without Ruby there to keep an eye on her, Bridget could be causing all kinds of havoc. On top of that, making a late entrance was such bad manners, since it meant Ruby would be interrupting the proceedings and drawing attention to herself.

Once she'd parked, she sprinted down the street—inasmuch as she could sprint in pink suede heels. She stopped at the front gate and searched through her bag for her mobile. She needed to turn it onto silent so that there was no chance of it ringing during the ceremony. Having found the phone, she realized there was no need to turn it onto silent as the battery symbol was registering empty yet again.

Fi's front door was open. The loud chatter coming from inside told Ruby that things hadn't yet got under way. Letting out a small sigh of relief, she stepped inside the little house, whereupon her nose was instantly assailed by the aroma of fresh deli. Despite the thicket of people congregated in the living room, she could just about glimpse the buffet table. It was loaded with Himalayas of bagels, not to mention platters of cold cuts, smoked salmon, coleslaw and pickled herring.

Ruby's first impression was that the guests were made up entirely of Saul's elderly Jewish relatives. Tiny old ladies with dowager's hump, cotton-candy hair and wonky eye shadow greeted elderly gents in fedoras and fawn car coats. She caught a few snippets of conversation, all of which seemed to concern the bountifulness of the buffet table and how much longer they might have to wait before somebody offered them a cup of tea.

Saul's mum and dad were at the far end of the living

room, trying and only partially succeeding to keep Ben occupied with a jack-in-the-box. They noticed her and waved hello. Ruby decided it was going to be almost impossible to fight her way through the crowd to reach them, so she waved back and mouthed "mazel tov."

Eventually Ruby picked out a few of Fi's relatives. They were the ones looking awkward and uneasy. It was pretty evident that none of them had been to a circumcision before and that they weren't sure what to expect.

Fi, Saul and the baby were nowhere to be seen. Ruby suspected they were upstairs and that Fi was having second thoughts about going through with the circumcision.

Although Fi always maintained that in principle she had no problems with circumcision, the procedure itself still upset her. Ruby remembered being told that minutes before Ben's circumcision was due to start, Fi had burst into tears because she felt so guilty about "mutilating my tiny baby." Bridget had made it worse by putting in her two cents. No doubt she had done the same today and Saul was probably trying to comfort Fi and calm her down.

Ruby decided to look for Bridget and make sure she wasn't attacking the rabbi with her rosary and accusing him of being a heathen. She decided to start with the kitchen. As she went to open the door, an old lady with a knobbly Jackie Stallone face-lift, heavy black eyeliner and a fuchsia trout pout that looked ready to burst, touched her on the arm. "I wouldn't go in there, if I were you," she said in a throaty American accent. "The grandmother's shooed everybody out because she wants to get the baby to sleep. Lord knows why. He's going to get a mighty rude wakeup call in a minute." The woman laughed and then made a series of exaggerated chewing motions, which made her look like a strange tropical fish. "Those pickles on the buffet table look to die for, don't you think? Actually, I'm something of a kosher pickle expert. You see my husband, Buddy, and I—"

"Sorry, I don't mean to be rude," Ruby interrupted, "but it's actually Connor's grandma I need to speak to."

"Well, don't expect a warm welcome. Between you and me, she seems like a bit of an old sourpuss."

"Oh, she's not so bad when you get to know her." Ruby smiled. She opened the kitchen door.

Ruby closed the door behind her and put the Patisserie Valerie cake on the kitchen counter, along with all the other cakes people had brought.

Bridget, who appeared not to have heard her come in, was standing at the sink, her back toward Ruby, dressed in the same black suit she had worn to Fi and Saul's wedding. In one arm she was cradling Connor, whose head she had positioned next to the trickling mixer tap.

"In the name of the Father, Son and Holy Ghost I baptize thee Connor Declan Weinberg." With that, Bridget filled her cupped hand with water and drizzled it over Connor's head. The baby let out a short, slightly disgruntled cry.

Ruby slapped her hand to her mouth to stop herself laughing. "Oh, my God," she muttered under her breath, "the woman's baptizing him under the kitchen tap."

"There, there, little man," Bridget said tenderly as she wiped the baby's head with a tea towel and began planting kisses on his face. "It's nothing to what that lot of heathens in there are about to do to you. Your poor little winky... What are they going to do to your poor little winky?" As she spoke she turned away from the sink and noticed Ruby.

"Fi's refused to get a priest in to baptize him," Bridget said simply, hugging Connor to her breast, "so I thought a little DIY one wouldn't hurt."

"I think it's a lovely idea," Ruby said, happening to notice how much tidier the kitchen was than when she'd visited the other day. She wondered if that was due to Bridget, too. She could just imagine her tearing round the house with a cloth and a bottle of bleach declaring the entire place a health hazard and making poor Fi feel even more inadequate.

"I had to do it," Bridget whispered conspiratorially. "If that rabbi's knife were to slip and he killed the poor little mite before he was in a state of grace, his soul would be in limbo." She gave Connor one final kiss and maneuvered him into his baby seat. Despite the shock of the water, he was starting to fall asleep.

Ruby wasn't about to get into a debate with Bridget about whether a compassionate God would allow an innocent baby's soul to suffer. Anyway, she didn't get a chance. Bridget was opening the fridge and taking out a bottle of champagne.

"It's meant to be for later, but there's plenty more on ice outside and I think I need something to steady my nerves. Will you join me?"

Ruby was never one to turn down a glass of champagne. "You bet," she said, completely forgetting that only an hour ago she had taken two powerful painkillers and that the instructions on the box were to avoid alcohol. The cork popped, briefly jolting Connor from his sleep. As Bridget filled two glasses, Ruby decided she would try to move the conversation away from circumcision and onto something more neutral.

"So, how was your trip to Vancouver?" Ruby asked, remembering Bridget had been there recently to visit one of Fi's sisters.

"Ah," Bridget replied wistfully, "now, there's a city. Did you know you can swim during the day and ski in the mountains at night? And the food...As you know, I don't eat much red meat as a rule, on account of it aggravating my rheumatics, but one night we went to this hamburger joint...Vera's, I think it was called. Ruby, I swear to God I've never tasted meat like it."

"Really? That good, eh?"

"Oh, like you wouldn't believe. I chose a cheeseburger. My son-in-law said I should go for the Veraburger, but that was plain and I like a bit of melted cheese on a burger—so long as it's not too stringy. Anyway, when it came, it melted in the mouth."

"Wow."

"You barely needed to chew. I'd say it was succulent without being too rare. I don't like my meat rare on account of the bacteria."

"Very sensible."

"And the fries. Done to a turn, they were . . ."

Bridget poured them a second glass of champagne. Fifteen minutes later she was still yakking. By now she had moved on to the superior health care, the superior tax system and various other superiors in Canada. Once again Ruby glanced surreptitiously at her watch and wondered why the ceremony hadn't got under way. She was just beginning to think Fi had decided she couldn't go through with it, when she walked into the kitchen. Relief spread across her face the moment she saw Ruby.

"Where have you been?" she said. "I've been trying to get you all afternoon, but your phone's been off. Did you get my messages?"

"No, my batt—"

"OK, you will never guess what's happened," she broke in, her arms flapping with excitement. "It's *the* most amazing coincidence . . ."

"What is?" Ruby frowned. She was picking up a strange vibe from Fi. Despite her friend's enthusiasm, Ruby could detect anxiety in her eyes. She was getting the distinct impression that Fi was about to try and sell her something that she knew full well Ruby wouldn't want to buy.

"Fi, why do I get the feeling I'm not going to like what's coming next?"

Fi swallowed hard. "All right, I admit it might be a bit awkward at first. But I'm sure it'll all work out. Please, promise me you won't get upset or embarrassed."

"Just tell me. What mustn't I get upset or embarrassed about?"

Bridget had been putting a blanket over Connor and was only half listening to what her daughter was saying. "How can people not get upset when you're about to cut into this little mite?"

Fi rolled her eyes. "Mum, please, stop it. I don't need this now. Ben was fine after his circumcision and Connor will be, too. Now can we just drop it?"

Bridget gave an exaggerated, long-suffering sigh.

At this point Saul came in. Bridget offered him a look that could have stripped paint. He merely smiled back at her. Ruby couldn't work out if his smile was one of contempt, or whether it was simply his way of keeping the peace. Knowing Saul it was bound to be the latter. "The rabbi's ready," he said to Fi. He gave Ruby a quick smile and a wave and said, "Speak to you later."

Fi told Saul she wouldn't be a moment. "You have to hang on while I tell Ruby what's going on. She didn't get my messages."

"I'm sorry, I know it's important, but it'll have to wait," Saul insisted. "Rabbi Sherman's got two more circumcisions after ours and he's running late. Plus my Aunty Faye is threatening to collapse into a diabetic coma if she doesn't eat soon or get a cup of sweet tea."

"So, offer to make her a cream cheese bagel. I'll be literally ten seconds."

"Fi, please... The rabbi just told me the medication to control his Parkinson's is about to wear off. I'm pretty sure he's joking, but... we really need you and Connor now."

"Oh, all right," Fi snorted. She scooped up the baby and followed Saul out of the kitchen. "Just don't be cross with me," Fi said, turning back to look at Ruby. "There was nothing I could do and I did try to warn you."

"OK, but just tell me what it is I need to be warned about," Ruby pleaded. "I'm starting to panic." But Fi was gone.

WHEN SHE ASKED Bridget if she knew what Fi was talking about, she said she hadn't the foggiest. "If I were you, darlin', I wouldn't take any notice. Her hormones are still all over the place after having the baby. Mark my words, it'll be something of nothing."

But Ruby was sure it wasn't nothing. A few moments later, when she began to feel a bit light-headed, she put it down to a combination of champagne and apprehension. Then, as she got up from the kitchen table, she felt the top half of her body starting to sway. It was only as she reached out and gripped the kitchen table for support that she realized the sensation had less to do with unease and more to do with the painkillers she'd taken earlier, which weren't meant to be mixed with alcohol. So much for her theory about them being less potent because they were past their use-by date. Now she was about to make a spectacle of herself in front of all those people and everybody would think she was drunk. Fi of course would never forgive her. Great.

"Are you sure you wouldn't rather stay in here?" Ruby said to Bridget, who was now weeping and crossing herself. Ruby desperately hoped Bridget would decide to boycott the actual circumcision. First, it meant that there was no chance of her making a scene and upsetting the ceremony. It also meant Ruby could sit in the kitchen, sipping water until she felt better.

But Bridget insisted on going into the living room. "That innocent child will not go through this heathen ritual alone. He needs my moral support and I will be there for him."

She began striding out of the kitchen, an unsteady Ruby close behind. For Bridget, "being there" meant standing right at the front, next to the rabbi, Saul, and Saul's brother, Jake, who as godfather was holding the baby. Fi couldn't bear to watch, so she was standing at the back of the room with Saul's mother.

Ruby had enough to contend with, what with keeping herself upright and making sure Bridget didn't cause any unpleasantness, that she didn't pay much attention to who was standing nearby. She heard more than she saw. First there was Bridget still calling on Our Lady to "stop these heathens mutilating this poor little man." Then there was one of Fi's brothers telling her to put a sock in it, and that if it was good enough for the royal family, it was good enough for her.

By now the prayers had begun and people were shushing Bridget. She responded with loud sobs.

In addition to the light-headedness caused by mixing painkillers and champagne, Ruby was also starting to feel slightly sick at the thought of what was about to happen to Connor. More than anything, she wished that Bridget hadn't insisted on taking a ringside position.

As she saw Connor's plump little legs splayed like an oven-ready chicken, she felt the nausea get worse. She didn't see what happened next because she closed her eyes. The next thing she knew, Connor was letting out the most almighty wail. While people exchanged mazel tovs and Fi's brother took Bridget to find a medicinal glass of whiskey, Ruby didn't move. She stood glued to the spot, her heart racing, her forehead covered in cold sweat, knowing that she was about to either upchuck or pass out or both and that there was nothing she could do to stop it.

As the spinning in her head began to gather speed, the

room took on a blueish tinge. Finally, she felt her legs give way.

"Whoa, it's OK, I gotcha," said a male voice. It seemed to be coming from miles away. She was vaguely aware that somebody was supporting her under her arms. "We need to get you lying down," the voice continued. She felt him scoop her up, walk the few paces to the sofa and lay her down. A pile of cushions was placed under her feet. "That'll get the blood flowing again," he said. It did, sort of—enough for her to risk opening her eyes. When she saw that the room was still a blue blur, she closed them again.

"You in any pain, Ruby?" the man asked. She shook her head.

"That's good. Means you just fainted. You'll be feeling better in a couple of minutes." By now, concerned guests were gathered around the sofa. The man said they should stand back to give Ruby air. Since tea was now being served, the old people in particular didn't need telling twice. "Fi said you would be here," he went on, "so I was looking out for you, but I didn't recognize you with your hair up." He was holding her wrist and taking her pulse. "Was it just watching the circumcision that made you feel faint or was it something else? Have you eaten today?"

Ruby managed a garbled explanation about accidentally mixing painkillers and champagne. "Youadoctor, then?" She was slurring her words. Although she was recovering from the faint, the effects of the champagne and painkillers seemed to be getting worse.

"Yes. Ruby, open your eyes and you'll see it's . . ."

"Sho . . ." She let out a loud hiccup. "How jew know my name?"

"Ruby, it's me . . ."

Another hiccup. "Me who? Who me?" She started to giggle. "You sound American. Funny, your voice sounds familiar. Can't quite place it though."

"I am American," the man said. "Come on, Ruby, try and open your eyes. Then you'll see why you recognize my—"

"Nah. When I open them, it'sh all bloooo." She hiccuped and put her arm across her eyes as if to emphasize her determination not to open them. "You know I met this American doctor the other day. He's a gyne... a gyne... how jew say it? A gynecolumnist, that's it." Another hiccup. "A gynecolumnist."

When Ruby drank too much, she became garrulous and utterly uninhibited. There was no knowing how much more garrulous and uninhibited she was about to become having mixed alcohol with strong painkillers.

"Anyway," she went on, "he wants to go out with me. At least he did, before I pissed him off by being rude on the phone. At first I thought the idea of dating a gyne... thingumy was dishgusting. I mean, do you know how they spend their days?"

"I've got a fair idea," he said.

"But I think I'm starting to change my mind." She started to giggle. "Come here." She snorted. "I've got something to tell you." He sat down on the edge of the sofa. "No, closer." He leaned in.

"You promise you won't tell?" she said.

"Promise."

" 'Cause it's really [hic] personal."

"OK."

"Right... well [hic] the other day when I was at the hospital having one of those well-woman checkups, the [hic] doctor found a stamp in my... in my... well, it was in a very [hic, hic] private place. Anyway, I was on the phone telling my friend Fi all about it... she's Connor's mother, you know... anyway, when I'd finished, there was thish other doctor standing next to me. I'm sure he overheard everything I said."

"Ah. I can see how that might be a tad embarrassing."

"Too blinkin' right. But you see, I did shome reeely quick thinking and pretended to him that me and Fi had been discussing something completely different."

"Smart move."

"I thought so. [hic, hic] But now there'sh a problem. If we go out, I'd feel compelled to tell him that I lied. Then I'd have to deshcribe what really happened and that..."

"...would be more than plain embarrassing, it would be downright humiliating."

"Thassit! You goddit."

"You know, I'm sure he'd understand." He was really teasing her now, but she was too high on her champagne-and-painkiller cocktail to notice.

"You reckon?"

"I'm positive. He sounds to me like the kinda guy who'd see the funny side."

"Maybe. I dunno... So, what short of a doctor are you?"

"Actually, I'm a gynecolumnist, too."

"No! Wadda coincidence...I'm...I'm dilated to meet you." She roared at her joke. "Jew geddit? Gynecolumnist... di-lated to meet you?"

"Yep, that's really funny," he chuckled.

"OK, you have to tell me something. My friend Fi reckons gynecolumnists make great lovers. Not that she's ever slept with one. She just thinks it makes sense, what with them knowing their way around women's bits. So [hic, hic] would you say you're an above-average lover? I mean, if you were to give yourself marksh out of ten, what would you score? A nine? A ten?" She burst out laughing. "Nah, you've got a sexy voice, I bet you're an eleven. Or even...a twelve!" She was cackling now.

"Thank you," he said.

"By the way, what's your name?"

"Sam."

"It's not," she giggled. "[hic] You're having me on."

"No. My name really is Sam."

"But, this American doctor I met, hish name's Sham, too. God, I know two gynecolumnists, both American and both called Sham. How weird is that?"

He didn't say anything.

"So," she said, "what's your last name?"

"Epstien."

Now Ruby roared with laughter. "Yeah, right. Very funny."

"Ruby, for the last time, please open your eyes. It's me, Sam Epstien."

"Don't be so ridiculous," she said lifting her arm from where it had been resting over her head. "How can you be...?" Slowly her eyes started to focus. The realization that the man sitting beside her really was Sam Epstien positively catapaulted Ruby back to sobriety. She sat bolt upright, eyes wide open. "Holy Mother," was all she said, before lying back down again because she still felt dizzy. "But I don't understand..." She swallowed hard, aware that her heart was pounding. "...what on earth are you doing here? And I said all those things to you about my...you know...the stamp thing...and about gyne...gyne..."

"Columnists," he prompted.

"Yeah, about gynecolumnists being good lovers. Omigod. Omigod." She slapped her hand to her mouth.

Just then a concerned-looking Fi appeared. She was clutching Connor to her. Courtesy of a teaspoon of sweet kosher wine, he was sound asleep. "You OK, Rubes? Don't worry, Saul's mum felt a bit queasy during the proceedings, too. You're not alone." She lowered her head to kiss Connor, who had let out a tiny whimper in his sleep.

At this point Sam disappeared to fetch Ruby some water.

"So, Rubes," Fi said, doing some uneasy throat clearing,

"erm, coming round and seeing Sam here must have come as a bit of a shock."

"Just a little," Ruby said by way of understatement.

"I'm so sorry. I shouldn't have let Saul bully me earlier. I should have insisted on telling you that Sam was here. It's just the most staggering coincidence. Remember the conversation we had the other day about Saul's American relatives—Buddy and Irene—the ones who are big in kosher pickles? I said I thought were called Ep-*stein*? Well, I got it wrong. They're Ep-*stiens* after all. Sam is Saul's cousin. Isn't that just amazing?"

"Amazing," Ruby said with a tight-lipped smile. "Totally amazing."

Chapter 9

Bridget, not one to be intimidated by a doctor, informed Sam that what Ruby needed wasn't water, but hot sweet tea. After two cups of her thick orange brew—the sort that you could stand a spoon in—Ruby decided she felt well enough to go home. Fi—who now knew about the painkillers-and-champagne combo, as well as the contents of Ruby's drunken conversation with Sam—tried to persuade Ruby that she was in no fit state to drive. When Ruby insisted, Fi started to panic and went to find Saul's dad to see if he would give Ruby a lift home.

Just then Sam appeared. "You know, Ruby," he said kindly, "you really shouldn't get behind a wheel." He'd clearly heard her talking to Fi.

"Didn't anybody ever tell you it's rude to listen in on other people's conversations?" Ruby replied tersely. She was still cross with him for the way he had been teasing her.

"I'm sorry, but I couldn't really help it. You and Fi were practically shouting. And Fi's right. With what's in your bloodstream right now, you'd be a danger on the road. Why don't you let me give you a ride home?"

"Thanks," she said, "but if I can't drive, I'd prefer to get a cab."

Ruby knew herself well enough to realize that the indignation she felt was only partly to do with his having teased her. She was also feeling cross with herself. It wasn't so much having fainted that bothered her. What upset her was that she had confessed to having mixed painkillers and alcohol and that he must now think she was the kind of ditzbrain who never read the directions on medicines.

She got up from the sofa and straightened her shoulders and back in order to make herself look as in control and unditz-brained as possible. A second later the room started to spin again and she fell back onto the sofa in a heap, aware that her skirt had ridden up her legs and was now practically round her waist.

"Don't worry, you'll be OK in a moment," Sam said. "You just stood up too fast."

As she maneuvered her skirt back to her knees, she felt the dizziness start to ease off.

"You know, you really need to take it easy for a few hours. And I'm not happy with you going home in a cab. You might start to feel ill again, and if you do, there should be somebody with you."

"I really can take care of myself, you know."

"Sorry. I'm coming on too strong. It's force of habit. As a doctor you get so used to handing out advice. You're right. I'm sure you'll be fine in a cab."

As he turned to go, she felt her heart sink. "I'm sorry, too," she said. "I was being rude and ungrateful. You were only trying to help."

"Look, I know you're pissed with me for teasing you back then," he said, "and you have every right to be. I apologize. You didn't know what time of day it was and there I was, taking advantage. That was wrong. Can you forgive me?"

Ruby could tell from his sheepish expression that he was

genuinely contrite. She managed a small, reluctant smile. "Yes, I can forgive you. Anyway it's me who should be apologizing. I was short with you on the phone the other day. It was because I was in the middle of a rather difficult conversation. Chanel, who works with me in the shop, and her husband had just found out they can't have children."

"I'm sorry to hear that. I know how hard it is to receive news like that. . . . Anyway, you weren't remotely short. I kept meaning to phone you, but I've lurched from one emergency to the next over the last few days. I didn't resurface until last night."

"That's OK. Look, there's another thing. I owe you another apology. I behaved badly when we met at the hospital. I should never have made up that daft post office story. I was so embarrassed, that's all. Did you realize I was lying?"

" 'Fraid so. I'd been standing at the coffee machine for quite a while without you noticing me, so I heard pretty much all of your conversation with Fi."

"Oh, God." She covered her face with her hands. "So you know how the stamp got inside me and everything?"

"Kinda," he said. His face was wrinkled in discomfort, but she could tell it was on her behalf. He crouched down in front of her. "I have an idea. Why don't we just pretend this stupid stamp business never happened, and start again?"

She looked at him doubtfully, taking in his navy cashmere jacket and lavender check open-neck shirt. "I'm not sure . . ."

"It's easy. Watch." He stood up and offered her a broad smile. "Hi, my name's Sam Epstien. I'm Saul's cousin."

She took his outstretched hand and shook it. "Ruby Silverman. Fi and I go way back."

"I couldn't help noticing you weren't feeling very well earlier. I'm a doctor, is there anything I can do?"

"Actually, I'm feeling much better, but I wouldn't say no to a lift home."

He grinned. "My pleasure."

IT TURNED OUT that Sam had already agreed to take his uncle and aunt—Buddy and Irene—back to their hotel in Kensington. "Would you mind if we dropped them off first?" he asked Ruby. She said she didn't mind in the slightest.

By now she had worked out that Irene was the elderly American woman with the knobbly Jackie Stallone face-lift and absurdly bloated trout pout who had tried to stop her going into the kitchen to see Bridget.

Buddy turned out to be overweight and in possession of a permanently perspiring bald head.

As he made the introductions, Sam explained that in the last few years, ever since his parents had died in a car crash in 1996, Buddy and Irene had been like a mother and father to him.

"You can't begin to imagine how much we adore this boy," Irene said to Ruby, at the same time squeezing Sam's hand. "We have three daughters, so he's the son we never had."

"And he has such a brilliant mind—like you wouldn't believe," Buddy added. "Sam, did you tell Ruby how you were top of your class at med school?"

"Er, we didn't quite get around to that yet," Sam said, starting to look distinctly pink around the gills. Ruby knew how he felt. Whenever her parents had a party, Aunty Sylvia would home in on couples who had sons about Ruby's age. Then she would drag her protesting across the room to meet each set of parents. "This is my niece, Ruby," she would gush. "Isn't she beautiful? Do you know she got three A's at A level and a distinction in her grade-eight piano exam?"

The four of them got into Sam's car—Buddy and Irene in the back, Ruby and Sam in the front.

"You know," Irene said to Buddy, as she grappled with her seat belt, "those pickles today, they weren't half bad."

"Neh."

"You don't think so? I thought so."

"Not enough snap. You got a handkerchief, Irene? The sweat's pouring off me. It was so hot in there. Did anybody else find it hot in there? I found it hot in there."

"I was fine," Irene replied. "Perfectly comfortable. I think maybe it's your thyroid. You should get it checked out." She paused. "Sam, you're the doctor. Tell Buddy he needs to get his thyroid checked out. He won't listen to me."

"You know, it's not such a bad idea," Sam said, looking at Buddy through the rearview mirror.

"I'm fine. Stop fussing. It was hot in there, that's all."

"You know," Irene went on, "maybe you're right about the pickles. They looked magnificent, though. I said to Ruby here how good they looked, didn't I, dear?"

"You did." Ruby turned round to see Buddy dabbing at his head with a folded handkerchief.

"Irene." Buddy sounded like an elderly schoolmaster about to reprimand one of his pupils. "How often have I warned you about being taken in by superficial appearances? What my wife sometimes forgets, Ruby, is that when it comes to deciding if a pickle is a great pickle or merely a mediocre pickle, only a fool lets himself be duped by what it looks like. Don't get me wrong. Naturally, the look of a pickle, its color and its texture are important, but at the end of the day, there's only two things that count: snap and flavor. A great pickle is like great sex. It should set your senses on fire. Don't I always say that, Irene—a great pickle is like great sex?"

"You do, Buddy. You always say that." Irene leaned

forward in her seat belt and tapped both Ruby and Sam on the shoulder. "He always says that."

"You see," Buddy said, "it's all about your sugar-to-vinegar ratio. Get that wrong and you're sunk. I've seen grown men, professional picklers who've been in the business for fifty years, break down and weep when a vat of sweet-and-sour pickles goes wrong. I always remind them you can't be too careful with your sugar-to-vinegar ratio. Don't I always say that, Irene? You can't be—"

"So, what do you do, Ruby?" Irene inquired.

Ruby explained.

"So, is there good money to be made selling baby clothes?" Buddy asked.

"I do all right."

"So, what do you gross in a year? In that kinda upscale neighborhood I'm guessing what, three quarters of a mil, sterling?"

"Buddy!" Irene reprimanded her husband. "Ruby's a stranger. How can you interrogate her like this?"

Buddy gave a shrug. "I was only asking."

"OK, we're here," Sam announced. Ruby couldn't have been more grateful. She'd been racking her brains to find a tactful way of avoiding discussing her business affairs with Buddy.

"We're back at the hotel, already?" Irene remarked, incredulous. Ruby turned round and noticed she was making the chewing motions with her mouth that she noticed when she first met her. "That was so quick. Wasn't that quick, Buddy? I mean, if you tried the George Washington Bridge into the city this time of day it would take twice as long."

"Three times. I always say the George Washington Bridge at rush hour is . . ."

"Don't get out of the car yet," Sam instructed Buddy and Irene. "It's raining. I have an umbrella in the trunk."

Ruby said good-bye to Buddy and Irene and wished

them a safe journey home. The pair got out, but she stayed in the car—not because she didn't want to get wet, but in order to give Sam a private moment with his aunt and uncle.

"You sure you won't come up?" she heard Irene say to Sam. "You wouldn't believe the view from our room."

"I'd like to, but I think I should be getting Ruby home. She really needs to get some rest."

"OK, Sam. You're the doctor." With this Irene motioned Ruby to lower her window. "A handsome Jewish doctor," she said, her eyes wide with eagerness. "What more could a beautiful, successful girl want?" She was chewing again. "Take it easy, Ruby, and let's meet up when Buddy and I come for Wimbledon next summer."

"It's a date," Ruby said.

"THEY'RE SWEET," Ruby said once they were on the move again.

"Yeah. Buddy's my dad's brother. He's a couple of years older, but he looks exactly like him. It's really weird. Every time I see Buddy, it's like looking at a ghost of my father. My dad wasn't so opinionated, though. You really have to be in the mood for one of Buddy's pickle lectures."

"I've never lost anybody close to me—apart from my grandma, but she was very old."

Pain shot across his face. "I think about them every day." He explained that his mother and father—both doctors—had been on holiday in the French Alps. "They were on a hairpin bend and their car collided with a speeding tourist bus. They never stood a chance."

"I'm so sorry," she said. "I can't imagine what it must be like to lose people you love, in that kind of circumstance. You must be so angry."

He shrugged. "I was. But it's hard to stay angry. Slowly

the grief and rage stops being all-consuming and you learn to live alongside it."

"I can see that," she said.

"Say," he said, pulling up at a red light, "you hungry?"

"Now that you mention it, I'm ravenous." She looked at her watch. It was past eight and she hadn't eaten since lunch. "I couldn't face anything at Fi's, but the nausea seems to have completely worn off."

"What do you fancy? Italian? French? Chinese?"

"Believe it or not," she said, "I could murder some sweet-and-sour pork."

"Me, too. I was hoping you'd say that."

"I adore Chinese," she said. "It does it for me in a way that posh French food never can. It's just got that . . . that . . ."

"Thing," they said in unison. Then they started laughing.

As they headed toward Chinatown, they passed a McDonald's and Ruby confessed that Big Macs were her secret vice.

He threw back his head and laughed. "I shouldn't be saying this—particularly not as a doctor—but after seeing *Supersize Me* I went straight to McDonald's and bought two large cheeseburgers."

"No! I did the same. Except with me it was a Big Mac. Didn't that film just get your juices going?"

"I hate to admit it, but it really did."

She asked him what other junk food he liked.

"I love sandwiches made with french fries."

"With ketchup or mayo?" Ruby asked.

"Ketchup, no contest."

"I disagree," she said, shaking her head. "Ketchup might be the obvious choice, but I think if you gave the mayo option a try, you'd see it was superior."

"You think?"

"Definitely."

For the next twenty minutes they exchanged junk food

confessions. It turned out that both of them had a weakness for supermarket cakes and cinema pick 'n' mix sweets.

"What about cheap bangers?" Sam asked. She was touched by his use of the word *banger*. He was really trying to get into the vernacular.

"Love 'em," she said. "It's the fat that gives them their flavor. You know what I also adore?"

"What?"

"Tinned spaghetti sandwiches on white bread with butter and Marmite."

"Now, that," he said, laughing, "is totally gross. The tinned spaghetti I can understand, but I just don't get this Marmite thing. It's disgusting. What is it about you Brits and rancid meat products?"

Ruby explained that Marmite was actually made of yeast, and that he was thinking of Bovril. "And anyway, that's rich coming from somebody whose countrymen invented southern pear salad. Do you mind telling me who in their right mind would mix pears with cheese and mayo?"

They started to compete about which country produced the most disgusting foodstuffs. She countered his jellied eels with American cheese product, but in the end they decided it was a tie because it was impossible to choose between black pudding and hog snout.

By the time they got to the restaurant, Ruby realized she hadn't laughed this much in ages. Certainly not since she and Matt split up.

When they sat down, the waiter came to take their drink order. Sam said he fancied a beer, but Ruby decided to stick to sparkling water.

"Somebody told me this place used to be much bigger," he said. "Apparently they sold part of it off to the undertaker's next door. I can't help thinking there's something odd about a Chinese restaurant becoming an undertaker's. You wonder if people die and two hours later they want to do it all over again." This made her almost choke with laughter.

They were chatting and laughing so much that it was ages before they got round to looking at the menu. It was only when the waiter came a third time to try and take their order that they decided they ought to think about food.

As she studied the menu, a thought occurred to her. How would she feel if Sam turned out to be a nonsharer? Whereas in French or Italian restaurants, nobody shared food, although tasting was allowed, strictly upon invitation (a rule Aunty Sylvia had yet to take on board), in Indian and Chinese places everybody shared. That way people got to taste a bit of everything. But every so often, Ruby came across somebody who either didn't know about the food-sharing rule or, more worryingly, refused to observe it.

She had worked out long ago that a reluctance to share had less to do with selfishness and more to do with being cheap. People who took a what's-mine-is-mine attitude seemed to think that if they agreed to share their food, it would end up being eaten by everybody else and they would end up with nothing but fish lips and chicken feet. What was more, they would have to pay for the privilege. To avoid this, they seized "their food" the second it arrived. They then lined up their glass of beer, the soy sauce bottle and the little white vase with the carnation to create a no-go area, the dining equivalent of the North Korean border.

She had no reason to think that Sam was one of the mean, neurotic nonsharer types, but in the past she had discovered that people she thought would be sharers turned out not to be and vice versa.

When their food arrived, she noticed that he looked a bit uncomfortable and seemed reluctant to help himself to anything. She offered him some of the sweet-and-sour pork she'd ordered.

"You're a sharer!" he said, relief flooding into his face.

He took the oval plate from her. "I've been sitting here worrying that you wouldn't be. You see, there are these two guys at the hospital and whenever we go out for Chinese food, they never share. I guessed it was a Brit thing. These guys are so weird. They build barricades around their food with the beer glass, the soy sauce bottle..."

"...and the little vase with the carnation," she added, laughing.

"You've seen it?"

"Once or twice," she said.

They had almost finished eating when a couple of pot-bellied middle-aged men came in and sat down at the next table. Sam had his back to them, but Ruby, who was facing the pair, had become aware that every so often they stopped talking to stare at her. At first she thought she must have food around her mouth, which Sam had been too polite to point out. She dabbed her lips with her napkin, but the leering didn't stop. Then they started laughing. She found herself straining to hear what the men were saying. It took her a while to work out they were speaking German. She'd taken German in school and had always been pretty good at it. How good it was now, she wasn't sure. She carried on listening.

"Sie hat melonen, ja?" said the more portly of the two. He started laughing and held out his palms as if he were weighing two massive watermelons.

"Nein. Zitronen."

"Orangen, vielleicht?"

By now Sam was waving a hand in front of Ruby's face to get her attention. "You feeling ill again?" he said.

"No, I'm fine. Sorry, I was miles away." But instead of turning back to talk to Sam she carried on watching the men and listening. At this point Sam glanced over his shoulder to see what she was looking at.

"They seem like pretty regular guys to me," he whispered. "What language are they speaking? Sounds like German."

"It is. They're talking about me."

"They are? What are they saying?"

She hesitated.

"Come on," he urged. "What is it?"

"OK..." She took a deep breath. "They seem to be discussing the size of my breasts."

"What? Are you sure?"

She nodded. "They can't seem to make up their minds whether they're more like melons, lemons or oranges." Ruby was used to workmen making "phwarrr, darlin', you've got more front than Southend" comments about her breasts, which were a C cup bordering on a D. She'd learned to ignore the remarks, while at the same time being quietly flattered. Somehow it felt different when the men making the remarks were sitting next to her in a restaurant.

"Right," Sam said, starting to get up. "Leave this to me."

She grabbed his hand. "No," she hissed. "Please. Sit down. I'll deal with it." It was about time, she thought, that she proved to him she wasn't a helpless ditz brain.

She stood up and placed her napkin on the table. Smiling brightly, she walked to the next table. The men smiled back, clearly thinking that despite her being with a man, she was giving them the come-on.

"Guten Abend," she said. *"Schoenes Veterinare in Anbetracht."* The smiles vanished and were replaced with expressions of shock and embarrassment. They had been found out. One of them managed to stammer a *Guten Abend.* Their faces having turned deep crimson, the men lowered their heads and began studying the froth on their beers. Ruby returned to her seat, grinning.

"Well, you certainly wiped the smiles off their faces."

She could tell by his expression that he was impressed. "So, what did you say to them?" Sam asked.

"Nothing really. I simply said that it was nice weather, considering." She took a sip of water. "But I think I made my point, don't you?"

"Absolutely," he said.

AFTER DINNER, SAM drove her home. "I had a great time tonight," he said as they stood outside her street door.

"Me, too."

"So..." She watched him shifting uneasily on his feet. "I was wondering if maybe we could do it again sometime."

"I'd like that," she said.

"How's about this Saturday? I'm free during the day."

"Saturday's good," she said—far too quickly, in her opinion. She could have kicked herself. Had reading *The Rules* three times taught her nothing?

"But what about the shop?"

"The shop?... Oh, yes, of course the shop. Er... that's not a problem. I can get somebody in to help Chanel." She stood there hoping and praying that Annie, the high school student who helped them out from time to time, would be up for a day's work.

"So, what did you have in mind for Saturday?" she asked.

"You know what? I've never been to the coast."

"Brighton," she declared. "It's sort of Venice Beach meets Coney Island meets Notting Hill. You'll love it."

"Sounds great. So it's a date?"

"It's a date."

He placed his hand gently on her arm. "Promise you'll call me if you start to feel ill again."

"I promise, but stop worrying. I'll be fine."

He planted a kiss on her cheek. She detected the faintest

hint of cologne. A sudden and powerful wave of desire washed over her as she realized how desperately she wanted to kiss him on the lips and have him kiss her back.

He made a move to go and then stopped. He was shaking his head and grinning. "The way you dealt with those guys back at the restaurant is still making me smile. I think your German is better than you think."

"Oh, it's not that good," she said, "believe me."

He insisted she was being modest. She decided not to shatter his illusion. There seemed little point in confessing that on the way home, a linguistic realization had struck her. Instead of remarking to the Germans that it was "nice weather, considering," she'd actually said it was "nice veterinarians, considering."

Chapter 10

Ruby was rubbing her forehead in frustration. "Look," she said to Ivan the Terrible as she switched the house phone to her other ear, "I know you're extremely busy, but if you could just see your way clear to fixing the loo today. The ball cock is acting up again. And although I really do appreciate your having made a start on the kitchen, the cupboards still don't have any doors." She explained that she was going to Brighton for the day and he would have the place to himself.

"I understand, but eet ees problyem. You see, my brother, he ees sick and he hef very big operation today. Not good. Three years his testicle has been on waiting list."

"Goodness. As long as that? Poor man. Look, I can see things are difficult. Don't worry about getting here today. I can manage with the loo as it is for a few more days. I hope your brother's OK."

"Tenk you. Look, there ees possibility I fit you in. After I see my brother in the hospital, I hef job in Edgware. Maybe I fit in bollock after I trim Mrs. Goldberg's bush."

RUBY WOULD HAVE been ready on time, but Fi rang just as she was getting out of the shower to tell her to switch on the TV. "It's a repeat of some stupid daytime chat show on Sky, but they're discussing the pressures on pregnant women to stay thin. They've got this doctor on from St. Luke's, so I thought you might be interested."

Ruby pressed the TV remote and sat down on the sofa. The obstetrician from St. Luke's was a handsome, blue-eyed patrician type in his early forties. His name was Tom Hardacre. He was being interviewed by a young female presenter—Kate somebody or other—about new government statistics that showed that anorexia among pregnant women and those who had recently given birth was on the increase.

"This is something new and quite startling," he was saying. "In my opinion the images of women shown in magazines as well as those coming out of Hollywood put intolerable pressure on women."

The mainly female studio audience began clapping. Then an actress in the audience responded by saying that Hollywood stars were themselves under pressure to remain thin, otherwise the work dried up. A discussion followed about why female celebrities weren't rising up and doing more to put a stop to the situation.

At one point during the discussion, the audience was shown giant black-and-white paparazzi photographs of ultrathin Hollywood mothers leaving the hospital with new babies.

"Of course, Dr. Hardacre," Kate the presenter said, "two of those mothers—China Katz and Mia Ferrari—gave birth at your hospital. One would have thought that a hospital like St. Luke's, committed as it is to promoting healthy pregnancy and natural childbirth, would be spearheading a campaign to educate expectant mothers about diet. Do you think you are doing enough?"

Ruby thought it was a slightly barbed but perfectly reasonable question. Tom Hardacre fielded it perfectly. His face formed itself into an expression of deep concern.

"Kate," he said, adding a condescending smile, "I don't want you or anybody watching this program to think for one minute that I and all my colleagues at St. Luke's aren't desperately worried about this issue. We are. What's more, all the medical staff go to tremendous lengths to explain to our expectant mothers that they are putting the health of their babies at risk by excessive dieting. I'd say we are doing everything we can, but if you, Kate, or indeed anybody thinks there is more we could be doing, I would absolutely welcome their suggestions."

Ruby gave a tiny shiver. "Euuh, smarmy or what?" She had only been watching this man for a few minutes, and as a rule she wasn't one to judge people so quickly, but she'd taken an instant dislike to him. She wanted to carry on watching the interview, but she knew that by now she must be running late. She switched off the TV and went into the bedroom to get dressed.

The door buzzer rang just after ten. Sam was right on time. She, on the other hand, was still in her bra and pants, indecisive about what to wear.

She dashed to the door and pressed the intercom button. "Hi, Sam, come on up." With that, she ran back to the bedroom and began rummaging through the pile of clothes on the bed in an effort to find something to throw on, so that she would look halfway decent when she let him in.

Her sexy black silk kimono would have been perfect. Of course it wasn't on the bed and the only thing hanging on the back of the bedroom door was her grungy, scratchy with dried-up food stains, pink terry number—the one she wore when she was getting her period and wanted to do nothing but curl up in front of *Dr. Quinn, Medicine Woman* and eat Marshmallow Fluff sandwiches. She couldn't possibly put it on to greet Sam. In desperation she pulled on one of her long, baggy T-shirts.

Sam greeted her with a kiss on the cheek. He was wearing a round-neck khaki-colored John Smedley over dark beige cargo pants. She couldn't help noticing how well the khaki matched his dark skin and eyes. Yet again she found herself thinking how seriously handsome this man was.

"Breakfast," he declared, presenting her with a large flat box with *Krispy Kreme* written across the lid. "I hope you haven't eaten. I didn't know what doughnuts you liked, so I bought a few."

"A few?" she said, laughing.

"OK, a dozen. C'mon, you know that in the Jewish system of weights and measures anything under a gross equals a few."

"Sam, thank you," she said, taking the box. "I adore Krispy Kremes." Since Harrods was the only place in London that stocked them and he'd probably had to drive round for ages to find a parking space before joining the queue in the bakery department, bringing Krispy Kremes was a truly lovely gesture.

"Great T-shirt, by the way." He was looking at her and smiling appreciatively. She beamed back at him. Matt used to remark on how sexy she looked in baggy T-shirts. She'd never really believed him, though. Having largish breasts, she always felt they made her look like she was wearing a tent. But maybe he was right. Perhaps she could carry off the baggy look.

As she led him into the kitchen he almost tripped over a box of wall tiles, which Ivan had left by the door. "Sorry," she said, pushing the box to one side with her foot. "Kitchen and loo are in total chaos." She explained about Ivan the Terrible and made him laugh with the story of Mrs. Goldberg's bush.

"Heaven knows when it's going to get finished."

"It's going to look great, though," he said, running his

hand over a beech-wood cupboard door, which was lying on the counter. "I like the stainless steel handles. You have a real eye."

"Thank you," she said, her lips forming another crescent. It had been ages since she'd received compliments from a man and she was really enjoying it. "Oh, by the way, a doctor from St. Luke's was just on the telly talking about the dangers of pregnant women going on diets."

"Yeah, I read the government report. It's really scary. These women have no idea the harm they're doing to themselves." He asked the name of the doctor.

"Tom Hardacre. What's he like? Seemed a bit patronizing..." She slapped her hand to her mouth. "Oh, God, he's not a friend of yours, is he?"

Sam gave a reassuring laugh. "No, I barely know him. Meant to be a great doctor though. Very forward-looking. Highly regarded."

"Oh, right," she said. "Maybe I got him wrong. Perhaps he was just nervous being on TV." She paused. "Tell you what, why don't you make coffee while I finish getting dressed."

She directed him to the coffee, milk and mugs and went back into the bedroom. Peering out the window, she saw that for once the sun was shining. She began rummaging through the pile of clothes lying on the bed, looking for something summery. Finally she decided on her baby-blue A-line skirt. She would team it with the frilly blue and pink peasant top she'd bought at the start of the summer. It would show off her still-tanned shoulders and midriff.

As she stood in front of the mirror, about to pull off her T-shirt, the realization dawned that the thing didn't make her look so much sexy as comical. It was the T-shirt Fi had bought her for a joke, two Christmases ago. Written across the front, in massive brown letters, were the words: *Say no to shampoo—demand real poo*.

• • •

THEY DIDN'T STOP talking all the way to Brighton. He seemed particularly interested to hear about Les Sprogs. He also asked her lots of questions about her family. Soon she was telling him about her Baby Organic plan and Ronnie's need to psychoanalyze everybody. She loved the way he listened and really engaged with her. So many men she'd been out with—poor old Duncan being an extreme example—always insisted on bringing the conversation back to themselves.

At one point he put a blues CD on the player. She told him how she'd got into blues after seeing the film *Ray* a couple of years ago. "I love the melancholy of the blues—the hot steamy moodiness just draws you in. And don't you just love the names of some of those blues singers? Muddy Waters. Lightnin' Hopkins."

"Blind Lemon Jefferson." He confessed he often spent hours in the bath making up names for blues singers. "There's actually a recognized method for doing it. I found it on this blues Web site. Blues singers often have three names. The first has to be some kind of an affliction—as in blind. The second must be a fruit—as in lemon. And the last has to be the name of an American president—as in Jefferson."

She thought for a moment. "OK. How's about Asthmatic Kiwi Nixon?"

"That's it! Or Flatulent Nectarine Bush."

Pretty soon they were beside themselves laughing.

"Ooh, ooh, I've got one," she squealed at one point. "How's about Horny Passionfruit Clinton."

"You know, you really are very funny," he said. For a couple of seconds he took his eyes off the road and turned toward her. "And I've been meaning to say that the blue in the top really suits you. It goes with your hair."

"Thank you," she said, feeling herself flush with pleasure.

IT WASN'T UNTIL they got to Brighton that Sam realized he'd left his jacket at Ruby's flat. But since the sun was blazing, they agreed there was no chance of him needing it.

Weather-wise, the late September day promised to be perfect. No doubt the cold and drizzle, which had been around for the last couple of weeks, would be back, but for now the only signs of autumn approaching were the long shadows and a quiet stillness in the air. Even the normally rough sea was calm. Sunlight bounced off what passed for waves, giving the impression that sparklers were burning on the horizon.

The hot dog and burger vendors, who had no doubt packed up for the season when the cold started, were out in full, hoping to make one final killing before the weather cracked up again.

Ruby and Sam strolled along the boardwalk, dodging stray toddlers, cyclists and tank-topped Rollerbladers. Every so often they would stop to watch a street magician or escape artist, or mooch around one of the New Age shops, which sold crystals and tacky Buddha prints and were run by holisticer than thou young men with earlobes full of piercings and dreadlocks the thickness of a Buddy Epstien pickled cucumber.

As they came out of a shop called Merlin's Cave, Ruby closed her eyes and sniffed the air. "Umm, ozone chips and fried onions. You can't beat it. It's over two hours since we had the doughnuts. How d'you fancy a cheap nasty hot dog, packed full of chemicals and carcinogens and offering a fifty-fifty chance of mild to serious gut rot tomorrow morning?"

"Bring it on," Sam said. "But I insist on extra carcinogen on mine." They found a hot dog vendor and Sam suggested she find an empty bench while he joined the queue. After ten minutes he came over to where she was sitting, bearing two large hot dogs dripping in ketchup, mustard and onions. "They were out of Coke," he said, "so I got us two cans of finest 'carbonated orange-flavored juice drink.' "

"Perfect," she announced.

After they'd finished eating they decided to head toward the pier. As they walked he told her how much he was enjoying having discovered a new branch of his family through Buddy and Irene. "Saul and Fi are lovely people. And they seem really happy together."

"They are. I think a lot of people would give anything to have what they have."

They walked on in comfortable silence. Eventually he asked her if she was getting used to the idea of having a baby brother or sister. She explained that she was still struggling with it. "I've had Mum and Dad to myself for thirty-two years. Now I've got to share them and I'm ashamed to say that the little kid in me really doesn't want to."

He said it was probably normal to feel the way she did. "I don't think it matters how old you are when a sibling is born. The first child always feels a sense of loss. I know I did. I can remember trying to suffocate my brother with a pillow when he was born. If my mom hadn't come into the room when she did, I don't know what might have happened."

"God, how old were you?"

"Twenty-five."

She roared with laughter.

When she asked him about his brother, Sam shrugged and seemed reluctant to say very much. "Josh is eight years younger than me and I think he was far more affected by our parents' deaths than I was. Buddy and Irene loved him as their own, but he kinda went off the rails. These days he doesn't have much to do with the family."

She didn't feel she knew Sam well enough to ask what "kinda went off the rails" meant, so she let it go.

"Sam," she said, changing the subject, "can I ask you something?"

"Sure. Go ahead." He had his hands in his pockets and his smile was causing appealing little crinkles to form around his eyes.

"What made you want to specialize in gynecology? I mean it's a bit..." she struggled to find a word that wouldn't offend him.

"Weird? Perverted? Misogynistic?" he said, sounding amused rather than offended. "Take your pick. I've been accused of all three." Ruby said that she thought *misogynistic* sounded a bit harsh.

"I agree," he said, "but some women believe male gynecologists are power-crazed woman haters who get sexual kicks out of dominating them."

"I'm not sure I'd go quite that far, but as you know—since I blurted it out the other day when I fainted—similar thoughts had occurred to me."

"I understand, and I wasn't upset by what you said." She could tell by his expression that he meant it. "Women are right to have reservations about male gynecologists. Once in a while you come across a gynecologist losing his license for what is politely referred to as 'inappropriate behavior.' The profession—like all branches of medicine—needs more women, but I went into it because mostly you're dealing with healthy young people rather than the sick and elderly. And if I do get a kick, it's not from examining naked women, it's from helping to bring a healthy baby into the world, or knowing that it's my skill that has made it possible for an infertile woman to conceive."

He paused. "Sorry, I was getting on my high horse. I have this tendency to lecture people sometimes." He was looking ever so slightly embarrassed and awkward. Seeing his vulnerable side like this made her feel even more drawn to him. She told him she didn't think he had got remotely on his high horse and that she could really understand a person wanting to go into a branch of medicine where the joy far outweighs the pain and misery. "And I suppose having lost your parents, you've had your fair share of pain."

She watched him sidestep a toddler. "Hey, little guy," he said, kneeling down and placing a gentle hand on the child's head. "Where's your mom?" In fact, she was no more than three or four paces behind the child. Sam stood up, offered the mother a smile and turned back to Ruby. "You're right. I'm sure my parents' deaths had something to do with me not wanting to specialize in something like cancer or heart disease."

She was desperate to ask him about St. Luke's celebrity patients and whether he'd treated any of them personally, but decided not to say anything. She knew he was obliged to respect his patients' privacy and she didn't want to put him in an awkward position. She didn't feel she could leave the subject entirely alone, though.

"It's amazing how those celebs give birth at St. Luke's and then appear in the newspapers a few days later looking so thin—as if they've never been pregnant."

"I know," he said, with a despondent shake of his head. "Don't get me started. They exercise and diet like crazy when they're pregnant. We do our best to explain the harm they're doing. But they don't seem to care. What worries me is that other women see these postpartum pictures, think they should look like that, too, and are starting to copy them. The whole thing is spiraling out of control. I just don't know what the answer is."

Ruby was glad and relieved that he felt the same way about this problem as she did. She wasn't sure how she would have reacted had he turned out to be one of these men for whom women could never be too thin.

• • •

BY NOW THEY had reached the pier. They were greeted by a low, rhythmic boom coming from the sound system. It was the kind of noise that seemed to get inside you and make your pancreas wobble. This was accompanied by the heavy metallic clatter of the amusement rides and intermittent screams as the Big Dipper took another dive.

"Is there an arcade?" he said. "I love arcades."

"I was hoping you'd say that. Follow me."

They swapped their loose change for tokens and headed for the flashing lights and bleeping Martian sound of the slot machines. Most had been commandeered by boisterous gangs of tracksuited, hooded teenagers. One or two were occupied by men with vacant bloodshot eyes and tatty leather jackets.

"I have a system for working the slot machines," Sam said. "It's a sure thing. You hover around a machine and wait until whoever's playing has spent all their money—hopefully without getting the jackpot. By then you know the machine is due to pay out, so you move in."

"C'mon," Ruby said. "Everybody's tried that and it's not that simple."

"Trust me," he said, with a sexy but distinctly self-mocking wink, "I'm a doctor."

They waited until one of the tracksuited gangs decided to cut their losses and move on to another machine.

"OK. Watch and learn," he said. For the next few minutes they stuffed tokens into the machine and lost every time.

"Sam," she said eventually, watching him shove in another token, "there isn't an Epstien system, is there?"

"How can you tell?"

This made her laugh. "And you've never won the jackpot, have you?"

"Not as such," he said, staring intently at the spinning fruit. "In fact, between you and me, I've never won so much as a dime on a slot machine."

No sooner had the words left his mouth than a rattling waterfall of tokens began spewing onto the floor.

"Omigod," Ruby exclaimed in disbelief. "We've won. We've actually won. There has to be fifty quid here." She found herself flinging her arms around his neck and kissing him on the cheek. People playing nearby machines had seen them get the jackpot and had turned to stare. For a moment she thought there was going to be trouble when the track-suited teenagers, who were still hanging around, yelled out "we woz robbed." But they simply pulled up their hoods and slouched off.

"See," Sam said, laughing. "And you laughed at the Epstien system."

Shaking her head with amusement, she got down on the floor and began sweeping the tokens into a pile. A second later he was kneeling in front of her, doing the same. "We can put them in my bag," she said.

It must have taken them over a minute to gather up all the tokens.

"Right, I think that's it," he said, dropping a final handful into her bag.

She looked round and checked that there were no strays lying on the floor.

"Yep, that seems to be the lot." He got to his feet, then took her hand to help her up. As her head came level with his, her eyes met his. Neither of them moved. What followed was one of those electricity-charged moments, which left them in no doubt as to what was about to happen. He began by cupping her face and drawing her toward him. Then he planted tiny kisses on her mouth. Before long his arms were tight around her and she was parting her lips for him. When his tongue found hers she felt her stomach flip with desire. He tasted of orange-flavor fruit drink. As she melted into him, she was aware of her breathing becoming much slower and deeper. She wanted him to ravage her here and now among the slot machines. It was only when some more kids yelled out "Gedda room," that they pulled away, giggling self-consciously.

In the end it turned out they'd won far less than they'd thought. Instead of being £50, it was just over £20. Neither of them minded, though. The surprise and fun of seeing the machine spewing tokens had been enough.

THEY SPENT THE afternoon lazing side by side on the beach. As they talked he would walk his fingers along her arm or start playing with her bangs. Every so often they would stop talking and start kissing again. Once when they were in the middle of necking, his mobile rang. "I'm sorry, Ruby, I have to get this. It could be the hospital."

"Of course. Go ahead."

He placed his finger in his ear to block out the beach sounds. "Hey, how's it going?... What? When did this happen? Are you OK?" She watched his face darken. Then he stood up and moved away and she couldn't hear what was being said.

When he came back she thought he looked agitated and preoccupied. "Problem?"

"Umm?" He was miles away.

"The call. Is there an emergency at the hospital?"

"Er... No. It's just some minor glitch with one of my patients. It's nothing to worry about. They're dealing with it."

She frowned. Sam seemed pretty anxious and perturbed for somebody who had just been told there was nothing to worry about. And did he usually ask colleagues if they were OK? He clearly took his work very seriously.

He sat down again. "You look stressed," she said gently. "You sure you're OK?"

"I was up until after two last night delivering twins. I'm just a bit tired, that's all. Sorry."

"Hey, you don't have to apologize for being tired.... Here, I know something that might help." She began massaging his shoulders. They were hard and knotted with tension.

THEY LEFT BRIGHTON around six. Sam was on call later that evening and needed to be close to the hospital in case there was an emergency. Before they left they went to a restaurant on the boardwalk called The Regent, and blew their winnings on a fish-and-chip supper. After a beer, Sam relaxed and returned to his usual bright self. Ruby forgot about the phone call and his odd reaction to it and spent most of the meal gently teasing him because he'd ordered mushy peas, thinking it was guacamole.

As they pulled up outside her flat, they kissed again. Deep urgent kisses that refused to end. At one point as they pulled away she remembered he needed to collect his jacket. "Do you want to come in and get it?"

"Do you want me to?" he said.

The serious tone of his question made her realize that her question had come out wrong. "What? God. No. Sorry. I meant 'it' as in your jacket. The one you left in my flat. I didn't mean 'it' as in... you know... *it*-it."

On the other hand, maybe subconsciously (she wasn't Ronnie's daughter for nothing) she had meant *it*-it. And if she had been asking him in for *it*-it, was it *it*-it that she really wanted? After all, this was their first date. She might hate herself afterward if she broke her strict no *it*-it until the third date rule. Then again, she wasn't sure if she could hold out until then, and the way she saw it, the meal they shared after Connor's circumcision was technically a date. So, by rights this was their second date. What was more, it had lasted all day—twice or even three times as long as a regular evening date. If she took the number of hours they'd spent together into account, surely there was an argument to be made for this being their third, or even fourth date.

"I think it would be OK if you came up . . ." she gave him a coy smiley look, "for . . . erm . . . the jacket."

"You sure you want me to come up for the jacket?" he said, playing along with her. "I mean, I don't have to have the jacket. I can manage perfectly well without the jacket. I am not a man so obsessed with getting the jacket that I would want to put pressure on a woman to give me the jacket. Particularly not on our first date."

The speech was pure Jerry Seinfeld. He had managed to make her laugh and feel sexy at the same time. "I'm sure," she said. "I really want to give you the jacket."

"I KNOW I'VE got some Ray Charles here somewhere," she said. As she carried on searching through a pile of CDs, Sam came up behind her and began kissing the back of her neck. She felt him slide the wide neck of her peasant top down over her arm. His kisses moved to her bare shoulder. Every nerve ending in her body was tingling. It was as much as she could do to concentrate on looking for the CD.

"Found it," she said, slipping the CD into the player and placing the rest of the pile on a low shelf.

"Come here, you," he whispered. Unaware that she had forgotten to hit "start" on the CD player, she turned to face him. The blood was pounding in her head. He cupped her face and drew her toward him. They'd been sharing passionate kisses all day, but this was different. There was an extra urgency about what was happening now, along with an absolute certainty about how it would end.

They moved to the sofa. Gently he pushed her back and soon he was on top of her, his erection hard against her. She let out tiny yelps of delight as he ran his hands through her hair and kissed the tops of her breasts. "Why don't I get that music going?" he said at one point as they pulled away briefly. Barely taking his eyes off her, he extended an arm over the back of the sofa and just managed to reach the CD player. A moment later a voice was blasting out at full volume and it wasn't Ray Charles. "I love and accept my body. I am beautiful and vibrant in my uniqueness. I am a child of the universe who has every right to love and be loved. I am capable of finding love."

No! Panic shot through her. After she'd listened to it the other day, she must have put the *Discovering True Love Through Inner Empowerment* CD back in the wrong sleeve.

Ruby felt herself freeze. Sam looked up from her breast.

"Correct me if I'm wrong," he said, a bemused look on his face, "but that doesn't sound much like Ray Charles."

She swallowed hard as she wracked her brain for a plausible explanation. "Just one of those stupid CDs that you get free with the Sunday papers," she blurted. "I listened to it the other day when I had nothing better to do, but only out of curiosity. Made me think how wretched it must be for all those pathetic lonely saddos out there who can never get a date."

"You know," he said, getting up to change the CD, "when I was much younger and just getting into dating, I could have done with something like this to boost my self-esteem."

"Oh, me too. Me too. But luckily those days are long gone. Long, long gone."

He was searching for the Ray Charles CD when the

phone rang. She decided to let the machine pick up. What she didn't realize was that she had forgotten to set it to silent.

"Oh, hi, darling, it's Mum. Just phoning up for a chat and to check you're OK. You never told me how you're getting on with the affirmation CD? Is it having any effect? Never give up hope, darling. Somewhere there's a man for you. I promise. Love you."

Chapter 11

"Omigod, you must have been mortified," Fi said, clamping the breast-pump funnel to her left nipple. "What on earth did Sam say when he heard the message?"

"Nothing. He didn't get a chance. He had to rush off." Ruby described how just as her mother's call ended, St. Luke's rang Sam to say there was an emergency and he was needed. Apparently the same patient who had been giving cause for concern when they were in Brighton had taken a turn for the worse.

"Emergency, my aunt Fanny," Fi snorted. "Probably just some celeb throwing a diva fit and threatening to sue because she'd found a postpartum hemorrhoid."

"No, I think it was pretty real," Ruby said. She explained that Sam had sounded pretty uptight while he was on the phone to the hospital and that he'd seemed particularly concerned for the nurse who'd phoned. "I could actually hear her crying on the end of the line and he was telling her to keep calm and not to worry. God only knows what must have been going on for a nurse to lose her cool."

"You'd cry, too, if you had to cope with these spoiled, self-centered women who can't cope with the tiniest thing going wrong in their lives. I'd hate to be in Sam's shoes. He must live in constant fear of a malpractice suit landing on his desk."

Ruby nodded. That probably explained Sam's initial anxiety after he got the phone call on the beach.

Fi lowered her head and watched milk squirt from her breast and into the baby's bottle. "I dunno why I don't just put a bell round my neck, change my name to Daisy and have done with it." She explained that Saul had offered to take over the night feeds for a while so that she could get some sleep. Since she was adamant that Connor should only have breast milk, she was forced to express it into a bottle.

Ruby offered her an affectionate smile and placed a hand on her shoulder. "C'mon, it won't be forever."

"I know. Look, don't mind me, I'm still fretting about how all these stars manage to stay so slim when they're pregnant." Two or three magazines were lying in a pile on the table. She picked up the top one. "Have you seen this?" She was holding this month's *For Her*. "There's an interview with Claudia Planchette. It's so bloody galling." She slid the magazine toward Ruby. "Look at the picture of her. Apart from her bump she's still as skinny as anything. And she has the nerve to say it's all down to genes. Yeah, right. She's clearly starving herself and her baby.... On the other hand, there's no denying the results."

"Fi, just listen to yourself. Are you saying that a bit of you wishes you had starved yourself when you were pregnant with Connor?"

"No, of course not," Fi shot back. "Claudia Planchette's obviously obsessed, but like they were saying on that TV show yesterday, the situation really is getting out of hand and stars like Planchette are to blame. I've got pregnant friends who are sane, grounded, professional women and even they are restricting their diets. Have you any idea where this could lead? I'm telling you, Rubes, if this situation gets any worse, we are going to start seeing educated, middle-class women giving birth to full-term babies who are severely underweight and malnourished. Why isn't somebody doing something?" Fi was so angry and exasperated that her face had become quite pink.

"You're right," Ruby said. "But what do you do? Women have to wake up and start seeing this madness for what it is. Until that happens nothing will change.... C'mon, cheer up. Why don't I pour us a glass of wine?"

Fi said she'd better not because the alcohol would get into her milk and make Connor tipsy. "On the other hand a drop of vino might make him sleep better." She said there was an open bottle of Chardy in the fridge. "I'm sorry I keep getting on my soapbox about this dieting thing, but it's really got to me."

"Don't apologize. If I'd just had a baby and put on a few pounds, it would get to me, too." Ruby opened the fridge door and took out the bottle of Chardonnay. Then she turned to Fi. "I assume you'll be wanting a bucket of freshly mown grass with your wine?" she giggled.

"Ha, blinkin' ha."

Ruby only poured herself half a glass. She wasn't planning to stay long. She was on her way to her parents' for dinner—Aunty Sylvia was bringing her new chap. She'd stopped off at Fi's to give her the new Les Sprogs catalogue. Fi was looking for a child's bed for Ben, which Saul's parents had offered to pay for.

"So, are you seeing Sam again?" Fi asked.

Ruby said she was. She explained that he'd phoned first thing to apologize for having to rush off and to ask if she was free on Friday. He'd also managed to ease her embarrassment over the CD fiasco by telling her how Irene had spent years placing lonely-hearts ads on his behalf in Jewish newspapers. Apparently, each time an ad appeared he would receive dozens of e-mails from ultra-Orthodox parents desperate to marry off their daughters to a nice Jewish doctor.

"So, you two must really be hitting it off."

Ruby became thoughtful. "Well, we don't stop talking. He makes me laugh. And I feel completely relaxed with him. It's like I've known him forever..."

"And he is incredibly sexy."

"There is that." Ruby smiled. She described how she'd barely slept last night because she kept rerunning the tape of their first kiss. "It was so sublime, it actually took my breath away. It never felt like that when I kissed Matt—not even at the beginning."

"That's because Matt wasn't a gynecologist. I'm telling you, gynecologists are great lovers. You wait. When you finally get to do the deed, it is going to be fabulous. You are so lucky."

Just then a little voice called out from upstairs. It was Ben. "Mummee, my done a ukky pooh in va twoilet! Come and wipe my bottom!"

"Gawd, I thought he was asleep," Fi said. She called out a "well done, poppet" to Ben and told him she would be up in a tick. "Hallelujah. First turd he's deposited in the loo for weeks." She pulled the plastic cone off her breast and examined the contents of the baby bottle. "If I add that to the lot I expressed earlier," she said, buttoning up her shirt, "there might just be enough for one feed." She took the bottle over to the fridge and poured the contents into a jug. "I think I've got some nuts somewhere," she said to Ruby, "if you fancy something to go with the wine." Then she disappeared upstairs to see to Ben.

Ruby had to admit she was feeling a bit hungry and began opening cupboards looking for the nuts. Courtesy of Bridget, the kitchen was still immaculate. Instead of a dozen coffee-stained mugs piled up on the draining board, there were now two perfectly straight rows of shiny, freshly bleached mugs in the crockery cupboard, handles all facing the same direction. Eventually she found a bag of peanuts stowed in a large clean Tupperware container alongside several packets of Monster Munch.

"Great, you've found them," Fi said, coming back into the kitchen, having put Ben back to bed. "I haven't been able to find anything since my mother started cleaning and reorganizing the kitchen. I wouldn't mind—in fact I'm really grateful—but she does it with such bad grace and makes me feel so inadequate."

Ruby offered her the open bag of nuts. Fi took a handful and sat down. "You know," Ruby said, "exasperating as it is, maybe you should try to let Bridget's comments wash over you. Just make use of her while she's around."

"I should," Fi said, noisily munching nuts. "And I do try, but with my mother it's easier said than done." She drained her glass and allowed Ruby to refill it.

"God, just think," Fi said. "If you married Sam, we'd be related."

Ruby burst out laughing. "We hardly know each other and you've already got us married off. You know, you are rapidly turning into a Jewish mother."

Just then, Saul appeared. "Saul," Fi said, "what relation would I be to Ruby if she married your cousin Sam?"

"Hang on," Saul said, frowning. "Have I missed something?"

"Your wife's getting a bit ahead of herself," Ruby replied. "Sam and I have been on one date, that's all."

"He seems like a really nice bloke," Saul said. "I hadn't met him until the circumcision. Turns out he's really into soccer." He turned to Fi. "Spurs are at home to Man U on Saturday. Thought I might see if he wanted to come."

"Great. Anything to keep you and my mother apart."

"By the way, where is she? Popped out to put gas in her broomstick?"

Fi shushed him, but she couldn't help laughing. "She's taken Connor for a walk. He's been crochety all day and she thought the fresh air might help him drop off."

"Let's hope so," Saul said, "but whatever happens I'm doing the feeds tonight. You have to get some rest." He took a swig of Fi's wine and a handful of nuts from the bag. "Right, I'm off to see Tony the Fascist. He's going to fit the car with a new exhaust. Shouldn't be more than a couple of hours." Tony the Fascist was Fi and Saul's car mechanic. He had political views that were Neanderthal to say the least, but he worked from home and was cheap as chips.

Just then Bridget came bustling in. She was holding Connor in her arms. "Sure now, Fiona, will you look at him? Sleeping like a lamb. I swear you don't give him enough fresh air. That's why he doesn't sleep through the night." She noticed the bottle of Chardonnay. "You're drinking wine."

"Yes. Fancy a glass?" Fi said.

Bridget ignored the invitation. Instead she gave a loud, disapproving sniff. "But it'll get into your milk and give Connor the runs," she said. "Poor little mite. Hasn't he been through enough?" She handed Connor to Fi and began unbuttoning her coat. "I'll take him upstairs in a minute and check on his wound." This last comment was directed specifically at Saul. Ruby and Fi saw the pulse going on the side of his head. "Let it go, just let it go," Fi whispered to him. Saul shoved more nuts into his mouth.

"And will you look at that husband of yours," Bridget went on. "With all that long hair."

"Mum, he's in *Hamlet*. He has to have long hair."

"But he looks like a woman," she said.

"Only when I stand beside you," Saul muttered so that only Fi and Ruby could hear. Fi's foot made violent contact with Saul's shin.

He winced, offered a general "see ya" and left, grabbing another handful of nuts on his way.

Ruby asked Bridget if she would prefer a cup of tea or coffee.

"Coffee would be grand." She asked Ruby how she was feeling.

"Oh, much better. Although in the end I decided not to drive home. Sam had to—"

"Lovely, dear. Lovely. Now then, what do you think of the way I've cleaned this kitchen? You can see your face in those taps. Encrusted with lime scale, they were. All they needed was a bit of elbow grease." She looked pointedly at Fi. For the next five minutes she delivered a lecture on how the education system was failing girls by not teaching them domestic science. Fi responded by knocking back a third glass of wine.

"Well, I have to say," Ruby said, placing a mug of coffee in front of Bridget, "that it all looks lovely."

Fi shot her a look as if to say "traitor." Ruby raised her look with a "what do you expect me to say" shrug.

"Of course the floor was particularly bad," Bridget went on. "I don't know the last time that saw a mop and soap. Four goes it took me to get it looking like this. Mind you, it wasn't as bad as the stove. I used a whole bottle of scouring cream on it. You know, Fiona, you need to get organized. You could get all your chores done if you got that baby into a routine. Do you think I picked you up every time you cried? Take it from me, young as he is, he's got you wrapped around his little finger."

She finished stirring sugar into her coffee and picked up the milk carton. "Empty," she snorted. Her world-weary expression suggested that this was just another in the long line of domestic failures she had come to expect from her daughter.

Ruby offered to get some more milk from the fridge, but Bridget was already on her feet. For some reason Ruby found herself watching as Bridget opened the fridge door and reached inside. When she brought out the milk jug, Ruby patted Fi's arm and jerked her head in Bridget's direction. "Omigod," Fi whispered, bringing her hand to her mouth. "She's got my—"

"I know. Shouldn't we stop her?" Ruby said.

"Stop her and I will never ever speak to you again. OK?"

"OK."

Squirming in an attempt to suppress their hysterical laughter, they watched Bridget pour the milk into her mug.

She came back to her seat and took a mouthful of her coffee. This was followed in quick succession by another and then another.

"How's the coffee, Mum?" Fi said.

"Actually, it's not at all bad. And the milk's not too creamy. Even semiskimmed is too creamy for me. I have a very sensitive palette, you know. What kind is it?"

"Oh, it's a new organic one," Fi said innocently. "It's, erm . . . it's imported from France."

"Really? Whereabouts in France?"

"Brest, I think." Fi had her hand clamped to her mouth in an effort to hold in her laughter. "They fly it over. That's why it's called Brest Express."

"Right. When I get home I'll be sure to ask for Brest Express milk."

RUBY ARRIVED AT her parents' just before eight. Ronnie was wearing a baggy sweatshirt with "Does My Bump Look Big in This?" written across it. She had an oven glove slung over her shoulder. Ruby admired the sweatshirt. "Great, isn't it? Your Aunty Sylvia bought it for me." She led Ruby into the kitchen. A half-roasted leg of lamb in its tin was sitting on the counter. "I'll be with you in a minute. I just need to finish basting the roast. Your dad's listening to music. He probably didn't hear you come in." Ronnie picked up a large basting spoon and began pouring meat juices over the lamb. "Help yourself to wine." As Ruby poured Merlot into a glass, she breathed in the delectable aroma of roasting meat, rosemary and garlic.

One of Ronnie's sketchbooks was lying on the table. Ruby sat down and began flicking through the pages. It was full of charcoal drawings of full-breasted heavily pregnant women. "Wow, these are lovely," Ruby said, taking in the stark unadorned images and fluid lines. Ronnie said they were no more than doodles at the moment. "The Tavistock Gallery is planning a new exhibition. It's going to be called 'Birthright' and they asked me to contribute some paintings or sketches. I thought it might be fun to have a go."

Just then Phil came wandering in, his brand-new iPod Shuffle round his neck. He was singing along loudly to his music and managing to hit about one correct note in seven. "We gotta install microwave ovens... Gotta move these refrigerators. Gotta move these color TVs..."

At this point Ronnie decided to join in. She began jigging her hips and singing into her basting spoon. Taking his cue from his wife, Phil started playing air guitar. Soon both of them were giving it their all.

"My God," Ruby said, shaking her head in amusement, "George and Gracie do Dire Straits."

"Blinkin' cheek," Ronnie laughed, tapping Ruby on the head with the handle of her spoon.

Phil took out his earphones and bent down to kiss Ruby hello. "You know, this Shuffle is wonderful. You should get one. You install all your music and it plays it at random. You never know what's coming up next. I love it. And look at it. The thing's the size of a cigarette lighter and I've got a thousand songs on it. A thousand." Still humming, Phil turned to Ronnie. "By the way, have you taken your passionflower and yellow dock root tincture? And I squeezed you that beet juice half an hour ago. Look, it's still sitting there. It's meant to be really good for you and you haven't touched it."

"Hey, Dr. Phil, have you ever tasted beet juice?" Ronnie said as she began taking cutlery from the kitchen drawer. "Ruby, tell your father to stop fussing. I'm fine."

"She is at the moment," Phil said to Ruby, "but geriatric multigravidas are more prone to health problems than younger women."

"Oy! Less of the geriatric if you don't mind. It makes me feel ninety."

He said he was sorry and turned back to Ruby. "Anyway, I've been on the Internet and discovered there are all these natural supplements your mother can take to prevent anemia and high blood pressure—"

"And they all taste like rancid bark," Ronnie piped up.

"Dad, stop panicking. St. Luke's is one of the best maternity hospitals in the world. Mum's being well looked after."

"I know, but I worry. You can never be too careful." He asked Ronnie if she'd shown Ruby the picture from the latest scan.

"I was going to after dinner," Ronnie said, giving Phil a handful of cutlery. "Look, maybe you could lay the table. Sylvia and Nigel will be here any minute."

Phil didn't move. "You know," he said to Ruby, "they use this amazing three-dimensional scanner now."

"Picture it," Ronnie interrupted. "There I am, lying on the table with this giant plastic penis inside me and your father's chatting away to the radiologist, going: 'So tell me, who makes this? Mitsubishi? Toshiba? And what kind of specification does it have?' "

Ruby started giggling. "What do you expect? He's a man. He can't help himself. And I'm sure he was interested in the baby, too."

"Your mother knows full well that I was," Phil said, depositing an affectionate kiss on Ronnie's cheek. He turned to Ruby. "Did you know that it's about ten and a half inches long now? It weighs nearly a pound and has eyebrows and eyelids. What's worrying me is that it should have started kicking, but it hasn't."

Ronnie rubbed her forehead in frustration. "Phil, please give it a rest. I'm meant to be the neurotic one round here. Everything's fine. The radiologist found a good strong heartbeat. Stop fussing. Now, please, will you go and lay the table?"

Giving another shrug, Phil disappeared into the dining room.

"You know," Ronnie said to Ruby, "I haven't been able to stop thinking about Claudia Planchette and that poor little girl of hers."

"I'm the same. It frightens me to think of the life she must have."

"I'd like to think that Claudia just gets a bit hormonal when she's pregnant, but I doubt it." Ronnie began spreading whipped cream over a Pavlova base. "You know, now I think about it, she was really irritable during that prenatal class. It was odd. Afterward, we all got to talking about whether the shape of your bump could indicate whether you were having a boy or a girl. It was all silly stuff and we were all giggling. Anyway, just for a laugh, the teacher suggested we compare bumps. So there we all were, lifting up our tops—only Claudia refused to join in. She was the only one. I thought maybe she had issues about taking off her clothes in front of other women. I mean, the teacher was crossing a boundary, I suppose . . ."

"Ronnie. Please. Get to the point. I'm aging here." It was Aunty Sylvia, looking stunning in a long rust-colored coat dress and matching wide pants. She had just walked in and seemed to have heard everything Ronnie had said. She went over to Ruby and pinched an inch of her niece's cheek flesh. "And how's my favorite niece?"

Ruby rubbed her smarting cheek and said she was fine.

"OK, the point is," Ronnie went on, giving Sylvia a gentle slap on the wrist for helping herself to strawberries that were meant for the Pavlova, "when I looked at Claudia's face, she seemed more than just embarrassed. I'd say she was terrified. I got the sense that there has been a time in her life when she's experienced some kind of trauma while being undressed in front of women. Some kind of abuse, maybe. I think she could be suffering from some kind of posttraumatic stress."

"Don't be daft," Sylvia said, stealing another strawberry and this time managing to dodge the slap. "You're reading far too much into it. Claudia was simply petrified that somebody was about to produce a camera, which would have meant a picture of her bump—which she hasn't been paid for—appearing in newspapers and magazines all over the world."

"Of course, you're right," Ronnie said. "I hadn't thought of that."

While the conversation had been going on between Ronnie and Sylvia, Ruby hadn't said a word. Her mind had shot back to the changing room in Les Sprogs and the glimpse she'd caught of Claudia Planchette's "bump." Was it remotely possible that her first instinct had been correct and that Claudia wasn't pregnant and had been wearing a prosthesis? But why would she want to make the world believe she was pregnant if she wasn't?

"Earth to Ruby. Come in, Ruby," Aunty Sylvia said, passing a hand in front of Ruby's eyes. She came to with a start.

"Sorry." Ruby blinked. "I was miles away."

"I was just saying," Aunty Sylvia said, "why don't you two come and meet Nigel? He's in the living room with your dad." Ruby wanted to mention her prosthesis theory to Ronnie, but she was busy yakking to Aunty Sylvia.

"Have you told him how old you are?" Ronnie hissed.

"Not as such," Aunty Sylvia said. "I haven't been able to find the right moment, but I'll do it as soon as I feel the time is right. I promise."

NIGEL WAS A stocky, mild-mannered man in an immaculate gray business suit and nondescript tie. He was the exact opposite of the loud, hugely entertaining—but ultimately emotionally damaged—types Aunty Sylvia usually went out with. There was no getting away from it: Nigel was dull.

Over dinner they were addressed on the difference between tax evasion and avoidance, the benefits of gifts and corporate bonds and how to invest them in order to derive the highest possible after-tax return. It didn't help that Aunty Sylvia, who wasn't quite pissed as a pudding, but well on her way, kept egging him on.

"Go on, Nigel. Don't be shy. Tell them how you helped the Osbournes with their tax planning strategy."

"Ah, well now, that wasn't easy," he said, leaning back in his chair and steepling his fingers. "You see, the change in tax law in 1998 means that gains made outside the U.K. can be taxable in the U.K. It was actually the March 1998 budget which extended CGT to cover expats for up to five years after their departure."

All the time Nigel was speaking, Ruby couldn't take her eyes off his face. When they were introduced, her first impression had been that Nigel possessed a warm, kind, if pudgy face, which smiled easily. She could see why Aunty Sylvia found him attractive. Having said that, there was something odd about his features. Something almost effeminate. Try as she might, she couldn't put her finger on what it was.

During one of the rare moments that Nigel paused for breath, Aunty Sylvia squeezed his hand and said: "This man has got the most brilliant financial brain. Tell them how you've helped the Stings."

"Sylvia, I'm not sure I should really say any more. It's meant to be confidential."

"Millions, he saved them. Millions. I tell you, anytime, and I mean anytime, you need financial advice, Nigel is your man. He's so gifted, they named a loophole after him. The Nigel Brompton Loophole."

"Ah well, you see, that was based on my discovery that each year the Inland Revenue . . ."

"More wine, anybody?" Phil broke in. Ruby could tell by the taut expression on her father's face that he was coming close to shoving Nigel's head up his own loophole. Phil began going round the table, filling glasses. "By the way," he said to nobody in particular, "you'll never guess what I'm working on at the moment. I'm designing the packaging for a heart defibrillator—you know the thing with the electric paddles that doctors use to restart people's hearts." He put down the wine bottle and went over to the coffee table. He came back with a brown cardboard box. He explained that the defibrillator company were making battery-operated machines for home use and had given him one to play with.

"Wow, this is fantastic," Aunty Sylvia enthused. She took another glug of wine and then began opening a plastic pouch.

It contained rubber gloves, a surgical mask and scissors to cut off the patient's clothes. "We have to test it out." She unfolded the instructions and cast her eyes over them. Bearing in mind how much she'd had to drink, it was doubtful that she was absorbing any information. "Right, come on, Phil, pretend to have a heart attack."

Nigel made the point that it had to be dangerous to pass an electric shock into a healthy heart. "You're right," Aunty Sylvia said, momentarily defeated. "Ah, but there is something here that we could try to bring back to life." With that she got up. "OK, everybody. Charging two hundred. Stand clear." A moment later she had clamped the paddles to what remained of the leg of lamb. Pausing for dramatic effect, she pressed the shock button. Then everybody—including Nigel, who it appeared wasn't entirely without humor—burst into helpless, hysterical laughter. "Do we have an output?" Aunty Sylvia said, warming to her part of Dr. Corday. Ronnie shook her head in reply.

"OK, let's try a shot of adrenaline."

"Sylvia," Ronnie said gravely, doing her best to play along and at the same time stifle her giggles, "you've done your best. I think we should stop." She placed her hand on her sister's arm. "We have to face it. The roast is gone."

Sylvia heaved a theatrical sigh and rubbed her forehead with the back of her hand. "You're right. OK, people, I'm calling it," Sylvia said. "Time of death, ten after eight."

Everybody roared.

"Nobody could have done any more," Nigel said, patting Aunty Sylvia's hand and grinning. Then he deposited a rather self-conscious kiss on her forehead and in a whisper that only Ruby overheard, he told her how funny and adorable she was.

"Ooh, ooh, Phil," Ronnie said, her hand clamped to her stomach. "It must be all the excitement. I just felt the baby kick."

• • •

"OK, BE HONEST, both of you," Aunty Sylvia said later on as she, Ruby and Ronnie scraped plates and loaded the dishwasher. "Do you think Nigel's boring?"

"Do you?" Ronnie asked, putting a dishwasher tablet into the dispenser. She hadn't been in therapy for donkeys' years without learning how to neatly lob a question back to the client.

Aunty Sylvia became thoughtful. A double helping of Pavlova had helped her sober up. "Maybe a little. He did go on a bit tonight, didn't he? But I think that was only because I was egging him on and he was nervous. He's not very good in company, but he did get more lively toward the end. When we're alone I see the real him. He's kind, grounded and completely trustworthy. With Nigel, I always know where I am."

"And he's got the most beautiful eyebrows," Ruby heard herself say. Ruby had figured it out. It was Nigel's perfectly shaped and arched eyebrows that gave him that strangely effeminate look.

"Yes, I noticed them as well," Ronnie said. She lowered her voice. "He doesn't pluck them, does he?"

"Ronnie, Nigel does not pluck his eyebrows." Aunty Sylvia seemed deeply offended by the suggestion. "They're completely natural. I admit it's an odd sort of look, but I'm getting used to it." She paused. "If I'm honest, the real thing that bothers me about Nigel is his lack of edge."

Still playing therapist, Ronnie asked her sister to define *edge*.

"I dunno. Emotional baggage. Hang-ups. Possessing deep dark secrets. All the men I've ever been out with have fallen into one of those categories. Nigel, on the other hand, is an open book. What you see is what you get. Nothing about him could surprise me."

"In other words," Ronnie said, "he's not a project."

"I was sure that I didn't want another project. Now I don't know. There's something missing. Maybe I'm just addicted to troubled men. I get such a kick out of trying to change them."

"But you know you can never change them," Ronnie said. "Pretty soon it all goes sour and they make you unhappy."

"You're right," she said. "You're absolutely right." But Ruby could tell she wasn't entirely convinced.

Chapter 12

At half past eight on Monday morning, Ivan the Terrible appeared on Ruby's doorstep.

"Sorry I not come Saturday." He was puffing like a worn-out steam engine. "I try to come, but I left bollock on bus. Today I hef new one. I ask man at plumber's merchants to geev me best bollock. Oh, and I make no charge for one I lost."

"That's very kind of you, Ivan," Ruby said. As she let him in she couldn't help noticing how pale he was. "Ivan, you seem incredibly breathless. You don't seem at all well."

"Pleez. Not to worry," he said. But she was worried. Ivan's hand was clamped to his chest and he was wincing in pain. She insisted he come into the living room and sit down. "I think we should call a doctor."

He waved a dismissive hand. "It's nothing. I eat too much herring and black bread thees morning. It geev me pain." With that he let out a loud and not unconvincing belch.

"All right. If you're sure you're OK."

"No worries. I em fine. You go."

Ruby left, but not before she had promised to phone during the day to check on him.

• • •

SHE ARRIVED AT the shop to find Chanel leaning on the counter reading the horoscope column in the *Daily Mail*—a sure sign that her spirits were improving and that she was getting back to her old self. The therapist Ronnie had recommended was clearly helping. The moment she heard Ruby come in, Chanel looked up.

"OK, get this: 'For months now, Saturn, the planet of structure and stricture, has been retrograde in your sign, but as it begins to move forward again and is joined by Jupiter, planet of growth and opportunity, things are really starting to look up. Prepare to celebrate.' "

"Wow, sounds great."

"Doesn't it?" Chanel chuckled. "Shame I'm not a Pisces."

Ruby burst out laughing. Chanel was getting her sense of humor back, too. It was going to take time for her to come to terms with not being able to have a baby, but she really was making progress.

"Oh, by the way, this might interest you." She closed the newspaper and slid it across the counter toward Ruby. "I remember you saying 'ow Sam 'ad to rush off the other night. I think this might explain why." Ruby stared at the headline on the front page: "Claudia Loses Baby."

"Oh, my God," Ruby said, truly shocked. She hadn't much cared for the woman, nor did she think she was the best mother in the world, but there was no way she would have wished this on her. "That's so awful. I can't believe it. I didn't tell you, she was here in the shop the other day, buying swimsuits." She read through the article. Apparently, Claudia had gone into premature labor on Saturday afternoon. Later that evening, doctors gave her drugs to try and stop the labor, but yesterday she finally gave birth to a boy. He had lived for three hours.

"No wonder Sam was in such a state when he left," Ruby said. "How could I have imagined for one minute that Claudia wasn't pregnant?"

Chanel frowned and asked what she meant.

"Oh, it's nothing. Just me getting carried away that's all."

But Chanel wouldn't let it drop and Ruby ended up telling her about the incident in the fitting room and how she'd imagined seeing Claudia wearing a prosthetic stomach. Chanel didn't have to think twice.

"You daft wally," she laughed. "It'll've been one of those new pregnancy girdles—the ones they're all wearing in Paris."

"I know. I know. Forget it. I was just being an idiot."

A few minutes later, the phone rang. It was Sam.

"Sam, hi. I've just been reading about Claudia Planchette losing her baby. It's so sad. I had no idea she was one of your patients and that's why you had to rush off the other night. It must have been awful. Bet it's a media circus outside the hospital, though."

"Just a bit. There have to be a hundred paparazzi here, desperate to get a shot of her leaving. She wasn't my patient, though."

"Oh, sorry. When you left you seemed so uptight. I just assumed."

"No, it was something else." He sounded exhausted.

"Sam, have you had any sleep recently?"

"I think I may have caught a couple of hours back in March," he said with a soft laugh, "but I'm actually on my way to bed now. I was just ringing to suggest that instead of going out Friday night, you come to my place. I'll cook. Real food. Not junk."

She said that would be great.

"Unless, of course you'd rather go out. I just thought staying in would be more relaxing."

She was pretty sure "relaxing" was a euphemism for wanting to ravage her. At least she hoped it was. "Staying in will be perfect," she said.

The following day, he paid a surprise visit to the shop. "I had a couple of hours to spare, so I thought we could maybe go for coffee."

She'd suggested several times that he pop in so that he could see where she worked, and she couldn't have been more pleased to see him. She also loved the way he surprised her by turning up unannounced.

The problem was that when he arrived, the shop was full of customers. Chanel insisted she could cope on her own, but Ruby felt guilty about leaving her.

In the end Sam said if they couldn't go out, he would go to Starbucks and bring back coffee for all three of them. Chanel, who was clearly smitten with Sam, gazed after him as he disappeared.

"Wipe away the drool," Ruby giggled. "The customers will see."

"Don't care," Chanel said dreamily. Ruby had never imagined that grounded, down-to-earth Chanel was capable of such girlish giddiness. "God, you're a lucky girl. 'Ave you seen those brown eyes? The way they draw you in? I bet 'e's a wonderful doctor. 'E's the kind of bloke you could really talk to."

Chanel went off to serve a customer. By the time Sam reappeared ten minutes later with cappuccinos, the rush had subsided and Ruby was kneeling on the floor unpacking a box of crib blankets that had just been delivered.

"You know," he said, "this place is so . . ." He was looking up at the giant crystal chandelier and the gold and brocade rococo crib that Stella had insisted Ruby buy from a manufacturer in Paris and put in the window.

"Like the infant Louis XIV's nursery?" Ruby suggested.

"I was going to say 'classy,' " he said. "But I guess that's a pretty good description. I can see what you mean when you say this place isn't you. I imagine a Baby Organic store being very minimalist. I could see white walls, huge color photographs of mothers and children maybe…"

He'd got her. Oh, he had so got her. Ruby felt her skin prickle with delight.

In the end she didn't get much time to talk to Sam, partly because the phone kept ringing and partly because Chanel seemed intent on telling him her entire gynecological history. While Chanel talked, Ruby carried on unpacking blankets. "So anyway, they removed the fibroids in '98. All the women in my family 'ave fibroids. Goes back four generations apparently. Then they checked me for polycystic ovaries. Now, apparently, you get 'airy with polycystic ovaries. So, my Craig—who admittedly was under a great deal of stress at the time—turns to this doctor and says, 'Excuse me, mate, are you accusing my wife of 'aving excess facial hair, because if you are, you'd better step outside.' 'E can be so sweet, my Craig."

Sam listened intently, asked questions and seemed to take a genuine interest in Chanel's problems.

"The upshot is they can't find nothing wrong with me. By rights I should 'ave no problems falling pregnant a second time, but there you go…"

Sam nodded slowly and offered Chanel a sympathetic smile. Ruby could tell from her expression that she was positively glowing. She wondered how many of the doctors Chanel had seen over the years had actually taken the trouble to offer her some comfort and warmth. "I'm really sorry," he said. "I do understand what you're going through. I also know what it's like to want answers and not get them. The point is that medicine has come a long way, but it doesn't know everything. What you need is support right now. Some counseling might be a good idea. I could recommend somebody."

Chanel thanked him and explained that she was already seeing a counselor. She seemed so moved by his kindness that Ruby thought she might be about to cry, but Chanel being Chanel, she wouldn't give in. "So, anyway," she said, managing a half-smile, "me and Craig are thinking about fostering. We thought we'd see 'ow we get on and then maybe think about adoption later on."

"You never mentioned fostering," Ruby said, flattening the cardboard box that had held the blankets. "I think it's a brilliant idea."

Eventually Sam said he should be getting back to the hospital. "I have a prenatal clinic in a half hour." He turned to Chanel. "Good luck with the fostering. I hope it works out." She smiled again and thanked him.

"OK," Ruby said to Sam. "See you Friday."

He put his arms round her waist and gave her a quick kiss and a squeeze. "I can't wait," he whispered into her ear. "And this time, I promise there won't be any interruptions."

RUBY WANTED EVERYTHING to be perfect for Friday. She booked an appointment at the überposh beauty salon round the corner, where she parted with over a hundred quid to have her brows and legs plucked and waxed and her skin exfoliated to the silky softness of an Hermès scarf.

Then, an hour or so before she was due to meet Sam, panic set in. She had just got out of the shower and was massaging moisturizer into damp skin, just like they told you to do in the mags, when the thought hit her.

Like most women, Ruby was insecure about her body. She thought her legs could do with being longer and slimmer. She was less than keen on her hair, which was so fine and wavy that every morning when she woke up, it looked to her as if a family of hamsters had been nesting in it. If hangups about the external parts of her body weren't bad enough, now she was starting to fret about her internal parts.

She wrapped herself in a towel and went into the living room. The phone was lying on the coffee table. She picked it up and dialed Fi's number.

"Fi, it's me. I think I'm suffering from vagina anxiety."

"What?" Fi giggled. "How d'you mean, vagina anxiety?"

"OK, Sam's a gynecologist, right?"

"Right."

"And he must have seen thousands of vaginas, right?"

"Right."

"So, what if..."

"Oh, I get it. You're thinking, suppose your vagina doesn't pass muster."

"Correct. I mean the vagina is practically the man's habitat. He must have seen some fairly amazing ones in his time."

Fi didn't say anything. "Forgive my ignorance, but what exactly constitutes an 'amazing' vagina? Apart from the obvious tightness factor, but since you've never given birth, you can't have any problems in that department."

Ruby made the point that it wasn't her vagina per se she was worried about, it was the look of the area in general. "I mean they must vary."

Fi said as far as she knew all vulvas looked like cross-sections of dried pear. Then she went into a long tale about how her friend Amy once went out with a bloke called Lawrence, a self-confessed chauvinist who liked to think of himself as a bit of a vulva connoisseur. "Poor Amy was so paranoid about having a substandard vagina that she used to spend hours squatting naked over a mirror. Look, Sam's a lovely, sensitive bloke who sees you as a whole person. He won't be anything like Lawrence of her labia."

Deep down, Ruby knew Fi was right about Sam, but it didn't stop her going hunting for a hand mirror. Of course it was nowhere to be found, and in the end, the only vaguely reflective surface she could find was the bottom of her Illy coffee tin.

She went into the bedroom and took off the towel. Anybody looking through the window just then would have seen a naked woman, legs akimbo, looking as if she were about to pleasure herself with a jumbo-size coffee container.

Of course, the metal tin wasn't remotely shiny enough and Ruby couldn't see more than a pinkish blur. She got dressed, still unsure about whether her vulva was quite top drawer.

As well as the hundred quid she'd spent at the beauty salon, she'd also gone to Selfridges and treated herself to a staggeringly expensive La Perla bra and panties set. The dusky cream lace bra had a deep plunge, which even if she did say so herself, made her breasts look rather magnificent.

She was in no doubt what she would wear on top. Her floaty, minty green gypsy dress with the short puffed sleeves would be perfect. She'd bought it from Whistles weeks ago and hadn't worn it, even though she'd been longing to.

Ruby always felt that one of the things that set her apart from the well-heeled women who shopped at Les Sprogs was their attitude toward clothes. Rich women found the idea of keeping an outfit "for best" completely alien. They bought clothes to wear. They didn't save them for special occasions. As a result they slobbed around the house in Gucci and went supermarket shopping in cream, dry-clean-only Prada and thought nothing of it. No matter how much money Ruby acquired, she knew she could never do that. She found it impossible to shake off the belief that expensive clothes, which might get stained or spoiled, were for keeping, not wearing. It was a class thing.

• • •

SAM'S FLAT WAS in one of those grand tree-lined avenues off Kensington High Street. He was renting it from an American friend who had bought it, only to have his company send him back to the States for a year.

He answered the door in jeans, a white T-shirt and bare feet. His hair was still damp from the shower and he smelled deliciously of shampoo and warm, clean skin. As he kissed her hello and told her how utterly stunning she looked, it was as much as she could do to not launch herself at him there and then.

Instead she remarked on the other glorious smell that was coming from the kitchen. "Puttanesca sauce," he said.

She said it was one of her favorites, which it was.

He led her into an enormous, high-ceilinged and oppressively cream living room. Her feet sank into the thick cream fitted carpet. She stood there taking in the cream feather-backed sofas and floor-length cream curtains with fancy tassels and draped pelmets edged in gold brocade. The walls were two-toned cream: oatmeal French silk wallpaper beneath the wooden dado rail, a lighter off-white above. Ruby looked up. "Wow, the chandelier's just like the one at the shop."

Sam rolled his eyes. "I know. Kristian, who owns this place, is heavily into crystal." He jerked his head toward a display cabinet. It was full of tiny crystal animals. "All Lalique, apparently," Sam said with a grimace. "But I have added some touches of my own."

He pointed to one of the alcoves next to the grand cream marble fireplace.

It contained a jukebox that looked as if it had come straight from a fifties coffee shop. In the other alcove was the largest plasma-screen TV she had ever seen, and at the far end of the room, in the bay window, was a miniature snooker table. In the center of the table stood a plaster bust of Joseph Stalin, to which Sam had added a baseball cap and a pair of Ray-Ban aviators. "I love it," Ruby giggled.

She sat down on the sofa next to a giant, shaggy-haired ginger tomcat.

"I'm not quite sure how to break this to you," Ruby said, "but he isn't cream."

Sam laughed. "That's because he's a stray. He came in one morning. I made the mistake of feeding him and he hasn't left. Meet Cat Damon."

As if on cue, Cat Damon half opened a lazy eye and closed it again. Ruby began stroking the animal's head. "Great name," she said. "I guess this place is sort of Joey and Chandler meet Liberace." She gave him a sexy look. "Although I think it's pretty clear you're not Liberace."

"Er, no. That would be Kristian," Sam said. He was standing by the mahogany dining table pouring champagne. "He's the one who curls his eyelashes and keeps a note of the first day of the Kenzo sale in his diary."

She went over to the jukebox. As she stood admiring the fake walnut and chrome cabinet, he handed her a glass of champagne. "Cheers," he said. She tipped the glass and felt the bubbles tickle her nose.

"The guy upstairs was moving and he didn't have room for it in his new place, so I made him an offer."

"It's beautiful," she said, running her fingers down the song list.

There was a pile of old sixpences on the table. He picked one up. "What would you like to hear?"

She sipped some more champagne and carried on looking at the song selection. "Hmm . . . I think it has to be 'Are You Lonesome Tonight?' "

"Good choice." He dropped a coin into the slot. Then he took her champagne glass from her and placed both glasses on the dining table. As the music started up, he pulled her toward him. She rested her head on his shoulder and they swayed gently in time to the music. As she breathed in his smell again, her head started to spin. At one point she lifted her face to look at him. His face seemed to be waiting for her, smiling, ready to kiss her. First his lips went to her forehead, then to her cheeks. Finally they found her mouth. She parted her lips, felt his tongue probing hers. He tasted of champagne.

She pushed her hips forward against Sam's erection. He responded by running his tongue down her neck and shoulders. She closed her eyes and let her head roll back. Her legs were about to give way under her. Sensing this he said, "C'mon." He took her hand and led her first to the kitchen, where he quickly turned out the flame under the puttanesca sauce, and then on into a cream bedroom. It was lit by three giant and exceedingly ornate gold candelabra. Tacky as Kristian's taste was, she had to admit the effect of the soft, flickering light was intoxicating. She kicked off her shoes and felt the soft deep pile of the carpet under her bare feet.

Sam's lips were on her mouth, her neck, her shoulders, the tops of her breasts. By now her heart was racing, her breath coming in shallow gasps. She felt his hand move up inside her skirt and he began stroking the inside of her thigh. Moisture was seeping from her. The next second he had pushed the crotch of her panties to one side and was pushing his fingers deep inside her. She parted her legs, laid her head on his chest and let out a deep, almost feral moan.

"Come onto the bed," he whispered.

The next thing she knew her head was sinking into a pile of soft pillows and he was lifting her dress up over her hips. As he went to pull off her panties, she felt a stab of vagina anxiety-induced panic.

"Sam?"

"What is it?"

"You see, the thing is—I was wondering what with you being a gynecologist and everything..." But he had already removed her panties and her voice trailed off. Her stomach quivered as he began kissing her belly and moved slowly south. Finally he began opening her legs. She made a feeble attempt to close them, but it was useless.

As his fingers teased her labia, the sensation was so sublime that she let out a tiny whimper. Gently he opened her. She opened her eyes and watched him gazing down at her.

"You are so beautiful," he said.

"Really?"

"Oh, yeah." He looked up at her. "You were about to ask me something just now. What was it?"

"Oh, it was nothing. Absolutely nothing."

His head was between her legs now. A second later she felt his tongue trail over her vulva and begin flicking her clitoris. She heard herself making more soft whimpering noises. As his tongue probed and teased, probed and teased, she felt the familiar unstoppable wave start to build inside her.

Afterward, he rested his head on her belly and she ran her fingers through his hair. Finally he moved himself up the bed so that he was lying next to her. She put her hand to his crotch. His erection was still straining under his jeans. She traced its outline with her finger. "I want you," he said. He sat up and she pulled off his T-shirt. His body was muscular and still tanned from the summer. A thick column of dark hair began at his navel and disappeared under his jeans belt. She undid the buckle and began unzipping his fly. The tip of his penis rose above the waistband of his boxers. She pulled them down, releasing his thick erection. A tiny seed of semen glistened at the tip. She wiped it away with her finger and, kneeling next to him, took him in her mouth. He reached out for her buttocks, ran his fingers between them and found her vulva.

She could feel he was about to come, when he pulled away.

"Move onto your knees," he said, almost commanding her. He reached for the pillows and placed them underneath her.

She gasped as, without warning, he reached inside her and spread her juices over her vulva. "Your clitoris is so hard," he said. "Like a little pea." He carried on teasing it, taking his time to build her toward orgasm. Then just as she was about to come for a second time, he pushed hard and deep inside her so that she cried out. He carried on thrusting, but not for a second did he take his hand away from her clitoris. She was finding it harder to come again so quickly after her last orgasm. He seemed to sense this.

"It's OK, there's no hurry," he whispered. "We have all the time in the world. Just let yourself float away."

She did just that. She closed her eyes and let the sensation she was feeling between her legs fill her entire being until, in a strange almost Zen way that she had never experienced before, she became it.

"There you go," she heard him whisper. "There you go." His fingers were gliding faster and faster on her clitoris. At the same time his thrusts became more rapid and deep. Finally they slowed and she felt one final movement inside her. "Come on, you can do it," he said. "You can do it." A few seconds later the tiny contractions started to build inside her.

They fell back onto the bed in a sweaty breathless heap.

"Oh, my God," she said into the pillow, "that was amazing."

He ran his hand over her bottom. "Glad to be of cervix," he said.

They made love three more times that night.

The next morning they sat in bed eating Pop-Tarts and

drinking coffee with Cat Damon curled up asleep at their feet.

"You know, you have the cutest morning hair," he said.

"Cute?" she said, running her fingers self-consciously through her hair. "Please. Most mornings I look like the progeny of Einstein and Phyllis Diller."

"Well, I think it's pretty," he said.

She wasn't sure if he was just being gallant, but she thanked him anyway.

"God, I've just remembered," she said. "We never had the spaghetti puttanesca sauce."

He said that when he got up in the night to pee, he put it in the freezer. "We'll have it another time."

She said she would look forward to it. "You know," she said, biting into her second Pop-Tart, "I cannot believe that I am dating a Jewish doctor." She sat chewing. "Here I am, the perfect Jewish daughter. The irony is that if I told my trendy, liberated Jewish mother, she wouldn't be impressed."

"That suits me fine," he said, laughing. "Have you any idea what it's like back home, being treated as a demigod by the members of Irene's mah-jongg group?"

She was laughing now. "Oh, come on. Be honest, you love it really."

"OK, maybe just a bit. Some of those seventy-something women are really hot."

She looked at the bedside clock and let out a long breath. "You know, I really do have to go home and get ready for work."

He took her plate and mug of coffee from her and put them down on the floor. Then he pulled her on top of him. "C'mon, just five more minutes."

"I'll be late," she giggled.

"No you won't." He was sucking her nipple. Just then

Sam's phone rang. "Christ, what now? Ruby, I have to get it in case it's the hospital."

"Sure."

He reached out for the phone. In a second his face had darkened exactly as it had when the hospital had called last time. He covered the mouthpiece to tell Ruby he wouldn't be long. Then he got out of bed and went into the hall to continue the call. She couldn't hear what was said, but he sounded tense. As he came back into the room she caught him telling whoever was on the end of the line to "hang on in there."

"Hospital?" she said.

"Er... yeah." He seemed lost in thought.

"You don't seem too sure."

"Sorry, I was miles away. I need to get to the hospital."

"That's OK. I understand. Look, I have to get a move on anyway."

"OK," he said. Then something seemed to jolt him back into the present and he pushed her back down onto the bed and kissed her very thoroughly, one last time.

Chapter 13

Six weeks later, Sam told Ruby he had fallen in love with her. It was a crisp, bright Sunday afternoon in November and they had been for a stroll in Kew Gardens. Afterward they decided to have tea at the Original Maids of Honour, a tea shop across the road.

"This place looks like something straight out of the 1940s," Sam said, eyeing the tired decor and dark wood fittings.

"Doesn't it?" Ruby agreed. She said that whenever she came here, she expected to see women wearing the "New Look" sipping tea at the next table.

These days, Ruby saw Sam two or three times a week. On her weekends off—when Annie the student helper filled in for her at the shop—she stayed with him at his flat.

Saturdays tended to be spent mostly in bed. In between making love, they would catch up with the week's papers, set the world to rights and eat fish-stick-and-brown-sauce sandwiches while watching execrable made-for-TV films. In the evening they would go out for dinner and then catch a movie.

On Sundays they forced themselves out of bed around two and usually went for a long walk by the river at Richmond.

Today they had swapped Richmond for Kew.

As Ruby poured Earl Grey from a pretty bone china teapot, she explained to Sam that Maids of Honour were tiny custard tarts originally made for Henry VIII. "Apparently he loved them so much that he had the chef who invented them imprisoned so that he couldn't pass on the recipe."

"He imprisoned somebody? Over a cake recipe? Even by ole 'Enry's standards, that sucks."

She giggled at his attempt at a Cockney accent and told him he sounded like Dick Van Dyke in *Mary Poppins,* but she was forced to agree with him about Henry. Imprisoning the poor chap did seem to rather suck. At this point she bit into her own Maid of Honour and custard burst out and oozed over her mouth. Sam reached across and wiped it away with his napkin. "I do love you," he laughed.

"Love you, too," she said.

Light as the exchange had been, it silenced them. Something more than banter had just passed between them and they both knew it. For a few seconds they sat looking at each other across the table. "When I say I love you," Sam said gently, reaching out and taking her hand, "I mean I'm in love with you."

"I'm in love with you, too," she said simply. "I think I knew it that first time you kissed me on Brighton pier."

"Really?"

"Really."

"With me it was when you got so confused that time at Connor's circumcision."

"You're kidding. But I know I sounded like some wittering bag lady."

"You did. But haven't I ever told you I've always had this thing for wittering old bag ladies?"

She laughed. "You know, when I'm with you, it just feels so natural."

"Same here." His face broke into a smile and he leaned forward to kiss her. "You taste of custard," he said. He stirred sugar into his tea. "I've been thinking. I'm due to go back to the States in a couple of months, right?"

Ruby hated it whenever he talked about going home. She knew she was about to be forced into another long-distance relationship, the way she had been with Matt. She was scared of history repeating itself.

She looked up at him, an almost plaintive look on her face. "Sam, do we have to talk about this now? It's been such a lovely weekend. We've just said we love each other and I don't want to spoil it."

"I'm not going to spoil it. The doctor I swapped places with on the exchange scheme isn't coming back. Apparently he's accepted a job in the Middle East. St. Luke's has offered me his job. It's only a year's contract but..."

"You'll take it, right?"

"I already said yes—if that's OK with you?"

Her entire face lit up. "OK? How could you possibly think it wouldn't be OK? Sam, this is brilliant. Totally, utterly and completely brilliant."

"I really want to be with you," he said.

"And I really want to be with you, too."

RUBY WAS AWARE that as well as being lovers she and Sam had become best friends. There was almost nothing she couldn't tell him. She had never felt so comfortable or relaxed in a relationship. When she'd been with Matt, all they'd ever talked about was their jobs. Work was what bound them together. She wouldn't say she and Sam never talked shop, but it didn't dominate the conversation the way it had with Matt.

The only downside to their relationship was the

inevitable phone calls from the hospital. Sometimes they would be in the middle of making love and the phone would ring. "Sorry, gotta go," he would say, leaping out of bed and pulling on his jeans. "One of my patients is about to push out a baby."

Then there were the other calls—the ones that always upset him—like the call he'd got that day in Brighton and later on back at his flat. When one of those calls came, he would always excuse himself and disappear to take it in private. Afterward he seemed distressed and distracted. "Bad news from the hospital?" she would say. He would gaze into the middle distance and mutter something in the affirmative. He never seemed to want to discuss it. Sometimes it would take him hours to recover. She always assumed there had been some catastrophe, like the death of a baby.

Time and again she had tried to encourage him to talk about what had happened. "I really worry about you bottling up your emotions like this," she said after he'd received one particularly distressing call. "I know I'm beginning to sound like my mother, but it isn't healthy."

He shrugged and offered her a weak smile. "It's the way I deal with bad news. I know it's asking a lot, but can you put up with me when I'm like that?"

"Of course I can. It's you I worry about. Not me." This wasn't quite true. When he received bad news, she did find his inability to communicate frustrating. She coped by convincing herself that Sam still carried the emotional scars from his parents' deaths. That was why other people's tragedy had such an effect on him. She had no doubt, though, that this would change with time.

The other subject Sam seemed reluctant to talk about was his brother. Ruby still had no idea what he had meant when he said Josh went "off the rails." She assumed that whatever had happened to his brother had compounded the grief Sam was already feeling about his parents and that was why he found it hard to discuss. Again, she decided he would open up with time.

AFTER TEA THEY walked into Kew Village and Sam bought her scented yellow freesias, which were her favorite flowers.

"You know what?" he said. "I think maybe it's time you introduced me to your mom and dad. They're such a big part of your life and I've never met them. It feels like there's a part of you I don't know."

"You're right," she said, inhaling the sweet scent of the freesias. "I think it is time you met them."

It was beginning to get dark, so they decided to head back to the car.

They couldn't have taken more than a dozen steps before Sam slowed to a stop. A woman was coming toward them. She had clearly seen Sam and was waving.

"Hey, Kim," Sam called out. His tone was friendly enough, but he seemed startled rather than pleasantly surprised to be bumping into her. A moment later they were exchanging double kisses. The woman was tiny with short dark hair and a wide-eyed gamine face. She looked vulnerable, Ruby thought, almost frail. Or maybe it was just her slight build that made her seem that way.

"You're a long way from Highgate," Sam went on. "What are you doing in these parts?"

"A friend of a friend is having a kids' birthday party." American accent. "She invited Todd and Amy. I've just been for a walk by the river and now I'm on my way to pick them up."

"You went to the river? Alone?" He was clearly alarmed by this. Ruby was confused. Kim wasn't a child. Why on earth was he so bothered about her taking a stroll by the river on a Sunday afternoon?

"Sometimes I just have to get out," she came back, her voice heavy with meaning.

Sam's expression softened. "I know you do." Suddenly he remembered Ruby. "This is Kimberley," he said, brightening. "She's a very, very old friend. She's over here with her two children."

"Oh, how long for?" Ruby said, shaking Kimberley's hand.

"I'm not too sure," she said. She cast Sam an anxious look, which Ruby picked up on.

Kimberley. Kimberley. Why did the name ring a bell? Then she had it. The night when she was in Sam's car with Buddy and Irene, Irene had asked after a Kimberley.

"So, Kim, how are you?" Sam said gently, the troubled look returning to his face.

Kimberley smiled a weak, careworn smile. "Yeah, I'm good. Things seem to have calmed down a little. Look, I really ought to be going. Todd and Amy will be wondering where I am. Nice to have met you, Ruby." She cast another meaningful glance at Sam. "See ya, Sam."

"See ya. And you take care." He gave her a hug and kissed her on both cheeks.

"I will."

"That all seemed a bit tense," Ruby whispered as they walked away.

"I know. I'm sorry."

She slipped her arm through his. "Look, if Kimberley is an old girlfriend, that's OK. You don't have to be embarrassed. Just so long as she isn't a new girlfriend, that's all." She didn't believe for one minute that Sam was cheating on her with Kimberley. There had definitely been a tension between them, but it hadn't seemed in the remotest bit sexual.

He gave a small laugh. "Kim and I have never dated. We go way back. Her mother is friends with Irene. And she's married."

"So, she's over here with her husband?"

"No, he's back in the States. The marriage hit a pretty rough patch recently and she decided to come over here for a few months to get her head straight and visit family. She's been through a lot and I've been very worried about her. She recently started having panic attacks. That's why I worry about her going out alone."

"I'm sorry she's having a rough time. She seemed nice."

"She is. Kim's great."

They carried on walking.

"I'm glad you're going to meet my mum and dad," Ruby said eventually. "You're right, they are a big part of my life. But there's a big part of you I don't know anything about."

"Surely not," he said, grinning. "You know all my big parts."

She whacked him playfully on the shoulder. "I'm serious. I mean your brother. You never talk about him. You're not in touch. What happened?"

Sam flinched. "I'll tell you what happened: drugs. Heroin, to be precise. Josh got into it big time. Had to drop out of law school. He was studying at Yale . . ."

"That is so sad. What a terrible waste."

She could see by his expression that he was distressed and she didn't want to make him feel worse by asking more questions. "You know, Sam," she said, "whenever you feel like really talking, I'm always here."

"I know. Thanks. That means a lot to me." With that he bent down to kiss her.

By now they had reached Sam's car. They decided to drive home through Richmond Park. It was almost four and getting dark, but Ruby thought they might just be able to slip in before the park gates shut. When they reached the entrance, the park police had just arrived. Any moment now, they would start directing traffic away from the gates and back onto the main road. Sam managed to get through, along with another car. These days, the speed limit in the park was down to twenty. Everybody found it irritatingly slow. Some drivers got so frustrated that they passed on the narrow road. Almost every time she drove through the park, Ruby saw cars passing. Some barely escaped colliding with the oncoming traffic. Those who didn't pass kept to just under thirty, hoping they wouldn't get caught by a speed trap.

They had been driving for less than a minute—Sam doing about twenty-five—when another vehicle, a monster-sized four-wheel-drive, drew level with them on the wrong side of the road. Ruby heard Sam mutter something under his breath as he slowed to let the vehicle pass. But the black Porsche Cayenne—which Ruby couldn't help thinking would surely have become the modern Gestapo staff car of choice—refused to pass. Each time Sam eased off the gas, it slowed down to match his speed. "What's going on?" Ruby said, looking at the Porsche, which towered above Sam's Audi.

"Just some jerk's idea of a joke."

She could just make out the driver. He was huge and apelike. Sitting behind the wheel he looked like a gorilla driving a toy car. He was also grinning at Sam.

"Why's he smiling?" Ruby said. "Does he know you?"

"I've never seen him before in my life."

"I don't like this," Ruby said with a shiver. "I'm starting to feel really threatened."

"Calm down. He's just some asshole getting his kicks. He's looking for a reaction. If we ignore him and do nothing, he'll get bored."

But a full minute went by and the Porsche didn't pass. The driver was still turning his head every few seconds to grin at Sam. Ruby could see Sam was starting to get rattled because his jaw muscle kept tightening. Then, suddenly, with no warning the monster vehicle swerved violently toward the side of Sam's car.

"Shit, he's trying to hit us," Sam cried, pulling down hard on the wheel to avoid a collision.

"Right," she said, reaching for her mobile.

"What are you doing?"

"What do you think?" Her voice was shrill, verging on the hysterical. "I'm phoning the police. This guy is a nutter. He could kill us."

Then, just as they were approaching Roehampton Gate, the Porsche overtook them, sped out of the park and disappeared. "Bugger," Ruby said, "I didn't get his license number, did you?"

"No, he was going too fast."

She put down her phone. There seemed little point in calling the police now. Sam asked her if she was OK.

"Yes. A bit shaken, that's all. I can't believe that bastard got away with doing something so evil. Look, maybe we should phone the police. He might be known to them."

"No," Sam snapped. "Leave it."

"But why? Why are you so anxious to let it go? We could have been killed back there."

"You're right, but I know how these things work. You spend hours making a statement to the police and then nothing happens. There's no point—particularly when we didn't get his number."

But she refused to let it drop. The moment they got back she phoned the local police station. The duty officer immediately asked if she'd got the car's license number. When she said she hadn't, the officer said there really wasn't much they could do.

"What did I tell you?" Sam said when she got off the phone.

"You seem almost relieved they didn't want to know," she said.

"Relieved? Why would I be relieved?"

The next day, feeling a good deal calmer after a night's sleep, Ruby phoned her mother to tell her that there was a new man in her life. She decided not to mention what had happened in Richmond Park, as it would only scare the living daylights out of her and cause her blood pressure to shoot up.

"Oh, darling, this is wonderful news," Ronnie said. "We haven't seen much of you lately. I guessed you were seeing somebody. Why don't you bring him for dinner on Saturday? No, scrub that. Dad and I are busy on Saturday. Our local branch of the National Childbirth Trust is having a Protect Your Perineum wine and sushi evening. How's about Sunday?"

"Great." She decided not to ask what happened at a Protect Your Perineum evening, as she was sure the answer would only make her feel queasy.

"So, Sam's a doctor, you say?" Ronnie was doing her best to sound relaxed about this fact and failing miserably.

"Yes. Actually he's a gynecologist at St. Luke's."

"Reee-ally? And he's Jewish?"

"Uh-huh. But he's not religious. I mean he's not so much Jewish as Jew-*ish*."

"I see. And is he good looking, this Jew-*ish* doctor of yours?"

"Very."

"And it's serious between the two of you?"

"Oh, yes."

"Wow. So, my beautiful, successful daughter is in love with a handsome Jewish doctor."

"And my trendy, liberated mother is suddenly sounding like Golde in *Fiddler on the Roof*."

"I'm sorry, darling, but I can't help it. I'm beginning to think that there is a whole part of my personality that I may have been repressing for years. Suddenly I seem to be getting in touch with my inner yenta."

Ruby swallowed hard. "Mum, please tell me you're kidding."

Ronnie burst out laughing. "Of course I'm kidding. Me, a yenta? As if. Look, I have to ring off. I want to phone Aunty Sylvia and then there's your grandmother in Marbella. Oooh, and your father's cousins in Montreal."

ON THE GROUNDS that Aunty Sylvia was so in touch with her inner yenta that she would burst into "Sunrise, Sunset" the moment she met Sam, Ruby suggested to Ronnie that it might be best if she wasn't invited to dinner on Sunday. Ronnie immediately took the point and agreed. In the end, though, she was forced to invite her. Apparently Aunty Sylvia had phoned Ronnie in tears on the Saturday to say she thought that Nigel was seeing another woman. She was in such a state that Ronnie felt she had no option but to invite her to dinner in an effort to cheer her up. "She won't say anything to embarrass you," Ronnie assured Ruby. "She's far too miserable."

Food-wise, Ronnie went to a great deal of effort and produced a magnificent chicken-and-mushroom risotto. Phil had bought half a dozen bottles of wine, and judging by the labels, he had spent a fortune.

Having spent ages on her feet, stirring risotto, Ronnie also managed to look particularly stunning. For once she had dispensed with her hippie, boho look and had opted for something more elegant. She was wearing a long, coffee-colored Ghost shirt over matching wide trousers. Aunty Sylvia kept telling her how fabulous she looked. So did Phil, who could barely take his eyes off her. Several times during dinner he placed a tender hand on hers and asked her if she was feeling all right.

"Doesn't it give you a kick seeing your parents so much in love after all these years?" Sam whispered to Ruby at one point. Ruby had to admit that it did.

For the first half of the evening, Aunty Sylvia's mood was pretty subdued, and as a result—just as Ronnie had predicted—her behavior toward Sam was impeccable. There was no gushing, no cheek pinching, not a whisper about wedding caterers.

Then, after she downed two glasses of merlot before the main course, glimpses of her normal self began to appear. As they all sat down to dinner she grabbed a handful of Sam's cheek and mouthed to Ruby that he was "gorgeous." Ruby colored up on Sam's behalf, but he seemed to take the cheek pinching in his stride. It probably reminded him of being with Irene's mah-jongg cronies, she decided.

"So, you're into all this natural childbirth then, Sam?" Aunty Sylvia said, tucking into her risotto: "You know, in my mother's day, natural childbirth just meant taking your makeup off." Clearly encouraged by his laughter, she carried on. "Mum was always saying how she was in labor for seventy-two hours with me. Seventy-two hours of agony. I couldn't imagine doing something I *enjoyed* for that long."

"So, Sam," Ronnie said, shooting Aunty Sylvia a sour look to indicate she was lowering the tone of the evening, "they say that the episiotomy rates at St. Luke's are the lowest in the country."

"Apparently so," Sam said. "It's really good for the hospital's reputation."

Aunty Sylvia put down her knife and fork and grimaced. "Ronnie, please, we're trying to eat."

"Oh, by the way," Ronnie continued, ignoring her sister, "after dinner I must show you all my belly cast."

Aunty Sylvia gave an incredulous blink. "Come again?"

"I've made a plaster cast of my bump."

"Now I've heard everything," Aunty Sylvia said, shaking her head.

"I felt I should pay homage to the way my body has changed to grow this baby."

"In other words, you wanted a souvenir," Aunty Sylvia said.

"It's much more than just a souvenir," Ronnie came back, clearly rattled.

Phil seemed to sense that the atmosphere between the two women was heating up. He steered the conversation toward Sam. "So, Sam, what are you driving while you're over here?"

Sam said he had use of Kristian's Audi, which had come with the flat.

"Oh, which model?"

"The V8."

"Lovely car. So is it the 3.7 liter or the 4.2?"

He had to think. "Er . . . the 4.2."

"And how are you finding the five-speed automatic? I don't know about you, but this Tiptronic technology just fascinates me."

"I can't say that I know much about it—"

"Me neither," a clearly bored Aunty Sylvia broke in. "You know, Sam, I need to pick your brains. I've had this brilliant idea for a TV health show."

Panic shot across Ronnie's face. "Sylvia, I'm not sure Sam wants to hear about . . ."

"Sure, I do," Sam said, brightly—clearly trying to avoid a lengthy treatise on Tiptronics. He turned back to Aunty Sylvia. "Please, go ahead."

"Well," she said, "it's a quiz show. I've called it *Name That Specialist.*"

"Oh... kay..."

"It works like this," she went on. "You have two families of hypochondriacs competing to identify a doctor from descriptions offered by the quizmaster."

"Uh-huh."

Ruby squeezed Sam's knee under the table to let him know how much she appreciated him humoring Aunty Sylvia like this.

"It works like this." Aunty Sylvia was warming to her theme now. "Imagine I'm the quizmaster, speaking to the panel."

"Right," Sam said.

"Gawd," Ronnie groaned, running her hand over her forehead.

Aunty Sylvia cleared her throat and sat up straight. "OK, everybody, fingers on buzzers. This doctor has consulting rooms in Harley Street and St. John's Wood. His specialty is gastroenterology. He is considered to be the top man in his field and is famous for his catchphrase: *I think we should try you on a proton pump inhibitor.* Name that specialist!" Aunty Sylvia started to cackle at her own brilliance. "Is that great TV or is that great TV?"

"Well..." Sam paused, clearly searching for a diplomatic response. "I think it's got, er... definite possibilities."

"Did you hear that?" Aunty Sylvia said, shooting Ronnie a look of disdain. "Sam said it has possibilities."

At this point Phil suggested that Sam might like to come upstairs and see the wireless camera he had fitted in the baby's nursery. "It's going to be fantastic for keeping an eye on the baby."

Ronnie gave an amused shake of her head and turned to Ruby. "As ever, your father's got his priorities sorted. We've got no furniture for the nursery, no carpet down, but we have a CCTV camera installed."

The two men disappeared upstairs. "My little Ruby with a handsome Jewish doctor," Aunty Sylvia squealed. This time it was Ruby's cheek she pinched. "Who would have thought?"

"Thanks, Aunty Sylvia. I'll take that as a compliment." Rubbing her cheek, she turned to her mother. "So, Mum, you haven't said what you think of Sam."

"Oh, darling, he's lovely. He's intelligent, charming, funny, and watching the two of you together, I can see there's a real emotional fit."

Aunty Sylvia took another glug of merlot. "And I bet you anything he doesn't half know his way around in the bedroom department." She laughed a dirty laugh. "He could invite me up to see his speculum collection any day of the week."

"Sylvia, please," Ronnie said. "Do you have to bring everything down to such a base level?"

"So, Aunty Sylvia," Ruby broke in, "Mum says things haven't been so good between you and Nigel."

"That's right. And before you say anything, it's got nothing to do with me being older than him. I haven't mentioned it yet. I still haven't been able to find the right time. This is something else. Lately, he just seems so remote, so distant, somehow. I keep asking him if he's got something on his mind, something he wants to tell me, but he says there's nothing and that he's just stressed at work."

"What makes you think he isn't?" Ronnie said.

"Just a feeling," Aunty Sylvia shrugged. "This isn't about work. I know it."

"OK, but it might not be an affair," Ronnie persisted. "The two of you really need to sit down and talk."

"I know. But a part of me doesn't want to hear the

answer. I know Nigel's not perfect. I know he comes across as a bit dull and he's not a project like all the other men I've been out with, but I've realized that I really do love him. If he's found somebody else, I don't know what I'd do." Her eyes began to fill with tears. She sniffed and wiped them away with a tissue. "So, Ruby, does Sam make you happy?"

Ruby nodded. "You have no idea."

"I'm glad, darling," Aunty Sylvia said, squeezing Ruby's hand.

"Of course, what worries me," Ronnie said to Ruby, "is that he comes with so much baggage. You know, losing his parents the way he did. I can't help wondering if he has dealt with his grief. I hate the idea of you doing what your Aunty Sylvia does and becoming his therapist."

"There's no danger of that. Honestly, Sam's pretty together, bearing in mind everything he's been through. But please don't bring it up. Don't start trying to analyze him. I know what you're like."

"Sweetie, as if I would. I wouldn't dream of embarrassing him like that."

At this point they heard Sam and Phil coming down the stairs. They didn't come straight back into the living room. Instead they hovered outside the door. "So," they heard Phil saying. "You don't think the pain is anything to worry about." Ruby exchanged a worried look with her mother, who didn't seem remotely troubled. Instead she gave an amused shake of her head. "What's going on?" Aunty Sylvia hissed. Ronnie told her to listen.

"I really don't think you should be alarmed," Sam was saying. "See your doctor by all means, but it's not uncommon for expectant fathers to experience sympathetic breast pain."

The three women clutched each other to stifle their giggles.

After dinner, they had coffee in the living room. Ronnie sat down on the sofa next to Sam. "So, Sam, tell me..." Panic shot through Ruby. Ronnie was going to do it. She was going to break her promise and start delving into Sam's psyche. Ruby cleared her throat noisily to get her mother's attention, but Ronnie ignored her and carried on. "Do you think Hillary will ever be president?"

THE FOLLOWING MORNING, just as Ruby arrived at the shop, the phone rang. It was Ivan to ask if it would be OK to come round to her flat that evening to lay the kitchen floor tiles.

"Absolutely," Ruby said excitedly. Once the tiles were laid, that was it—there was nothing left to do. Ivan had kept promising to finish the tiles, but every day there would be a phone call to say he was very sorry, but he had got called away to another job and could she just hang on a bit longer. Even though she had lost count of the splinters she had in her feet from walking on rough floorboards, she always said yes. She was so worried about his heart giving out and didn't want to complain or put pressure on him.

Having said that, over the last few weeks Ivan's health seemed much improved. He had finally been to see his doctor, who had put him on some new medication, which he said was making him far less breathless.

"OK, Ivan, bye," she said. "Catch you later."

As soon as she put the phone down there was a tap at the door. It was a deliveryman. Next to him were two giant cardboard boxes. She knew what they contained: baby clothes from Guatemala. She signed for them and dragged the heavy boxes across the floor into the middle of the shop.

Ruby had decided that the following month—in the run-up to Christmas—the shop would hold a "Guatemalan

Week." Since the Guatemalan baby clothes and accessories sold so well during the rest of the year, she was buying extra stock, including toys, crib mobiles and even Christmas decorations. The idea was to give the profits to a charity that rescued street children in Guatemala City.

"Please tell me you've cleared this plan with the Nazi in nylons," Chanel said as she took her coat off a few minutes later. Ruby didn't say anything. She simply carried on unpacking baby clothes. "Oooh, just look at this," she squealed, holding up an exquisite multicolored romper suit. "Isn't it fabulous?"

"You 'aven't told 'er, 'ave you?" Chanel persisted.

Again, Ruby didn't reply.

"You 'aven't, 'ave you?"

Ruby took a deep breath. "OK, not as such." She'd kept meaning to phone Stella to bounce the idea of the Guatemalan week off her, but since Stella wasn't exactly one of life's philanthropists and Ruby knew exactly what her reaction would be, she'd decided to keep quiet.

"Gawd, she is going to go mental when she finds out."

"She won't find out if nobody tells her."

"Duh. Ruby to earth, come in, Ruby. Stella does look at the accounts, you know. She'll see exactly what's gone on behind her back."

"I know. You don't have to tell me. It's just that it's coming up to Christmas. The shop's made a huge profit this year. We can easily afford to give some of it away and I don't want Stella putting her foot down."

"I know, but you've gotta phone 'er. You've got no choice."

"I will, but I've got to think up some way of selling her the idea. Maybe we should get some celeb involved. That way we get press coverage and loads of PR for the shop."

"Sounds good to me."

Chanel had to leave early that afternoon because she and Craig had an appointment with their social worker. They were going to find out if their application to foster a child had been approved.

"Good luck," Ruby said, giving Chanel a hug before she left. "Not that you'll need it. You and Craig are going to make wonderful foster parents."

Since the shop was quiet, Ruby decided to phone Stella in New York. She couldn't put it off any longer. As the phone rang, Ruby rehearsed what she was going to say. She would go on about how giving to charity was good for the company image. Then she would tell a white lie and say she had a list of celebs willing to launch Guatemalan week. Surely that would work. After half a dozen rings or so, Stella's voice mail kicked in.

The message was typically brusque and to the point. "I'm in the Maldives without my cell phone until mid-December. In the case of a life-or-death emergency you can call Chrissie, my PA, who knows how to reach me." Chrissie's number followed.

Ruby decided that since what she wanted to discuss didn't begin to qualify as a dire life-or-death emergency, she would go ahead with Guatemalan week in the hope that once Stella knew that she had persuaded a celebrity to launch the event and achieved some excellent publicity for the company, she wouldn't be too put out.

She had just put the phone down when the shop door opened. A young woman—she couldn't have been more than twenty—was struggling to get in with a stroller. Ruby ran over to hold the door for her.

"Thanks." She smiled. Ruby couldn't help noticing the girl's appearance. Her long dark hair was hanging flat and greasy round her face. She looked thin, pale and exhausted. She wasn't badly dressed—in fact she looked pretty trendy, but her jeans, coat and handbag were clearly chain-store bought rather than designer. Her scuffed boots clearly hadn't been bought new this season. She was by no means the usual Les Sprogs customer.

"Is it OK if I look round?" Although she was well spoken, she seemed tense and ill at ease with her surroundings—as if she knew she didn't quite belong.

"Of course. Just ask if you need any help." Ruby bent down to look at the baby in the stroller.

"Just got him off," the girl smiled. "He's been howling all afternoon. Plus I was up with him all night. I really don't know what's got into him."

Ruby looked at the sleeping infant. He had a mop of bright ginger hair. "Wow, look at all that hair. It's gorgeous."

The girl smiled. "I know. The only problem is that everybody calls him Ginger Nut or Carrot Top. I wish they wouldn't. His name is Alfie."

"Hello, Alfie," Ruby whispered, stroking his tiny hand. The baby responded by making little chewing motions in his sleep, but didn't wake. Ruby suggested she leave the stroller by the counter. "I'll keep an eye on Alfie while you have a browse."

Ruby watched the girl as she wandered round the shop, tentatively picking things up. At one point she picked up a pair of Baby Gucci dungarees, looked twice at the price tag, because she clearly hadn't taken it in the first time, and quickly put them down again. She clearly couldn't afford anything and seemed to be thinking she was committing some kind of social trespass. Then she started to gather her confidence. Still ignoring the Gucci range, she picked up a fur-lined jacket with a hood, three or four T-shirts and several sleep suits. Ruby did a quick sum in her head. The girl was holding at least £300 worth of stock. When she'd chosen everything she wanted, she came over to the counter and put the clothes down next to the till. "And I'd like to look at your strollers please."

"Sure," Ruby said. "They're over here." She led the way toward the display of prams and buggies.

The girl explained that she needed a triple buggy.

"A triple? Wow." Ruby wanted to say she didn't look old enough to have one child, let alone three, but she kept her thoughts to herself. It was none of her business.

"It's a long story." The girl smiled. "I have two-year-old twin girls as well. They're at home with my mum."

"Goodness, talk about having your hands full," Ruby said.

"Tell me about it."

There were three triple buggies to choose from. The girl chose the most expensive. It was just over £800. Ruby explained that the only one she had in stock was the display model and she would have to order another one. "It shouldn't take more than a couple of days."

The girl didn't seem bothered. "I'll pay now if that's OK."

The stroller plus the clothes came to nearly £1,200. The girl put her hand into her bag and pulled out a roll of notes. Ruby couldn't help blinking in surprise. The usual Les Sprogs customers might pay cash for a small item—a £10 furry animal, say—but when it came to larger amounts they generally produced a gold or platinum American Express card. Still, Ruby thought, it was none of her business why she was paying in cash. Money was money.

"You can come back for the stroller," Ruby said. "Or if you'd prefer, I can arrange for it to be delivered to you."

"I think I'd prefer to pick it up," the girl said as Ruby handed her a large Les Sprogs carrier bag full of clothes. Ruby took her name—Hannah Morgan—and phone number and said she would call her the moment the stroller came in.

Ruby helped her out with the buggy. As Hannah disappeared down the street, Ruby couldn't help wondering what her story was.

Chapter 14

Chanel came into work next morning bearing apricot Danish, two skinny cappuccinos and a double-shot grin. "Don't tell me," Ruby said, "social services has said yes."

"I can't believe it. The report said me and Craig would make ideal foster parents. Off the record our social worker told us that all being well, we should 'ave no trouble adopting in a year or so—if that's what we decide to do."

"That's fantastic," Ruby said, giving Chanel a hug. "Well done. I knew you'd do it."

"It's most likely we'll get a school-age kid, which means I can work school hours and you won't be left in the lurch."

"God, I can't tell you what a relief that is. I was dreading having to replace you. It just wouldn't be the same." They realized weekends and school holidays would be a problem, but had decided to leave sorting out arrangements until Chanel knew when her first foster child was arriving. She seemed to think it was highly unlikely anything would happen before Christmas. Since Christmas was obviously their busiest time of the year, this was even more of a relief to Ruby.

As they got ready to open the shop, Ruby told Chanel about trying to phone Stella. Chanel agreed it didn't make any sense trying to reach her while she was on holiday. "You know what she's like about her 'me time.' Isn't worth the aggro."

Around midmorning, Fi popped in to say hi. When Chanel told her about being accepted as a foster parent, Fi was genuinely delighted, but her smiles couldn't hide the tension in her face.

"Wassup?" Ruby said. "Connor still not sleeping?"

Fi shook her head. "It's not that. He's doing fine, bless him. He's been sleeping through the night for weeks now. No, it's money. We're flat broke." She explained that Saul had finished his *Hamlet* stint at the National and still didn't have another acting job lined up.

"He's going for two or three auditions a week and each time he's being given the bums. You know, with his looks he'd make a fabulous Old Testament hero. Shame nobody's thought about doing a remake of *The Ten Commandments*. Anyway, things are looking pretty bad. Even the singing jobs have dried up. Soon we'll be in arrears with the mortgage. I've got the bank and Barclaycard on my back every five minutes demanding money. Saul's talking about jacking it all in and taking up minicabbing."

"He absolutely mustn't do that," Ruby came back. "He's so talented. He's got a great singing voice. His luck will change. He just has to sit it out, that's all."

Chanel said if he was desperate, Craig had just fired his apprentice. "I'm sure Saul could do the job. It pays bugger all, but if it would help . . ."

"And I can always lend you a bit," Ruby said. "You only have to ask."

"You are both very kind and I really appreciate the offers, but if it comes to it, Saul will have to retrain and get a proper job and I'll have to go back to teaching. It's as simple as that."

Just then Fi's mobile rang. She looked at the caller display and let out a sigh. "It's my mum. I can't cope with her on top of everything else."

Ruby suggested she ignore the call, but Fi said she daren't in case Bridget was ill or there was some kind of emergency. She pressed "connect." "Hi, Mum, how are you?... An ingrown toenail? Oooh, poor old you. That can be really painful.... What? Hang on. You cannot possibly blame Saul being out of work for your ingrown toenail.... He will get another acting job. It just takes time. I know you're stressed about it. So am I.... Yes, I know Lindsay O'Connor from school has a stable, a four-car garage and a château in the Perigord.... Yes, I know she's done well for herself. She's also got what?... A giant plasma-screen TV?... Really? Well, good for her. It's called an STV? You sure? I've never heard of an STV. Wait a minute. I think you might find that's STD, which stands for sexually transmitted disease. Lindsay's famous for putting it about.... Mum? Mum?..." Fi shrugged and turned to Ruby and Chanel. "She's hung up."

The three of them burst out laughing.

"I've just had a thought," Ruby said as Fi was leaving. "When Chanel gets her first foster placement, I'm going to need some extra help in the shop. I've got Annie, our student who does the odd weekend, but maybe you could help out, too, and Saul could babysit."

Fi hugged her and said she would definitely think about it.

TWO DAYS LATER, Hannah Morgan came back to collect her triple buggy. She was still minus her twins and this time she was carrying Alfie in a baby sling.

"It's the girl I was telling you about," Ruby whispered to Chanel as the door opened. "The one with the wad of cash." Chanel, who was in the middle of wrapping a christening shawl for a customer, looked up. "Maybe she's a gangster's moll," she whispered back. Ruby dug her in the ribs and shushed her.

As Chanel's customer walked away with her carrier bag, Hannah reached the counter. But it was Alfie who grabbed Chanel's attention.

"Oh, what gorgeous hair," she gasped. "It's exactly the same color as my Craig's." While Ruby greeted Hannah, Chanel walked round to the other side of the counter and began cooing at Alfie, who was gurgling and blowing saliva bubbles. " 'Ello precious," she cooed, stroking his tiny chubby hand. "Aren't you a big boy? Yes, you are." She turned to Hannah and asked how old he was.

"Two months," she said.

"So that would make him a Virgo or a Libra."

"He's a Libra."

"Ooh, right little flirts they are when they grow up. I bet 'e's going to break a few 'earts."

Ruby couldn't help noticing Hannah's expression. She was smiling, but there was an emptiness in her eyes.

"I could eat you, little man, yes, I could," Chanel carried on. "Oh, I love them at this age. They're so perfect."

"He's still a bit small, though. He was eight weeks premature."

"Couldn't wait, eh?" Chanel said. "You silly sausage. I bet you didn't 'alf give your mum a fright coming into the world that early."

Ruby went to fetch Hannah's triple buggy from the storeroom. When she got back, Chanel was cradling Alfie and blowing raspberries on his cheek. When sick trickled down his chin, she produced a clean tissue from her trouser pocket and gently wiped it away. "That's better, isn't it? We don't want to send you home smelling of sick, do we?" She turned to Hannah. "Look, why doesn't Ruby show you 'ow to put up the buggy while I look after Alfie."

Hannah nodded. Chanel carried him across the shop and stopped next to a crib mobile. She turned the dial and it began to tinkle "Brahms Lullaby."

"THESE TRIPLE BUGGIES are real contraptions, I'm afraid," Ruby said, cutting away the plastic covering with scissors. "But I'm sure you'll soon get the hang of it."

"I'm sure I will." Hannah's exhausted expression reminded Ruby of Fi when Connor was refusing to sleep.

"So, it must be really hard going with three little ones."

"To be quite honest, it's a total nightmare. My mum's brilliant, but she lives in Leeds with my stepfather and doesn't get down too often. When she goes home, it's just me. No dad to help out, I'm afraid. I'm a single parent." She must have seen the quizzical look on Ruby's face. "I got pregnant with the twins while I was at university. I decided I could just about cope with a baby and carry on studying. The scan didn't pick up that it was twins until I was five months gone. I was in shock for about a month afterward. I love them to bits now they're here, but I had to give up uni. It hasn't been easy."

"I don't know how you do it."

"That's what my mum says."

"Listen," Ruby said, "do you fancy a cup of tea? I was just about to put the kettle on."

"I would absolutely love a cup of tea," she said.

Ruby told Chanel to shout if a customer came in, then she disappeared into the kitchen. When she emerged carrying a tray of tea, Chanel was still playing with Alfie. Hannah seemed happy to leave them to it while she sat flicking through an old copy of *Hello!,* which had been lying on the counter. Ruby had just put the tray down when she became aware that Hannah had stopped turning the pages and was sitting staring at one particular picture. A full five seconds must have passed and she didn't move.

"You OK?" Ruby said eventually.

Hannah jumped. "Yes. Fine... Actually, forget the tea. I really should get going." With that she got up, took Alfie from Chanel and without stopping to put him in his harness, almost ran out of the shop.

"But, but... you've forgotten the stroller," Ruby called after her, but she was gone.

"What was that about?" Ruby said to Chanel.

"God knows. Seems totally crazy if you ask me."

Ruby said she didn't think that Hannah was mad, just exhausted. She picked up the copy of *Hello!* It was still open at the page Hannah had been reading. There was a picture of a grief-stricken Claudia Planchette leaving St. Luke's after losing her baby. Ruby slid the magazine toward Chanel. "It was an appalling thing to have happened, but I wonder why it upset Hannah so much."

"Dunno. Maybe she knows her."

Ruby said it seemed unlikely.

THAT NIGHT, RUBY had dinner with Sam and he told her that now he was staying on at St. Luke's, he had been given a new office. "It's huge and it's on the fifth floor with views over Holland Park."

She said she'd love to see it.

"OK. I have some papers to pick up from the hospital. Maybe we could go after we've eaten." No sooner had Ruby agreed to the plan when her mobile trilled. It was Phil to say Aunty Sylvia had turned up in floods of tears. "Your mother's at yoga, then she's going out with some of her girlfriends for something to eat. Sylvia's in a real state. I wouldn't normally ask, but you couldn't come over, could you?"

"Dad, it's a bit difficult. I'm in a restaurant having dinner with Sam and then he wants me to see his new office."

"What is it?" Sam whispered.

"Hang on, Dad." Ruby put her hand over the phone and explained to Sam about Aunty Sylvia.

"Look, we've almost finished eating," Sam said. "You go. You can see the office anytime."

"You absolutely sure?"

"Positive."

Ruby dropped Sam home, and then drove on to her parents' house. When she arrived, Aunty Sylvia was sitting on the sofa sobbing. Her eyes were red and swollen. "I'll make some more tea," Phil said, sounding flustered and clearly preferring to leave Ruby to deal with Aunty Sylvia.

"Aunty Sylvia, what on earth's the matter?"

She sniffed and then reached into her handbag. "These. These are the matter."

She was holding up a pair of women's knickers. "I found them in Nigel's underwear drawer."

"But why were you looking through his drawers?"

"He's away for a couple of weeks on business and I was watering his plants."

"And you thought you'd hunt for evidence that he was seeing another woman."

Aunty Sylvia dabbed her eyes and nodded. "And I found it." More loud sobbing.

Ruby put her arm round her aunt. "Well, whoever he's been seeing certainly doesn't go in for sexy underwear," Ruby said, relieving Aunty Sylvia of the flesh-colored Bridget Jones–style big knickers. "And she's not exactly petite. Look at the label. Size eighteen."

"I know. She's even fatter than me. How could he be seeing somebody so fat and sexless? I don't get it."

Ruby asked if she had managed to speak to him.

"I phoned him and he's adamant he hasn't been seeing anybody. He says he can explain the pants and it isn't what I think. What does he take me for, a complete idiot? Why are men such cowards? He's clearly cheating on me. Why hasn't he got the balls just to come out and say so?"

Ruby took a long deep breath. "Who knows?" When Aunty Sylvia started weeping again, Ruby sat holding her and rocking her back and forth. Phil hovered and generally looked out of place and awkward. By the time Ronnie arrived home just after eleven, he must have made half a dozen cups of tea.

"Good God," Ronnie said when she saw the state Aunty Sylvia was in, "what on earth's going on?"

By way of explanation, Aunty Sylvia held up the knickers again. Ruby described how Sylvia had come by them and what she suspected.

"Oh, Sylvia. I'm so sorry. You don't deserve this." She turned to Ruby. "All right, sweetie, you go home. You've done brilliantly. I can take over now."

"You sure?"

"Absolutely."

Ruby kissed Aunty Sylvia good-bye and said she would phone to check on her in the morning.

"This man is a total, utter and complete bastard," Ronnie snarled as she sat down and hugged her sister. Ruby couldn't help observing that for once her mother wasn't trying to analyze the situation, she was just reacting, which was precisely what Aunty Sylvia needed.

RUBY LAY IN bed thinking about what a piece of work Nigel really was. How dare he treat Aunty Sylvia like this? It was odd because he'd come across as such a decent bloke. Admittedly he could bore on rather, and then there were his eyebrows. Aunty Sylvia had insisted they were natural, but they hadn't looked natural to Ruby. As she gazed up at the shadows dancing on the bedroom ceiling, an idea—and an unsavory one at that—started to take shape in her mind. Effeminate eyebrows. A drawer full of big knickers. No. Surely not. He couldn't be. Could he? Poor old Aunty Sylvia. Then again, she'd read that loads of apparently normal heterosexual men were; and man-wise, Aunty Sylvia was always up for a project. She was the first to admit that Nigel was a bit lacking in this department. Having said that, Nigel might turn out to be a project too far.

THE NEXT MORNING, half an hour before opening, Hannah turned up at the shop with Alfie. She tapped on the door, and Chanel went to open it.

"I'm so sorry about running out yesterday," she said as Chanel invited her in. "It was so rude of me. I got rather upset, that's all."

"Don't worry," Chanel said. She began stroking Alfie's head. "Mornin', poppet." They went over to the counter where Ruby was standing.

"Your stroller's all ready," Ruby said brightly. "I'll get it."

"No, wait. I'd like to say sorry to you, too."

"Forget it." Ruby smiled. "You're a single mum. You've just had a baby. Your hormones are all over the place and you just got a bit stressed, that's all."

"I wish I could stop it, but it keeps happening. The thing is, I'm not coping very well with Alfie. Trying to look after three children under three on my own isn't easy. Sometimes I get so tired and emotional that I feel like I'm falling apart." Hannah ran her fingers through her hair.

"Come on, let me take Alfie," Chanel said gently. "You sit down."

Hannah eased a wriggling Alfie from his sling and handed him to Chanel.

"It was also the picture of Claudia Planchette that upset you, wasn't it?" Ruby said. The girl gave a "maybe" shrug.

"It was so awful, her losing her baby," Ruby went on.

Hannah didn't say anything, but her expression had changed suddenly. It was clear that she was anxious to say something.

"What is it?" Ruby said gently.

"No, it's nothing."

But it was obvious that it wasn't "nothing." "Come on," Ruby urged, "you might find it helps to talk."

Hannah rubbed her hand across her forehead. "I need to tell somebody. My mum knows, but not being able to talk about it to anybody else is driving me mad."

"Not being able to talk about what?" Ruby asked.

"OK..." Hannah paused and inhaled deeply. "What would you say if I told you that Claudia Planchette never lost her baby?"

"Of course she lost it," Ruby said. "I'm going out with a doctor who works at St. Luke's. I know for a fact that she lost her baby."

"I'm telling you she didn't. After Claudia gave birth to Avocado, she was petrified that a second pregnancy would ruin her figure, so I carried her baby instead."

"You're saying that she used you as a surrogate?"

"Yes."

Chanel shot Ruby a look as if to say "the woman is totally bonkers."

"I'm not mad," Hannah said, picking up on Chanel's expression. "And I'm not lying, either. OK, I was a fool to get involved in the first place, but the money I was being offered was going to allow me to move into a bigger flat, go back to university and finish my English degree."

"Go on," Ruby said, intrigued now.

"It all happened so fast. The mother of a friend of mine is a midwife at St. Luke's. She knew how hard up I was and she asked me if I was interested in earning some really big money. Usually surrogates only get paid enough to cover their expenses. She was talking tens of thousands, so long as I signed an agreement not to speak to the press."

"So, who was the father?" Ruby asked. "The newspapers said it was some French movie star, but she was refusing to name him so that he could grieve in private."

"There was no movie star. That was just gossip. Claudia hasn't had a relationship since her divorce. She had her eggs fertilized by an anonymous donor—a Mensa member, I think. Apparently he has a thing about spreading his seed for the benefit of humanity."

"But the embryos weren't implanted in her?"

"That's right. They were implanted in me. There were three. Two died early on. I carried the remaining baby while she wore a series of body suits and convinced the world she was pregnant."

"Good God," Ruby muttered. She shot a look at Chanel as if to say: "See, I told you I was right. That day in the fitting room, she was wearing a body suit."

"Claudia's not the only star hiring surrogates. I know for a fact that Mia Ferrari and China Katz used them. There are bound to be others. It's all about vanity. Can you believe these women are so scared of putting on weight during pregnancy that they are actually hiring other women to carry their babies?"

"Bloody 'ell," Chanel gasped. "So that's 'ow they keep their figures. They never lose them in the first place." Alfie started to whimper. She put him over her shoulder, shushed him and began gently rubbing his back.

Ruby was leaning on the counter, trying to take in what Hannah had just told her.

"I know my story sounds absurd and I don't really expect you to believe me, but it is the truth. I promise."

"Yes, I know it is," Ruby said. She began telling Hannah

about the day Claudia came into the shop to buy a maternity swimsuit. "Ever since, I've been trying to convince myself I was seeing things."

"You weren't seeing things," Hannah said.

Ruby was still shaking her head in disbelief. "So, these stars leave St. Luke's, apparently having just given birth. They pose for the paparazzi in their skimpy little jeans, smug as you like with their perfect babies and perfectly flat postpregnancy stomachs and tell the world it's all down to sensible eating and good genes. The upshot is that they make every new mother on the planet feel gross and hideously inadequate for having put on a few pounds. And all the time, they weren't even pregnant. Even by Hollywood standards, it's beyond belief."

Chanel hadn't said anything for a few minutes. "So," she said to Hannah. "If you carried Claudia's baby and it didn't die, Alfie must be . . ."

". . . Claudia's baby. That's right."

"So why is he with you?"

"That's the really twisted part. Alfie was born by emergency cesarean. There he was, this tiny, two-month premature scrap lying in an incubator and Claudia decided she didn't want him."

"What? She didn't want her own baby? You're saying she rejected this precious little mite? Why?"

"He has a deformity."

Chanel frowned. "What deformity? He doesn't 'ave a deformity. You can see he's totally perfect."

"No he isn't. He has ginger hair. She didn't want her baby because he has ginger hair."

"Oh, come on," Ruby shot back. "That I don't believe. There has to be more to it."

"Nope. Claudia hates ginger hair. She finds it repulsive. It seems there was some mix-up over the coloring of the sperm donor. She was led to believe he had dark brown hair. In fact his hair was ginger."

"But I thought it was only the British who had hang-ups about ginger hair," Ruby said. "I didn't realize Americans disliked it, too."

"I'm fairly sure they're less than keen on it," Hannah replied. "It's just that they don't make jokes about it like we do. Think about it, though. When did you last see a ginger-haired man take the romantic lead in a Hollywood film? It's not sexy. The last thing Claudia wanted was a son who would grow up to be unsexy."

Ruby said she got the point.

"Anyway," Hannah continued, "Claudia came into my room shortly after I had Alfie, took one look at him, threw an almighty hissy fit and left. Hollywood stars like Claudia think of themselves as royalty. They demand total perfection."

"But this wasn't a designer dress with a wobbly hem," Ruby said. "It was a baby. Her baby. Her flesh and blood."

"I know, but as far as she was concerned, Alfie wasn't real. He was just another lifestyle accessory—one that didn't meet the required standard. Her parting words were: 'I'll pay you to keep him. Anything you want. Name it.' She paid me half what I was owed for the surrogacy, but I've seen nothing since Alfie was born."

"But I saw you had all that cash," Ruby blurted before she could stop herself. "Oh, God, I'm sorry. That was so rude of me. Your money is none of my business."

Hannah smiled. "It's OK. It came from my uncle. He's ancient and doesn't trust banks. He isn't rich by any means, but he keeps what money he has stashed down sofas and under mattresses. He adores Alfie and insisted I buy him a few really special things. I'd never even heard of Les Sprogs, but I just happened to be passing, so I came in."

Ruby went over to Alfie, who was now fast asleep on Chanel's shoulder. She began stroking his cheek. "It's beyond insane. How can anybody reject their own flesh and blood because they have the 'wrong' color hair? I have to say that when I met her she seemed a bit emotionally unstable, but to do something as wicked and cruel as this . . . The woman has to be completely, seriously ill. No wonder her ex is fighting her for custody of Avocado."

"I didn't know that," Hannah said. Ruby picked up a copy of the *Daily Mail* and showed it to her. The headline read: "Planchette Unfit Mother—ex-husband claims."

Hannah shook her head. "She is an unfit mother. I've got no doubts about that. It's why I didn't go to court to force her to take Alfie. What kind of a life would he have had with her? And if she had still refused to take him, he would have ended up in foster care. I couldn't do that to him."

Ruby let out a long breath. "But why would St. Luke's put its reputation at risk to get involved with something like this? It doesn't make any sense."

"You can never underestimate people's greed," Hannah said. "Even doctors in private practice can be dazzled by dollar signs. And we all know how underpaid midwives are." To her instant shame, it occurred to Ruby—albeit for no more than a second or two—that Sam might be involved. It would certainly explain all the secrecy and phone calls.

"And of course," Ruby added, purging her appalling thought about Sam from her mind, "what they're doing isn't actually illegal. It just stinks morally."

"So," Chanel chipped in, "the too-posh-to-push brigade 'as gone a stage further. Now they're 'too-fabulous-to-fertilize.' "

"Absolutely," Hannah said with a bitter laugh.

She explained that from what she could work out, the

hospital acted as the agent for Hollywood stars looking for women to carry their babies. They charged tens of thousands to find surrogates, arranged for them to be artificially inseminated and supervised the pregnancy and birth. "Not that anybody will ever prove what's going on. These people are very clever. They've got every angle covered. The insemination doesn't happen on the hospital premises. They will have gone to huge lengths to make sure all payments look legitimate."

Ruby suggested that maybe the midwives would be prepared to blow the whistle.

"Are you kidding?" Hannah said. "They're making a great deal of money. Why would they risk losing it? On top of that, they would be struck off the nursing register."

"So, who was your obstetrician?" Ruby asked.

"His name is Hardacre. Tom Hardacre."

"You are kidding," Ruby cried. "He's involved in this? But he's a leading authority on natural childbirth. I grant you he comes across as a bit arrogant and pleased with himself, but loads of doctors are like that. There's no way he could be connected to this."

"Well, I assure you he is."

"OK, so why haven't you reported him to his superiors?"

Hannah started laughing. "Because for all I know, his superiors are involved as well. And even if they're not, my allegation sounds absurd. Do you really think anybody at St. Luke's would even listen to me?"

"You could go to the newspapers."

"I could, but then we're back to square one. As soon as the story became public, the courts would get involved. Any judge would insist on DNA tests to prove Alfie is Claudia's, but like I said, I can't risk her taking him—and I also couldn't bear the thought of him put into care."

"So you're prepared to keep 'im?" Chanel said.

"I'm prepared to, yes."

"Does that mean you don't really want 'im?" she persisted, but not unkindly.

Hannah sat considering her response. "I want to want him," she said finally. "After all, I'm all he's got. But the truth is, I'm not his biological mother and I haven't bonded with him, like I did with the twins. I know that makes me sound heartless and wicked, but it's how I feel." Her eyes began to fill with tears. "I'm just not coping. My mum's still staying with me, but even with her help, I'm not up to this."

"Hey, come on," Ruby said. "You're doing brilliantly and nobody thinks you're remotely heartless or wicked. We'll sort something out. Just you see."

Chapter 15

"Look," Ruby said, rooting through Sam's kitchen cupboard for the pepper grinder. "I know Hannah's story sounds like some mad fantasy, but if you met her, you'd see she's isn't mad, just exhausted; and I think probably very angry about what's happened to her." She found the pepper behind a jar of honey and passed it to Sam.

"I have no doubt that she comes across as totally credible," he said holding the grinder over the pan of Bolognese sauce and starting to turn the handle. "But what she's saying is inconceivable. If you're asking for my opinion as a doctor, it sounds like she's suffering from postpartum depression. She needs to see a shrink." He put the grinder down on the counter and began stirring. "She's also a very convincing actress—so much so that she's managed to draw you and Chanel into her crazy world."

"But what about the body suit?" Ruby persisted. "I saw Claudia in a body suit and now Hannah's confirming she wore one."

"Taste this," he said, putting the wooden spoon to her lips. "What do you think?"

"Very nice," she said. "A touch more oregano, maybe... but you haven't answered my question."

Sam shrugged. "You said yourself the suit could have been some kind of maternity girdle."

"But it clearly wasn't. Hannah saw it. And my mum said there was this time when they were all messing around after her prenatal class and she refused to show off her bump."

"OK, I admit I don't have all the answers, but believe me there will be a rational explanation." He then asked—exactly as she had asked—why a hospital like St. Luke's would risk its reputation by getting involved in some kind of morally suspect surrogacy scam. "St. Luke's is synonymous with natural childbirth worldwide. Arranging for women to use surrogates purely because of vanity is way beyond hypocrisy. The press would lynch us. Our patients would lynch us. And quite rightly."

"Hannah said the people involved are making massive amounts of money."

"But if something like this were going on, don't you think there would have been rumors? Gossip? I've been working at St. Luke's for more than eight months and there's been nothing. Surely something would have leaked by now."

"So you've really heard nothing?"

"Not a whisper."

"And this Tom Hardacre, the obstetrician who was on TV, the one Hannah saw when she was pregnant..." As she took a step back, her foot came down on Cat Damon's tail. He let out a long loud squeal.

"*If* she saw him."

"OK," Ruby said reluctantly, bending down to comfort Cat Damon. "*If* she saw him. So, you reckon he seems like a decent enough chap?"

"As far as I know. Like I said, he is very highly respected. I admit that some people at the hospital don't like him because he's a bit flashy. He's independently wealthy and he buys and sells property. Not just houses—commercial property. Apparently he's made millions. The guy owns two

Porsches, for crying out loud. Don't you see? He can't possibly be involved. He simply doesn't need the money."

"But he is involved. I just know it. Hannah is not a liar or a mad fantasist."

Sam started to laugh. "You really have got the bit between your teeth, haven't you?"

"Too blinkin' right I have."

"OK, would you like me to do some digging? See what I can find out?"

"About Hardacre?"

"About him and this whole surrogacy thing. I'll ask around discreetly. Who knows—maybe there is something going on and I'm the only one who doesn't know about it."

Ruby's face lit up. "You'd do that? Even though you think I'm totally bonkers?"

He put down the wooden spoon he was using to stir the pasta sauce, drew her toward him and kissed her.

"You know what?" he said as they pulled away.

"What?"

"You're very sexy when you're bonkers."

She swatted his arm playfully. "You just wait. When it turns out I was right all along, you won't be calling me bonkers." She kissed him briefly on the lips. "You will be careful, won't you? We don't know who's involved in this, or at what level. The last thing either of us wants is for you to lose your job."

"Don't worry. I'll be discreet. All I can say is that I hope to God you're not right about all this. The consequences for the hospital would be dire." He opened a cupboard and took out a couple of plates. "For now, though, I think we need to take a break and stop thinking about all this."

"You're right," she said. "Listen, why don't we go for a drive after dinner? I still haven't seen your new office."

• • •

RUBY HAD NEVER seen Sam's old office, but apparently this new one on the fifth floor was luxurious by comparison.

"It has to be three times the size," Sam said.

Ruby looked round, taking in the huge window overlooking the park, the light gray carpet, the ultramodern dark mahogany-and-steel desk and black leather swivel armchair. "Umm, very Philippe Starck," she said, running her hand across the desktop. Spread out over the desk were dozens of photographs of newborns. She began sifting through them. "Oh, Sam. These are gorgeous. All from grateful customers, I presume?"

He nodded. "I thought I'd put them up on the wall."

She went over to the picture window and pulled back the vertical blinds. The lights of London were twinkling like a box of spilled jewels. "Wow, look at this view. You can see the very top of Big Ben."

Eventually she turned away from the window. It was a moment or two before she noticed the screen. No doubt there. And... stirrups. Memories of her experience with Dr. Double Barrel came flooding back. Beside the screen was a metal stand. On top, there was a box of rubber gloves and a tray of instruments. She felt herself tense. "Omigod, is that a speculum? I've never seen one up close."

He started laughing. "Ruby, what do you expect? I'm a gynecologist."

"Yes, but you know that gynecologists' consulting rooms make me squeamish."

She moved back to the desk. She was looking for something to divert her attention. She noticed a stethoscope lying next to the photographs. She picked it up and draped it around her neck. "What do you think?" she said, adopting a sexy pose. "Do I look the part?"

"Very professional. You know I could really fall for you in that."

He was half sitting, half leaning against the desk. "C'mere," he said, smiling at her.

She went. He put his arms around her.

"I thought you'd already fallen for me," she said coyly.

"What I mean is that if I hadn't already fallen for you, I would have just then."

"I see. That's all right, then." She was aware that he was running his hand over her bottom.

"Hey," he whispered, "you want to play doctors and nurses?"

She burst out laughing. "I *cannot* believe you just said that. You'll have me in suspenders and a white cap next."

"Ooh, now there's a thought."

Still laughing, she went to swat his arm, but he caught her wrist in midair and started kissing her. She made a feeble attempt to fight him off, but quickly gave in.

"Take off your top," he said, starting to undo the buttons on her blouse.

"What? No! Don't be ridiculous." She clamped her hand over his. "Somebody might come in."

"It's late. Who's going to come in?"

"Dah. This is a hospital. Anybody could come in."

Somehow he had managed to undo all her shirt buttons. The stethoscope was back on the desk. She let him slip her shirt off her shoulders and start unhooking her bra. A moment later he was flicking one of her nipples with his tongue. "You're right," he said at one point. "I should lock the door. Somebody might barge in." He moved to go.

She caught his arm. "No, no. Please don't stop. Forget about the door."

"But you just said . . ." His face became a grin. "Oh, I get it. The danger's turning you on."

She felt herself blush. "Maybe."

"OK, but let me turn off this bright light. It's not exactly romantic."

He moved to the panel of switches by the window and flicked one. The room was suddenly bathed in darkness, broken only by the glow and twinkle of the lights of London.

He came back and slipped his hand under her skirt. Her entire body shuddered in delight as his fingers skimmed over the crotch of her panties. Any second he was going to make her take off her skirt. What was she wearing underneath? She racked her brain to remember what she'd put on that morning. She was behind with her laundry and there had been virtually nothing to choose from in her underwear drawer. She prayed she wasn't wearing her flesh-colored Bridget knickers or the red thong Chanel had bought her the other Christmas with "Hey, Santa Baby" written across the front. No, it definitely wasn't the red thong. She would have remembered that.

SHE LET HIM unzip her skirt. It fell over her hips, revealing cream lace panties.

"Come with me." He was leading her toward the screen.

"Oh, Sam, I'm not sure about this." Making love on a gynecologist's table might have been Fi's idea of erotic heaven, but it definitely wasn't Ruby's.

"It's either that or the floor," he said. "Under this carpet, it's solid concrete."

She eased herself up onto the table. He stood beside her, tilted her face and kissed her lips. "I love you," he said, smiling at her as he trailed a finger over her breast.

"I love you, too."

Soon their kissing became more urgent. His tongue was probing hard and deep into her mouth. With one hand he was easing her panties down. He put his hand between her legs. She was aware that this was the most kinky thing she had ever done in her life, but she was way past caring. She closed her eyes, let herself float away and waited for him to touch her. She let out a gasp as he gently parted her and began caressing her. She thought she would come in a matter of seconds. He seemed to sense she was close to orgasm and eased up the pressure. At one point he stopped completely, making her cry out in frustration. Then, slowly, barely touching her at first, he began again.

As her orgasm approached she became vaguely aware of someone singing. She could swear that somewhere way off in the distance, a male voice was belting out Bob Marley's "One Love." The singing seemed to be getting louder. Then footsteps kicked in. Sam had clearly heard them and was beginning to panic. "Shit. C'mon, Ruby, are you almost there?"

"Al... most. Just... just give me another couple of seconds."

"One love, one heart. Let's get together and feel all right."

"He's getting closer. It could be one of the security staff. He might come in."

"I know, but don't stop. Please don't stop now. I'm almost there. I can do this. I know I can."

She came in short, electrified jerks, just as the door opened. Aware that she was prone to call out during orgasm, Sam had clamped his hand over her mouth. "Not a sound," he whispered, his voice steely with tension.

The screen surrounding the examination table was made up of strips of curtain. There was a gap between two of the strips, wide enough for them to peer through. As their eyes focused, it was as much as they could do not to cry out in shock. Standing in the doorway, backlit by the light from the corridor was a six-foot-tall, grinning skeleton. A violent shiver shot up Ruby's back. She was so petrified that she couldn't think straight. She knew they shouldn't have done this. Now they were being punished. As over-the-top as it seemed, the Grim bloody Reaper was coming for them. Every instinct told her to get the hell out of there. So what if she was caught running naked and screaming around the hospital parking lot.

After a few seconds she noticed that—oddly, for the Grim Reaper—he wasn't carrying a scythe or wearing a hood. On the other hand, what he did have was a mop of thick black, Afro-style dreadlocks. Her fear was turning to confusion. She watched as the thing rattled into the room, legs and arms bouncing and waving like a ghoulish-looking string puppet.

"One love, one heart. Let's get together and feel all right." And since when did the Grim Reaper announce his arrival by singing Bob Marley songs?

It was then that the dreadlocks became separated from the bones. A Rastafarian porter—six-six if he was an inch—eased the skeleton into the corner of the room and checked that it was safely balanced on its stand. "There we are, bro'. Now you can rest in peace, even if you are made out o' plastic... *One love, one heart. Let's get together...*" And with that, he left the room and gently closed the door behind him. *"... Let's get together and feel all right..."*

Sam instantly exploded with laughter. "It's my new skeleton," he cried, rocking back and forth. "All the doctors are being given them for their offices. The hospital bigwigs thought they added a touch of class. God only knows why mine arrived at this time of night... I'm sorry if you were scared."

"Me? Scared? I wasn't scared. I was taken aback, but I could see what it was right away." For some misguided feminist reason, she always got defensive around men when they suggested she might be scared.

"Well, I'm glad you could," he said, running his hand over his head, " 'cause I tell you, for a second back there, I actually thought the Grim Reaper had come to get us. Can you believe that?"

"Don't worry," she soothed, "fear and guilt can do strange things to the brain."

"I guess."

Just then there was a sudden, shrill noise. Ruby let out a short but piercing shriek. "Omigod, what was that?"

Sam started laughing again. "Hey, Ruby, take it easy. It's just my phone... So you weren't scared, eh?" He reached into his pocket for the phone.

"OK, well I might have been. Just a bit."

She prayed that it wasn't an emergency call from the labor ward. No sooner had he pressed "connect" than his face fell in that all-too-familiar way. As she began getting dressed, she watched him stride over to the other side of the room. "OK, do what you have to do... let me know." She couldn't hear what he said next but she was sure she heard the word *police*. Clearly, it wasn't the labor ward calling.

"God, what's happened?"

He seemed to hesitate, almost as if he wasn't sure what he was about to say next. He was clearly distressed. He ran his hand over the top of his head. "It's... erm. It's Buddy. He's had a stroke."

"Omigod. Is he OK?"

"They don't know. The hospital's still doing tests. Irene's going to phone me later when they know more."

"So how were the police involved?"

"Police? What do you mean? I didn't mention the police."

"Really? But I'm sure you did."

"Oh... yeah. Sorry. I remember. Buddy collapsed in the street. The police called the ambulance."

They went back to his flat and had an early night. Sam was restless beside her. She cuddled him, stroked his head and did her best to comfort him. Several times she asked if he wanted her to make him a hot drink, but he said he was OK. Then about seven, the phone rang next to the bed. His arm shot out to grab it. He mouthed to her that it was Irene. "OK, I think I'd better come. There's a flight that leaves Heathrow at ten."

"Buddy's really bad, then?" Ruby said after he'd come off the phone.

"Yes. It's not looking good. I'm sorry, Ruby, but I've got to go to him."

"Of course you have. I know how close you are to him. Is there anything I can do?"

"I don't think so." He was staring up at the ceiling. Even in the half-light she could see the distress on his face. She asked how Irene was bearing up. "She's doing OK, but she wants me to be there to make sure he gets the best treatment."

"Makes sense."

He rolled over and began stroking her hair. "I'm going to miss you."

"I'm going to miss you, too." She knew he probably wouldn't be gone for very long, but she couldn't stop her eyes filling with tears.

"And remember," he went on, "that whatever happens, I will always love you." With that he got out of bed and headed for the bathroom.

Her brow wrinkled. "How do you mean 'whatever happens'?" But the shower was already running and he couldn't hear her. She shrugged and assumed—not that it made sense—that he'd been referring to the possibility of Buddy dying.

It was touch and go for a few days, but finally his doctors said that Buddy was out of the woods. Sam phoned to say he wanted to stay in New York for a couple of weeks to monitor his progress and keep Irene company. "St. Luke's has been very understanding about me taking time off." He paused. "Look, I'm really sorry about breaking my promise to you."

"What promise?"

"I said I'd do some digging at the hospital about the surrogacy thing."

"Sam, please don't even think about it. You have far more important things on your mind. Stay in New York as long as you like. Irene's probably still in shock and I'm sure she could do with you being around. By the way, is she there? I'd really like to speak to her and pass on my best to Buddy."

"Actually she's just gone back to the hospital to see Buddy, but I'll tell her you called." His voice sounded tense, she thought. She asked him if he was all right.

"I'm fine. It's all been a traumatic few days, that's all. I haven't had much sleep."

While he was away, Ruby wrestled with her thoughts about Hannah's story. Reluctant as she was to admit it, since her conversation with Sam, she was starting to have second thoughts. Suddenly she wasn't sure what to believe. Sam was clearly the voice of reason and common sense. And yet, and yet. Hannah seemed so convincing. She came across as somebody who was worn out—but she didn't seem like a delusional nutcase. Not that Ruby had met enough delusional nutcases to know what one might sound like.

"The thing is," Ruby said to Fi the night she phoned to tell her that Buddy was on the mend, "I keep coming back to the issue of the bodysuit. It's not as if I put the idea into Hannah's head. She brought it up before I'd even mentioned it."

Fi said she got the point. "On the other hand, you have to admit her story does sound pretty preposterous." It was clear to Ruby that Fi was more convinced by Sam's argument than by hers, but didn't want to upset her by saying so.

• • •

EVERY FEW DAYS, Hannah would pop into the shop for a chat. Now that her mum had gone back to Leeds, she would come in with all three children. Her identical twins, Ellie and Ruth, were reassuringly robust little souls with permanently smiling moon faces. They charged around the shop on their chubby legs, stopping occasionally to climb in the prams and cribs or throw soft toys around. Hannah was forever apologizing on their behalf, but Ruby and Chanel kept telling her that they were quite used to two-year-olds causing mayhem about the place.

The two women also took turns visiting Hannah. Ruby had been expecting to find her living in some graffiti-covered housing project with used condoms and syringes in the lift.

Although Hannah's flat was public housing, it was brand-new. It was airy and bright and outside there were trees and grass and a children's play area. Each time Ruby went she was amazed at how tidy Hannah managed to keep the place. Hannah laughed and said it was so small that she had no option.

Whenever they saw her she seemed to be worried about the twins' boisterous behavior. She was convinced they were more unruly than other toddlers and that it was all her fault because she was exhausted and not giving them enough attention. Ruby put her in touch with Fi, who reassured her about the terrible twos and told her all about Ben depositing turds behind the sofa and under the kitchen table. When Fi suggested Hannah might like to come along to her postnatal support group, she jumped at the invitation.

Hannah's feelings about Alfie were still ambivalent, though. Whenever she came to the shop she was always more than happy for Chanel to take him. Chanel made an enormous fuss of him. She would kiss and cuddle him, give him his bottle, change him. She was clearly getting attached to the little mite. When he laughed—apparently for the first time—it was because Chanel had been blowing raspberries on his tummy.

Now that Sam was in New York and couldn't do any investigating into the surrogacy issue, Ruby had been thinking about what she could do on her own. One night while she was lying awake because her mind refused to switch off, she found herself thinking back to her first conversation with Jill McNulty. She remembered Jill's overreaction when she made a joke about celebrities leaving St. Luke's looking so thin. Her jumpiness had been out of all proportion. At the time, Ruby had put it down to her living in fear of losing her job if she was caught gossiping. Maybe there was more to it. Was it possible she knew what was happening at St. Luke's?

The following day, Ruby told Hannah about her conversation with Jill. "It wouldn't surprise me if she knew something, but I can't see much point in confronting her. She's not going to say anything. She's clearly petrified of getting the sack."

A light seemed to go on in Hannah's head. "I think I may have met this Jill. Forties. Blonde. Smartly dressed."

"That's her."

"It was just after I had Alfie. She came into my room. We had a brief conversation about my payment and she asked me to sign something. Then she left. I never saw her again."

"So she is involved," Ruby said. "I bet you anything she keeps records of all the payments to surrogates. She's the obsessively tidy type that would. I wonder if there's some way of finding out."

"But you've said yourself she's not going to say anything. What are you thinking?"

"I'm not sure yet."

• • •

WHEN RUBY WENT round to Fi's and told her she was planning to sneak into Jill McNulty's office one lunch hour and have a hunt through her files, Fi practically had a fit.

"You're mad. If you got caught, this woman would have every right to call the police. This is pure recklessness. Don't do it. This isn't your fight."

"But somebody has to get involved. If I don't, nobody else will."

"But you don't even know if Hannah's story is true."

"It is. I just know it is."

"So how are you going to get into this McNulty woman's office?"

"I'll have a key. Despite all the security and ID cards at the hospital, the office keys are kept on hooks in the cleaners' cubbyhole. I remember passing it and seeing them hanging there."

"But even if by some miracle you don't get caught and you manage to find the names of the people involved in the surrogacy scam, they will deny everything. If it gets into the newspapers, you will be made to look ridiculous. Have you thought about the shop and the repercussions this could have on the business?"

"Of course I have. I've also been thinking about how it could affect Sam. I love it that you worry about me, but these celebrities and the doctors who pander to their vanity must be exposed. Look how you've been affected by seeing all these pictures of skinny Hollywood women leaving St. Luke's. These celebrity mothers are making ordinary women feel like failures because they don't look stick thin and toned immediately after giving birth. You know that a new mother—particularly a breast-feeding mother—needs all her strength. God knows how many of them are starving themselves, just to get their figures back. Somebody has to put a stop to it. Why shouldn't it be me?"

Fi sat thinking. Ruby could see she was coming round. "OK, but why not break in after work? Surely that would be safer."

Ruby explained that her talks always finished around lunchtime. "I couldn't hang around the hospital without people noticing and asking me what I was doing."

"You seem to have it all worked out," Fi said, allowing her face to break into a smile. She stood up and put her arms round her friend. "You are very, very brave, Ruby Silverman. Insane, but brave, and I'm extremely proud of you."

Chapter 16

The day after her discussion with Fi, Ruby gave her second talk at St. Luke's. Even more women turned up this time. Clearly word had got around.

Afterward, pleased with how the session had gone, Ruby locked up. Then, heart racing, loins fully girded, she headed down the corridor toward the cleaners' cubbyhole. As usual the door was open and the office keys were on their hooks for all to see. "Anybody in here?" Ruby said tentatively. No answer. She slipped inside, navigating her way around various buckets and mops. Her nose registered the strong smell of disinfectant. She scanned the row of hooks. The one to Jill's office was at the end. A tag hung from it marked with her name. Congratulating herself on how easy this sleuthing lark really was, she turned to leave. As she did so, her elbow made contact with a mop, causing it to fall onto a metal bucket with what sounded to her like an almighty crash. Ruby's heart almost stopped. She put her head round the door to see if anybody had noticed the disturbance. To her huge relief, the corridor was empty. Trembling, she let out a long, slow breath and made her way toward Jill's office.

Even though it was lunchtime, there was no guarantee that Jill would be away from her desk. Ruby would knock first. Only if there was no reply would she let herself in. If Jill was there, Ruby had a story prepared. She would say that one of the windows in the room where she gave her talks was refusing to open, and could Jill ask one of the hospital handymen to take a look at it.

She gave two gentle knocks.

"Come in." It was Jill. Ruby's heart sank. She opened the door. Jill was sitting behind her immaculately tidy desk wearing a charcoal-gray jacket and crisp white blouse. She looked up at Ruby and smiled.

"Hello, Ruby. Come on in. What can I do for you?" Jill motioned her to take a seat. As usual, Ruby noticed her perfectly painted pale pink nails.

Ruby sat down and delivered her spiel about the window.

"No problem," Jill said. "I'll make sure it gets done. Now is there anything else you need, because after today I'm on leave for a week. I'm going walking in the south of France with my chap. I can't wait to get away."

"So your office will be empty?" Ruby blurted.

"Y . . . es. That's what usually happens when people go away."

Ruby had to think on her feet. "No, erm . . . I er . . . I er . . . What I meant to say was, will there be anybody filling in for you?"

"No. Nobody. I'm sorry about that. If you need anything urgent you can always speak to the chief administrator's secretary."

"That's good to know. Thank you."

She insisted on writing down the secretary's extension and e-mail. "Now, if she's not around, the receptionists at outpatients will always be able to find somebody to help you in an emergency."

"Thanks. I'm sure I'll be fine."

"Look, what about if I leave you my mobile number, so you can always reach me."

Ruby said she wouldn't dream of disturbing her while she was on holiday.

"Of course, I've got to pack up all my files and papers before I go," Jill went on. "My office is being redecorated while I'm away. My stuff's being put into storage."

"What? All of it?" Ruby was cursing the fates that had built her up and then a moment later let her down so cruelly.

"Yes." Jill was looking quizzically at Ruby. "Why do you ask?"

"Oh, nothing. I was just thinking how inconvenient it is for you, having to pack it all up."

"It is a bit," Jill said, "but these things are sent to try us. I'm sure I'll manage."

Ruby stood up to go.

"Oh, by the way," Jill said, "I hear the gorgeous Dr. Epstien is staying on."

Ruby colored up. "Yes, he's been offered a permanent post. So, you know about us?"

"Everybody does," she said with a conspiratorial giggle. "The nurses and midwives are madly jealous, of course. They're all a bit in love with him."

Ruby wasn't quite sure how to respond to this. "Right, well, have a great holiday," she said. "I'll see you when you get back."

Ruby closed the door behind her and trudged down the corridor. Jill's files were going to be moved and she had no idea where. The only way to get access to them was to wait until she got back from holiday. Great. Just great.

She opened the door to the cleaner's cubbyhole and replaced the office key as easily as she had removed it.

• • •

RUBY DEALT WITH her frustration—not to mention the fact that she was missing Sam hugely, even though he was phoning and e-mailing—by throwing herself into getting Guatemalan week up and running.

She had fancy invitations printed, inviting her regular customers, including dozens of celebs, to the launch on the second Saturday in December. In the meantime, boxes continued to arrive from Guatemala. They were full of baby clothes, exquisite handmade toys, crib mobiles and nursery knickknacks. Added to this were Christmas cards and decorations.

One evening after work—a few days before the launch—she drove over to see her mother. Phil was in Munich meeting a client. He was staying overnight and Ruby had offered to come for dinner and keep Ronnie company. Ronnie was making her English curry, which was beyond sublime even if it wasn't quite authentically, or even vaguely, Indian. It consisted of chicken fried with onions and mixed with curry powder, hot mango chutney, raisins, apples and bananas. When Ruby was a child and her mother didn't have much by way of housekeeping money, she cooked it all the time. Ruby had never lost the taste for it.

"Oh, by the way," Ruby said as they walked down the hall toward the kitchen, "I've brought the nursing bras you ordered. They're two sizes up from what you're wearing now, but I thought it made sense because you're bound to get bigger when your milk comes in."

Ronnie took one look at the flesh-colored, double-D-cup nursing bras and grimaced. "Ooh—sex-ee. Are these meant to be for breasts or udders?" she said.

Ruby laughed. "If you really want something to turn Dad on, come and see my new range of breast pumps. Now, they really are for udders. The last time I saw Fi hooked up to one, she was threatening to change her name to Daisy." Ronnie chuckled and said she couldn't wait.

Ronnie poured Ruby a glass of wine. She stuck to sparkling water, which she said was the only thing that eased her almost permanent heartburn. As ever, the curry was divine.

At one point, Ruby asked what was happening with Aunty Sylvia and Nigel. Ronnie said Aunty Sylvia had had a monumental row with Nigel about the big knickers she found in his drawer and now they weren't speaking. "But you know what Sylvia's like. She can never keep up the silent act for long. I'll keep you posted." Ronnie took a sip of water. "You seem preoccupied," she said. "It must be hard with Sam away?"

"It is. I'm really missing him."

"But it's not just Sam, is it?" Ronnie frowned. "There's something else troubling you."

By way of reply, Ruby said: "Your obstetrician at St. Luke's—this woman..."

"Dr. Beech?"

"Yes. You really like her, right?"

"She's wonderful. I couldn't ask for a better doctor."

"So, you think she's completely straight."

"What, as opposed to gay?"

"No," Ruby giggled, "as opposed to crooked."

"Dr. Beech, crooked? The idea is absurd. What are you suggesting?"

"Oh, nothing."

"Ruby, this is me you're talking to. What's going on?"

"It's a long story."

She patted her bump. "Me and Sigmund aren't going anywhere."

"Sigmund—that's a therapy joke, right?"

"No, actually we thought Sigmund Silverman had a bit of a ring to it." Ronnie started laughing. "Yes, of course it's a joke. Now, tell me what's been going on."

Ruby went back to the beginning when Claudia came into the shop to buy a swimsuit. She then recounted the entire surrogacy saga. Ronnie got so excited that she had to have a glass of wine. Every so often she would interrupt with a "No!" or an "Omigod! You couldn't make it up." Finally she sat back shaking her head. "Do you realize these ridiculous women have set the feminist movement back fifty years? It's appalling. Utterly, utterly appalling."

"I'm wondering if you should switch hospitals again. I don't like the idea of you being at St. Luke's with all this going on."

Ronnie became thoughtful. "I can't see much point in changing hospitals. It's late in my pregnancy and I'd trust Dr. Beech with my life. I'd bet everything I own that she's not involved in this thing."

"But I'm sure you could easily find a doctor at the Portland who would take you on—even at this late stage."

"No, I'm comfortable with Dr. Beech. I'll stay where I am." She paused. "But, sweetie, you must not get involved trying to expose people. Have you thought how it could backfire if you got caught?"

She gave her mother the same speech that she had given Fi, but whereas in the end Fi had sort of given her blessing to Ruby turning detective, her mother couldn't. "You're my daughter. I'm scared. I mean, suppose it were to get nasty, I mean really nasty?"

"You mean violent?"

"Maybe not actual violence, but I could see you being threatened. You can never underestimate what people are capable of when there's money involved—particularly big money."

"Oh, come on, Mum, I think you're being a bit melodramatic."

No sooner had the word left her mouth than Ronnie clamped her hand to her bump and winced in pain.

"Mum, you OK?"

"I'm not sure." Ronnie sat up again and let out a breath. Whatever it was appeared to have passed.

"You don't think you could be going into labor, do you?"

"But Sigmund's not due for another six weeks."

"I know, but he might be early."

Ruby went to fetch her mother a glass of water. Five minutes passed and the pain came again, causing Ronnie to double up. Three minutes later, there was another one.

"Ruby, I think perhaps we need to go to St. Luke's." Ronnie asked her if she would mind going upstairs and throwing a nightdress and a few toiletries into an overnight bag, just in case. "Ooh, and don't forget my perineal massage oil. And the whale music CD is on the dressing table."

On the way, Ronnie started to panic about the baby arriving when she was only thirty-four weeks pregnant.

"Mum, it will be fine. Babies survive at twenty-six weeks these days. I promise you, this is not going to be a problem."

But Ronnie wasn't convinced. "I wish your dad were here." She kept trying to get Phil on his mobile, but it was going to voice mail.

At the hospital, Ronnie was greeted by a bustling Jamaican midwife who radiated calm. She could see that Ronnie was anxious, so she sat on the bed, holding her hand and telling her everything was going to be fine, that she was in good hands and had no reason to be frightened. She was everything you would expect from a midwife at St. Luke's. Nevertheless, Ruby couldn't help looking at her—as she'd looked at all the other nurses and doctors she and Ronnie had passed since they arrived—and wondering if she was involved in the surrogacy affair.

"You cervix naht even dilated, my darlin', and I'm getting a good strong heartbeat." The midwife carefully rearranged the bedclothes. In her opinion, Ronnie had simply been having Braxton-Hicks practice contractions, but she wanted to get the duty doctor to examine her, just to make sure. "And if she say everything OK—we get you a nice cup of tea." With that she bustled out of the room. If this woman was involved in anything corrupt, Ruby would eat her one and only and extremely precious Philip Treacy hat.

It turned out that the doctor on duty was Dr. Jane Anderson, the motherly woman gynecologist Ruby usually saw when she had her checkups at St. Luke's. She had clearly got over her virus. "Dr. Jane's great. You'll really like her," Ruby said to Ronnie.

She arrived a few minutes later. As usual her appearance was comfortingly messy. Her hair looked like it had been styled by Bob Geldof. Her clothes—a scarlet fleece over a brown pleated skirt—looked as if they had been pulled out of a drawer during a power outage. Her face lit up when she saw Ruby. "The moment I saw the name Silverman I wondered if Ronnie could be any relation to you."

"She's my mum." Ruby grinned.

"Goodness. Surely not," Dr. Jane said, sitting down on Ronnie's bed. "You don't look nearly old enough." Ronnie was visibly relaxing. She laughed and explained that she had been a teenage mum. It turned out that Dr. Jane was one of ten children and that her mother had given birth to her first at sixteen. Soon the two women were chatting away as if they'd known each other for ages.

Dr. Jane confirmed the midwife's diagnosis.

"You mean these really are nothing more than practice contractions?" Ronnie said. "But I don't remember them being this painful with Ruby."

Dr. Jane patted Ronnie's hand and smiled. "How long ago did you have Ruby?"

"OK, I admit it was thirty-two years ago."

"Enough said," Doctor Jane chuckled. "The pains were probably just as strong then, but you don't remember."

Because the pains were continuing and Ronnie still seemed anxious, Dr. Jane decided to keep her overnight for observation.

After Dr. Jane left, Ronnie turned to Ruby. "You go home and get some rest," she said. "I'll be fine."

"No, it's still early. I'll stay for a bit and keep you company."

They watched TV in Ronnie's room, but the pains weren't easing off. Ronnie was getting more and more concerned that she was going into real labor, even though the midwife kept reassuring her she wasn't. Her anxiety wasn't helped by her not being able to reach Phil.

By about ten, Ruby was feeling hungry and suggested getting them something to eat from the cafeteria.

Ronnie didn't fancy anything to eat, but insisted Ruby get something for herself.

Ruby headed down the long corridor toward the cafeteria. She'd only gone a few paces when she remembered that access was cut off. The decorators who were painting Jill's office and several others on her corridor were also painting the corridor itself. They'd just started on the ceiling and there was scaffolding up.

Ruby followed the handwritten sign directing people downstairs to the basement corridor. It followed the identical path to the one above. At the end was a flight of stairs, which came up just outside the cafeteria.

The dimly lit basement, with its municipal dark green paint and oppressively low ceiling snaked with thick pipes, gave Ruby the creeps. To make matters worse, it was completely empty, apart from a couple of abandoned carts left standing against the wall. She strode out, anxious to get to the next staircase, which would take her back to the bright light and comfort of the cafeteria. She was almost there and beginning to feel a little less spooked, when she noticed a door marked "storage." She slowed down. What if...? No, the thought was ridiculous. It was too easy. On the other hand, Jill had said her files were going into storage and this appeared to be a storage room. She turned the handle. The door was locked. What did she expect—that the door would swing open, and sitting in front of her would be a box marked "Jill McNulty's Top-Secret Surrogacy Files"?

She went into the cafeteria and bought a mint tea for Ronnie and a KitKat for herself. Still wondering what might be behind that door, she went back to her mother.

When she walked into the room, Ronnie was sitting up in bed, smiling broadly. "You look better," Ruby said.

"I am. Thank God we didn't worry your father."

"So, the pain's gone?" Ruby said, putting the cup of mint tea down on the bedside locker.

"Let's put it this way, I've been to the loo five times since you left. For some reason the curry seems to have upset my stomach. The midwife said it can happen and that some women become sensitive to certain foods in pregnancy." She insisted she would be fine now and that Ruby should go home.

"OK, if you're sure. Ring me anytime if you need me. Promise?"

"Promise."

Ruby leaned over the bed and kissed Ronnie good night. "Love you."

"Love you, too, darling. And thanks for looking after me."

"My pleasure," Ruby said.

As she headed toward the main exit, Ruby broke off a piece of KitKat and popped it into her mouth. A few moments later, she had demolished the entire thing. After all the stress and tension of the evening, she was desperate for a sugar fix.

As she carried on walking, she became aware that she was about to pass the cleaners' cubbyhole. She felt her pace slow down. The door was open and the keys were hanging on their hooks. Screwing up the KitKat foil and shoving it in her pocket, she looked first to the right and then to the left. Deciding that the coast was clear, she slipped into the tiny room.

There were six keys marked "storage." That meant the hospital had six storage rooms. With so many to choose from, the chances were slim that the room she had just discovered contained Jill's files. "Oh, what the hell," she muttered. She picked up all six keys. Putting her head round the door to check that nobody was coming, she began walking toward the basement stairs.

As she reached the bottom a loud clanking sound almost had her charging back up again. Then she realized it was just the noise of the water pipes. She headed toward the storage room, looking over her shoulder every few seconds to check that there was nobody following her.

The fourth key fitted the lock to the storage room. It was a largish room—maybe twice the size of her living room. It was filled with office furniture. She decided that the desks, filing cabinets and swivel chairs belonged to the offices that were being decorated. Under each desk was a cardboard packing case. Ruby went over to the first one. A name she didn't recognize had been scrawled across the top in black felt tip. She didn't recognize the name on the second one either. Feeling a bit like Goldilocks, she looked at the third. Bingo! Just right! The box was marked with Jill's name.

Ruby slipped the door keys into her pocket and lifted the flaps on the packing case. It contained three or four old-fashioned box files full of papers, mainly invoices marked "paid" or "outstanding." She sat down on the linoleum-tiled floor and started sifting through the papers. If they weren't invoices, then they were financial forecasts or lists of maintenance work needing to be carried out.

She was halfway through the second box file when she came across a typed sheet that looked different from the rest. It was divided into columns. The first was headed up "name of patient." Then came the time of delivery and sex of child. The final column contained the signature of the attending doctor or midwife.

Ruby studied the sheet and noticed that in the column marked "patient," there were always two names. The second was in brackets. She went through the list. Many of the names meant nothing to her, but several did. They were the names of celebrities. The first one she spotted was China Katz. Ruby's heart rate began to speed up. In brackets next to the star's name was another name: Kate Murphy. Somebody had written the words "baby girl" and then there was a signature.

She carried on scanning the list. Farther down was a second name she recognized: Mia Ferrari. As usual, a woman's name was bracketed next to it. "Oh, my God," Ruby muttered, hand shaking. "These have to be the names of the surrogates." Her eyes widened. There had to be more than a dozen women here who had used them.

Her eyes carried on down. When she finally found the name she was looking for, she let out a gasp. She ran her finger across the columns. Claudia Planchette . . . [Hannah Morgan] . . . Boy. Finally her eyes came to rest on the signature of the doctor who had performed Hannah's cesarean. The signature read: S. Epstien.

She thought she must have read it wrong, but she hadn't. She must have watched Sam sign dozens of credit card slips. There was no doubt in her mind. This was his signature all right.

Shocked and confused, Ruby stuffed the piece of paper into her bag. Then she carried on hunting through the papers. She came across a photocopy of the original list. She thought about leaving it, but instead she put it in her pocket. Having made sure that the rest of the papers were arranged tidily in both box files, so that they didn't look as if they had been tampered with, she closed the lids. Then she put them back in the packing case and secured the flaps. She was convinced that there had to be a rational explanation. There was no possible way that Sam could have been involved in this. He must have been set up in some way. She had to speak to him.

Her adrenaline flowing overtime now, she switched off the light and opened the door into the corridor. Since she was looking down, it was the woman's shoes she saw first: sensible black slip-ons with a tiny heel. Ruby's entire body went rigid. Her eyes shot to the woman's face. "Jill! What on earth are you doing here?"

Judging by her stunned expression, Jill was as shocked as Ruby.

"I have an important meeting tomorrow," Jill spluttered nervously, as if she were the guilty party. She cleared her throat. "I came to collect some papers."

It was then that Ruby realized Jill wasn't alone. Standing beside her was Tom Hardacre. She recognized him from the TV. He was even more good looking in the flesh. On the other hand, he was wearing a rugby shirt with the collar turned up. The supposedly rakish public school look tended to attract sporty fillies from the shires, but always left Ruby thinking "Dodgy Fulham estate agent."

"This is Ruby Silverman," Jill said to Tom Hardacre. "She has been giving talks to some of our expectant mums."

Hardacre nodded slowly. "Ah, yes, I remember you mentioning her." His tone was languid and aloof.

"I thought you were on holiday," Ruby said to Jill.

"There have been heavy storms in the south of France. Tommy and I decided not to go, didn't we, darling?" So, Tom Hardacre was her "chap." That was something Ruby hadn't known.

Hardacre ignored Jill and turned to Ruby. "Your turn to answer a question," he said icily. "What exactly are you doing here?"

Ruby considered her options. She could make up some story and attempt to lie her way out of the situation, or she could attempt to overcome the shock and fear she was feeling, pull herself up to her full five feet four and a half inches and confront this pair.

"I've been doing some detective work," Ruby heard herself say.

"In this dreadful place?" Hardacre smirked. His expression contained all the sympathy of a shark ambushing lunch. "Goodness. What could you possibly have been looking for?"

"Evidence," Ruby said.

"Evidence," he repeated chirpily. "I see. Might I ask, what sort of *evidence*?"

Ruby noticed that Jill was looking petrified and practically hyperventilating.

"Evidence that proves you and Jill were involved in finding surrogates to carry babies for rich women who didn't want to lose their figures by getting pregnant themselves."

Hardacre put his hands in his pockets and roared with laughter. "I've never heard such utter piffle. This hospital and all the doctors in it are committed to natural childbirth."

"Really? So, what do you make of this?" Ruby reached into her pocket and pulled out the copy of the list she had found.

"What is it?" Jill said, voice trembling. Ruby handed her the paper. Jill began reading—but clearly far too slowly for Hardacre's liking. He snatched it from her.

"The names of the surrogates are in brackets," Ruby said.

Hardacre started to laugh. "None of this implicates us. The only signatures I see here belong to Sam Epstien and the other foreign doctors working here. Quite a little scam they've got going, I would say."

"Absolutely," Jill echoed.

"But I found it among your papers," Ruby said to Jill.

"I . . . I have no idea how it got there. Maybe you planted it. That's it. You could have planted it."

"What! Don't be absurd. Why would I do a thing like that?"

"I don't know," Hardacre said. "To blackmail us, maybe?"

"What possible reason could I have to blackmail you?"

At this point a young porter approached, pushing an empty cart. He kept his head down, pretending not to have heard the raised voices. The three of them responded with silence.

Ruby watched as Hardacre slipped the paper into his back pocket. It was clear he now thought he had retrieved the evidence against him. Of course he hadn't. Ruby still had the original list in her bag.

"Right, this conversation is over," he said. "I don't know who put you up to this, but I would suggest you go home and forget all about it. Although you might want to have some words with Sam Epstien, who clearly isn't the honest straightforward type you thought he was. In fact I am tempted to pay a visit to the hospital's chief executive myself."

Ruby wasn't about to be browbeaten. "I suggest you take that form out of your pocket and look more closely at it."

"I'm not sure you heard me," he came back at her. "I said this conversation is over."

"Indulge me." She smiled. "Just look at it."

He took the paper out of his pocket.

"OK, look down the list until you get to Claudia Planchette. The name next to hers—the one in brackets—belongs to a woman called Hannah Morgan."

"What of it?"

"Hannah was one of your patients, wasn't she? It was Hannah who gave birth to Claudia's baby."

"What? You're mad." Hardacre crossed his arms defensively in front of him. He was trying to retain the upper hand, but it was clear that he was losing it.

"Hannah claims she was Claudia's surrogate and I believe her. So, are you telling me you knew nothing about it?"

"Yes, I am. This form is rubbish. It has nothing whatsoever to do with me and I have no interest in some madwoman who might be trying to extort money from Claudia Planchette."

"Did you know that Claudia still owes Hannah a great deal of money?" Ruby persisted.

Hardacre stared her straight in the eye and said: "I have absolutely no idea what you're talking about."

Even in the poor light, it was clear that the color had drained from Jill's face. She looked as if she might throw up from nerves at any moment.

"What's more," Ruby went on, "Claudia rejected her son because she didn't like the color of his hair. He is ginger and Claudia doesn't *do* ginger. Even when it comes to her own child."

"This is madness. I've never heard such utter bilge."

"You know, my guess is that at some stage—sooner rather than later—Hannah will go to court to get the money

Claudia owes her. DNA tests will be required and I fail to see how you and Jill and, more to the point, St. Luke's, won't be implicated. Of course, technically you may have done nothing illegal, but bearing in mind St. Luke's commitment to natural childbirth and your public comments about anorexia in pregnant women, you have done something morally outrageous. By caving in to these women's vanity and allowing them to have babies using surrogates, you are perpetuating a vile culture in which women are only acceptable if their bodies look emaciated. Not only will St. Luke's reputation be ruined if this goes to court, but I doubt you will ever work as a doctor again."

Jill hadn't said anything for a while. Suddenly it was clear that her anxiety had turned into full-scale panic. "My God, what are we going to do? How many times did I try to tell you that Claudia Planchette was a loose cannon and not to be trusted?"

"Shut up," Hardacre spat. "You don't know what you're talking about."

But Jill wouldn't or couldn't shut up. "I knew we could trust all the others, but I begged you not to get involved with Claudia. As usual you refused to listen to me. Your greed and arrogance got the better of you. Now look what's happened."

Ignoring Jill, Hardacre touched Ruby's arm and took her to one side. "You know, Ruby, I'm sure we could come to some arrangement that would benefit both of us."

"What? You're trying to buy me off?"

"Let's put it this way, I have considerable funds at my disposal. On top of that I am sure I could persuade Claudia to pay Hannah everything she is owed, as well as a substantial allowance if she agrees to keep the baby. The last thing Claudia wants is a scandal. If you agree to my terms, we all benefit and St. Luke's reputation is saved into the bargain. What do you say?"

Ruby was clenching her fists with outrage. "I say no." She paused. "Just tell me one thing. Why did you get involved in this thing? By all accounts, you're a very rich man. You didn't need the money."

He stood there, refusing to say anything. Something approaching a snarl had formed on his face.

"Ah, but that's just it," Jill piped up. "He did need the money."

He turned on her and once again barked at her to shut up.

Suddenly something seemed to snap inside her. "No. I won't shut up. I will not let you control or shout at me anymore. I've had enough. Do you hear? That's the last time you tell me what to do." Jill was standing next to them now. "You see, Tom was bankrupt." Even though she was looking directly at him, she continued to refer to him in the third person. "He'd invested all his money in some shady Iranian construction company. It went bust and left him penniless. Everybody had warned him it would happen, but he refused to listen and went ahead. Money is like a drug to Tom. The more he has, the more he wants. It's the only thing he cares about." She started to cry. "And soon I became like him. I was weak. He dragged me into his reality. He convinced me there was nothing wrong with these women using surrogates. I can't believe what an idiot I've been."

Ruby was beginning to feel some sympathy for Jill. Hardacre was a domineering monster who preyed on frail women.

Hardacre looked contemptuously at Jill, but didn't say anything.

"Just tell me one thing," Ruby said to Hardacre. "Was Sam Epstien really involved in all of this?"

"Scales beginning to fall from your eyes, are they?" She took that as a yes. Hardacre brought his face to within an inch of hers. “Remember, I may have been bankrupt, but I am not bankrupt now.” His tone was menacing. “I am rich again, and if you choose to take me on, I will fight dirty and I will prove to be a formidable adversary.”

Ruby didn’t doubt it for a second.

Chapter 17

When she got home, Ruby was still shaking with shock and fury. She was also thinking about Sam. She refused to accept he was part of this despicable surrogacy gang. She opened a bottle of wine and sat on the sofa, knocking back Sauvignon and trying to calm down. She wondered what Hardacre and Jill would do now. Would they disappear? She doubted it. Hardacre was an arrogant bully and Jill would probably calm down eventually and carry on doing as she was told. The pair would wait for her to go to the newspapers. Then they would hire lawyers and come out fighting with injunctions and writs. What they didn't know, of course, was that she still had the original list containing the names of the celebrities and their surrogates.

At one point she got up to listen to her phone messages. There was one from Sam saying how much he was missing her and that Buddy had suffered no long-term effects from the stroke. "So, I'll be home the day after tomorrow. The plane gets in at 6 A.M. Don't bother meeting me. I'll get a cab to your place and maybe we could have breakfast together before you leave for work. Love you."

She must have played the message half a dozen times.

She was looking for an awkwardness in his voice, any sign that might indicate he had something to hide. But he sounded so relaxed, so happy, so in love with her. What was more, Sam was a virtual slave to medical ethics. He never discussed patients with her. It was inconceivable that he could be involved in the surrogacy business.

A couple of hours later adrenaline was still pumping inside her. She decided some warm milk might calm her down. Having put a mug of milk into the microwave, she went to her handbag and took out the list with Sam's signature on it. Her back resting against the kitchen counter, she stood staring at the handwriting. On some pretext or other, Jill must have convinced Sam, as well as the other foreign doctors, to sign their names in the last column before any of the other details were filled in. The other information must have been added later. It was obvious why Jill and Hardacre wanted the names of foreign doctors on the list. If the scam ever came to light, the foreign doctors, who usually only stayed for a few months, would get the blame. The likelihood was that they would be long gone and nobody would bother pursuing them.

She took the mug out of the microwave and looked at the kitchen clock. It was past three—ten in the evening New York time. She decided to phone Sam. Somebody was trying to cover up their own involvement in the surrogacy affair by implicating Sam. He absolutely had to know what was going on.

She kept trying his mobile, but each time she got his voice mail. After half an hour or so, the effects of the warm milk started to kick in and she started to feel drowsy. She left an urgent message for him to call her and took the phone to bed with her.

She fell asleep almost immediately. Two hours later she was wide awake again, her mind buzzing. What if the press somehow got hold of the surrogacy story and Sam couldn't prove his innocence? He wouldn't just lose his job. He would lose his career. She tried phoning him two or three more times, but there was still no answer. When she couldn't get back to sleep, she got up and made another hot drink, but she couldn't get it down. She felt too sick.

She rang St. Luke's just after eight to check on Ronnie. She spoke to the Jamaican midwife who was just going off duty. She said Ronnie was absolutely fine and had left in a taxi a few minutes ago. Ruby immediately called Ronnie on her mobile. "Mum, what are you doing going home on your own? I said I'd pick you up."

"I know, darling, but I'm fine and I didn't want to put you to any trouble. It would have meant you getting to work late and I know this is your busiest time of year."

Ruby said she would phone to check on her later. "That's sweet of you, but don't worry. Your dad's back from Munich this lunchtime."

WHEN CHANEL ASKED her what was wrong, Ruby put her off by saying she had slept badly and had a headache—both of which were true. She didn't want to tell Chanel—or Fi for that matter—what she'd discovered until she'd spoken to Sam. It felt too disloyal.

Around midmorning, Fi phoned to ask Ruby if she fancied meeting up for lunch. Chanel was happy to mind the shop, so Ruby accepted.

They went to Carluccio's and ate comfort food—steaming hot minestrone, into which they dipped thick chunks of heavily buttered ciabatta.

"Rubes," Fi said quietly as she moved vegetables around in her soup, "there was actually a specific reason I wanted us to have lunch."

"Sounds ominous," Ruby said, raising her eyebrows. "Go on."

"Look, you know I love you and that I wouldn't say or do anything to hurt you."

Ruby held her ciabatta in midair and frowned. "Blimey, this is starting to sound really heavy."

"It is. I haven't slept for nights thinking about whether or not I should tell you, but in the end I decided I had to."

"Tell me what?"

"It's about Sam."

"What about him?"

"Well, it's not so much about Sam—well, it is, but..."

"Fi, come on. Whatever it is, just say it."

"OK." Fi put down her soup spoon and steepled her fingers. "I have just found out that Buddy never had a stroke. He hasn't been ill at all. In fact, for the past month, he's been in Boca Raton with Irene."

"What are you talking about? Of course he's had a stroke. Sam's been in New York making sure he gets the right treatment."

"Sam may have been in New York, but he hasn't been with Buddy and Irene." She picked up her bag, took out a postcard and handed it to Ruby.

Ruby glanced at the picture of a palm tree–fringed beach and turned the card over. It was addressed to Fi and Saul. She looked at the postmark. It had been sent about a week ago. There were just a couple of lines: "Buddy and I having wonderful vacation soaking up the sun. Back in NY after New Year's. Hoping to see you soon. Love, Irene."

"I don't know what's been going on," Fi said gently, "but it looks as if Sam has been lying to you."

"Lying?" The suggestion was outrageous. "He can't have been lying. There has to be some mistake."

"There's no mistake. I phoned Irene, just to double check. Buddy's absolutely fine."

"But I don't understand. What could possibly be going on?" Ruby's confusion and panic was causing her heart to pound in her chest. "And to lie about somebody being close to death. It's an appalling thing to do. I can't believe Sam would be capable of such a thing." Fi didn't say anything.

"So, what does this mean?" Ruby went on. "That Sam's got another woman back home?" The name Kimberley shot into her head. She was the rather forlorn friend of Sam's they had bumped into at Kew. Could Sam be having an affair with her? Had he whisked her off to some love nest in New York? It seemed unlikely, but she supposed it was possible. Maybe she had been missing something when she decided there was nothing going on between them.

"I think you'll have to ask him that," Fi said.

Ruby sat shaking her head and feeling sick. "I don't know what to do. Suddenly this is all getting too much."

"What do you mean? Has something else happened?"

Ruby decided the time had come to tell her what had happened last night. Fi listened quietly as Ruby explained about finding the paper with Sam's signature on it. "If you had asked me even a minute ago, I would have said that Sam was one of the most honorable, trustworthy people I know. It's one of the reasons I love him. Now I'm not sure what to think."

After lunch, the two women stood on the pavement saying good-bye. "I feel so guilty having to be the one to tell you this," Fi said. "But I couldn't live with you not knowing the truth."

"Don't feel guilty," Ruby said. "If I had been in your position, I would have done the same."

"And you'll let me know as soon as you've spoken to Sam?"

"Promise."

Ruby gave Fi a final hug. Afterward the two women set off in opposite directions. Even though the air was bitter and it was starting to rain, Ruby walked slowly, tears stinging her cheeks.

She arrived at the shop and for the first time since it had opened, she was relieved to see there were no customers. She sat down heavily on one of the chairs they reserved for expectant mums and told Chanel everything that had happened. “I thought I knew Sam,” she said, finding it impossible to choke back the tears. “I can’t believe he lied to me about Buddy being ill.”

Chanel was typically upbeat. “Look, I know it looks bad, but you ’aven’t spoken to Sam yet. You need to give ’im a chance to explain.”

Ruby agreed that she did, but she couldn’t prevent the words *straws* and *clutching* coming into her mind.

THAT NIGHT, SHE tried Sam again. When she still couldn’t reach him, she phoned Hannah. It was important that she was kept up to speed with developments.

When Ruby told her how she had acquired the list of surrogate mothers, Hannah was gobsmacked. “Bloody hell. That’s amazing. God, you’re brave. I couldn’t have done something like that. I’d have been petrified. So where do we go from here? For Alfie’s sake, I’m still not sure I want to go to the newspapers with this.”

“I know. We have to be really careful about what we do next.” Ruby said she needed to think. By saying this, she was playing for time. Mindful of Chanel’s advice not to mention her own feelings, she refused to make any decision about how to proceed until she had spoken to Sam about how his signature came to be on the form.

“Hannah, before you go, I want to check a couple of details with you about Alfie’s birth.”

“Sure.”

“You had an emergency cesarean, right?”

“Right.”

"And Doctor Hardacre performed the op?"

"No. He was on holiday. Somebody else did it."

"Who?"

"I don't know. There was such a fuss and commotion because I was losing so much blood. All I can remember is being wheeled into surgery and being given an anesthetic."

"What about the rest of the time you were in the hospital? Which doctor saw you?"

She said she didn't know his name. "But he was young. American. Very good looking as I remember."

"Was his name Epstien?"

"It could have been. I really don't remember."

IT WASN'T UNTIL the early hours of the morning that she finally reached Sam. He said he hadn't called her because the phone network had been down all day and he had only just got her messages. "I'm really sorry not to have gotten back to you. And I can't speak now, because my plane's boarding. You said it was urgent. Can it possibly wait until I get back?"

"Yeah, sure." She'd waited this long to speak to him. A few more hours weren't going to make much difference.

"Rubes, you sound a bit down. You OK?"

"Let's talk when you get back." She managed to wish him a safe journey.

She went to bed, but once again sleep refused to come. Just after seven, she decided to get up and have a shower. She had just got out when she heard the door buzzer go. She opened the door, wearing her old terry dressing gown. Sam was standing in front of her beaming, bearing freshly baked croissants from the French baker round the corner. He threw his arms round her. "Gee, I have missed you."

"Me, too," she said, aware of how cold her voice sounded. She made no attempt to put her arms around him.

"Has something happened? You sound weird, just like you did last night on the phone. What's going on?"

"I'll make some coffee," she said.

He dragged his bag into the hall and closed the front door. "Ruby, talk to me. You're making me nervous. Have I done something?"

She stood filling the kettle with water. "I'm not sure where to start."

"You could try the beginning."

She flicked the switch on the kettle and handed him the stolen paper. "Take a look at this."

"What is it?"

"Just read it."

He was clearly jet-lagged and couldn't quite take it in. "Yeah, OK, this is one of the forms all doctors sign at St. Luke's after they've attended a birth. Where did you get this?"

"I'll explain in a minute. Do you see anything odd about the form?"

He squinted. "There are some names in brackets. I've never seen that before."

"Suppose they were the names of surrogate mothers."

He shrugged. "I guess that's a possibility. But it makes no sense that the hospital would keep records of surrogates for somebody to find."

"Or steal."

His eyes were bulging with disbelief. "You stole this?"

"From Jill McNulty."

"Jill? What's she got to do with all this? And how could you take a risk like that? If you'd got caught..."

"I did get caught."

"For crying out loud. What happened?"

She explained about Jill's relationship with Tom Hardacre—both personal and professional—and how they'd caught her leaving the storage room.

"So, you were right. Hardacre is involved."

She directed him back to the paper. "Look down the list of doctors. What do you see?"

"Hold up. That's my name. It says I attended the birth of Hannah Morgan's baby."

"And did you?"

"No, I did not." His voice was raised in indignation.

"Tom Hardacre seems to think you did."

"I don't give a damn what he thinks. The man is a liar."

"Hardacre suggested that he and Jill weren't working alone and that you were part of their little team."

Sam's eyes were wide with fury. "Surely you don't believe that? It's absurd. I admit it's my signature on the form, but I have no idea how it got on there. Somehow I've been set up. I must have thought I was signing something else. If I get hold of Hardacre, I'll break the bastard's neck. Christ, my entire professional reputation is at stake here. I swear to God, Ruby, the night Hannah's baby was born, I was nowhere near the hospital."

"That's not true. That was the night we got back from Brighton and you got a call from the hospital asking you to go in to attend an emergency. I remember we even had a conversation about it on the following Monday. Why are you lying?"

He took a deep breath and let it out slowly. "I'm not lying now. I was lying then. That call wasn't from the hospital. I never went near the place."

"Really? Hannah says that while she was in hospital, she was seen by a young, good-looking American doctor. Was that you?"

"No. It absolutely was not me. There are several American medics at St. Luke's."

"OK, but why did you lie to me about going to the hospital?"

He couldn't look at her. "I had to see somebody. They were in trouble."

"Who was it?"

"I can't tell you that."

She blinked with astonishment and let out a soft laugh. "What do you mean you can't tell me?"

"I just can't, that's all. You have to believe me."

"What? Like I believed you when you said you were going to New York because Buddy had had a stroke?"

The color drained from his face. "You know about that?"

She picked Irene's postcard up off the kitchen unit and handed it to him.

"I cannot believe Buddy could have been so stupid. He was supposed to tell Irene."

"Tell Irene what? That they were meant to be your alibi? That they were meant to be covering up for the fact that you were seeing another woman?"

"Ruby, I swear to God that I wasn't seeing another woman."

"Then what were you doing? Was it tied up with the surrogacy thing?"

"No! I had nothing to do with that. I can't tell you what I was doing there."

"Rubbish. The truth is it was a woman. I've caught you with your guard down—not to mention your pants—and you can't think up another story that might convince me you weren't seeing somebody else?"

"That's not true."

"Sam, this is absurd. Now you've been found out, you could at least have the balls to admit you were having an affair in New York. Was it with Kimberley?"

He winced—as if she had suddenly wounded him. She

interpreted his reaction as guilt. "I am not having an affair with Kimberley," he said softly. "I had some business to attend to in New York, but I can't talk about it right now."

"What business?"

"Just business. OK?"

"No, it's not bloody *OK,*" she shot back. "If you weren't seeing somebody in New York, what were you doing?" She was vaguely aware of the kettle coming to a boil and switching itself off.

By way of reply, he rubbed his hand over his eyes. "I can't tell you. I'm sorry. I am so sorry." He tried to put his arm round her, but she pushed him away. "Believe it or not," he said, "this is tearing me apart, too, but right now I need you to trust me."

"Trust you? That's a laugh. How can I trust you, when you've lied like this? You let me think Buddy was at death's door. That was an evil thing to do. I can't believe he was in on it as well. Until now, I'd thought he was such a sweet man. And as for you . . . I loved you. I still love you." Tears were starting to tumble down her cheeks.

He tried to wipe them away, but she pushed him off again. "I love you, too," he said. "You have no idea how much I love you."

"But love is about trust and I can't trust you. You've lied to me. You lied to me about what you were doing in New York. I can only assume you lied to me about your involvement with this surrogacy affair and that this is your signature on the form." She was waving the paper in front of him.

"Ruby, as God is my witness, I don't know how it got there."

"I'm sorry, Sam," she said softly. "I simply don't believe you. Now, I think you'd better go," She was surprised by how calm and in control she felt.

He stood in front of her, his face etched with pain.

"And I can't see much point in you coming back." She wiped her eyes with her dressing gown sleeve.

He nodded. "You're right. I think maybe it's best that I go."

She expected him to protest, to fight for her, to beg her not to end it. Instead he was simply walking away. A few moments ago he had been telling her how much he loved her. If he really loved her, he wouldn't be letting her go like this.

After he had gone she lay on her bed, curled up in a ball, and sobbed until it was time to drag herself up for work. Her emotions veered from disbelief and shock to utter disgust. Sam cheating on her was bad enough, but to discover he was some lowlife who was making a fortune helping vain, self-absorbed starlets keep their figures by using surrogates to carry their babies, made her sick to her stomach.

OVER THE NEXT few days she battled to hold herself together. She would have fallen apart had it not been for her determination to keep going and the love and support she received from Chanel and Fi. They talked to her for hours and encouraged her to cry and rage against Sam as much as she wanted. Fi even came to the shop with a homemade lasagne and a casserole to help keep her strength up. She also offered to phone Buddy and Irene to see if she could get any more information about Sam's affair, but Ruby persuaded her not to on the grounds that Buddy and Irene's loyalty was to Sam and she would only get put off with more lies.

Fi also kept insisting Ruby come for dinner. She would make huge comforting casseroles or lasagnes and Saul would keep her wineglass filled up and later on, when she was pleasantly tipsy, he would drive her home.

One night when the three of them were having dinner,

Ben woke up and came downstairs. He climbed onto Fi's lap and sat listening to the adults discussing Sam.

"Huh," Ben announced gravely at one point. "Dat Sam I Am, dat Sam I Am, I do not like dat Sam I Am."

"You're not the only one, darling," Ruby responded with a bitter laugh.

Ruby assumed that after Tom Hardacre's promise to fight dirty, he and Jill would carry on working at the hospital. She was pretty sure they would be happy to play a waiting game and sit tight until she finally let the surrogacy matter drop through lack of concrete evidence. When her curiosity got the better of her and she phoned the hospital to check if Hardacre and Jill were still there, it came as a surprise to be told that they were both on extended leave. She was forced to consider that maybe she had them against the ropes after all. When she asked the girl on the switchboard if Sam was still working at the hospital, she discovered that he was. For whatever reason, he was standing his ground it seemed.

The frantic preparations for Guatemalan week also turned out to be a powerful anesthetic to Ruby's emotions. The night before the launch, Ruby, Chanel and Fi were at the shop until eleven, getting the place ready.

Earlier on, Craig, who had taken the day off work, spent hours tramping up and down in the perishing cold, handing out flyers. Ruby was aware that in PR terms, handing out flyers was a bit downmarket for a shop like Les Sprogs, but she didn't care. The event was for charity and anything that brought in the customers was fine by her.

In the evening Craig took charge of draping the walls in vivid cotton fabrics and hanging fairy lights and brightly painted Mayan Christmas masks. He also went out to fetch pizza and beer.

The women decided to devote three racks exclusively to Guatemalan baby clothes. They dotted the shelves with worry dolls, beaded angels, Santas and hand-carved nativity scenes. Finally, Ruby hung some very powerful black-and-white images of Guatemalan street children. "Just to remind people what this event is all about," she said.

They were just about to leave when Craig noticed that a few of the fairy lights had started to flicker. While he went off to fix them, the women stood around talking. "No word from Sam, I take it?" Fi said. Ruby shook her head. "Every time the phone rings, I think it's going to be him, wanting to talk."

"What's to talk about?" Chanel said. "The bloke's a liar and a cheat. End of story. If you ask me, you 'ad a lucky escape."

"One of the things I find hardest to accept," Ruby said, "is what a pathetic judge of character I am. I used to think I was really good at getting the measure of people. Can you believe that?"

Fi put an arm around Ruby's shoulder. "Come on, we were all taken in by Sam. He seemed so charming and decent. I still find it almost impossible to believe he has done the things he's done. The man is a total creep."

"Too right," Chanel said. "You're best off out of it."

"I know," Ruby agreed, "but I loved him so much and it's so hard to stop."

ON SATURDAY MORNING, an hour before opening time, Ronnie and Phil arrived at the shop laden with trays of Guatemalan food. They had brought Guatemalan doughnuts as well as borrachos—cakes soaked in rum. On top of all this, there were plates and plates of chicken tamales and several liters of Guatemalan punch.

"Oh, Mum! This is amazing. A few nibbles, you said. You really didn't have to do all this. You must have been at it all week."

"My pleasure," Ronnie said waving away Ruby's words. "You know what a sucker I am for a good cause."

For the time being at least, Ruby had decided not to tell her mother that she and Sam had split up. It would only upset her. With the baby due in a few weeks, she had enough to worry about.

Aunty Sylvia turned up a few minutes after Ronnie and Phil. She had agreed to be in charge of handing out juice boxes and Christmas crackers to the children. She still looked sad, but if her appearance was anything to go by—full makeup, calf-length olive suede skirt and matching cashmere top—she was coping very well. "So, have you had it out with Nigel yet?" Ruby asked.

"Sort of. I'll fill you in later."

Ruby suspected the shop would be busy. She had no idea quite how busy. From about eleven, customers started pouring in. Handing out flyers had clearly been a brilliant move. Even though she'd already thanked Craig profusely for all his hard work, she made a mental note to buy him a very large and very expensive bottle of malt.

Ronnie's food was a tremendous hit, but the punch went down particularly well. Once the posh mummies were sufficiently lubricated, they couldn't part with their money fast enough. The Guatemalan clothes and toys flew off the shelves.

Ruby was disappointed not to see any famous faces, but she hadn't been counting on too many stars turning up. She knew how reluctant most of them were to mix with "civilians." On top of that, it was almost Christmas, and she knew that by now most of them had abandoned London in favor of Mustique or wherever.

As more and more people arrived, the din grew louder. On top of the Latin American music coming from the CD player, there were the braying mummies, babies crying and older children screeching as they careened about the place, knocking over glasses of punch and stealing characters from the nativity scene.

Things were well under way when Fi and Saul arrived with Ben and Connor. "Right, what can we do to help?" Fi said. Ruby put Fi on the register with Chanel while Saul took a gang of children, including Ben and a sleeping Connor, over to the play area.

Just after twelve Ivan appeared. He had finally finished laying the floor tiles in Ruby's kitchen. Since she had missed him the night before, because she had been busy decking out the shop, and since Ivan worked on a strictly cash-only basis, she asked him if he would mind popping in the next day to collect the money she owed him. He'd been looking much better lately, but this morning he was more breathless than she had ever seen him. He was also rubbing his chest.

"Ivan," she said as she handed over several fifty-pound notes, "are you having chest pains?"

"Eet's nothing. I be fine. I have pulled mus-kle, that ees all."

"Really?" She wasn't convinced.

"Da. I hef slice of kek and a leetle punch, maybe. Then I feel much better." She invited him to help himself.

The one person she hadn't remotely been expecting was Nigel. He came in looking rather self-conscious—presumably because he knew that Aunty Sylvia had told the family about their tiff. He acknowledged Ruby with an awkward wave and went over to Aunty Sylvia. At this point a small child began fiddling with the volume control on the CD player and turned the music off. As a result, everybody could hear the exchange that followed between Aunty Sylvia and Nigel.

"I thought I told you not to come here," Aunty Sylvia hissed.

"I know, but I had to see you. We need to sort this thing out."

"But this isn't the time or place. It will have to wait."

"It can't."

Their voices grew louder. Soon people were exchanging uncomfortable glances.

Then, just as Ruby was about to go over and ask them to take their argument outside, Aunty Sylvia, clearly sensing they were causing a scene, steered Nigel behind the counter and into the kitchen.

No sooner had Ruby completed her sigh of relief than she heard her father cry out: "Oh, my God, he's collapsed." Ruby swiveled round to see Ivan lying on the floor. He was curled up into a fetal position, gasping for breath.

"Omigod," she cried.

As she dashed over to Ivan, who was surrounded by a small group of people, she could hear arguing coming from the kitchen. "You never told me you were seventeen years older than me," Nigel was shouting at Aunty Sylvia. "How do you expect me to feel?"

Deciding that people overhearing Aunty Sylvia's tiff with Nigel was the least of her worries, she knelt down beside Ivan, whose lips were starting to turn blue. "Ivan, can you hear me?" she said urgently, tapping his face. "Please speak to me."

"I'm a nurse," a female voice said. "Let me take a look at him." Ruby got up to make room for the woman. She felt the pulse in his neck. "He's had a heart attack! Somebody call an ambulance!"

In the background, Aunty Sylvia and Nigel were still going at it. "Why does it matter how old I am?" Aunty Sylvia was yelling at Nigel.

"It doesn't matter. What matters is that you didn't tell me. Why can't you understand," Nigel said, "that a relationship has to be built on trust?"

"You're a fine one to talk about trust."

By now, the nurse had gone into what seemed to Ruby

like a controlled panic. "OK, I can't find a heartbeat!" She began pressing down hard on his chest. Every few seconds she would stop to breathe into his mouth and check if there was a pulse.

"What do you mean I'm a fine one to talk about trust?" It was Nigel.

"You know precisely what I mean."

Ruby, Phil and Ronnie were standing next to the nurse. "Is there anything we can do?" Ruby said to her. The nurse shook her head. "We need the paramedics. They might be able to restart his heart electronically."

Suddenly Ronnie's eyes widened, like an insect. "Omigod. Quick, Phil, the defibrillator! It's in the trunk of the car!"

Phil tore out of the shop and was back in less than a minute. The nurse practically snatched the machine from Phil and began scanning the instructions.

"What do you mean, you feel cheated?" Aunty Sylvia was barking at Nigel.

"Stand clear!" shouted the nurse. She placed the paddles on Ivan's chest and pressed the shock button. His upper body rose in the air. "Still nothing. Let's try again." She repeated the procedure. When there was no response, she tried for a third time.

"Yes, we have an ouput!"

There was loud cheering, clapping and shouts of "thank God."

"OK," Aunty Sylvia was shouting, "how do you think I feel, discovering I'm going out with a man who likes to dress up in women's clothes?"

For a few brief seconds there was a stunned silence, followed by a few giggles. The silence was broken by Ben, who was standing next to the nativity scene: "Mummy, Mummy," he piped up, "my have swallowed va baby Jesus."

Before Fi had a chance to rush toward him, another voice could be heard booming: "Would somebody care to tell me exactly what is going on here?"

Heads turned. Stella was standing in the doorway, an Armani-clad human pressure cooker on the point of parting with its lid.

Chapter 18

Although Stella gave every impression of being about to fly into a rage, she didn't. Losing control wasn't her style.

Ronnie and Aunty Sylvia took her to one side, well away from where the paramedics were attending to a now fully conscious Ivan and sprang to Ruby's defense.

Aunty Sylvia wasn't remotely scared of cousin Stella and didn't mince her works. "Stella, none of what happened here is Ruby's fault. She was doing this for charity. I admit it got out of hand, but that was partly my fault. I will not have you bullying and victimizing her. Is that clear?"

Stella looked Aunty Sylvia up and down. "Sylvia—long time no see. So, you stopped going to Weight Watchers, then." She turned to Ronnie and did the same. "Ruby mentioned you were pregnant. How very brave at your age."

"Good to see you're still so full of charm," Aunty Sylvia snarled.

At this point Ruby intervened and suggested to Aunty Sylvia that maybe she wasn't helping and that perhaps she and Ronnie should go home.

Once everybody had left the shop, Stella finally turned to Ruby and glared at her as if she were a side order of vegetables she hadn't ordered. At no point did she raise her voice or make any attempt to remonstrate with her. When Ruby tried desperately to apologize, Stella merely raised a hand to silence her. "I have very little to say, other than this . . ." Her voice was like stone. "Never in my life have I felt so let down. What I have seen here today is an outrage. I'm not interested in hearing explanations or excuses. Suffice it to say that my association with Les Sprogs is at an end."

"What? I make one mistake and you decide to walk out? Stella, don't do this. Can't we at least sit down over a cup of coffee and talk?"

"I have made my decision."

"So, where does that leave me?" Ruby said in what was little more than a whisper.

"That isn't my problem. You can choose to buy me out of the business or kiss it good-bye." She turned to go.

"But you own over 90 percent of the business. Where am I supposed to find money like that?"

"I have no idea."

"Stella, please. You can't just walk out like this. At least let me explain."

"Explain what? That you organized some cheap tawdry event behind my back and allowed it to turn into a soap opera?"

"I tried to reach you to ask you about doing a Guatemalan week, but you were on holiday. I thought you would be angry if I disturbed you."

"Guatemalan week?" Stella sneered. "What do you think you are running here with my money, a business or some kind of third world charity?"

"A business, but one with a heart and a social conscience—particularly at Christmas."

The words went over Stella's head. "You will be hearing from my attorney," she said. With that she turned on her heel and headed toward the door.

"Stella, please . . ." But she was gone.

Ruby bent down and picked up an empty juice box left by one of the children. She'd lost Sam and now she might be about to lose her business. She crumpled the box hard in her hand and felt tears stinging her eyes.

She trudged into the kitchen and put the kettle on. While she waited for it to boil, she phoned the hospital to find out how Ivan was doing. It took her ages to find anybody who had any information. When she finally found a nurse who did know what was going on, she was reluctant to tell Ruby anything because she wasn't a relative. The nurse took some persuading, but eventually she told her that Ivan was in surgery having an emergency bypass. She suggested Ruby phone back the next morning when they would know more about his condition.

No sooner had Ruby put down the phone than Chanel reappeared. Once all the customers had gone, Chanel had left as well, to give Ruby and Stella some space to talk. She had returned with Alfie, who was asleep in his stroller. For the moment, Ruby was too taken up with her own affairs to ask where Hannah was or how Chanel came to have Alfie.

"So, what did Stella 'ave to say?" Chanel said.

Ruby told her.

"Whadda bitch," Chanel muttered.

"I'll go to my bank to see what they're prepared to lend me, but I'm pretty sure they won't let me have the entire amount. But I absolutely refuse to let the business go without a fight. Not after I've worked so hard to build it up. I have to raise the money somehow. Thing is that right now I haven't the foggiest what I'm going to do."

"That makes two of us," Chanel said.

"What do you mean?"

She explained that after leaving the shop, she'd bumped into Hannah in the street. Hannah and Alfie had been on their way to the launch party. They went for coffee and

Hannah burst into tears, saying she was exhausted and couldn't cope with looking after Alfie. She begged Chanel to have him for a week or so.

"Look at 'im, lying there—all innocent and perfect," Chanel said to Ruby. " 'Ow could I possibly have said no?"

"But what are you going to do? Shouldn't you tell somebody? The authorities?"

Chanel shrugged. "Don't see why. 'Annah has the right to ask a mate to look after 'er baby for a few days. And I'm 'appy to do it."

"But has it occurred to you that she might want you to have him for longer than just a few days? What if she asks you to keep him?"

Chanel began stroking Alfie's head. "No point jumping the gun. Let's just wait and see 'ow she feels after she's 'ad a break."

RUBY'S BANK MANAGER said the bank would be willing to lend her half the amount she needed to buy Stella out. That meant she still had to come up with £200,000. Her parents immediately suggested remortgaging their house, but supremely grateful as Ruby was for their offer, she wouldn't hear of them risking their home. Fi and Chanel insisted something would turn up, but short of a miracle, Ruby couldn't see what.

From then on, Chanel brought Alfie to work for a few hours each day. He slept most of the time, but when he was awake Chanel couldn't have been more loving and attentive. When she wasn't cuddling him, playing with him or blowing raspberries on his tummy, she was showing him off to the customers. Everybody could see what a perfect mother she would make. "You've fallen in love with him, haven't you?" Ruby said.

"It's not just me," Chanel said, gazing at the sleeping child. "Craig 'as, too."

"Have you spoken to Hannah?"

Chanel nodded. "I 'ad her on the phone for two hours last night. She loves 'im to bits, but you were right—she isn't sure she can take 'im back."

"What are you going to do?"

"Give 'er more time to think. At least until after Christmas."

"What if she still doesn't want him back?"

"Then we 'ave to inform Social Services."

"What do you think will happen to him?"

She stroked Alfie's cheek. "Once the authorities know that Claudia Planchette is his real mother, they'll try to reunite 'im with 'er. I keep trying to convince myself it would be for the best."

"Would you and Craig take him if you could?"

"You mean adopt 'im?"

Ruby nodded.

"In a 'eartbeat."

EVERY LUNCHTIME, CHANEL and Alfie went home and Fi arrived to take her place. Fi couldn't have been more grateful for the work. Saul was still jobless and she was desperate to earn a few extra pounds to pay for Christmas. Helping out in the shop also gave Fi a break from her mother. Bridget had already arrived for her annual Christmas visit and was causing her usual mayhem. "Mum and Saul aren't speaking after she heard him on the phone telling one of his friends he was leaving me because of another woman—my mother. The only light on the horizon is that Saul has got a couple more auditions lined up. We've got the bank and the Inland Revenue on our backs. I'm praying he gets something before Christmas."

While Ruby was busy at work, she didn't have time to think about Sam. It was only when she got home in the evening and opened a bottle of wine that she allowed her emotions to take over. The problem was that despite everything, she couldn't stop loving him. It was that along with her overwhelming sense of loss that made her cry herself to sleep every night.

Every morning when she woke up, it took a few seconds before she remembered that Sam was gone from her life. The realization hit her like a wrecker's ball. From time to time, she thought about calling him, but there seemed no point.

Her spirits lifted a little when she discovered that Guatemalan week had raised £10,000 for the street children. A few of the celebrities, who had been invited to the launch but couldn't make it, had sent extremely generous checks.

It also turned out that one of Ruby's customers knew a journalist on the *Evening Standard* and had mentioned to her how much Ruby had raised. The next thing Ruby knew, the features editor was on the phone saying they wanted to run a full-page article on Les Sprogs. Ruby got straight on the phone to Stella. She hoped Stella would be so impressed that she had managed to raise money for charity as well as achieving a PR spinoff for the shop that she would change her mind about pulling out of the business. In fact she barely reacted. Her only memorable comment was: "Have you heard from my attorney yet?"

After she put the phone down from Stella, Ruby turned to Chanel. "She won't budge."

"C'mon, don't let 'er get you down. We'll sort something out. I'll talk to Craig. Some of 'is customers are loaded. Maybe you could touch some of them for a few grand. You never know."

"Yeah, you never know." She smiled.

• • •

CHANEL AND FI insisted Ruby take off the weekend before Christmas. "We've got all our child care sorted," Chanel said. "You go 'ome and rest."

Ruby put up a fight, but not much of one. Not that she planned to rest. Christmas was only a few days away and she hadn't done any shopping.

On Saturday morning she woke up and waited for the now-familiar pain to engulf her. She let the tears come. Then, after a few minutes she forced herself out of bed. She put on her dressing gown, went into the kitchen and made a strong cup of coffee.

As she sipped it, her thoughts turned to Jill McNulty and Hardacre. She wondered where she went from here. With Hannah's testimony, Jill McNulty's list and her own evidence that Tom Hardacre had tried to bribe her to keep quiet, she clearly had enough information to take to the newspapers. So what was stopping her? She knew it could only be loyalty to Sam. Even with all the evidence against him, part of her was still struggling to accept that he was involved.

The other thing bothering her was that the moment the story appeared in the newspapers, St. Luke's reputation would be ruined. Despite her fury about what was happening there, Ruby didn't want to be responsible for bringing down a world-famous maternity hospital. Once the story made the headlines, it would be almost impossible to convince people that the entire medical staff wasn't on the take from the surrogacy scam. Then again—as she'd told Jill and Hardacre—it was bound to leak out eventually if Hannah decided to sue Claudia for the money she owed her. Even if she didn't go to court, Alfie's true identity would have to be revealed when Chanel handed him over to Social Services.

It wouldn't be long before some opportunistic employee sold the story to the newspapers.

Once the press got wind of the story, Hannah would be hounded by tabloid journalists. They might choose to ignore the fact that she became a surrogate mother to help pay her university fees. Instead they might accuse her of greed and of being an unfit mother to her twins. Fingers would be pointed and her life could be ruined.

At the same time Claudia might end up taking Alfie simply because her fans would hate her and her career would be finished if she didn't. Ruby dreaded to think what sort of a life he would have with her as a mother.

Much as Ruby wanted Jill McNulty, Hardacre and Claudia exposed, she couldn't help thinking that this was one story that should never see the light of day.

After she'd finished her coffee, she decided to give Hannah a call to see how she was doing.

"Do you think I'm really wicked for not wanting to take Alfie back?" It was clear from her voice that she was deeply troubled.

"No. I don't think you're wicked." Ruby could hear what sounded like both twins crying in the background. "You're a single mum and you've got two young children of your own to care for. I think you're making the right decision."

"I've been a complete idiot getting involved with this surrogacy thing, but I really thought Claudia couldn't have any more children and that I was helping her. I had no idea what was really going on. Having said that, the moment I met her I could see she was crazy."

"Look, you were trying to earn some money to finance going back to uni. There's absolutely nothing wrong with that. You were a bit naive, that's all."

"A bit? That's an understatement."

"C'mon, you made a mistake. A pretty big one, I'll admit, but you have to stop beating yourself up."

She asked if Ruby had given any more thought to how they were going to expose Jill and Hardacre. Hannah seemed happy to leave all the decision making to Ruby. It was clear she didn't have the time or energy to take it on. Ruby told her what had been going through her mind. They agreed it needed more thought and that they would speak again after Christmas.

AS CHRISTMAS DREW closer, Ruby thought she might get a call or at least a card from Sam, but nothing came. She was sad not to hear from him, but bearing in mind the ease with which he had left her, she wasn't surprised.

She spent Christmas Day with her parents. Ronnie, who looked almost ready to pop, wasn't allowed to lift a finger.

On Christmas morning, Aunty Sylvia and Ruby arrived early to start preparing lunch. Phil had done all the food shopping a few days before. He'd bought everything apart from the turkey. That, along with several bottles of vodka, had been delivered courtesy of Ivan. The presents were a thank-you to Phil for helping to save his life. Apparently Ivan had also located the nurse who'd managed to restart his heart and sent her a turkey and vodka, too.

Aunty Sylvia took control in the kitchen. Ruby, who hated cooking roasts—even when it wasn't Christmas—because she could never get the timing right, was perfectly happy to be her sous chef.

"You know," Aunty Sylvia said, wiping the end of her nose with the back of a stuffing-coated hand, "I never really apologized for the dreadful scene Nigel and I caused the other day in the shop. We just got carried away. I'm so sorry. I feel so guilty that I was responsible for Stella pulling out of the business."

"Don't worry," Ruby said, cutting another cross at the base of a Brussels sprout. "It wasn't just you. Stella thought the whole event was tacky and she hated the fact that I'd organized it behind her back." She put the sprout in a bowl of water and took another one from the bag.

"So, how's Ivan?" Aunty Sylvia asked. Ruby said she had spoken to him and that he was back home and doing fine.

"Thank the Lord for that. Have you given any more thought to buying Stella out?"

Ruby shrugged. "I've had plenty of thoughts. What I need is the money. Stella's attorney is putting pressure on me to pay up or agree to sell."

"You know, I've got a bit of money put away. It's not much, but if it would help."

"That's kind and I appreciate the offer, but you haven't got enough to gamble with. If for some reason the business went belly-up, I wouldn't be able to repay you and I couldn't live with that."

Aunty Sylvia grabbed another load of stuffing and shoved her hand back up inside the bird. "There's always Nigel," she said. "He's pretty loaded."

"Nigel? I'm not sure I'd feel comfortable asking your ex for money."

"My ex? Who told you we'd split up?"

"Nobody. I just assumed . . . after the . . . you know . . . the whole underwear thing."

"We're working it out. He's seeing a therapist. She's helping him look at his relationship with his father. Apparently he was very domineering. As a result Nigel grew up feeling the need to reject his masculine side and embrace his feminine one."

"So at least he's stopped wearing women's clothes."

"Oh, no," Aunty Sylvia said waving her hand carelessly so that a great lump of stuffing fell to the floor. "He'll probably always want to do it. But I can live with that."

"You can?"

"That's your Aunty Sylvia—only happy when she's got a project." It was Ronnie. She made her way over to the sink and began filling the kettle.

"You know what, Ronnie? Maybe you're right. Maybe I do enjoy trying to help the men in my life. But it seems to work for me. We've joined a support group for couples in our position and Nigel thinks I'd be brilliant at advising the men how to dress and do their makeup. He thinks I should go into business selling women's clothes designed especially for men. I'm thinking of calling it Girls with Big Hands."

"Well, as long as you're OK with the situation," Ronnie said. "That's all that matters."

"I am," Aunty Sylvia said defiantly. "Now, if you'll excuse me, I'm going upstairs to wash my hands."

After she'd gone, Ronnie turned to Ruby. "And how are you coping, darling?"

Ruby hadn't wanted to worry her mother by telling her how she had broken into the storeroom at St. Luke's, or what had happened between her and Sam. The problem was that Ronnie, whose antennae were always on full alert, could tell that Ruby was keeping something from her. She'd kept pestering Ruby to tell her what was going on and eventually Ruby had given in.

"I'm having second thoughts about exposing the surrogacy story," she said.

"I can see that. The hospital would be finished."

"And I'm worried that your care might be put in jeopardy. You and I have the same surname. Some bent midwife could easily make the connection."

Ronnie nodded. "If you do decide to go ahead with the story, I'll arrange for Dr. Beech to deliver the baby at the Portland."

Ruby agreed that might be for the best.

"Darling, I'm so sorry about you and Sam. I know it sounds trite, but the pain will ease sooner or later."

Ruby said she just wished it could be sooner rather than later. Ronnie put her arms round her daughter. "You know your dad and I are always here if you need us. I don't want you to think that little Sigmund's arrival is going to make any difference to that."

Ruby smiled. "I know it won't. I love you."

"Love you, too." Ronnie kissed her daughter on the forehead.

Just then the switch on the kettle clicked itself off. "You stay there," Ruby said. "I'll make the coffee." She had taken no more than a couple of steps when she felt herself starting to slide across the floor. She reached out to grab the counter, but it was just out of reach. Several times she almost righted herself. Finally she fell backward and landed hard on the floor.

"You OK?" Ronnie gasped, heaving herself off her chair.

Ruby had managed not to bash the back of her head, but she had landed awkwardly. Somehow her foot had ended up underneath her. As she eased it out, she grimaced with pain. She also noticed that it was covered in sage and onion stuffing. "Actually, no, I'm not. I've done something to my ankle."

Aunty Sylvia, who was her company's official "first-aider," diagnosed a bad sprain and wrapped up the ankle. For the rest of Christmas Day, Ruby sat next to Ronnie on the sofa, her foot up on the coffee table. At one point Ruby and Ronnie needed to go to the loo at the same time. Phil said watching the pair of them trying to climb the stairs was like watching two old-age pensioners trying to rock-climb.

Nigel, who'd had Christmas lunch with his elderly parents, arrived chez Silverman around teatime. Phil, who knew all about Nigel's penchant for ladies' lingerie, barely knew where to look. His awkwardness wasn't helped by the fact that he had downed a substantial amount of Ivan's splendid vodka before lunch, not to mention several glasses of wine with lunch. "What can I get you, Nigel? A glass of champagne or a cuppa?"

Nigel said tea would be great.

"So what cup size would you like? Sorry, I mean would you like a mug or a D cup. I mean teacup."

His faux pas didn't stop there. A few minutes later he was asking Nigel if he'd seen the Manchester United game the previous week. "What a load of big girls' blouses. If you ask me they were complete rubbish."

Before anyone could stop him, he began admiring Nigel's new tawny-colored sweater, which Aunty Sylvia had bought him for Christmas. "So what color is that, Nigel? Sort of gusset, would you say?"

As usual Ruby had no plans to reopen the shop until after the first week in January. People who shopped at Les Sprogs tended to go away just before Christmas or shortly after and were never back before the fifth of January. Since her ankle was still very swollen and painful and she couldn't drive or stand on it, she was grateful for the time off.

On New Year's Eve she took a taxi to Chanel and Craig's. Earlier in the week Chanel had rung to say they were planning a quiet dinner and would she like to join them. She'd been invited to Fi and Saul's, but they were having a family evening with his parents and loads of other relatives, and even though they assured her she wouldn't be intruding, Ruby still felt she might.

She had also been invited to a couple of parties, but since she was still getting teary over Sam and her ankle hurt, she wasn't exactly in the mood to party. She decided that a quiet evening with friends was just what she needed.

Chanel and Craig were still looking after Alfie. Hannah was sure she didn't want him back and the couple was about to contact Social Services. "I'm not sure 'ow the law works in these cases," Craig said to Ruby while Chanel was in the kitchen making coffee. "It's possible we may not 'ave this little fella much longer. If Chanel is forced to give 'im up, 'er whole world's gonna come tumbling down... not to mention mine."

After they'd had coffee, Chanel asked Ruby if she'd like to come upstairs and see Alfie.

"I'd love to."

The nursery was perfect. Of course it hadn't been created for Alfie. Craig had decorated the room during Chanel's only—and very brief—pregnancy. "We never 'ad the 'eart to change it."

Ruby looked up. Minuscule electronic stars twinkled in the dark blue ceiling. There was just enough light to make out the Winnie the Pooh mural Craig had painted. In his crib, Alfie had kicked off his duvet and was lying on his back in a white sleep suit covered in rabbits. He was making tiny snoring sounds.

"I keep trying to prepare myself for losing him, but it's so 'ard."

Ruby put her arms round Chanel and hugged her. "Oh, sweetie... I hope you get to keep him, but there's so much to sort out. You can't rely on it. You have to be prepared for Claudia to want him back."

"I know, and I'm trying to be realistic, but Claudia 'asn't been in touch with 'annah. She 'asn't seen 'er or spoken to 'er since she refused to take Alfie 'ome from the 'ospital. If she took 'im now, what sort of a life would 'e 'ave with 'er? You've seen what she's like with Avocado. She's a dreadful mother."

"Yes, but she still has rights."

"Rights she bloody gave up months ago when she rejected 'im for 'aving ginger hair."

"I'm afraid that's not how the law sees it."

"Well, the law needs bloody changing."

Ruby gave her another squeeze. "Come on. Let's go downstairs and have some more coffee."

Chapter 19

Ruby spent the next couple of days resting her ankle, which had started to swell up again because she'd been putting too much weight on it too soon. She passed the time reading and watching trashy TV. Every so often she would get up off the sofa and hobble to the loo or the fridge.

By lunchtime on the second day, she decided that if she watched another *Will and Grace* rerun, or based-on-a-true-story made-for-TV movie, she might be forced to eat her head.

She picked up the latest David Baldacci, which Aunty Sylvia had got her for Christmas, but she couldn't settle. She began flicking through *Hello!* and put it down. Then she phoned Ivan to wish him a Happy New Year. He sounded full of beans and was talking about being back at work by March. "Doctors ver' pl'zed with me. I phone you soon. You hef more jobs maybe? I could build bookshelves in lounge, yes?"

Much as she liked him, the last thing she needed was Ivan farting around for another three months trying to do a job that should take three days. But she felt sorry for him. Even though he sounded pretty upbeat, his heart attack must have shattered his self-confidence, and the last thing she wanted was to make him feel useless and unwanted. "Good idea," she heard herself say. "Bookshelves would be great. Why don't you give me a ring when you're ready to start?"

She said good-bye to Ivan and went into the kitchen to make yet another cup of coffee. When she came back she sat with the mug in one hand and the TV remote in the other. For a full five minutes she channel-surfed. When nothing took her fancy, she lay back on the cushions and closed her eyes. Eventually she dozed off with CNN still on in the background. She could only have been half asleep because all the time, she was vaguely aware of a voice talking about some court case or other. A name kept being repeated over again. Even in her semi-asleep state, she was aware that the name meant something to her. Suddenly her eyes were wide open.

"... and that was Dan Rozenberg reporting from New York on the Josh Epstien retrial, which begins Tuesday."

Ruby sat up too fast, causing her head to swim. She blinked at the screen, but the report had finished. The anchorman had moved on to an item on oil prices. "Hang on," she said out loud, "did he say Josh Epstien?" Was it possible he was referring to Josh Epstien as in Sam's brother, Josh? Surely not. She knew Sam's brother was a drug addict, but Sam had said nothing about him being a criminal. Then again, there were quite a few things Sam hadn't told her about his life. All she could think was that if Josh Epstien's trial was being reported on CNN, he must be one hell of a villain.

She hobbled into the bedroom and sat down at the computer. Then she Googled Josh Epstien, clicking on "images." Before she went any further she wanted to see if the face that came up looked anything like Sam. She needed to be certain this was the same Josh Epstien.

The first photograph showed a twenty-something man

and woman on their wedding day. The dark, good-looking man in his late twenties was the image of Sam. Her eyes went to the woman standing next to him. The joy on her face left Ruby in no doubt that this was the happiest day of her life.

Long blonde curls lapped at her bare shoulders. Of course she'd cut her hair since then and had it dyed. She was also a lot plumper now. Even so, Ruby recognized her at once. Underneath the picture, the caption read "Josh and Kimberley Epstien on their wedding day in 1999." So, that explained Sam's link to Kimberley. She was married to his brother. What it didn't explain was why Sam had kept this fact a secret.

She clicked out of images and into text. There were hundreds of references to Josh Epstien, but the first told Ruby all she needed to know.

Two years ago Josh had been tried and sentenced to life imprisonment for murdering a New York mafia boss in some kind of drug turf war. At the time he had pleaded guilty. Now he was claiming that he had been arrested simply for being in the wrong place at the wrong time and that the real killer—a billionaire New York businessman named Herbert Garcia with gangland connections—had threatened to kill Kimberley and the children if he didn't take the murder rap.

For the last few months, Josh's lawyers had been fighting to get the case reopened. During this time, Kimberley had been receiving death threats. Eventually she and the children had fled abroad. Very recently, DNA evidence linking the businessman to the killing had been discovered. He had since disappeared.

Ruby sat back in her chair. Now she understood. Kimberley had come to London because she thought she would be safe. On top of that, Sam was there to look out for her and offer what protection he could.

It was then that Ruby remembered the black Porsche Cayenne that had tried to run them off the road in Richmond Park. Was it possible the gang had followed Kimberley here and that they knew Sam was helping her? Were they trying to threaten him in the same way they had been threatening her? It was dawning on her that the reason Sam went back to New York was connected to Kimberley and Josh and the new murder trial. But why had he lied? Why hadn't he trusted her with the truth? He must have assumed she wouldn't stay with him if she knew his brother was a convicted murderer.

She needed to speak to Sam. It was only just dawning on her that all the time they were going out, he must have been under the most unbearable pressure and stress. He must have been so frightened—not only for Kimberley, but for himself as well.

Ruby needed to make him understand that whatever Josh had or hadn't done, she still loved him. She picked up the phone and dialed Sam's mobile, only to be told the number was no longer valid. She tried his flat. The phone had been shut off. Finally she called the hospital. "I'm sorry," said the woman on the switchboard, "but Dr. Epstien no longer works here."

Ruby could only assume that with the new trial coming up, Sam wanted to be near his brother and had decided to go back to New York. Since he'd left his job, he clearly wasn't planning to come back.

Moments later she was on the phone to Fi. "Have you got a number for Buddy and Irene?"

"Yes. Why?"

"I'm trying to find Sam. I think he might be on his way back to New York."

"Ruby, why on earth would you want to speak to Sam?" She sounded really concerned. "You have to let him go. The man is bad news. He's done you nothing but harm."

"But I'm not convinced he has. At least not intentionally. Please, Fi, could you just let me have the number?"

Fi went off to find it.

"Thanks," Ruby said after she had read it over. "I'll phone you when I know more."

"What more? What is it you're trying to find out?"

"I'll explain later. Promise. Bye."

Buddy picked up the phone on the first ring. Before he said anything Ruby heard him muttering to Irene about who could be phoning so early.

"Buddy, it's Ruby Silverman. You remember we met in London, after Connor's circumcision?"

"Ruby, hello. Great to hear from you." She thought she detected a slight edge to his bonhomie—as if he didn't quite know what was coming next. "So, to what do I owe this pleasure?"

"I know all about Josh, the murder, everything," she said.

"I see." His voice was grave suddenly. "How did you find out?"

She explained.

"I'm sorry we lied to you, Ruby, but we both thought it was for the best. Sam thought that by telling you the truth he would lose you. The reason he left London was to bring Kimberley and the children home. Those sons of bitches had followed her to London and were threatening her. They kept saying that if she didn't get Josh to change his story, they would kill her and the children. We had to fight to get it, but in the end she was offered round-the-clock police protection in New York, so she decided to fly back. Sam came with her and stayed on for a few weeks to keep an eye on her."

"But if he'd told me the truth, I would have understood."

"Maybe. He wasn't prepared to take that risk."

"Do you know where he is now?"

"Isn't he at his flat?"

"No, I've tried him there and at the hospital. He seems to have changed his cell number as well."

"Then I have no idea where he could be. He's due back here for the retrial, but we're not expecting him for a few days."

Ruby was starting to feel sick with dread. "Buddy, do you think these people could have hurt Sam in order to stop Josh testifying?"

"My God," Buddy muttered. She imagined him collapsing into a chair, fearing the worst. "Find him, Ruby. Please, please find him."

"OK. I'll start with his flat. I still have a key."

"And Ruby."

"Yes?"

"Be careful."

"I will."

HER FIRST INSTINCT was to phone the police, but it would take too long to explain everything and lose her precious time. She needed to get to Sam's flat now. She still had the set of keys he had given her. She grabbed her coat and bag and made her way gingerly and frustratingly slowly down the stairs. She was just about to hail a cab when she saw her mother coming toward her. She was holding a large dish covered in silver foil. Whatever was inside was enough to feed ten people.

"Mum! What are you doing here?"

"I knew you couldn't get to the supermarket and I was worried you might not have much in, so I brought you a lasagne. It just needs heating up."

"That's really kind of you, but I'm kind of in a hurry."

"Where are you going?"

"Sam's."

"What on earth for?"

"He's changed his mobile and he's left his job. I think he might be in danger."

"What do you mean, 'danger'? What possible danger could Sam be in?"

"It's a long story."

"It's something to do with this surrogacy thing, isn't it?"

"No. It's nothing to do with that."

"OK, but if he's in danger we have to call the police."

"There isn't time. I have to get to his flat now."

"God, I wish you'd tell me what's going on. Look, if you have to go to his flat, at least let me take you."

"No chance. You're almost nine months pregnant. I don't know what I'm going to find there."

Ronnie's face was full of concern. She put her hand on Ruby's arm. "Darling, are you really suggesting somebody might be out to hurt Sam?"

"Possibly."

"Right, pregnant or not, I'm coming with you."

"Mum, please . . ."

"If you get a cab, I'm only going to follow you. So make up your mind."

"God, you're an obstinate woman when you choose to be."

Ronnie smiled. "I'm parked at the end of the road."

The two women, one heavily pregnant and carrying a giant lasagne, the other half walking, half hopping, made their way to Ronnie's car. They put the lasagne on the back-seat and headed for Kensington. Since it was only two days into the New Year and people were still off from work, the roads were practically empty.

"Mum, I don't suppose you could put your foot down a bit, could you?"

"God, who are we? Cagney and Lacey?" She hit the accelerator. "So come on, tell me what's going on."

Ruby told her what she had found out. "I don't care what you say," Ronnie said. "We have to tell the police. We don't know what we're going to find at Sam's flat. What if he's being held hostage? Or worse?"

Ruby was adamant that there was no time. "Tell you what, you wait outside. If I'm not out in ten minutes, then you call them, OK?"

"OK."

They practically screeched to a halt outside Sam's flat. Ruby let herself into the building and began the slow, painful climb to the second floor. Over the years she must have sneered at hundreds of TV cops and movie heroes for doing what nobody would think of doing in real life—going into a life-threatening situation alone. Now, here she was doing precisely that. Only this wasn't TV. It was real life.

Ruby put her ear to the door and listened. There were no sounds coming from inside. She rang the bell and waited. Nothing. Heart racing, hand trembling, she tried to slide the key into the lock. She was in such a state that it took three attempts. She turned the key. Slowly, she opened the door. The first thing she saw was the junk mail scattered over the mat. She left the front door open in case she needed to make a quick getaway. Then she took a few steps down the hallway. There were no signs of a disturbance or a struggle. There was no upturned furniture. More to the point, there were no blood-spattered walls or carpet. She poked her head round the living room door. It was perfectly neat and tidy. Ditto the bedroom. Even though she still had no idea where Sam was, for the moment at least, she started to relax.

Then, as she turned to go back into the hall, she collided with a granite-hard, T-shirt-clad chest. For a beat, maybe two, she stood staring at the faces of Wallace and Gromit. Frozen with fear, her eyes moved upward. The giant, unshaven man had his arm raised above his head. His hand was wielding a hammer. She couldn't move. She couldn't scream. She was quite literally paralyzed. So this was it. This was what it felt like in that moment before death. Before the lights went out. She closed her eyes and waited for the hammer blows to rain down on her head.

"Blimey, you gave me a bleedin' fright. Who are you? What do you want?"

Ruby opened one eye and then another. The hammer was now down by the man's side.

"I might ask you the same question," she said.

"I'm the electrician. Bloke who owns this place got me in to fix some dodgy wiring before the new tenant comes in." She was pretty sure he was telling the truth because he had one of those tool belts round his waist.

"Sorry," she said, voice trembling. "I did ring the bell before I let myself in. Didn't you hear me?"

He pointed to his iPod headphones, which were draped round his neck.

"My boyfriend..." she began, "well, ex-boyfriend, actually used to live here. I...er, I left some of my stuff here and I wanted to see if it was still here. Mind if I take a look round?"

" 'Elp yourself," he shrugged.

The electrician wandered off into the kitchen. A few moments later she heard him banging away with his hammer.

Ruby stood thinking. If Kristian, who owned the flat, had called in the electrician because he was about to relet it, then it probably meant that Sam had told him he was moving out. This was a good sign.

She went into the living room. The bust of Stalin and the jukebox were gone. She assumed he had either sold them or shipped them back to the States. In the bedroom, all his clothes were gone from the wardrobe. The idea of

Sam having been attacked or kidnapped now seemed highly unlikely. Unless, of course, the gang had got to him while he was on his way somewhere.

She looked around the bedroom. The carpets needed a vacuum. There were cup rings on the bedside table. It was obvious that the cleaners hadn't been in yet. Suddenly she noticed the wastepaper bin. It was full. She ran over and tipped the contents onto the carpet. In movies the detectives always found out where somebody was from evidence left in the waste bin. Usually it was a crumpled piece of paper with an address on it. Or an old notepad with the imprint of an address. She sifted through the rubbish. There was an empty toothpaste tube, a pair of socks with holes in, a few chewing gum wrappers and an old newspaper. Nothing of any consequence.

She began putting everything back. Then, as she was about to ram the newspaper into the bin, she noticed a large advertisement. One of the airlines had a deal on New Year's flights to New York. Sam had circled it. Beside it he had written today's date. Ruby took her mobile from her bag and phoned the contact number at the bottom of the ad. "Excuse me, I saw your ad in the *Evening Standard*. Could you tell me what time your New York flight leaves today? . . . No, no, it doesn't matter that it's fully booked, I was just curious, that's all. Yes, I know it's a strange thing to be curious about if I'm not planning to travel, but could you tell me anyway?"

There was a flight leaving Heathrow two hours from now. She had no idea if Sam was intending to be on it—the woman had refused to say if his name was on the passenger list—but it was the only lead she had.

She was just about to leave and was thanking the electrician for letting her look round, when another thought struck her. "God," she said, "where's Cat Damon?"

The electrician looked at her as if she was raving. "Er, in Hollywood, I presume."

"No, that's *Matt* Damon. I'm talking about *Cat* Damon. He's a ginger tom. He lives here. At least he did."

"There is a cat in the building. Huge shaggy thing. Can't tell one end from the other."

"That's him."

"Seems to be living with the old lady downstairs. I saw 'er this morning letting 'im in. Only she calls 'im Mister Fluffy."

"Oh, well at least he's gone to a good home. I was worried he'd been abandoned."

"SO, ARE YOU thinking," Ronnie said, starting the car engine, "that Sam decided to leave London early?"

"It would make sense. As far as he's concerned, he and I are finished. What would be the point of hanging around? I'm surprised he stayed for Christmas."

They headed out onto the M4. At one point Ronnie took her eyes off the road briefly and looked at Ruby. "Has it occurred to you that the real reason Sam is running back to New York is to escape being implicated in the surrogacy affair? You are forgetting that his name is still on that list you found."

"But I've always thought he was set up in some way."

"Hmm," Ronnie said doubtfully, "just like this brother of his was *set up*."

"You think I'm being stupid chasing after Sam, don't you?"

"Not stupid. Just naive. You're living in hope that this Buddy was telling the truth and that Sam will turn out to be the honest, honorable man you always hoped he was. You've been through one hell of a lot recently and I just don't want you to be let down again."

They carried on in silence. Ruby gazed out of the window. There was no way that Buddy had been lying to her.

She just knew it. At one point she reached into her handbag and took out the list she had stolen from Jill McNulty. Ronnie glanced across at it. "Are you really suggesting that somebody convinced an intelligent man like Sam to sign a blank document? I find that highly unlikely, don't you?"

"OK, I admit I don't have the answer, but I know he wasn't involved in the surrogacy thing. After everything else I've found out, I'm certain of it now."

"I need to pee," Ronnie said.

"Oh, God, Mum. Not now. Can't you hold on until we get to the airport?"

"Ruby, I've got a baby sitting on my bladder. If I don't pee in the next few minutes, I'm going to wet myself."

"I'm sorry. I was being selfish. Are you feeling OK?"

"I'm fine. There's a rest area up ahead. I'll be literally two minutes."

As they pulled in, it started to drizzle.

Ruby insisted on fetching Ronnie's umbrella from the trunk. She held it over her mother as she got out of the car. As Ronnie set off toward the loo, Ruby walked back round to the passenger door. She was just about to get into the car when she saw her precious Jill McNulty list lying on the ground. It must have slipped off her lap when she got out of the car. Cursing herself, she bent down and snatched it up. It was covered in rain spots.

She was about to put it back in her bag when something—or rather a lack of something—caught her eye. Sam's signature had quite clearly been signed in fountain pen. So, how come the ink hadn't run in the rain?

She began rubbing at the signature with her finger. The ink didn't budge. "That's because it isn't bloody ink," she muttered to herself as a light went on. "It's print." Jill had clearly been busy with a scanner and photocopier. Her feelings were tumbling over themselves now. She loathed Jill McNulty and Tom Hardacre more than ever for implicating

Sam in their scheme. She was elated that she now had proof that Sam hadn't been involved in the surrogacy affair, but at the same time, she was furious with herself for doubting Sam.

The moment Ronnie got back from the loo, Ruby demonstrated her theory to her. "My God," Ronnie said, shaking her head. "So, your instinct was right all along. Sam was never involved with the surrogacies. Come on, let's get going. I just pray he's at the airport, because if ever two people needed to talk, it's you two."

As soon as they got back onto the motorway, Ronnie hit the gas. Ruby watched the needle on the speedo pass ninety.

"Mum, I know I asked you to step on it earlier, but we do want to arrive in one piece."

"I know, darling, but there's another reason we need to get a move on."

"What's that?"

"When I went to the loo my water broke."

"Omigod! Why on earth didn't you say something?" Ruby insisted they get off the motorway and head back to St. Luke's. "There's no traffic, we can do it in forty minutes."

Ronnie wouldn't hear of turning back. She said that since she wasn't getting any contractions, she would drop Ruby at the airport, leave the car in the parking lot and get a taxi back to St. Luke's.

Ruby agreed, but only if she phoned Phil and got him to meet her at the airport. "At least then you'll have somebody with you on the journey back."

Ronnie dialed Phil's mobile. As luck would have it, he was seeing a client in Hammersmith. He said the quickest thing would be for him to get the tube out to the airport.

"So long as there are no holdups," Ronnie said, "he'll arrive just after us."

Ruby said she hoped Ronnie knew what she was doing.

"I may not know much about childbirth," she said, "but I know how important it is to get to the hospital once your water has broken. If you delay getting there, you risk the baby getting an infection."

Ronnie told her to stop fussing and insisted she would be fine. She parked the car in the short-term lot at Terminal 4.

As she maneuvered to get out of the car, she stopped and inhaled sharply through her teeth.

"What is it?" Ruby said, grabbing her mother's arm.

"Nothing. Just the baby moving. Let me sit for a moment to get my breath back."

They sat there for maybe half a minute. "OK, I'm fine now," Ronnie said. They got out of the car and took the lift to the departure area.

Every step Ruby took was causing her pain. As she concentrated on her own discomfort, she failed to notice the taut expression on her mother's face. It was only when they reached the check-in area—which was pretty quiet, since the mass exodus out of the country had happened before Christmas—and Ronnie said she needed to sit down, that she noticed. "Bloody hell, Mum, you look white."

"I'll be fine after another rest."

"No you won't. You're in labor. You know you are."

"No I'm not. It's probably just more of those Braxton-Hicks contractions like before." Suddenly her hand went to her belly and her face contorted. "Ooh, that was a strong one."

"Mum, don't be ridiculous. These aren't practice contractions. You are in labor. We have to get you to a hospital. I'm going to find a member of the ground staff and get them to call an ambulance."

Ronnie nodded, but didn't say anything because she was having what appeared to be another and even more painful contraction. "Tell them to hurry," she gasped. "Please tell them to hurry."

Her thoughts and feelings about Sam shoved to the back of her mind, Ruby did an Olympian limp toward the information desk. The middle-aged woman in charge told Ruby not to panic, that she would make a call and that the airport ambulance would be along in a few minutes. Ruby described where she and Ronnie would be waiting and ran back to her mother. She heard the commotion before she saw what was going on. A small crowd had gathered round Ronnie. Somebody was shouting for a doctor. "This woman's about to give birth. Is there anybody who can help her?" Somebody else was telling Ronnie not to push. Ruby barged her way through the crowd. Ronnie was lying down on the bench, her head propped up on a pile of coats, crying out in pain and begging for somebody to help her.

"Mum, Mum, it'll be OK. The ambulance is on its way."

"Where the sodding hell is it? This baby's about to be born. And where's your father? Why isn't he here yet?"

"Don't worry, he'll be here. Mum, please try to keep calm."

Just then Ruby's mobile went. Assuming it was her father, she didn't bother to look at the caller display.

"Rubes, it's me." It was Fi. "You'll never guess what. We've just had the most wonderful news. Saul's got a job. And it isn't just any old job. Get this, he's got the lead in..."

"Fi, this sounds like wonderful news, but now isn't a good time. I'm at the Terminal 4 check-in at Heathrow and Mum's about to give birth any second."

"What are you talking about? What are you doing at Heathrow? Is she all right?"

"Not really. Look, I have to go. I'll phone you."

"Did you find Sam?"

"No. Fi, I really have to go."

As she hung up, Phil appeared. He came running over, red faced, sweating and breathless. The crowd parted like the Red Sea to let him through.

"I've been looking all over for you. What's happening?"

"What does it look like?" Ronnie said. "I'm about to have a baby."

"What? Here? You can't. We have to get to the hospital."

Ruby explained that it was too late. Ronnie cried out in pain as another contraction hit. Phil knelt down and took her hand. "Remember all your relaxation techniques. Come on, let's focus on your mantra."

"Bugger my sodding mantra."

"OK, then just breathe with me. Hah, hah, hah, heeh, heeh, heeh."

"I don't want to breathe! It hurts! I want drugs! I want an epidural! Now! Please, can somebody get me a doctor?"

"I'm a doctor," an authoritative male voice said. "Please let me through." Ruby froze. She knew that voice. It was Sam.

"Ruby?" he said, before she'd even turned round. "What on earth is going on?"

She turned round. As her eyes met his, she was aware of the overpowering relief she was feeling at having found him—not just for Ronnie's sake, but for her own, as well. "It's Mum. The baby's coming." Sam nodded hello to Phil and crouched down beside Ronnie. "How often are the contractions coming?" Before she had a chance to reply another one came. "Aaagh. I want to push. I want to push."

"OK, I think I have my answer."

He took off his jacket and rolled up his shirtsleeves. Then he asked if anybody had any clean towels in their luggage. Somebody undid their suitcase, found a couple and passed them to Sam. He said that he needed to examine Ronnie. To protect her modesty he asked everybody to stand with their backs to her and form a circle around the bench. "Hang on," Ruby whispered to Sam, tugging at his arm. "You are going to examine my mother internally?"

"I have to."

"Oh, God! The man I've been dating for the last four months is about to feel my mother's cervix. How modern is that?"

He told her she didn't have to watch.

"OK," he announced a few seconds later, "the head's crowning. Try not to push. I want you to pant for me while I check the cord."

Ronnie panted.

"Is the baby all right?" Phil said. He was white faced with fear. "Everything's fine," Sam reassured him. "One more push, Ronnie. When you're ready."

"Uuuuurggghhhhh!"

"Mum! The head's out!" Ruby gasped. She'd overcome her squeamishness and was standing beside Sam, watching everything. "Sigmund Freud's got loads of black hair."

"Sigmund Freud?" Sam was looking quizzically at Ruby.

She explained it was just a nickname. He seemed relieved. "OK, Ronnie, chin on your chest and one final push!"

Ronnie took a deep breath and held it. As she pushed one last time, her face turned scarlet and she dug her nails hard into Phil's hand. "Keep pushing," Sam urged. "... Keep pushing... And again ... OK, it's here. It's all over, Ronnie. Good job. You can relax." A few moments later the baby let out its first tiny, squeaky cries. As the crowd clapped and cheered, Sam wrapped the baby in a towel and laid it on Ronnie's chest. "What is it?" somebody asked.

Phil, who was looking overwhelmed and more than a bit vacant, mumbled: "It's a baby. It's a little baby."

Sam suggested gently that he might like to check what kind of baby it was. "Oh, yes," Phil said. He opened the towel. "It's a girl! It's a girl baby!"

Ronnie lay gazing at her new daughter, her eyes filling with tears. "Hello, little baby," she said.

Ruby knelt down next to her father. "She's beautiful," she said, tears filling her eyes, too. "Just beautiful."

By now the paramedics had arrived. They quickly took control, wrapped the baby in a foil blanket and got Ronnie onto a stretcher. "You're going to need a few stitches," Sam said to her, "but otherwise everything's completely OK."

"Thank you," Ronnie said to Sam, taking his hand. "Thank you for being there and for being so wonderful." She turned to Ruby. "I don't want you to come in the ambulance. Your dad and I will be fine. Now then, I think you two have some talking to do. Lack of communication is the main reason relationships break down, you know. Active listening, that's the key..."

"Mum," Ruby chuckled, "you had a baby five minutes ago and already you're therapizing."

She grinned. "It takes more than childbirth to put me off my stride."

Ruby kissed her mother good-bye and said she would see her later on that evening.

A few minutes later Ronnie, Phil and the baby were on their way to the nearest maternity hospital. Since Sam had missed his flight to New York, he and Ruby headed for the Terminal 4 Starbucks.

"You were brilliant back there," Ruby said.

Sam's face broke into a smile. "Thank you." He opened a packet of sugar and watched the tiny cascade of crystals sink into the froth on his cappuccino. "So, why did you come looking for me?"

"I know about Josh and the trial," she said, putting her coffee mug to her lips. "I happened to be watching CNN. Then I phoned Buddy and he told me the real reason you went back to New York."

He didn't seem particularly surprised. "I guess I knew you'd find out eventually. It was just a matter of time."

"So, where have you been? I phoned Buddy. He had no idea where you were. We've been so worried."

"I went to stay with friends in Devon. I got the train

back this morning. I kept meaning to phone Buddy and Irene, but a bit of me just wanted to forget everything for a few days. I didn't want to discuss Josh and the trial. I just wanted to be normal." He began stirring his coffee. "I'm sorry I lied to you about why I went back to New York. I hated myself for doing it. I still hate myself, but I had no choice."

"Of course you had a choice," she came back. "You could have trusted me."

"Right. So I should have taken you out for a romantic dinner and over the seared tuna I should have turned to you and said: 'Hey, by the way, my brother's a convicted killer and there are people out there threatening to kill his wife and kids, but this won't make any difference to our relationship, will it?' "

"But it wouldn't have. Sam, I don't care if your brother is the spawn of Hannibal Lecter, it's you I'm having a relationship with, not him."

"Josh is innocent, you know. He got involved with some bad people. He was a drug dealer for a time. He did some bad things, but he isn't a murderer. I believe that with every ounce of my being. The whole family does."

She drained her coffee mug. "I just hope he realizes how lucky he is to have all of you," she said.

"I just wish this whole Josh thing hadn't affected us the way it has."

"You know what hurt the most?" she said. "The way you left me. You made it look so easy. It was as if you didn't care."

"It wasn't remotely easy. Walking out on you was the hardest thing I have ever done in my life. It almost killed me to leave you, but all the time we were together I was scared for you. These goons wouldn't have stopped at threatening and intimidating Kim. Eventually they would have gotten to you. What happened that afternoon in Richmond Park convinced me of that. By then they were on to me. I couldn't risk you getting hurt. And by then everything got complicated. I'd started lying to you. You thought I was having an affair. You suspected I was involved in the surrogacy thing. It all got too much for me to handle."

"But you could have let me decide for myself if I wanted to be with you."

"And what would you have said?"

"I would have said that we were in this thing together and that I loved you."

"You would have risked your life to be with me?"

"Tell me something, if the tables had been reversed, would you have risked your life to stay with me?"

"Absolutely."

"The same goes for me." She reached out and took his hand.

"I couldn't let you do that," he said.

"And look where that's got us.... Talking of evidence, I can now prove that you had nothing to do with the surrogacies."

"You can? Well, that's more than I have been able to do. I went to see a lawyer—along with the two other foreign doctors involved—but he wasn't much help. He said that without concrete proof that we'd been set up, there wasn't much he could do. I tried to find Jill and Hardacre to confront them, but they're on extended leave. So, I've just been sitting here waiting for you to go public and for my professional reputation to be shot to pieces."

Ruby shook her head. "Sam, I can't begin to tell you how sorry I am. What with this and everything else, you must have been going through hell.... Anyway, I found out that Jill scanned your name onto that form. She did the same to some of the other doctors from abroad. The idea was that if the surrogacy affair ever came to light, you would have taken the rap. Nobody would have questioned it.

Hardacre is highly respected and you would have been seen as some opportunistic foreigners on the make."

They agreed that, along with Hannah, their next job was to report Jill and Tom Hardacre to St. Luke's board of governors.

"So," Ruby said, after making a mental note to phone Hannah as soon as she got home, "all those calls you kept getting while we were seeing each other, they weren't from the hospital, were they?"

He shook his head. "They were from Kimberley. Even in London, the threats never stopped. She was scared for her life. All the time she and the kids were here, she hardly slept."

"So, these villains—are they still after you? Buddy seemed to think they were."

"No. This is the great news and I haven't even told you. It's over. I called Josh's lawyer just before I reached the airport. He was just about to get on the phone to Buddy. I've never heard him so excited. Apparently Herbert Garcia, the real murderer, committed suicide a couple of hours ago. He was already on the run. He left a note saying he knew he would be going down for life and he preferred to take the easy way out. Now the retrial will simply be a formality."

"My God. That's amazing. How do you feel?"

"Like a huge weight's been lifted. It's been a long haul."

She squeezed his hand. "You look exhausted. I just wish you'd let me help you."

"I couldn't. This wasn't your fight. I know you're angry that I shut you out and I'm sorry. I will always be sorry, but if I had to do this all over again I'd still want to protect you."

"I understand," she said, smiling. She knew he wasn't going to shift his position on this, so she decided to let it go. "So, how was Devon?"

"Wet. And I missed you. I tried calling you this morning on your cell, but there was no answer."

"I'm sorry. I didn't hear it ring. What were you going to say?"

"That I was sorry about everything and that I love you."

"I love you, too. I never stopped loving you."

"Really?"

"Really."

"I have to go back to New York for the trial. How would you feel about coming with me? I could really do with the support."

"Like you have to ask. Of course I'll come with you."

"But what about the shop? Could Chanel manage without you for a week?"

She gave a weak smile. "She and Fi could probably manage it between them, but it won't be necessary. There's something I haven't told you. The future is not looking exactly rosy for Les Sprogs."

"How come?"

She told him about the Guatemalan-week debacle. "I still have a few weeks to raise the money to buy Stella out, but I'm not hopeful. I'm pretty sure I'm going to have to wind up the business. It might as well be sooner rather than later."

"I can't believe this. Les Sprogs meant everything to you."

"Yes, but you know that owning a posh shop in Notting Hill was never my ultimate goal. It was only ever a means to an end. Maybe this will force me to think seriously about how I can get Baby Organic off the ground."

"What about asking some of your wealthy Les Sprogs customers to put up some of the money?"

Ruby said she'd already tried. "No go, I'm afraid. The word's out—via Stella, of course—that I'm a reckless businesswoman and that potential investors would do well to avoid me at all costs."

He shook his head in dismay. "You know," he said, "if I had that kind of money, it would be yours."

"You really are the most lovely man, Sam Epstien. Did I tell you I love you?"

"You did, but I don't mind hearing it again. So, shall we give us another chance? What do you say?"

Her mouth formed a smile that threatened to swallow up her entire face. She leaned across the table and kissed him. "I say definitely."

The following summer . . .

After weeks touring the provinces, Saul's show finally hit the West End. The first night was a triumph. Saul received a five-minute standing ovation, followed by at least half a dozen curtain calls.

As she'd stood in the front row, cheering, whooping and applauding with the rest of the audience, Fi had wept tears of pure joy.

Afterward, the cast, their families and friends, not to mention thickets of mwawwing celebrities gathered at Soho House for the opening night party. Ruby and Chanel were desperate to reach Saul to tell him how spectacular his performance had been, but he was caught up in a tight throng of showbiz reporters and people patting him on the back and congratulating him. From the moment he walked into the party, his face had been one permanent grin, but Ruby could tell by the way he kept his arm wrapped tightly round Fi that he was a bit dazed and bewildered by all the attention.

In the end Ruby and Chanel decided it was going to be impossible to penetrate the posse surrounding Saul and so they retreated to the bar and the free champagne. There would be time to congratulate Saul later, once the hubbub died down.

"I always knew he'd make it one day," Ruby said to Chanel as they eased themselves onto tall bar stools.

A waiter appeared with a tray of hors d'oeuvres. Chanel passed, but Ruby couldn't resist helping herself to a small paper cone containing a munchkin-size portion of fish and chips.

"Wonder how he'll cope with all the fame, though," Chanel said, reaching across and stealing one of Ruby's chips.

"He'll be fine. He's pretty grounded. And if by some chance he does let the fame go to his head, Fi will soon put him in his place."

When Chanel disappeared to the ladies' room, Ruby stayed at the bar, people-watching, sipping her champagne and thinking back over the last six months.

Gradually, bit by bit, things had come right for almost everybody she knew. As her thoughts drifted from person to person, she felt as if she were watching one of those happy-ever-after montages at the end of a sloppy romantic comedy. She, of course, was the heroine who had finally won her man. Then there was Saul, who had become an instant overnight success—after fifteen years. Hannah had received the outstanding money she was owed by Claudia Planchette and, much cheered up, had gone back to university. Sam's name had been cleared and he was back at St. Luke's. His brother was just out of rehab and thinking about going back to law school. After her traumatic journey into the world, baby Maya was now a chubby, giggling six-month-old who was sitting up and learning to "self-soothe" at night. Ronnie and Phil were permanently exhausted, but adoring every minute of their new life, and Aunty Sylvia was taking bets on the little mite's first word being either *transference, avoidance* or *denial*.

Chanel was convinced that these "positive shifts" in people's lives were all tied up with Saturn changing direction.

"You see, Saturn is yer planet of structure and stricture," she'd explained when Ruby brought up the subject with her. "When it's retrograde, as it 'as been for the last couple of years, you might as well pack up and go to bed." Apparently Saturn had resumed its forward journey the previous January, which meant it was responsible for—among other things—Social Services allowing Chanel and Craig to foster Alfie with a view to adopting him. The process would take a few more months, but since Claudia had now given up all parental rights to the child and since Chanel and Craig had received a glowing home study report from their social worker when they originally applied to become foster parents, it seemed unlikely that anything could prevent the adoption from going through.

Claudia's lawyers had also benefited—in some part, at least, from this new, benign sky. They were able to keep the surrogacy story out of the newspapers by dealing directly with Chanel's local director of Social Services.

They had no such luck when Claudia finally lost custody of Avocado and ended up in the hospital suffering from exhaustion—clearly code for a nervous breakdown. The tabloids were practically printing pull-out-and-keep Claudia supplements.

"I think it's brilliant that she's having a breakdown," Ronnie had declared to Ruby, with the authority of somebody who had been in therapy since she was in diapers.

"Er—sorry, how can a nervous breakdown ever be 'brilliant'?"

"I'll tell you how. When a person hits rock bottom, they have no alternative but to confront their demons. It's wretched and painful but in the end it can be a wonderfully healing experience. I think Claudia will grow from this."

"You do?"

"Absolutely. Don't get me wrong, I'm not trying to make excuses for her, but I think she's probably had a very rough time. I know these Hollywood stars are rich and pampered, but I can't imagine how it must feel to have the media constantly scrutinizing and criticizing every aspect of their appearance. The pressure to be permanently beautiful and thin must be unbearable."

Ruby got the point. "Fall short of perfection and nobody wants to employ you. Endeavor to be perfect and you go mad."

"Something like that."

"You think she could turn her life around?"

"Absolutely. Some good might come of this yet."

"Oh, God," Ruby said, screwing up her face. "I can see it now: Claudia Planchette sells the film rights to her surrogacy story—the proceeds go to charity of course. Meanwhile she sets up a pressure group, demanding the film studios start using plus-size women in romantic leads. You can just see her organizing cookouts on Rodeo Drive and candlelit vigils outside Calista Flockhart's house."

OCCASIONALLY—USUALLY AFTER receiving yet another refusal from a potential investor—Ruby would start muttering to herself about being the only bloody person on the planet who hadn't benefited from Saturn's supposed change of direction. Then she'd think about the poor and starving, the terminally ill. She would remind herself that she had just found the love of her life and that she had no right to complain. But sometimes, it wasn't easy.

As she'd feared back in January, none of the banks had been prepared to lend her the money she needed to buy Stella out of the business and she had been forced to walk away. She'd come away with her initial investment, plus a reasonably decent payout from Stella, but it wasn't nearly enough to get Baby Organic up and running.

Aware that she had to earn a living while she carried on

trying to raise the money to start her new business, she had reopened her baby-wear stall in Camden market, where she now worked six days a week.

At night, while Sam slept—he had moved in with her in January—she paced around the flat, trying to think up new money-making schemes. There was still no question of her accepting loans from family or friends—or Sam—even though they were offered repeatedly. She was petrified that if something went wrong, she wouldn't be able to repay the money.

Sometimes, in the small hours, Sam would hear her moving about. Then he would get up, make her a cup of hot milk and try to persuade her to come back to bed. He was clearly worried about how little sleep she was getting. "Ruby, you can't go on like this. You have to let the people who love you help you financially." But she insisted there had to be another way and that she would eventually find it.

It wasn't that the banks and venture capitalists she'd approached were telling her that her business plan sucked, or that she wasn't up to the challenge of setting up Baby Organic. Quite the reverse. Practically everybody had said it was a superb idea, that she had discovered a gap in the market and that she clearly had talent.

"Then why won't you back me?" she had pleaded again and again. The response was always the same: palms were turned heavenward, spectacles were removed, pens were laid down on legal pads. The sticking point was always her lack of capital. The men in suits were prepared to put in 50 percent of what she required, but she needed to provide the other 50 percent. She simply didn't have it.

When Ruby asked Chanel—by way of a joke—why she wasn't reaping the rewards along with everybody else from Saturn's change of direction, Chanel looked grave. "I was hoping you wouldn't ask."

"Why's that?"

Chanel inhaled and let out a long, slow breath. "You're a Capricorn, right?"

"Right."

"Well, you see, the thing is, Saturn's actually yer ruler."

"Which means..."

Chanel hesitated. "Well, it sort of means that even when Saturn's moving forward, yer life's always going to be a bit of a struggle."

"Oh, great."

"You see, yer goat is born to climb mountains, and those mountains tend to be very high and 'ave paths which are full of rocks and obstacles. Goats always get to the summit in the end, though. It just takes them longer than other people."

"Like how long? I mean are we talking sometime before menopause?"

"Impossible to tell. You just 'ave to carry on working and trying to raise the money. But the really brilliant news is that in old age, Capricorns always look younger than everybody else."

"Well, that's something, I suppose. Must be the lack of free radicals in all that mountain air."

BACK AT SOHO House, Ruby was craning her neck, looking for Bridget. As she had before Connor's circumcision, Fi asked Ruby if she'd mind keeping an eye on her and making sure she didn't misbehave.

Just then Chanel returned from the loo. "If you're looking for Bridget," she said, "she's over there, chatting up some bloke." Chanel squinted, trying to make out who he was. "Omigod, it's David Schwimmer."

"Are you sure?"

"Positive."

Ruby insisted they move closer so that they could hear

what Bridget was saying and rescue David Schwimmer if it became necessary.

"You know, Mr. Schwimmer—or may I call you David? Has anybody ever told you you're much shorter than you are on the telly?" Bridget was giddy with excitement and too much champagne. Ruby rolled her eyes at Chanel.

"No. Actually they haven't."

"You know, David, I loved you in *ER*."

"Actually, I wasn't in *ER*."

"You weren't? Are you sure?"

"Pretty sure, yes."

"Huh. I could have sworn it was you. So who am I thinking of? "

"George Clooney, maybe? . . . Anyway, it's been nice talking to you." He moved to go.

"You don't know who I am, do you?"

"Er, no, I don't."

Bridget patted her newly coiffed hair. "I'm the mother-in-law of Christ."

"Is that so?" David Schwimmer seemed to be looking round for somebody to rescue him from the madwoman. Ruby picked up on this and moved forward, but Chanel grabbed her arm. "Leave her," she whispered. "Let her enjoy her bit of fame." Ruby was a bit reluctant, but she stepped back.

"No, you misunderstand," Bridget was saying to David Schwimmer. "I'm Bridget Gilhooley. Saul, who plays Jesus in the show, is married to my daughter, Fiona. You might have heard of me. *The Catholic Herald* ran an in-depth interview with me last week."

"Actually, no. I didn't get to see it."

"That's a shame. Well, next week you must listen out for me on the radio. I'm the star guest on *Cozy Confessions with Sister Assumpta*."

"That sounds fascinating. I'll be sure to catch it if I can."

"Of course, when I found out Saul had been given the lead in the revival of *Jesus Christ Superstar,* I thought how could they give it to a Jew? I mean, a heathen playing the Son of God. It's an affront to the Holy Spirit. But of course, I was forgetting that our Lord was a Jew. They're wonderful people, the Jews. After all, when you think about it, it was the Jews that invented God. And I believe they even invented the bagel."

"Yes, I believe that's so." As he humored Bridget, David was looking round as if to say "Is she for real or am I on *Candid Camera*?"

"And the thing about the Jews is, they take the family very seriously. Apart from being a great actor, Saul is the perfect husband and father. I've never been able to fault him on that score. I love him like one of me own."

"That's good to hear. So many men have problems with their mothers-in-law."

"Oh, not us. I can truly say Saul and I have never uttered a cross word. So, with your swarthy, Middle Eastern looks, David, would you be of the Jewish persuasion yerself?" She didn't wait for him to reply. "Of course Jews do insist on circumcising their baby boys. I can't say as I approve, but they do say it's a lot healthier. Would you be circumcised yourself, David?"

At this point, Ruby leaped forward and grabbed Bridget's arm. "Bridget! Please! We must let Mr. Schwimmer go. I'm sure there are lots of other people here he wants to speak to."

"Well, it's been interesting talking to you, Bridget. I can't wait to tell people I just met the mother-in-law of Christ."

"And you'll listen for me on *Cozy Confessions with Sister Assumpta*?"

"Wouldn't miss it."

Chanel guided Bridget back to the bar. Ruby turned to

David Schwimmer, who she had to admit was supremely dishy. "I'm so sorry about that," she said. "Saul's success has gone to her head a bit."

"No problem," he smiled, making him look super-plus dishy. "Listen, believe it or not, I don't know too many people here. I was wondering, would you like to go somewhere maybe and get a drink or a cup of coffee?"

"Who? Me?" Ruby looked over her shoulder, assuming he was directing his question at some gorgeous starlet who had just sashayed into view.

"Yes," he said.

"Oh, that is so kind of you and I'm very flattered, but actually I'm here with my chap."

"Well, your *chap* is a very lucky guy, that's all I can say. Nice to have met you..." He was inviting her to fill in her name.

"Ruby. Ruby Silverman."

"Nice to have met you, Ruby Silverman." He held out his hand, which she took.

"You, too," she said.

As he turned to go, he was accosted by Joan Collins. "David! Dahling!"

He offered Ruby a final pleading look.

"I'll leave you to it," Ruby smiled, nodding good-bye to David.

Tingling and positively giddy with excitement, Ruby went to find Chanel and Bridget. "Omigod," she cried, "I was asked out by David Schwimmer. Can you believe it?"

"You're 'aving me on," Chanel said.

"No. Honest. I think Saturn's change of direction could be starting to affect me after all."

"Are you sure he's not that one from *ER*?" Bridget said, draining yet another glass of champagne. "Oooh, look, is that Madonna over there? Now, if anybody needs a good hiding, that brazen hussy does. I ask you, what decent Catholic girl flaunts herself in her corsets and brassiere? She'll end up burning in the fires of hell, she will, but not before she's developed a nasty chill on her kidneys. Has the woman never heard of vests? If you ask me, that Guy Bitchie needs to take her under control. . . . Now then, where's she gone? Oh, there she is. . . ." Before anybody could stop her, Bridget had disappeared into the crowd.

"Leave 'er," Chanel said, smiling. "Why don't we let 'er enjoy her moment in the spotlight."

Ruby nodded.

Chanel picked up her champagne flute. She looked thoughtful. "You know, me and Craig would never 'ave got Alfie if it 'adn't been for you. I'm not sure we'll ever be able to thank you."

Just then Fi appeared. She looked stunning in a pale blue silk Vivienne Westwood dress. Ruby gave a comedy wolf whistle. Fi responded with a giggly twirl. Then she sat down next to them at the bar and scooped up a handful of nuts. "I've just got to get something inside me to soak up all the champagne. If I don't, I'm going to keel over." She turned to Chanel. "I heard what you were saying just then. You're right. Quite a few things wouldn't have ended up as happily as they have if it weren't for Ruby."

"Oh, stoppit, both of you," Ruby cried, turning scarlet.

But it was true. Frustrated and sad as she was that she couldn't get Baby Organic off the ground, she would always be proud that she'd been responsible for Jill McNulty and Tom Hardacre receiving their just desserts.

Before she and Sam flew off to New York for Josh's retrial, Ruby, Hannah, Sam and the two other foreign doctors who had been implicated in the surrogacy scam sent separate letters to the hospital's chief executive. A couple of weeks ago they were invited to attend a meeting with the board of governors. This was followed by several more and eventually resulted in the hospital conducting a lengthy, but secret internal inquiry into the surrogacy affair.

Hardacre, who, as Ruby had suspected, was the only doctor involved in the surrogacy business, had the arrogance and effrontery to deny everything and threatened to sue the hospital for slander, but Jill and the two midwives involved were much more easily intimidated and cracked under interrogation from hospital bigwigs. Naturally they implicated Hardacre. He, Jill McNulty and the midwives were duly sacked for "gross misconduct." None of them would ever work in the medical profession again.

Jill had left Hardacre. She had never been a particularly enthusiastic accomplice and had only taken part in the surrogacy affair because she was infatuated with him and he had bullied her into it. The last Ruby heard, Jill was atoning for her sins working on the checkout at Wal-mart.

Even though Tom Hardacre had been sacked, Ruby couldn't help thinking that he had got off lightly. His medical career was over, but unlike Jill, he had his substantial "immoral earnings" to fall back on. Ruby was so outraged by this that she didn't sleep properly for weeks. Then, one night as she lay tossing and turning she came up with an idea.

The following morning, after getting Hardacre's phone number from one of the hospital governors, she phoned him. When Hardacre heard it was Ruby on the line, he tried to hang up.

"No, please don't put the phone down. You see I've just had this brilliant idea."

"Really," Hardacre replied, his tone flat with disinterest.

"Yes. I think you should make a very large donation to the hospital. I'm sure they would accept."

Hardacre roared with laughter. "Why on earth would I do that?"

"Let's put it this way: I'm not sure how much money you've made out of your surrogacy business, but I'm certain your services didn't come cheap. It also wouldn't surprise me to discover that you received all payments in cash."

He was silent for a few moments. "What are you suggesting?"

"I'm suggesting you haven't paid a penny in tax since you started up this business. I am also suggesting that if you don't give St. Luke's all the money, I fully intend to report you to the Inland Revenue."

"I see."

"I thought you might."

A week later, a quarter of a million pounds was deposited anonymously into St. Luke's bank account.

The governors decided to put the donation toward building an eating disorders unit at St. Luke's, as well as spearheading a national campaign to educate women about the dangers of dieting during and right after pregnancy. Ruby couldn't help thinking it was poetic justice for Hardacre's money to end up helping to build an eating disorders unit.

It wasn't long before all fifteen of the Hollywood stars who had used surrogates sent threatening letters to St. Luke's via their attorneys, saying they would sue for libel if the story was leaked to the press and they were named in the affair. The hospital agreed on the understanding that they make a "voluntary" contribution to the eating disorders unit and paid any outstanding money owed to their surrogates. They all coughed up.

"WHO ARE YOU looking for now?" Fi said to Ruby, who was casting her eyes around the room again.

"Sam. He seems to have disappeared. I haven't seen him for ages. I think I might go and look for him."

Ruby stood up and straightened her skirt. "By the way, Fi, I couldn't be more happy for you and Saul. He was brilliant tonight. Nobody deserves a break more than he does. He's worked so hard for this."

"I know. I'm so proud of him."

Ruby gave her friend a kiss and a tight hug. "I won't be long. If Sam shows up, tell him I'm looking for him."

RUBY THOUGHT SAM might be outside on the terrace, but he wasn't. In fact the terrace was practically empty. A light drizzle was starting to fall and people were wandering back inside.

The spitting rain didn't bother her. She was happy to enjoy the silence for a few minutes. She sat down at one of the tables and breathed in the smell of fresh summer rain on London pavement. Having resisted it all evening, she reached into her bag and took out her phone. She wanted to check her voice mail. Maybe the venture capitalist chap she'd had a meeting with yesterday about investing in Baby Organic had changed his mind.

She dialed her voice mail. Nothing. No change there, then.

"Hey, what are you doing sitting all alone in the drizzle?" It was Sam. He was coming toward her, his face full of concern. "You OK?"

"I'm fine. Actually, I've been looking for you. When I couldn't find you, I decided to check my voice mail."

"No news from this financier you saw yesterday, I take it?"

She shook her head.

Still looking concerned, Sam pulled a chair out from under the table and sat down. "Sorry I disappeared. Buddy called. Irene has persuaded him to retire. He's selling the pickle business."

"You're kidding. That business is his life."

"I know, but he's not getting any younger. I think he realizes deep down that the time has come to sell up." He paused. "Ruby?"

"What?"

"Do you believe in miracles?"

She laughed. "I'm not sure. Of course, Chanel would probably say that miracles don't happen to Capricorns."

"Is that so?"

Sam took his phone out of his pocket and tapped out a number. "Hey, Buddy, I've got Ruby here. Let me put her on."

Ruby frowned. "Why does Buddy want to speak to me?"

Sam handed her the phone. "Why don't you find out?"

"Hello, Buddy. How are you?"

"Lousy, thank you for asking. My wife has forced me to retire. Do you know how many years of my life I spent in the pickle business?"

"No, I don't."

"Fifty-seven! Fifty-seven years, man and boy."

"Don't lie," Irene was squawking in the distance. "It was forty-two. You always have to exaggerate everything. Ever since I've known you, you have to exaggerate."

"Yeah, yeah. Whatever. Anyway, Ruby, here's the thing: I may be retired, but I'm still a businessman and I'm looking for a new project. Sam told me about this business venture you're trying to get off the ground. Sounds like a great idea. How's about I loan you the money you need?"

"You want to invest in Baby Organic?"

"Why not? Organics are the future. You'd have to be a schmuck not to see that."

"It's a sweet offer, Buddy, and don't think I'm not grateful, but I'm determined not to borrow money from friends. If the business went belly up, you'd lose your investment and I wouldn't be able to live with myself."

"Ruby, listen up. One thing I've learned from fifty-seven years in the pickle business..."

"I thought it was forty-two years."

"Fifty-seven, forty-two. It was a lot of years and what I learned in that time is that in business you can't make decisions based on what-ifs. Business is all about taking risks. I'm prepared to take a risk on you. The question is—are you prepared to take a risk on borrowing from a friend?"

Ruby sat, processing, the phone pressed to her ear. "I'm not sure. You see, my last investor was a member of my family and she ended up wanting to control everything..."

"I have no interest in controlling anything. After all, what does an old man like me know about babies?... Take the money. You'd be doing me a favor. You'd be easing my conscience. I still feel guilty about the way I encouraged Sam to lie to you. And I know you'll make a success of the new business."

"Look, it really is very kind of you, but I'm still not—"

"Please?... C'mon, what do you say?"

She looked at Sam, who was frantically mouthing at her to accept Buddy's offer.

"OK... you've got a deal, but if something goes wrong, I swear you'll get back every penny you put in. That's a promise."

"And if, as I suspect, you—correction, we—make a killing, I'm expecting a substantial share in the profits. Do we still have a deal?"

She hesitated. Then: "OK."

"Good girl. You've made an old man very happy."

"And an old woman," Irene piped up in the background.

"Thanks, Buddy."

"My pleasure, darling. My pleasure."

Ruby handed Sam back his phone. "You set this up, didn't you?" she said half smiling, half accusing.

"I admit I brought your problem to Buddy's attention, but it was his idea to help you."

She screwed up her face.

"What?" he said.

"Look, it's not that I'm not grateful. I am, but I can't have you stepping in to rescue me every time my life gets difficult. I need to be able to sort things out on my own. It means a lot to me."

"Ruby, for crying out loud. Why are you so stubborn? You've spent the last few months sorting out everybody else's lives. You uncovered the surrogacy scandal. You helped Hannah. Chanel wouldn't have gotten to keep Alfie if it hadn't been for you. St. Luke's wouldn't have gotten the quarter of a million if it hadn't been for you..."

"My mother wouldn't have given birth in an airport if it hadn't been for me."

He laughed. "OK, there is that... Come on, Ruby, ease up on yourself. Please don't change your mind about taking Buddy's money. You deserve it."

"OK," she said eventually, "maybe you're right."

"I *am* right."

"What can I say other than thank you and that I love you?" She reached up and kissed him on the lips.

"And I love you, too."

Her face broke into a grin. Then she tilted her head heavenward. "So, Saturn finally gave me a break. Who'd have thought?"

"Saturn? I'm not with you. What are you talking about?"

"Oh, nothing," she giggled. "Private joke... Come on, we ought see where Bridget's got to. I'm meant to be keeping an eye on her."

They didn't have to look far. While Ruby had been on the phone to Buddy, a band had set up and started playing with Bridget as their vocalist. "Omigod," Ruby gasped, "she must have insisted on doing a turn." She stared at Bridget, who was standing on a table top, her bra outside her dress, singing atrociously out of key and gyrating for all she was worth. "Like a vir-ir-ir-ir-gin, touched for the very first time," she squawked. Even more surprising was that everybody in the room had gathered round her and they were all clapping and singing along.

"Like a vir-ir-ir-ir-gin . . . Come on Madge, you brazen hussy!" she yelled to Madonna. "Up you get and join me."

And she did.

One woman.
Two hot men to choose from.
Let the games begin....
Breakfast at Stephanie's
a novel
SUE MARGOLIS
AUTHOR OF APOCALIPSTICK

BREAKFAST AT STEPHANIE'S

on sale now

"Elizabeth Arden?"

It was the third Saturday before Christmas and Stephanie Glassman, resident pianist at the Oxford Street branch of Debenhams, was sitting at a white baby grand on the ground floor, playing "Winter Wonderland." She couldn't have looked less Elizabeth Arden–like if she'd tried. Unless, of course, Miss Arden used to celebrate the festive season by dressing up in a tacky Mrs. Claus Christmas outfit, which included a fur-trimmed thigh-high skirt and Teutonic blonde wig with plaited Alpine shepherdess-style earphones.

As she carried on playing, Stephanie looked up from the keyboard and saw a bulky, tweedy woman standing at her side. She was weighed down with carrier bags, and her face exuded faint desperation and the urgent need of a large gin. Stephanie had been at Debenhams for two weeks now and the haunted, get-me-out-of-here Christmas shopper look was one she had come to recognize only too well.

"I'm looking for her Perpetual Moisture," the woman panted, desperation rising. "It's for my sister-in-law in Stoke Poges. She swears by it. Lord knows why she bothers. Got a face like a fossilized custard skin. Harrods and Selfridges have both run out. Of course, if I had my way the poisonous old boot would get a box of Newberry Fruits and a Jamie Oliver video and be done with it."

While the woman paused for breath, Stephanie gave her a warm, sympathetic smile.

"The Elizabeth Arden counter is just over there." She nodded. "Behind Dior."

"Right, well, if they haven't got it I think I'll plump for a foot spa. That way I can always live in hope she might electrocute herself." Stephanie thought it best to remain noncommittal—at least regarding the electrocution bit. "A foot spa's always useful," she said. "Or gardening gloves and a pair of pruning shears, maybe."

With that the woman huffed off toward the Elizabeth Arden counter and Stephanie segued into "Have Yourself a Merry Little Christmas."

Being Jewish, Stephanie's family didn't do Christmas—something for which she knew her mother, Estelle, had always been eternally grateful. The spring cleaning, shopping, baking and fish frying frenzy of Passover was enough to send her racing for the Valium—without having to cope with Christmas as well. Stephanie, on the other hand, had always rather resented the family's lack of Christmas celebrations.

Traditional as they may have been where Passover was concerned, her parents weren't particularly observant. For a start, they ate nonkosher food. When she was a kid they went out for Chinese dinner nearly every Sunday night. Her father was a ferocious advocate of cha siu pork, believing its medicinal qualities to be infinitely greater than those of chicken soup. Her grandmother, who usually accompanied them on these jaunts, refused to touch the pork. On top of this she always insisted on going through what Stephanie called her preening ritual, whereby she painstakingly picked out all the pork and prawns from her yung chow rice and piled them up in her napkin.

Christmas was like pork. You could "have it out"—like the turkey lunch at the Finchley Post House, even the midnight carol service at The Blessed Virgin down the road (her mum loved the tunes)—but on no account was it to be brought into the house.

As a child, Stephanie ached to take part in all the Christmas excitement and always felt jealous of her non-Jewish friends. Each year at junior school, just before they broke up for the holidays, all the kids in her class (except her, David Solomons and the Qureshi twins) would stand around in groups, busy competing about what they were getting for Christmas and having impassioned debates about whether Father Christmas really existed or whether the fat old bloke who delivered presents was just your dad dressed up.

She could still remember walking home from school on those dank December afternoons. It was teatime and in all the non-Jewish houses, the tree lights were being switched on. Every so often she would stop and stare at the twinkling windows, feeling she was peering into a never-never land. Ordinary houses, with their boring tarmac drives and UPVC window frames, became enchanted fairy grottoes. Her eight-year-old heart quite literally ached not just for Santa and the pillowcase of presents, but for the tinsel, the Christmas tree baubles, the crackers, the ritual of leaving mince pies outside for the reindeer—the sheer wondrous, sparkling magic of it all.

Of course she had Hanukkah, which happened around the same time as Christmas, but it wasn't the same, lighting a few pathetic candles and getting a fiver pressed into your hand by some whiskery old aunt.

When she gave birth to Jake, two and a half years ago, she promised him three things: her unconditional love and support, that she would never allow him to own a motorbike while he lived under her roof, and that he would have a childhood full of brilliant Christmases. Although this was his second, it was the first he was old enough to appreciate. As a result, Stephanie's living room ceiling was thick with paper chains, streamers and balloons. In the alcove next to the fireplace stood a garish, overdressed, six-foot-tall Norway spruce, which—since there was no husband or boyfriend to do it for her—Stephanie's father, Harry, had insisted on schlepping back from the greengrocer's around the corner, on the strict understanding it was to be referred to as a

Hanukkah bush. Deciding that she shouldn't look a gift horse in the mouth, Stephanie agreed.

SHE LOOKED DOWN at her watch. Almost three. Time for her break. Although she loved Christmas, she loathed her Mrs. Claus getup. What she hated even more was walking through the store wearing it. She didn't mind the short skirt so much because it showed off her long—and even if she did say so herself—shapely legs, as did the long stiletto-heeled boots she'd been given. No, what she loathed was the earphones wig. It made her look like that woman in *The Sound of Music* who, having been handed second prize at the Salzburg Music Festival, refused to stop bowing.

Women who noticed the earphones tended to smile in sympathy, but blokes always made some kind of smart remark. "Can you get the football on 'em, then?" Yesterday a shaven-headed youth in a Manchester United football shirt, loitering suspiciously with his mates by the watches, had yelled out: "Whassit like shagging Santa, then?"

"Not that good, actually," she'd replied, grinning. "He only comes once a year." Ho bleeding ho.

What worried her most about being Mrs. Claus was the thought of being seen by somebody who knew her, such as her parents' rabbi, or an ex-boyfriend, or perhaps some girl from school she hadn't seen for years and who now looked like Gwyneth Paltrow and was in mergers and acquisitions. It wasn't just the costume she would have to explain away. Far more important was why, more than ten years after leaving university (English, honors) and a successful stint at drama school—not to mention her great singing voice—she could aspire to nothing more elevated, careerwise, than a temp job as a cheesy, piano-playing Mrs. Claus in a middle-market chain store.

Stephanie finished with a quick burst of "Jingle Bell

Rock" and then stood up. The place was teeming with the fraught and the frazzled. A few feet away, a middle-aged couple seemed to be having a major fight about driving gloves. Then: "Coooeee."

Her heart sank to her stiletto boots. It had finally happened. Somebody had recognized her. OK, she could always say her dad played golf with Mr. Debenham and she was just helping out because the store's regular piano player had come down with Ebola.

She turned toward the voice. Instant relief. It was only the tweedy woman bent on electrocuting her sister-in-law in Stoke Poges. She was holding up a Debenhams carrier bag.

"Mini carpet bowls," she cackled. "Byeee. Merry Christmas!"

"You too."

Stephanie gave her a small wave and watched the woman disappear into the crowd. She was just trying to work out whether she had time to go to the loo and get to the toy department to buy Jake his main present—a Bob the Builder tool belt, on which she was entitled to a 20 percent staff discount—when she saw someone even more embarrassing than Rabbi Nodel.

She recognized Frank Waterman at once. Dark, swept-back hair, eyes the color of conkers, just a hint of well-tended stubble. They'd been in *Cabaret* together at the Nottingham Playhouse, six or seven years back. Stephanie had been in the chorus and he'd played Cliff Bradshaw, the romantic lead. During their time together, she developed *the* most almighty crush on him, but nothing ever happened between them. They exchanged hellos at rehearsals, went drinking with the same gang after the show, but since he was so resoundingly A-list to look at and always had stacks of women (not to mention a couple of blokes) sniffing round, she'd never plucked up the courage to flirt with him.

The show had been on for a couple of weeks when the message filtered down to London that the production was particularly excellent and a theater critic from one of the broadsheets turned up. He raved about the show and Frank's performance in particular, saying he possessed that indefinable quality common to all great actors and that celebrity undoubtedly beckoned. Frank had never looked back. These days, he was the Royal Shakespeare Company's rising star—and she was Mrs. Claus with earphones.

Now he was coming her way, but since he was busy chatting to the woman with him, Stephanie was pretty certain he hadn't noticed her. Plus it had been years since they'd last met and it wasn't as if they'd had much to do with each other back then. Chances were that even if he saw her, he wouldn't recognize her. Nevertheless she sat back down on the piano stool and buried her head in her music book.

"Steph?" Bugger. OK, play it cool. Do not let him see you're flustered. She looked up and forced her mouth onto full beam. "Frank? Frank Waterman?"

"I don't believe it," he said. "I knew it was you. I said to Anoushka"—glorious cheekbones, Fulham highlights—"I'm sure that's Steph from *Cabaret*. God, it must be what, four, five years ago?"

"Nearly seven."

"No. As long as that?"

"Yup. Time flies."

"God, doesn't it? So, you're Mrs. Christmas."

He was looking at the wig and smiling. Her hand sprang self-consciously to her left earphone. "A bit Heidi, I know." A smirk of agreement from Anoushka. "Still, it's only until Christmas Eve. Pays the bills."

"But what about the singing? Don't say you've stopped. You had such a fantastic voice. You were into blues and jazz, if I remember. Ella, Peggy Lee, that sort of stuff."

"That's right." She was gobsmacked. Utterly astounded

that he remembered. He turned to Anoushka. "One night in the pub when we were touring, Steph got up and sang 'My Melancholy Baby.' She was outstanding. Had us all in tears."

"Really?" Anoushka said with a brief, polite smile.

There was a moment's silence. "Wow, stunning earrings," Stephanie said to Anoushka, noticing the glistening pinkish-red stones. "I love rubies."

"They're pink diamonds, actually."

"Anoushka designed them herself," Frank said. "She runs her own jewelry business."

"Oh, right." Stephanie nodded. Then the penny dropped. Anoushka didn't run a mere business. It was a full-frontal corporate empire. "God, of course, you're Anoushka Holland. I read that piece about you in last month's *Vogue*. Didn't your company just get bought out by Theo Fennell for eleven million quid?"

"Eleven point five," Anoushka corrected. Having been put in her place, Stephanie didn't quite know what to say next. Frank picked up on her awkwardness.

"So," he said to Stephanie, "are you still singing?"

"Yes. I do a couple of gigs a week at the Blues Café in Islington. And I've had the odd bit in *Chicago* and *Les Mis*. Nothing major, though."

"Oh, it'll happen one day," he said. "With a voice like yours, it has to."

"But what about you? The critics loved you in *Othello*."

He blushed ever so slightly. Before he had a chance to reply, Anoushka broke in: "We really ought to be going, Frankie. I need to pick up a few bits at the General Trading Company." She put a proprietorial arm through his. "We only popped in to buy that Dustbuster thingy your grandmother was after." That last remark was clearly for Stephanie's benefit—to explain why the likes of Anoushka, her highlights and her eleven point five million, were slumming it at Debenhams.

"And don't forget," she went on, "we're due at the wedding planner's at six."

"Tying the knot in the spring," Frank explained.

"Wow, congratulations."

"Thanks. We're off to discuss harpists and doves. Bit bloody camp if you ask me. Plus I've got visions of two hundred guests turning up to the reception covered in bird turd."

"Frankie," Anoushka said, laughing, but Stephanie could tell she was cross, "how many more times? Otto has promised faithfully they don't feed the doves for three hours before the ceremony. Now then, we really must get going."

"Yes, we must," he said. "Sorry, Steph. It's been great seeing you."

"You too."

"Sweetie," Anoushka simpered.

"Perhaps Anoushka and I could catch you at the Blues Café one night?"

Anoushka had already started walking away. "Yeah. That'd be good," Stephanie said.

"Catch up on old times."

"Excellent."

He gave her a soft smile.

"Bye," she said. A moment later he had caught up with Anoushka, who turned her head and gave a little wave. "Bye Beth, lovely meeting you."

ORIGINAL CYN

on sale now

"Elizabeth Taylor died? Ah. Still, the old girl was getting a bit past it." As Cyn switched her mobile to the other ear she felt the taxi slow down and turn left. "Are you sure you're OK?" her mother asked tenderly. "I know how much she meant to you."

"I'm fine," Cyn said, rubbing at the condensation on the rain-speckled window and peering out. "I mean, it wasn't entirely unexpected."

"The vet did all he could," her mother was saying. Cyn's mind immediately conjured up a frantic scene in pet *ER*. She could hear the vet instructing everybody to "Stand clear" as he turns poor Elizabeth onto her shell and shocks her scaly chest with two tiny tortoise-sized resuscitation paddles. Half a dozen attempts later he wipes his brow and announces, "OK, I'm calling it. Time of death, ten after four." His face etched with failure, he snaps off his rubber gloves and throws them into the bin. Meanwhile, a tearful nurse sniffs and covers Elizabeth with a tiny white sheet.

"I remember the day I found her," Cyn's mother went on. "It was February 1981. The Canadian cousins were over and I'd gone to the garage to get some vol-au-vent cases out of the freezer. And there she was, hibernating inside a pile of sunlounger covers."

Elizabeth Taylor was by no means the only animal her mother, Barbara, had "rescued." In the years before and since the tortoise joined the Fishbein household, there were assorted stray cats, lost budgies and the odd hamster. There had even been an actual lame duck, which, having been attacked—probably by a fox—had somehow managed to waddle the half mile from the park pond to find sanctuary in the Fishbein kitchen. Barbara found homes for all the other animals. Even the duck was nursed back to health and eventually, with much ceremony, released "back into the wild" of the local park. She wasn't so lucky with the tortoise. Despite "tortoise found" notices stuck on virtually every lamppost in the neighborhood, nobody came to claim her. In the end the Fishbeins adopted her, but it was Cyn who loved her. It was Cyn who spoiled her with slices of tomato and painted ET Fishbein on her shell in Wite-Out, and it was Cyn who worried obsessively every winter about her not waking up from hibernation.

CYN CARRIED ON looking out the window, vaguely aware of her mother chortling to herself. She was pretty sure the car showroom was about half a mile farther down on the right. Her heart rate started to pick up. Her very own shiny, freshly minted, brand-spanking-new Smart Car was sitting there, waiting for her to claim it. What's more—and this was the truly amazingly fabulous bit—she was getting it for free.

Cyn was a junior copywriter at a cutting-edge and very much on the up advertising agency, Price Chandler Witty. Occasionally, companies whose accounts they handled would, after a particularly successful campaign, express additional gratitude and appreciation by offering the agency a car for an employee to have on long-term loan. The "long-term" bit was fairly ambiguous, but it pretty much meant that unless the recipient left the agency, nobody would ask for it back. The deal was that the car would carry advertising for whatever it was the donor company manufactured. Of course nobody at the agency minded, since it was generally thought that driving around advertising a sleek PalmPilot, digital camera or laptop was a pretty fair exchange for a new car.

Whenever a car came up—usually once or twice a year—the names of all the agency staff, from the directors to the cleaners, were put into a hat. The draw always took place in the function room at the Bishop's Finger across the road and afterward there would be a bit of a party. Last week there had been a couple of cars up for grabs. Although they were from different companies, both happened to be Smart Cars.

Cyn took no more than a passing interest in cars. It was partly that like many women she found the subject less than fascinating and partly that taking a proper interest would have led to yearnings, and yearnings ended up costing money. She had just bought her first flat. What with the mortgage payments and the loan on her new Ikea kitchen, she couldn't even contemplate replacing her old Peugeot. Nevertheless she adored the Smart Car. Its tiny, almost cartoonishly cute wedge shape made her laugh. She liked the way its straight back gave the impression that it was in fact the front end of a much larger, longer vehicle from which it had somehow been severed. Even though it looked like the transport of choice of a circus clown, there was no doubt that the Smart Car had style. She was aware, of course, since it was the coolest, most must-have two seater on the market, that everybody who drove one looked like a fashion victim; but that night, as she'd sat in the pub drinking with her little gang from the office, Cyn had decided that if she were ever lucky enough to own one, she would find a way to live with the shame.

Until last Friday Cyn had never won anything in her life, apart from the Yardley lavender bath soap selection box, which didn't count because she'd secured it in the school fete raffle when she was nine.

The first name out of the hat was Chelsea Roggenfelder. Chelsea was from New York and another junior copywriter at PCW. Since she had only been with the agency six months, it was spectacularly good luck. Chelsea managed to look utterly bowled over. A few meaningful looks were exchanged among PCW employees. Everybody knew she was

loaded and that deep down she probably wasn't
much more than mild amusement. The truth was th
she the inclination, Chelsea could have afforded to g
and buy a dozen Smart Cars. Chelsea's father was Sar
Roggenfelder, the Madison Avenue tycoon who had b
behind the advertising for a successful presidential campai
and several gubernatorial contests. Although she never sa
as much, it was perfectly clear that he paid the rent on he
Sloane Street flat and had bought her the BMW Z4, the perfect zipping-down-to-the-country accessory.

Her face on full beam, Chelsea stood up and pulled at the cuffs of her exquisitely tailored black jacket. With a flick of her Nicky Clarke highlights, she sashayed over to the tiny podium where Graham Chandler, one of the CEOs, was standing at the mike waiting to present her with her car key. On her way she stopped for a few seconds to smile and wave at everybody. One of the blokes sitting next to Cyn mumbled something about Chelsea's performance reminding him of Catherine Zeta-Jones dispensing largesse at the Oscars.

The applause was trailing off when Cyn heard her mobile ringing. She rushed outside where she could hear, only to discover it was somebody flogging plastic window frames. As she walked back into the pub she was met by loud cheering. It was a few seconds before she realized it was being directed at her. She frowned and looked questioningly at one of the temps from the office, who happened to be standing next to her. "It's you! You've won the other car!"

"Geddout."

"No, really." Then she saw Graham Chandler nodding and laughing.

After Graham had kissed her on both cheeks and handed her the car key, and Natalie, one of the PAs, had come rushing up to her, thrown her arms around her and made her do that jumpy up-and-down thing like kids in the playground, she went back to her table and just sat there with a daft grin on her face, completely overwhelmed. She was suddenly aware of how good news can be as much of a shock as bad news. Chelsea, on the other hand, was swanning around doing her best to convince people how stunned and delighted she was and that she simply couldn't believe her luck. "This is just too perfect," she simpered to Cyn, at one point. "Now I can keep the Z4 for driving to the country on the weekend and use the Smart Car in the city."

"Lucky old you," Cyn said, with just a hint of sarcasm.

"Yes. Lucky old you." The slurred Welsh accent belonged to Keith Geary, another copywriter. Keith, who was lanky and awkward, with jutting-out hips and shoulder blades, had been brought up in a small mining town. He liked to think of himself as a Marxist and was forever taking the piss out of what he described as Chelsea's Saks and the City lifestyle, particularly after he'd had a few, like now. Chelsea always gave as good as she got, though. "You know, Keith," she said, making use of her elegant nose, which had been perfectly engineered for looking down, "in you, I really do see a face unclouded by thought." Her tone made Camille Paglia sound affectionate.

"And on you, Chelsea," he said, "I see a head so big that your ears have separate zip codes."

Ouch, Cyn thought, suppressing a giggle. For once Chelsea was lost for words. Her mouth opened and closed a few times, goldfish-style. Then she turned on her long, spiky-toed Kurt Geiger heels and walked away.

"That showed her," Keith snorted, digging Cyn in the ribs. Then he staggered off, back to the bar.

Chelsea had come to advertising relatively late in life. She never talked much about herself, but a couple of people had found out that after university, she'd spent ten years in L.A., trying and failing to make it as a screenwriter. Finally, she decided to make a fresh start in London. There was no doubt that she had found her niche at Price Chandler Witty. Even though this was her first job in advertising, she was creating a considerable reputation for herself among PCW's clients. When it came to thinking up advertising slogans or designing campaigns, witty, razor-sharp ideas seemed to spill out of her like jackpots from a slot machine. It was quite obvious that she had inherited her father's talent.

Chelsea refused to be intimidated by the fact that nearly all the bosses at PCW, all the people she had to pitch ideas to, were men. From the off, she had never been scared to go into meetings and argue her corner. She was highly competitive and absolutely refused to be cowed. Fear simply wasn't part of her vocabulary. "You know, Graham," she would say, insisting on pronouncing Graham like most Americans do, as Grahm, to rhyme with ham, "I think we really need to start thinking outside the box here. I mean, it seems to me that you guys just haven't considered the click-through rate on this thing. And have you calculated the cost per click? . . . I figured not. Well, I have some preliminary data here which I've printed out and would like to pass round." The way it usually worked was that everybody would sit there examining her figures and come to the conclusion that she had a point.

While she wasn't exactly easy to warm to, women forgave her because they were in awe of her New York hey-mister-don't-bullshit-me feistiness. A few women—Cyn included—made no secret of wishing they had her balls. Some of the men felt the same. Mostly though, with the exception of Messrs. Price, Chandler and Witty, from whom she commanded considerable respect, the blokes referred to Chelsea behind her back as "the Terminator."

Cyn's relationship with Chelsea hadn't gotten off to a good start. Before she was taken on by PCW, Chelsea had three interviews over a four-week period. During that time the coffee machine kept going on the blink and Cyn, along with everybody else, took her turn at doing a coffee run to the sandwich bar over the road. By pure chance, each time Chelsea arrived for an interview, Cyn was handing out cups of coffee. On the day she started work, Graham Chandler took Chelsea round the office and introduced her to everybody. "And this is Cyn, another of our junior copywriters."

"Ah, yes, I've seen you getting the coffee. Be a sweetie, would you, and fetch me a skinny cappuccino, hold the chocolate." Had Graham not introduced Cyn as another copywriter it might just have been reasonable for Chelsea to assume she was one of the office juniors, but even then, her puffed-up, snooty manner was inexcusable. What made the whole thing worse was Graham standing there and saying, "I know it's not really your job, Cyn, but maybe you wouldn't mind."

"Of course not." Cyn smiled thinly, realizing she had no option but to go and get Chelsea her coffee.

As the weeks went by, though, Chelsea's manner changed where Cyn was concerned. It never became warm, exactly, but she seemed to be making a real effort to be more friendly. Cyn put it down to guilt over the coffee incident. Soon Chelsea was inviting her out to lunch, and Cyn decided it would be churlish to refuse. She had even got round to apologizing over the coffee incident, claiming she didn't realize at the time that Cyn was a fellow creative. "You know, I'm perfectly aware of how the men at PCW see me," she said on one occasion, referring to the "Terminator" epithet, "but the fact remains that women still aren't getting the opportunities they deserve in this business. The only way for us to push through the glass ceiling is to fight. You are clever and talented, Cyn. Women like us need to stick together—to keep faith with the sisterhood. Say, if you ever want to brainstorm some ideas with me or have me give you my opinion on something, feel free."

"That's so kind of you," Cyn said. "I really appreciate